BITTER GREENS

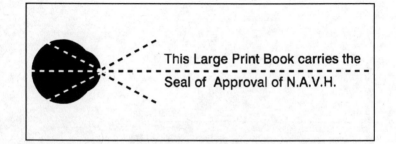
This Large Print Book carries the Seal of Approval of N.A.V.H.

BITTER GREENS

KATE FORSYTH

THORNDIKE PRESS
A part of Gale, Cengage Learning

 GALE
CENGAGE Learning·

Farmington Hills, Mich • San Francisco • New York • Waterville, Maine
Meriden, Conn • Mason, Ohio • Chicago

GALE
CENGAGE Learning®

LIBRARY OF CONGRESS CATALOGING-IN-PUBLICATION DATA

Forsyth, Kate, 1966–
  Bitter greens / by Kate Forsyth. — Large print edition.
    pages ; cm. — (Thorndike Press large print historical fiction)
    ISBN 978-1-4104-7425-4 (hardcover) — ISBN 1-4104-7425-9 (hardcover)
    1. Women—Fiction. 2. Scandals—Fiction. 3. Renaissance—Italy—Venice—
Fiction. 4. Italy—Civilization—1268–1559—Fiction. 5. Rapunzel (Tale)—
Adaptations. 6. Large type books. 7. Fairy tales. I. Title.
  PR9619.3.F59B58 2014b
  823'.914—dc23   2014029710

Published in 2014 by arrangement with St. Martin's Press, LLC

Printed in Mexico
1 2 3 4 5 6 7 18 17 16 15 14

This book is dedicated to all my dear friends who are both women and writers — we are living the life that Charlotte-Rose dreamt of.

FOREWORD

The first known version of the Rapunzel fairy tale was 'Petrosinella' ('Little Parsley'), by the Italian writer Giambattista Basile (c.1575–1632), published posthumously in 1634.

Sixty-four years later, in 1698, it was retold under the name 'Persinette' by the French writer Charlotte-Rose de Caumont de la Force (1650–1724), written while she was locked away in a nunnery as punishment for her scandalous life. She changed the ending so that her heroine's tears healed the eyes of the blinded prince and the witch was redeemed.

Fairy-tale scholars have always been puzzled by how Mademoiselle de la Force could have come to know Basile's story. His work was not translated from his native Neapolitan dialect for many years after Mademoiselle de la Force's death, and, although she was unusually well educated for her time, she never travelled to Italy, nor could she speak

Neapolitan. It is her version of the tale that we now know as 'Rapunzel'.

As well as being one of the first writers of literary fairy tales, Mademoiselle de la Force was one of the first writers of historical fiction and was known to be a major influence on Sir Walter Scott, who is commonly regarded as the 'father' of historical fiction.

CONTENTS

PRELUDE

All day, all day I brush
My golden strands of hair;
All day I wait and wait . . .
Ah, who is there?

Who calls? Who calls? The gold
Ladder of my long hair
I loose and wait . . . and wait . . .
Ah, who is there?

She left at dawn . . . I am blind
In the tangle of my long hair . . .
Is it she? the witch? the witch?
Ah, who is there?

'Rapunzel'
Adelaide Crapsey

A HEART OF GALL

I had always been a great talker and teller of tales.

'You should put a lock on that tongue of yours. It's long enough and sharp enough to slit your own throat,' our guardian warned me, the night before I left home to go to the royal court at Versailles. He sat at the head of the long wooden table in the chateau's arched dining room, lifting his lip in distaste as the servants brought us our usual peasant fare of sausage and white-bean cassoulet. He had not accustomed himself to our simple Gascon ways, not even after four years.

I just laughed. 'Don't you know a woman's tongue is her sword? You wouldn't want me to let my only weapon rust, would you?'

'No chance of that.' The Marquis de Maulévrier was a humourless man, with a face like a goat and yellowish eyes that followed my sister and me as we went about our business. He thought our mother had spoilt us, and had set himself to remedy our faults. I loathed him. No, loathe is far too soft a word. I detested him.

My sister, Marie, said, 'Please, my lord, you mustn't mind her. You know we're famous here in Gascony for our troubadours and minstrels. We Gascons love to sing songs and tell stories. She means no harm by it.'

'I love to tell a gasconade,' I sang. 'A braggadocio, a fanfaronade . . .'

Marie sent me a look. 'You know that Charlotte-Rose will need honey on her tongue if she's to make her way in this world.'

'*Sangdieu,* but it's true. Her face won't make her fortune.'

'That's unfair, my lord. Charlotte-Rose has the sweetest face . . .'

'She might be passable if only she'd pluck out that sting in her tail,' the Marquis de Maulévrier began. Seeing that I had screwed up my face like a gargoyle, waggling my tongue at him, he rapped his spoon on the pitted tabletop. 'You'd best sweeten your temperament, *mademoiselle,* else you'll find yourself with a heart of gall.'

I should have listened to him.

Palais de Versailles, France — January 1697
Full of regret, I clung to the strap as my carriage rolled away from the Palais de Versailles. It was a bleak and miserable day, the sky

bruised with snow clouds. I was sure my nose must be red; it certainly *felt* red. I drew my fur-edged cloak closer about me, glad that I would not, at least, arrive at my prison looking like a pauper.

I still could not believe that the King would order me to a nunnery. Apparently, it was in punishment for some impious Noëls that I had written, but all the women of the salons made subtle mock of the church. It seemed a harsh punishment for such a petty crime. Surely the King did not believe the rumours that I was having an affair with his son? The Dauphin and I were friends, drawn together by our love of art and music and novels, and our hatred of the King. Perhaps I had been too bold in expressing my views. Perhaps my tongue — and my quill — had grown a little sharp. I had thought myself safe under the Dauphin's protection. The Dauphin always said, though, that the one way for him to ensure his father punished someone was to beg his father to offer that person a favour.

Perched on the other seat, my maid, Nanette, gazed at me unhappily but I would not meet her eyes. 'It's all a great misunderstanding,' I said. 'The King will soon summon me back.' I tried to smile.

'Couldn't you have gone to him and begged his pardon, Bon-bon?' Nanette asked.

'I did try,' I answered. 'But you know the King. He must be the most unforgiving man

14

in Christendom.'

'Bon-bon!'

'It's no use scolding me, Nanette. I'm simply telling the truth.'

'But to be locked up in a convent. To become a nun.' Nanette's voice was faint with horror. 'Your parents must be rolling in their graves.'

'What were my choices? Exile or the convent. At least, this way, the King will still pay my pension and I'll be on French soil, breathing French air. Where else could I have gone? What could I have done to support myself? I'm too old and ugly to walk the streets.'

Nanette's face puckered. 'You're not old or ugly.'

I laughed. 'Not to you, perhaps, Nanette. But, believe me, most people at Versailles consider me a hideous old hag. I'm forty-seven years old, and not even my closest friends ever thought I was a beauty.'

'You're not a hideous old hag,' Nanette protested. 'Not beautiful, no, but there's better things than beauty in this world.'

'*Belle laide,* Athénaïs calls me,' I replied with a little shrug. The expression was usually used to describe a woman who was arresting despite the plainness of her looks. My guardian had spoken truly when he said my face would never be my fortune.

Nanette made a little *tsk tsk* with her tongue. 'You're worth twice the Marquise de

Montespan. Don't you listen to a word she says. And don't you go thinking you're a hideous old hag either. *I* wouldn't permit anyone to say that about me, and in my case it's true.'

I smiled despite myself. Nanette was not the most attractive of women. She was tiny and gaunt, dressed always in black, with sparse white hair screwed back into a knob at the back of her head. Her face and body were so thin that you could see all the bones underneath her withered skin, and she had lost quite a few teeth. Her black eyes were fierce, but her hands were always tender and her brain quite as nimble as it had ever been.

Nanette had been my maid ever since I was weaned from my wet-nurse. As a child, I would lie in my vast shadowy bed, a flame floating in the old glass lantern, and sleepily listen as she sang, 'You have searched me, Lord, and you know me. You know when I sit and when I rise; you perceive my thoughts from afar. You discern my going out and my lying down; you are familiar with all my ways.' Nanette was like the Lord in that psalm. Before a word was on my tongue, she knew it completely. She hemmed me in behind and before, and her hand held me fast.

'You'd best write to your sister straightaway and let her know what's happened,' Nanette went on. 'Marie's not clever like you, but

16

she's got a good heart. She'll beg that fat husband of hers to petition the King.'

'I'll write to the Princesses too,' I said. 'They'll be furious with their father. He simply cannot go around banishing all the most interesting people from court, can he?'

Nanette humphed, but the thought of the King's three pipe-smoking, bastard-born daughters lifted my spirits a little. Born of two of the King's mistresses, they had been legitimised and married off to various dukes and princes, and they enlivened the court with their scandalous love affairs, their extravagance, their gambling and their constant bickering over precedence. Although they were much younger than me, we had become good friends, and I often attended their soirées and salons.

My smile slowly faded. The Princesses de Conti were no longer in favour with the King and his reigning mistress, Françoise de Maintenon, who had been queen in all but name for more than fifteen years now. Some even whispered that Louis had married her in secret. Yet Françoise had none of the beauty and brilliance of the King's earlier mistresses. Not only was she over sixty, but she was also rather plain and dumpy, and altogether too pious for the King's bastard daughters.

Remembering the Princesses, it occurred to me that their mothers, the royal mistresses, had all ended their dazzling careers within

17

the austere confines of a convent.

Louise de la Vallière, the King's first mistress and mother of Princesse Marie-Anne, had been transformed into Sœur Louise de la Miséricorde.

Athénaïs, the Marquise de Montespan, mother of Princesse Louise Françoise and Princesse Françoise Marie, had been forced to the nunnery by scandal and rumours of black magic and poison.

The frivolous Angélique de Fontanges, the girl who had supplanted Athénaïs in the King's affection, had died in a convent at the age of nineteen. Poisoned, it was said.

I was a fool. Why would the King hesitate to banish *me* to a nunnery, when he had no problem sending his discarded mistresses, the mothers of his children? Women were locked up in convents all the time. Younger daughters sent as babies, so their parents did not have to pay so rich a dowry as they would for their wedding day. Rebellious young women, cloistered away as punishment for their disobedience. Widows, like my poor mother, banished by the King to a convent, even though she was a Huguenot and so feared and hated the Roman Catholic Church with all her heart.

Although I was pretending not to care, my stomach was knotted with anxiety. I knew little about convents except that once a woman disappeared inside, she stayed inside.

Nanette had often told me the story of how Martin Luther's wife, a former nun, had only been able to escape by hiding in an empty fish barrel. Certainly, I had never seen my own mother again.

The only life I knew was the court of the Sun King. I had lived at court since I was sixteen years old. What did I know about spending my days on my knees, praying and clicking away at a rosary?

I'd never make love again, or dance, or gallop to the hounds, or smile as I made a whole salon of Parisian courtiers laugh and applaud one of my stories. I'd never rest my folded fan against my heart, saying in the silent language of the court that my heart was breaking with love. I'd never be kissed again.

The tears came at last. Nanette passed me the handkerchief she had kept ready on her knee. I dabbed at my eyes, but the tears kept coming, making my chest heave in its tight cage of lacing, and no doubt making a terrible mess of my maquillage.

The carriage paused and I heard the sound of the palace gates being opened. Casting down the handkerchief, I swung aside the curtain that hid the view from my sight. Footmen in curly wigs and long satin vests stood to attention as the side wing of the golden gates was swung open by guards. Crowds of shabby peasants shoved forward, eager to see which fine lord or lady was leaving Versailles.

Holding my lace headdress in place, I leant out the coach window for one last glimpse of the palace at the end of the avenue, the marble forecourt, the prancing bronze horse, the green triangles of topiary in pots marching past like dragoons. The carriage rolled forward, the sounds of the wheels changing as they left the smooth marble flagstones and began to rattle over the cobblestones of the Avenue de Paris. I sank back into my seat. 'Adieu, Versailles, adieu,' I cried.

'Come, my little cabbage, you must stop.' Nanette took her handkerchief and mopped my face as if I was a child. 'I thought you hated court. I thought you said it was filled with empty-headed fools.'

I jerked my face away and stared out at the tall crowded houses of Versailles. It was true that I hated the royal court. Yet I loved it too. The theatre, the music and dancing, the literary salons . . .

'I should've whipped you more often as a child,' Nanette said sadly.

'More often? You never whipped me, though you threatened to often enough.'

'I know. That's what I mean. Such a tempestuous little thing you were. Either up in the boughs or down in the dumps — there was never any middle ground for you. I should've taught you better.'

'Well, Maulévrier did his best to beat some sense into me.'

'That cold-hearted snake.'

'I always thought he looked more like a goat.' I took the handkerchief back from Nanette and blew my nose.

'Yes, a goat, an old devil goat. I bet he had horns under that velvet hat of his.'

Normally, I would have said, 'Yes, and cloven hooves instead of feet, and a tail sticking out of his arse.' Instead, I sighed and leant my aching head against the cushion. All I could see out the window were dreary fields under a dismal sky. Snow floated past, melting as soon as it hit the wet cobblestones. The clop of the horses' hooves and the rattle of the wheels were the only sounds.

'Ah, my poor little Bon-bon,' Nanette sighed, and I passed her back her handkerchief so she could mop her own eyes.

Soon, we passed the turn-off to Paris, and I caught my breath with pain. *Would I ever see Paris again?* I remembered when I had first come to the royal court, still resident then in Paris. My sister had warned me to be careful. 'It's a dangerous place, Bon-bon. Keep a guard on your tongue, else you'll be in trouble, just like the Marquis says.'

I had been on my best behaviour at first, charming and amusing at all times. I had thought the court like a gilded cage of butterflies, all beauty and wonder and movement. I had grown careless. I had enjoyed my own sharp wit, my boldness. I had played with words like a jongleur juggled swords, and I had cut myself.

A fool's tongue is long enough to slit his own throat, the Marquis de Maulévrier had always said. I hated to admit that he could be right.

We crossed the River Seine and headed south through a dark and dripping forest. Although Nanette had packed a basket of provisions, I could not eat. The carriage came slowly down a hill, the postilion dismounting to lead the horses, and then we swayed and jolted forward on execrable roads into an early dusk. I shut my eyes, leant my head back against the wall and determined to endure. My name meant strength. I would be strong.

When the carriage came to a halt, I jerked awake. My heart constricted. I peered out the window but all I could see was the hazy yellow light of a single lantern, illuminating a stone wall. It was freezing.

'Quick, my powder, my patches!'

Nanette passed me my powder box and I flicked the haresfoot over my face, squinting into the tiny mirror at the back of the box. My hands were deft and sure; this was not the first time I had had to repair my maquillage in the dark.

I snapped my powder box shut and thrust it at her, snatching the small jewelled container in which I kept my patches, the little beauty spots made of gummed taffeta that were very useful for hiding pimples or small-pox scars. My fingers were trembling so much I could hardly pluck out one of the tiny black shapes. For a moment, I hesitated. Normally, I would press my patch to the corner of my mouth, *à la coquette,* or beside my eye, *à la passionnée,* but it was a convent I was about to sweep into, not a salon or ballroom. Carefully, I fixed the patch in the centre of my forehead, just under my hairline, *à la majestueuse.*

I was Charlotte-Rose de Caumont de la Force. My grandfather had been the Marshal of France, my cousin was a duke, my mother second cousin to the King himself. If I must enter a nunnery — quite against my own wishes — it would be in my finest clothes, with my head held high and no traces of tears on my face.

The postilion opened the carriage door. I descended as gracefully as I could in my high heels, though my feet were numb and my legs trembled after the long hours rattling over potholes. Nanette caught up my train to stop it dragging in the snow.

The yard was deserted, a lantern hanging above a barred oaken door providing the only light. Above the door were carved rows of stern-faced saints sitting in judgement upon cringing devils and sinners, who pleaded for mercy below. In the wan and flickering light, the sinners' stone limbs seemed to writhe and their faces grimace. Some had bat wings and goblin faces. One was a woman on her knees, hair flowing unbound down her back. Many had their noses smashed away, or their pleading hands broken. It looked as if the Huguenots had been here with their hammers and slingshots, seeking to destroy all signs of idolatry.

The postilion rang a bell beside the doorway, then came back to heave my trunk off the roof of the coach. Then we stood waiting, the postilion, Nanette and I, shifting from foot to foot, rubbing our hands together, our breath hanging frostily in the air before us. Minutes dragged by. I felt a surge of anger and lifted my chin.

'Well, we shall just have to return to Versailles and tell the King no one was home. What a shame.'

As if in response to my words, I heard keys being turned and bolts being drawn. I fell silent, trying not to shiver. The door opened slowly, revealing a bent woman shrouded all in black. The glow of the lantern showed only a sunken mouth drawn down at the corners by deep grooves. The rest of her face was cast in shadow by her wimple. She beckoned with a bony hand and reluctantly I moved forward.

'I am Mademoiselle de la Force. I come at the bidding of the King.'

She nodded and gestured to me to follow.

Gathering up the folds of my golden satin skirt, I swept forward. Nanette came after, carrying my train, while the postilion struggled with my trunk and portmanteau. The bony hand was flung up, in a clear gesture of refusal. The postilion halted, then shrugged, letting fall the end of the trunk.

'Sorry, *mademoiselle,* I guess no men allowed.'

I stopped, confounded. 'Who, then, will carry my trunk?'

The black-clad nun did not speak a word. After a moment, Nanette released my train and bent to take hold of the end of the trunk. The postilion saluted and ran back to his horses, standing with heads bowed in the dusk, snorting plumes of smoke like ancient dragons. Biting my lip, I draped my portmanteau over my arm and seized the other end. Thus burdened, we crossed the step into a dimly lit corridor, as cold as the yard outside. The nun slammed the door shut and bolted it, secured three heavy iron locks and returned the jangle of keys to her girdle. I saw a flash of a scornful eye and then the nun jerked her head, indicating I should follow her. As we walked, she rang a handbell, as if I was a leper or a plague-cart. Swallowing angry words, I followed her.

I now understood what my guardian had meant by a heart of gall.

DEVIL'S BARGAIN

The Abbey of Gercy-en-Brie, France —
January 1697

The portress led the way down a corridor intersected by archways, which held up the curving vaults of the ceiling. Each of the pillars was crowned with intricate carvings of leaves and faces and animals, the paving stones below worn in the middle by centuries of shuffling feet.

I followed close on her heels, propelled by anger and pride, while poor Nanette struggled to keep up behind me. When we came to a junction, with steps curving upwards on one side and an archway leading into another corridor on the other, the portress indicated that Nanette could remain here and leave the trunk at the base of the stairs. The old nun still did not speak, but her gestures were so peremptory that her meaning was clear.

Gratefully, Nanette dropped her end of the trunk and rubbed her lower back. I put down

26

my end but kept a tight hold of my portmanteau, for it held my strongbox with my few
jewels and coins, and my quills and ink and
parchment. The portress led me through the
archway, leaving Nanette alone in the corridor, her poor old face knotted up like a
purse.

'Will she be all right? Will someone look
after her?' I asked. The portress did not reply.
I smiled back at Nanette reassuringly and
followed the nun past a door that stood half-
open. Glancing in, I saw a kitchen with
women in plain brown robes busy around the
table and bench, the familiar sight of pots
and pans and skillets and kettles looking
strange and dwarfish under the high vaulted
roof. The servants looked up as we passed,
and the portress clanged her bell and drew
the door shut with a snap. There were more
doors standing open, one showing barrels of
wine, the next a storeroom filled with sacks
and crates, and jars of preserves.

At the end of the corridor, the portress
unlocked an iron-studded door with another
key from the bunch at her waist. We passed
through and she locked it again behind me.
The sound of the lock clicking home caused
my chest to tighten and my hands to clench.
This place was indeed as bad as a prison. I
wished I had not made my devil's bargain
with the King. Was it worth being locked up
in this place of stone and old women, just so

27

I could keep receiving my pension?

But what else could I do? Flee to England, that miserable damp country where no one knew how to dress? How would I make my living? No one there would be interested in my novels, which were all about the scandalous secret lives of French nobles.

Ringing her bell, the portress led me through an archway to a long walkway, open on one side to a square garden. I could see little more than a patch of lawn, brown and sodden with moisture, and what looked like a well in one corner with a pointed roof. Benches lined either side of the walkway, under beautiful graceful arches open to the wind. Snow whirled in and stung my face. I quickened my step.

Across the garden, I saw a great hulk of a building, its lancet windows shimmering with candlelight. Faintly, I heard the sound of singing.

'Is that the nuns?' I asked, for the portress's silence made me nervous. 'What are they singing?'

She did not respond.

'It's beautiful.'

Still she did not respond, so I gave up and followed in silence. At last, she led me into a small room, where a fire burned on the grate. I went to it and held my gloved hands to it thankfully. Without a word, the portress went out and left me there alone, shutting the door behind her.

Once again, I was kept waiting a long time and once again my temper was running hot, when the door opened and in came a group of nuns, their faces pale and sober within the black wimples. One carried a pewter bowl, another a steaming jug, the third a basket.

'Welcome to the Abbey of Gercy-en-Brie, Mademoiselle de la Force,' the one in the lead said. She was small and bent, with a sad face like a monkey's. 'I am the Reverend Mother Abbess. You may call me Mère Notre. This is the mistress of our novices, Sœur Emmanuelle; our bursar, Sœur Theresa; our refectorian, Sœur Berthe; and our infirmarian and apothecary, Sœur Seraphina.'

At the sound of her name, each nun bowed her head. The first was a tall aristocratic-looking woman with hunched shoulders and a hard white face. The second looked weary and haggard. The third was round-faced, plump and smiling, with the fresh rosy skin of a countrywoman.

The fourth, Sœur Seraphina, made the strongest impression on me. Once upon a time, she must have been a great beauty. Her face was a perfect oval, her nose slim and straight. Although her eyebrows and eyelashes were now sparse, their golden colour intensified the brilliance of her eyes, which were the colour of new honey. Her skin was like worn muslin, faintly spotted with age. She gazed at

29

me with a troubled expression, taking in my luxurious gown, the lace *fontanges* on my head, fully a foot tall, and the heavy maquillage.

'You have been ordered to take refuge at the Abbey of Gercy-en-Brie at the order of his most Christian Majesty, the King. Are we to understand that you enter our cloister willingly?' Mère Notre said.

I did not know how to answer. No postulant had ever been more unwilling, but it was treason to defy the King. I could only hope that if I obeyed, he would soon relent and allow me back to the royal court. So I answered reluctantly, 'Yes, Mère Notre.'

'But are the de la Force family not . . . Huguenots?' Sœur Emmanuelle's nostrils flared.

'Not any more.' I did my best to repress my anger and shame, but it sounded in my voice nonetheless.

'You abjured?' she asked.

I shrugged one shoulder. 'Naturally.'

Yet the question raised many a rattling skeleton. My grandfather had only survived the dreadful St Bartholomew's Day massacre of the Huguenots because, when brutally stabbed, he had fallen to the ground and pretended to be dead. His father and his brother had not been so lucky; they were both stabbed till all life was gone. My grandfather had been a proud and fervent Huguenot all

30

his life, as had all my family — at least until the King had later revoked the Edict of Nantes and made it illegal to worship according to your conscience.

After the revocation, many Huguenots had fled France rather than convert to Catholicism. My uncle, Jacques-Nompar, the fourth Duc de la Force, had refused to either flee or convert. He had been thrown into the Bastille, his daughters locked up in convents, his son given a Catholic education. Eventually, my uncle had died, and his son, my cousin Henri-Jacques, had abjured and sworn obedience to His Most Catholic Majesty, and so had been permitted to become the fifth Duc de la Force.

I too had abjured. What else was I meant to do? Follow other Huguenots into penury and exile? Allow myself to be burnt at the stake, like so many of my fellow *réformés*? The King had offered me a pension of a thousand silver *louis* to convert. I thought a thousand silver *louis* a year worth a mass or two. And it's not as if I was the only one. Twenty-four thousand of us had abjured our faith.

'You must come to this abbey with a willing heart, *ma fille*,' Mère Notre said. 'Is it your desire to submit to our Rule?'

'Yes, Mère Notre,' I said through stiff lips.

She looked doubtful. 'You do understand what is required of you, *mademoiselle*? Perhaps, Sœur Emmanuelle, you will instruct

31

our postulant?'

The novice mistress fixed me with her scornful dark eyes. 'You must swear to abide by the Rule of this house, to be obedient and faithful and seek humility in all things. The first grade of humility is to keep the face of God always before you. Remember that He is always watching.'

'Yes, of course,' I replied.

'The second grade of humility is to love not your own will or satisfy your own desires but only to carry out the will of God.'

Not wanting to repeat myself like an idiot child, I bowed my head.

She went on without pause. 'The third grade of humility is to submit to your superiors in all things . . . the fourth is to patiently bear all hard and contrary things . . . to hide no evil thoughts but confess all . . . to be content with the meanest and worst of everything . . .'

By this sixth grade of humility, I was no longer nodding my head or murmuring acquiescence but staring at her in dismay. Sœur Emmanuelle went on inexorably. 'You must not just call yourself lower and viler than all but really believe it.'

'Surely you jest,' I exclaimed, though of course I knew she was all too serious.

Do nothing that was not authorised. Do not speak unless spoken to. Do not laugh. Do not raise your voice. Do not lift your eyes from the ground. Remember every hour that you are guilty of your sins.

'Well, that I can gladly do,' I said in a tone of less than subtle insinuation.

A little flutter went around the circle of nuns, and Sœur Berthe blushed.

'We must be honest with you, Mademoiselle de la Force,' Mère Notre said. 'It is against our practice to take court ladies into our house. It is rare that they have a true vocation, and they unsettle our sisters and disrupt the life of the cloister. However, we appealed to His Majesty the King for help, as we had suffered greatly during the recent upheavals. His response was to send you.'

'A gift from God,' I replied, folding my hands and turning my eyes up to heaven. From the corner of my eye, I saw Sœur Seraphina shake her head in warning.

Mère Notre's wrinkled face was troubled. 'I fear His Majesty may have made a mistake. Although it is true we are in need of your dowry, I cannot in good conscience accept a postulant . . .'

'Mère Notre.' Sœur Theresa wrung her hands together. 'The roof! The altar plate!'

Mère Notre hesitated. I felt a sudden clutch of anxiety. What would happen to me if I was turned away from the abbey door? Nothing made the King more furious than having his will thwarted.

'I'm sorry, Mère Notre, I didn't mean to be

flippant. I have spent too long at the court of the Sun King, where the quick and empty answer is always valued over more measured and thoughtful responses. I beg you to give me time to learn your ways.'

She bent her veiled head. 'Very well. You come among us as a postulant. There is no need yet to swear eternal vows. If you find your call to God is mistaken, you may always return to the world you have left behind.'

I bowed my head, wondering to myself how best to frame a letter to the King so that he would relent and allow me to return. Begging letters were all too common at the court.

'St Benedict himself said not to grant any newcomer easy entry but to test their spirit to see if they are from God. So we shall give you time to adjust to life here at the abbey, though I think it best if your instruction as a novitiate begins at once. The sooner you leave your old life behind you, the better.' Mère Notre blessed me and then went slowly from the room. She was so small and bent she looked rather like a hunchbacked child.

As soon as the door had thudded shut behind her, the other nuns closed around me. 'Now,' Sœur Emmanuelle said in a voice of deep satisfaction, 'it is time for the shedding of all temporal goods. Let us start with the dowry.'

'Four thousand *livres*,' Sœur Theresa said, 'plus two hundred *livres* per year for board,

34

three hundred *livres* for clothing, and ninety *livres* for food.'

'But that's outrageous. I paid less for my room at the palace.'

'Once you have taken your vows, you shall be with us for all of your natural life,' Sœur Emmanuelle replied.

I set my teeth. 'What if I should change my mind and decide not to take my vows?'

'The dowry need not be paid until the day you take your vows,' Sœur Theresa said, 'and, in any case, His Majesty the King has offered to cover that expense for you.'

Relief filled me. Imagine going into debt to pay for a cell in this cold draughty place.

'However, we shall need you to pay us your board and lodging costs now.' Sœur Theresa held out one hand.

Biting my lip, I dug in my portmanteau for my purse and handed over almost six hundred *livres,* nearly two-thirds of my entire year's pension.

'Now, you must give up all your clothes, right down to the last stitch. You have no need of such wanton luxury here,' Sœur Emmanuelle said.

I stared at her. 'I beg your pardon?'

'You may not keep even a pin. Strip it all off and pass it to me. We have brought you a postulant's robe.' She indicated a small pile of rough homespun clothes that the refectorian, Sœur Berthe, had laid on the side table.

'I shall not. Do you have any idea how much this dress cost?'

'It'll fetch a pretty penny,' Sœur Theresa agreed. 'Maybe even enough to have the church roof repaired.'

'That's stealing. You can't sell my clothes.'

'Oh, we'll only sell them once you've taken your vows. They'll belong to the abbey then.'

'They'll be long out of fashion by then.'

'Not in Varennes,' she answered. 'Really, I wish Mère Notre was not so particular about the waiting period. If you were to take your vows straightaway, we'd be able to claim your dowry from His Majesty the King and sell all your clothes and jewels, and get that roof fixed. Then we wouldn't have to celebrate the midnight office with snow swirling down on our heads.'

'I'm sorry,' I said as calmly as I could. 'I'm afraid I cannot permit you to pawn my belongings for your repairs. I am here at the request of His Majesty the King, but I am sure it will not be long before I am missed at court and called back. So, you see, I shall have need of my jewels and my clothes.'

Sœur Emmanuelle snorted. 'I've never heard it said that His Majesty the King was prone to changing his mind.'

'Are you so well acquainted with the King that you know his habits? Have you spent much time at court? If so, I am surprised not to know you. I have been at court since I was a girl.' I smiled at her sweetly.

'It is not something to boast about. Obviously, you are as frivolous and pleasure-loving as the rest of those fools at court, if you prefer to hoard what little you have of worth against an uncertain future instead of dedicating it to the glory of God. You'll learn soon enough. Now, remove your garments else we shall strip you ourselves.'

I set my jaw and stared around at the circle of black-cloaked women. They closed in on me, Sœur Berthe seizing my shoulders. I tried to wrench myself away, but she was too strong.

'Have a care for the dress,' Sœur Theresa cried anxiously.

'*Bon grè, mal grè,*' Sœur Seraphina whispered in my ear, a gentle hand on my arm.

I knew she was right. It made little difference whether I submitted with good grace or ill grace. Either way, I would be forced to strip, and surely to do so gracefully would be a lot more dignified.

'Besides, you don't want your beautiful clothes to be ruined.' Sœur Seraphina smiled at me. She had a faint foreign accent, which I thought might be Italian as she sounded rather like the Mazarinettes, the seven nieces of Cardinal Mazarin, who had scandalised Versailles for years. 'You would not wish to work in the laundries or the kitchens in such glorious golden silk.'

I gazed at her in dismay.

'An idle brain is the devil's playground,' Sœur Emmanuelle said. 'Strip.'

I sighed. 'Someone will have to help me. I cannot undress myself.'

Sœur Seraphina gently removed my lace *fontanges.* It was named for the King's mistress Angélique de Fontanges, who had lost her hat while hunting one day and had hastily tied up her curls with her garter. The King had admired the effect, and the next day all the court ladies had appeared with their curls tied back with lace. Angélique was dead now, of course, and had been for sixteen years, but we still all wore the *fontanges,* vying with each other for height and elaborateness.

One by one, Sœur Seraphina unfastened my skirts. First *la secrète,* of heavy gold embroidered all over with honeybees and flowers, and then *la friponne,* of golden tulle, clipped to the outer skirt with jewelled clasps in the shape of butterflies, and last *la fidèle,* of pale gold silk brocade. The dress had cost me a fortune, but I had gladly paid it as a subtle compliment to His Majesty, who, like the King Bee, ruled the hive.

'If you'd like to finish disrobing . . .' Sœur Seraphina held up a black cloak for me to hide behind as I pulled off my fine chemise and put on the one of coarse unbleached linen that she passed me. I then unrolled my silk stockings and passed them to her, then stood waiting for more clothes to be passed back to me. None came.

'I am sorry, *mademoiselle,*' Sœur Seraphina said. 'I must examine you to make sure you are not with child. Our abbey cannot afford the scandal of a baby being born within our cloisters.'

I stared at her in disbelief. 'I'm not pregnant.'

'I need to make sure. If you would please lie on the table.' Sœur Seraphina indicated a sturdy table behind me, a white linen cloth spread over the dark oak.

'My word should be enough.'

'You may not know yourself.'

'*Zut alors.* If I don't know, how will you?'

'I am the convent's apothecary. Believe me, I can tell if a woman is with child.'

'And no doubt tell her how to get rid of it too.'

Sœur Seraphina said nothing, though her face was grave. Sœur Emmanuelle hissed, 'That would be a mortal sin. You sully our walls with your words.'

'Please,' Sœur Seraphina said. 'I will not hurt you if you submit, but, if you fight, my sisters will need to hold you down and then it will be much harder for me to be gentle.'

I huffed out an angry sigh. 'Make it quick then.'

'Please lie down and lift your chemise.'

I lay down on the table, my legs pressed together, and shifted my body so I could lift up my chemise. Sœur Seraphina must have warmed her hands at the fire, for her fingers were not as icy cold as I had expected. Quickly, she poked and prodded my stomach and then gently squeezed my breasts. A flippant comment sprang to my lips. I shut my teeth and said nothing. She pulled the chemise down over my belly, saying softly, 'Her womb is not distended.'

'No. I did tell you.'

'I need you to open your legs now.'

I squeezed my knees together. 'Surely that's not necessary.'

'I'm sorry,' she said again. 'I need to make a full examination.'

'We know what the court of the King is like,' Sœur Emmanuelle said.

'Do you? For I must admit I wonder how. For your information, His Majesty the King is a pious man indeed these days and the whole court in an agony of ennui.'

'If you please.' Sœur Seraphina pushed my knees apart. For a moment, I resisted, gritting my teeth together, but once again I reminded myself I had nowhere else to go. I could only endure as she gently slid her fingers inside me. It lasted just a moment but I felt scalded with humiliation.

As she removed her hand and turned away to wash herself, I sat up and pulled my chemise down over my knees. 'Satisfied?'

'She is not with child,' Sœur Seraphina said to Sœur Emmanuelle.

'And?' the novice mistress demanded.

Sœur Seraphina shook her head.

'If she means am I still a virgin, then I must let you know that I . . . I was once married.' I had to force the words out through a large lump in my throat. Tears were burning my eyes.

'Once? Where then is your husband?' Sœur Emmanuelle demanded.

I pressed my hands together. 'My . . . my husband is . . .' I could not say the words.

Sœur Seraphina made a soft sympathetic sound.

'I'm so sorry,' Sœur Berthe said. 'We didn't know you were a widow. The letter from the King called you *"mademoiselle".*'

'I am *mademoiselle,*' I answered harshly. 'Must I sit here shivering in this dreadful cold? Pass me some clothes.'

The nuns exchanged wondering glances. Sœur Emmanuelle's face was alive with curiosity. I swear I saw her nostrils flare at the scent of scandal like a pig's at the smell of deep-buried truffles.

I gave her my coldest glare, standing stiffly as Sœur Berthe tied up my stays for me. I then allowed Sœur Berthe to help me into a heavy black dress, which smelt unpleasantly of the lye in which it had been washed. Added

41

to this was a long apron, like a peasant might wear, dark stockings in thick itchy wool, tied above my knee by a length of leather string, then the ugliest sabots I had ever seen.

I cannot describe the revulsion I felt wearing these clothes. They made me feel ill. It was not just their smell, their itch, their roughness; it was their ugliness. I have always adored beautiful clothes. I loved the sheen of satin and the sensuousness of velvet. I loved the beauty of the embroidery, the delicacy of the lace, the shush-shush-shush of silk moving against the floor. I liked to lie in my bed in the morning and think about what I might wear that day. With my choice of clothes, I could pay a subtle compliment to the King or win the attention of a man I wished to become my lover. I enjoyed planning some daring new fashion, like catching up my skirts with a ribbon to reveal my high-heeled slippers, or being the first to wear a dress of black 'winter lace' over a pale cream satin the same colour as my skin. I felt like a butterfly stripped of its gaudy wings by some cruel boy.

Sœur Seraphina carefully removed the pins from my hair and let the artificial curls tumble down. She then removed a pair of shears from her basket and, before I could utter more than a startled cry, chopped off all of my hair with a few quick decisive snaps. It fell to the floor in writhing black snakes.

'*Mordieu!* Not my hair.' I clutched at my head, dismayed to feel my hair bristle against my palm like the spines of a baby hedgehog.

'I'm sorry,' Sœur Seraphina said. 'All postulants must have their hair cropped.'

'Much easier to keep it free of lice,' Sœur Berthe said.

'You didn't say . . . no one warned me . . .' My hands were still clutching my head. *I'll have to buy a wig like an old lady,* I thought. *I can't appear at court with cropped hair! But wigs are so expensive . . .* Tears prickled my eyes. 'You had no right. You should have warned me. I'd never have agreed to let you cut my hair.'

Sœur Theresa began to gather up the shorn locks.

'Don't do that!' I seized her by the arm. 'That is my hair. You probably plan to sell it to a wig-maker. Well, it's mine. If anyone is to sell it, it's me.'

Sœur Theresa shrugged and let me snatch the locks of hair and thrust them into my portmanteau. 'You must give up your bag to us also. We shall keep it safe for you in the storeroom.'

'But I have my writing tools in there. My quills, my ink, my penknife . . .'

'You have no need for such things here,' Sœur Theresa said.

'Novices are not permitted to write letters,'

Sœur Emmanuelle said.

'But I must write. I must write to the King, and to my friends at court. I must write to my sister so she knows where I am . . . and my stories. How am I to write my stories?'

'Stories?' Sœur Emmanuelle spoke scornfully. 'You think you may waste your time here writing such frivolous stuff? Think again, *mademoiselle.*' She seized my portmanteau, trying to wrest it away from me.

I struggled against her. 'You have no right. How dare you?'

Sœur Berthe came to her assistance. The portmanteau was wrenched from my arms and emptied on the table. Sœur Emmanuelle snapped my quills in half, emptied the bottle of ink into the pail, and crumpled the sheets of parchment and threw them in the fire.

I tried to stop her but was held back by Sœur Berthe's brawny arms. She did not release me, no matter how hard I kicked her with my heavy wooden clogs. *'Salope,'* I cried, and, *'Putain,'* and all the other curses and maledictions I could think of, but it did no good.

My quills and ink and parchment were gone, and with them any chance of writing my way out of this prison.

CASTLES IN THE AIR

The Abbey of Gercy-en-Brie, France —
January 1697

That night, I lay in my bed and wept.

The tears came like summer storms, shaking my body and snatching away my breath. Eventually, I would stop, exhausted, but then I would think again of all I had lost, and the tears would flow again.

My writing tools were my most precious belongings. My best quill pen was made from a raven's feather. When my husband, Charles, gave it to me, he told me it was as black and glossy as my hair, and as sharp as my wit. I only used it to write my stories; letters, gambling IOUs and *billets-doux* were all written with goose quills I had trimmed and shaped myself with my silver penknife, which had been the last gift from my mother. I was often so poor that I could not pay my mantua-maker, but I always invested in the best ink and parchment. I smoothed it with pumice stone till it was as white and fine as my own skin, ready to absorb the rapid scratching of my quill.

At least my bundles of precious manuscripts were safe in my trunk. Or were they? Perhaps the nuns had gone through my trunk as well and thrown all my manuscripts on the fire. The thought caused me actual pain, as if my chest was being compressed with stones. So many dark hours of the night spent writing by the light of a single candle instead of sleeping. So many hours stolen from my duties as maid of honour, writing instead of standing for hours on aching feet and pretending to smile at the antics of the royal dwarves. Three of my novels had been published — anonymously, of course, to avoid the King's censors. To my surprise and delight, they had sold well enough and had even brought me in a little money. I had been working on another, a secret history of Gustave of Sweden, which I had hoped to publish soon. What would I do if it was all burnt to ashes?

As I moved my head restlessly on my limp pillow, I felt acutely the lack of my hair. I put up one hand and brushed it against the bristles.

My hair had always been my one beauty. Even when I was only a little girl, it had been Nanette's pride and joy. Every night, she would loosen it from its ribbons and brush it for me, while I told her all about the triumphs or petty tribulations of the day. In those days,

Nanette was only a young woman, with more tenderness than fierceness in her black eyes. Under her white cap, her hair was fine and fair, and she had a soft bosom I liked to lean against.

Once a week, she would massage my head with rosemary oil and carefully brush it with a fine-toothed comb, squashing any nits she found on an old linen rag.

'Here's a big one,' she'd say.

'Let me see. Oooh, it's a grand-papa. He's big enough to be a great-grand-papa.'

'I don't know where you get them all from. I could've sworn you were swept clean of the little beasts last week. Have you been playing with the miller's children again?'

'Well, yes, Nanette, but then who else do I have to play with?'

'Not with snotty-nosed lice-ridden peasants.'

'We've built a fort, Nanette. We're playing the religious wars.'

'Oh, my little cabbage, that's not such a good game to play. Can't you play something nice? Can't you just play houses?'

'But that's so boring. We like to have battles. I'm the leader of the *réformés* and Jacques is the leader of the scarlet whores . . .'

'Bon-bon! Don't you speak like that. You must be careful.'

'Of what?' I twisted my head around to look at her in surprise.

47

'Not everyone in France thinks like your mother, Bon-bon. The *réformés* lost the war, remember, and the King — God bless his soul — is Catholic.'

I sighed. It was so hard to understand how the King could be both our monarch and our enemy. Nanette was perturbed, I could tell, her hand heavy on the comb. 'Ow. That hurts! Don't dig so hard.'

'Oh, I'm sorry. Is that better? Look, another big one.'

'That one's the great-grand-mama. Look behind my ears, Nanette. That's the nursery, where all the babies are. Do you think nits have nurses too, Nanette?'

'They'd need them with this many babies,' Nanette grumbled, tilting my head to one side as she combed behind my ear.

'When nits are all grown up, they climb the hill and look out for enemies.'

'Invaders from the heads of the miller's children.'

'Yes. And then they fight them off . . . What would nits use for weapons, Nanette?'

'Their teeth, I expect. Stop squirming, Bon-bon. If you sit still, I'll tell you a story.'

Nanette had a great storehouse of stories in her head: funny stories about a wicked fox or a fisherman whose wife wished his nose was a sausage; scary stories about giants that ate little girls, and ghosts, and goblins; and sweet stories about shepherds and shepherdesses

48

falling in love. Whenever Nanette wanted me to sit still — while doing up my boot hooks or sewing up a dragging hem — she knew that all she had to do was promise me a story and at once I would stop wriggling and complaining and sit as quietly as she could wish.

Where was Nanette tonight? Had she been given a bed or forced to endure the long journey back to Versailles with the carriage? She was so old and frail now, the journey would have exhausted her. I hoped she was sleeping comfortably somewhere. I would have to beg the nuns for some of my money back so I could pay for her to go home to the Château de Cazeneuve. She had left the chateau with me thirty-one years ago, when I had been summoned to court, and, like me, had never been back. I knew I could trust my sister, Marie, to have a care for her. How shocked Marie would be to hear I'd been banished to a nunnery. The thought brought a fresh rush of tears. I wanted Marie to be proud of me, her clever sister who served the royal family.

I heard a shuffle of feet, and then someone came into my cell. I tensed and lifted myself on my elbow. It was Sœur Emmanuelle. I could just see her long white face with its high-bred nose in the dim light of the lantern that had been left burning in the corridor. She was dressed in a loose chemise, with a shabby old shawl huddled about her shoulders.

Wiping away my tears, I rose higher on my elbow and opened my mouth to speak, but Sœur Emmanuelle lifted her finger to her lips and shook her head. I shut my mouth again. She nodded briefly, lifted the little clay pitcher next to my pallet and poured me a cup of water. She then sat beside me on the bed, passing me the cup. I drank obediently. The water was icy cold, but refreshing. I felt my shudders ease a little. She took the cup away and put it back on the table. Then she laid both hands beside her cheek, like a child pretending to sleep.

Exhausted, I lay down again. She dampened my handkerchief and gently washed my face as if I was a child. I felt tears rise again at this unexpected kindness but tried to smile at her in thanks. She smiled, a small grim compression of the corners of her mouth, and passed me a triangle of folded cloth that she had carried tucked inside her sleeve. I mopped my eyes and then blew my nose. When I shamefacedly offered her back her handkerchief, she shook her head and refused it. I scrunched it in my hot damp hand under my cheek. I felt her hand on my brow, stroking my forehead. I heaved a sigh, shut my eyes and felt my body slowly relax.

I was almost asleep when I felt the edge of my blankets lift. Cold air rushed in. Even as I

stirred and opened my eyes, Sœur Emmanuelle crept into my bed, one cold claw of a
hand sliding around my body to clutch my
breast, her gaunt body pressing itself against
mine.

I knew, of course, that women could have
female lovers as well as male. I had friends at
court who had been married against their will
to ageing roués or vicious rakes, and who
sought escape from their unwanted attentions
in the tender arms of their women friends.
Madeleine de Scudéry, whom I revered, was
famous for her weekend salons, 'Saturdays of
Sapho', which only women were permitted to
attend. We all read each other love poems
and wrote stories of a land of peace and
harmony, where men were forbidden and
women could be free of their brutish desires.
I had even been propositioned by a woman
once or twice, and had always refused with a
smile. There was a difference, though, between the raising of a suggestive eyebrow and
a cold bony hand groping at my breast, when
I was already strung tight as a lute string with
fear and dread and grief.

I spun around, shoving at her so violently
that she fell to the floor. 'Don't you dare,' I
cried. 'Get out!'

Sœur Emmanuelle landed on her bony arse
with a thump that must have hurt. I heard a
startled cry from the cell beside me. I sat up,
clutching my blanket to me, and stared at

51

her. I might have tried to say something but the look on her face thickened my tongue. It was a bleak black look, promising me that I would suffer for my rejection. For a moment, she stood there, looming over me, then she lifted the curtain and disappeared. I lay back, trembling inside.

Sœur Emmanuelle punished me every day.

I was made to empty all the chamber pots in the morning and scrub them out with water so cold that it formed a crust of ice in the bucket overnight. I was assigned to the kitchen and set to washing dishes in scummy water, and peeling endless mounds of vegetables. It was also my job to clean the ashes and charred remnants of wood out of the kitchen ovens and the fireplace in the parlour, the only room in the convent where a fire was permitted. I also had to keep the baskets of firewood replenished, staggering out into the snow to chop logs into kindling until my hands were blistered and sore. Sœur Emmanuelle kept a cane by her at all times and was quick to strike me on my back and shoulders if I did not obey her orders readily enough.

As a small child, I had never been struck, despite all Nanette's threats. Once the Marquis de Maulévrier became my guardian, however, I had been beaten regularly, to drive the devils out of me, he said. He had failed spectacularly. Each encounter with his birch rod only made me more devilish.

This was true of Sœur Emmanuelle too. The more she struck me and humiliated me, the more proudly I lifted my head and the more slowly I moved to obey. Once, she caught me rolling my eyes.

'On your hands and knees,' she cried. 'You shall crawl to the church like the worthless worm you are.'

I smiled and dropped at once to my hands and knees, gaily shaking my head and arching my back as if playing a game with a child. She struck me a stinging blow across the rear end, and I pretended to rear and buck like a donkey, braying loudly. The other novices smothered giggles.

'Enough!' she cried. 'You are insolent. I'll teach you to be humble.'

She hit me again, across the face. At once, anger surged through me. I leapt up and seized her cane and snapped it in two, flinging the pieces down. The novices all fell silent, looking scared. Sœur Emmanuelle bent and picked up the pieces of her cane.

'To defy your superior is to defy God himself. You must do penance. Come with me to the church.' Her voice was low and filled with menace.

I stood for a moment, my breath coming quickly, wanting to shout, 'I shall not,' as I had once shouted at the Marquis de

Maulévrier. I was not a rebellious disobedi-
ent child any more, though. I was a grown
woman. I could not afford to be thrown out
of the convent, not until I had the King's
pardon. Disobedience was treason, and the
penalty for treason was death.

'I'm sorry. I lost my temper. You shouldn't
have struck me, though.' I put one hand to
my smarting cheek.

'To the church,' she answered, her face
whiter than ever.

I nodded my head and moved towards the
door. She pushed in front of me, making me
follow behind her. I did so without protest. It
was freezing cold in the cloisters, snow on
the ground and in the sky. The church was
just as cold. Sœur Emmanuelle told me to lie
down with my arms spread wide in the shape
of a cross and my face pressed to the icy
floor. I obeyed. She knelt nearby and prayed
for my immortal soul. It was unendurable.
The minutes dragged past. At long last, she
rose, and I lifted my head.

'Stay there,' she ordered. 'Stay till you are
given leave to rise.'

She did not give me leave until midnight,
when the nuns all came to the church for
nocturns. She came in silently and stood over
me. All I could see of her was the black hem
of her habit. Then she made a sharp gesture,
bidding me to rise to my feet.

But I could not. My limbs were stiff and

frozen, locked in the shape of a cross.

She bent and seized me by the arm, dragging me to my knees and shaking me. She could not speak; Sœur Emmanuelle would never break the Great Silence, which lasted all night, from the evening service of compline to the morning service of matins. But she shook me violently and tried to make me get up.

My feet were like lumps of stone, my legs as weak as an old woman's. I managed to stand for a moment, but then the paving stones shifted sideways and I fell. I heard a quick flurry of steps, then Sœur Seraphina was beside me, her hands lifting me up. I staggered, but she supported me strongly, half-carrying me out of the church. She did not speak but helped me to my pallet in the novice dormitory. She wrapped me in her own cloak, which smelt sweetly of lavender, tucked a hot brick wrapped in flannel in bed with me and stood over me while I drank a cup of herbs steeped in hot water, my teeth chattering against the rim. Then she smiled at me, pressed one hand against my cheek in comfort and left me.

I was soon warm again and drowsy. My thoughts drifted. I imagined my mother bent over me, stroking my hair away from my forehead. 'Oh, Bon-bon,' she sighed. 'What trouble have you got yourself into now?'

I wrenched my mind away. I did not want

55

to think about my mother. It grieved me to imagine her up in heaven with the angels, looking down and seeing me here. It was better to disbelieve in heaven altogether.

I had not prayed to God all those long cold hours. I had not prayed since I was a child. I had simply gritted my teeth and set myself to endure. It had seemed important to me that Sœur Emmanuelle realised she would not break my will. I could have got to my feet once Sœur Emmanuelle was gone. I could at least have huddled on one of the wooden pews, perhaps even wrapped myself in the richly embroidered altar cloth. I'm sure that is what she expected me to do. Yet to do so would have been to allow her, somehow, to triumph over me.

The Marquis de Maulévrier used to lock me in the caves under the Château de Cazeneuve. They were as cold as the church, and much darker. A hermit had once lived there, many hundreds of years before, and had died there. I wondered if his skeleton was still there, hidden under the stones. I imagined I heard his footsteps shuffling closer and closer, then I felt his cold breath on the back of my neck, the brush of a spectral finger. I screamed, but no one heard me.

Surely he was a good man, that long-ago hermit, I told myself. *He would not hurt a little girl.* I imagined he was taking my hand because he wanted to show me the way to escape the cave. Perhaps there was a secret door down low in the wall, a door only large enough for a child. If I stepped through that door, I would be in another world, in fairyland perhaps. It would be warm and bright there, and I would have a magical wand to protect myself. I'd ride on the back of a dragonfly, swooping through the forest. I'd battle dragons and talk to birds and have all kinds of grand adventures.

Later, I found that small door into fairyland could be conjured any time I needed it. The world beyond the door was different every time. Sometimes, I found a little stone house in the woods where I could live with just Nanette and my sister, Marie, and a tabby cat who purred by the fire. Sometimes, I lived in a castle in the air with a handsome prince who loved me. Other times, I was the prince myself, with a golden sword and a white charger.

When I went to Paris, I gave that door to fairyland as a gift to the real prince I met there. The Dauphin was just five years old when I was appointed maid of honour to his mother, Queen Marie-Thérèse, but I did not meet him for another two years. I saw him many times, of course, dressed in frothing white gowns, with his hair hanging in blonde ringlets down his back. When he was seven, he was breeched, baptised, and taken from the care of his nurse and put in the charge of the Duc de Montausier, a former soldier who thought any sign of emotion a weakness to be repressed.

One day, the Queen sent me to bring her son to her for their daily meeting in the Petite Galerie. I hurried through the immense cold rooms of the Louvre, my heels clacking on the marble. My wide skirts swished. When I had first arrived at the Louvre, I had been utterly overwhelmed by the vastness and grandeur of the King's residence. I had always thought the Château de Cazeneuve was imposing, and indeed it was one of the largest estates in Gascony. It seemed small and medieval in comparison to the Louvre, however.

I understood then why everyone at court wore such full-bodied wigs and totteringly high heels and full skirts with trailing trains, and beribboned petticoat breeches and immense embroidered cuffs and hats flouncing with feathers, and why everyone's gestures and antics and tragedies were on such a large scale. It was an attempt to be undiminished.

As I reached the Dauphin's apartments, I heard the Duc de Montausier's voice along with an all too familiar *swish-crack* as he brought his cane down upon the little boy's body.

'You're a fool . . . *swish-crack* . . . an imbecile . . . *swish-crack* . . . an affront to His Majesty . . . *swish-crack* . . . you shame me . . . *swish-crack* . . . and yourself . . . *swish-crack* . . .* stupid as any peasant boy . . . *swish-crack* . . .'

I stood still, shaking, unable to move or speak. In the past two years, the memory of those dreadful years under the Marquis de Maulévrier's care had slowly faded to a mere bruise. The sound of that *swish-crack* brought it all back to me. I hunched my shoulders and set my jaw. At last, the Duc stopped and came shouldering past me like an angry bull. I waited a while, but the sound of the boy within weeping broke my heart. I gently pushed open the door and went inside.

The Dauphin was lying on his stomach on his bed, his curls all in disorder, his eyes swollen and red. His lacy shirt was only half-drawn over his shoulder. His thin back was covered in red weals. I took my handkerchief and dampened it in the bowl. 'You know, my guardian used to beat me too. I don't know why. Sometimes, he beat me because I spoke, and sometimes because I didn't.'

The boy looked towards me but did not speak. I offered him the damp handkerchief but he made no move towards it.

'I never knew what I was meant to do. If I cried, he beat me harder. If I bit my lip and refused to cry, that only made him angrier and the beating would be even worse. Is that the same with you and the Duc?'

He nodded his head slowly. I knelt beside the bed and passed him the handkerchief again. He took it and pressed it against his eyes.

'I think being locked up in the cellar was worse than being beaten, though. It was so dark I couldn't see my hand even if I held it right before my eyes. I was afraid of the spiders and the cockroaches too. And I heard squeaking and squealing and scritching and scratching, and thought there must be rats in there as well. Or maybe bats. Once, I saw little red eyes glowing in the darkness. They came closer and closer and closer . . .'

The prince's eyes were fixed on my face. When I paused, he said, 'What did you do?'

'I took off my boot and threw it at the eyes as hard as I could.'

He smiled.

'Worse than the spiders and the cockroaches, worse than the rats and the bats, though, was the ghost.'

'A ghost?'

I nodded. 'You see, the cellar used to be a cave where a hermit lived. He was said to be so holy that when he was challenged by a heretic to prove his saintliness, he hung his cloak on a sunbeam.'

The prince sat up on his elbow.

'He lived in that cave for a great many years and eventually died there. His bones were found there, in the very cave where my guard-

60

ian had locked me up.'

'Weren't you scared?'

'Terrified. But in the end I thought that a man who was so good he could hang his cloak on a sunbeam wouldn't hurt me and I'd rather be safe in his cave than where my guardian could get me.' Then I told the Dauphin about the secret door into fairyland that I had imagined, and how it didn't matter how hard my guardian beat me or how cold and dark the cave was, I was always able to pretend I was somewhere else.

By this time, the Dauphin was sitting up and his eyes were eager. 'Do you think maybe you could find a door like that here?' I asked, taking up his comb and tidying his hair for him. 'It's not a real door, you understand, just a pretend one. But it might make it easier to bear the Duc, at least until you're grown up and you can have him banished.'

'Or thrown in a dungeon,' the Dauphin said. 'With rats and bats.'

'Don't waste the secret door on thinking up awful punishments for him,' I advised. 'You want it to be a good place, the sort of place you can always go to, whenever you need to. Here, let me help you get your coat on. Your mother wants to see you.'

He sighed and pouted. 'I don't want to go. I want to stay here and think about the secret door.'

'You can think about it on the way. That's

the beautiful thing about the secret door. You can open it anywhere, any time.'

In later years, the court ladies often laughed behind their fans at the Dauphin, saying cruelly that he could spend a whole day tapping his cane against his foot and staring into space. I knew, though, that he was building castles in the air.

Midnight Vigils

The Abbey of Gercy-en-Brie, France —
April 1697

The midnight bell tolled, jerking me awake.

I lay for a moment, disorientated and afraid. My mind was filled with the flapping rags of dreams. I opened my eyes and felt my spirits sink as I recognised the dirty curtain that divided my bed from the others in the dormitory. Wearily, I sat up, sliding my poor cold feet out, seeking my night shoes. It seemed a long time since my feet had last felt warm. Every night, I slept curled in a ball like a wood mouse, my feet wrapped in the hem of my chemise, my dress and my cloak spread over the top of my thin blanket for added warmth. Perfect for quick dressing in the middle of the night.

I wish I had known nuns were woken up at midnight to pray. I'd have taken my chances with being exiled. Somehow, I had thought that nuns lived a life of idle luxury, with servants to wait on them and nothing to do all day but say the occasional rosary and make the occasional genuflection. I had heard stories of nuns who kept lapdogs, held parties in their cells at night and smuggled their lovers in with the laundry.

Perhaps such stories were true of other convents, but sadly they were not at all true of Gercy-en-Brie. Mère Notre and the other senior nuns took the laws of *clausura* seriously indeed. The windows were kept shuttered and barred, the gates were double-locked, and the walls were so high that I had not seen a bird or a cloud since I had arrived here. In all the weeks I had been here, I had seen no one but nuns and lay sisters — women who had come to the abbey without a dowry and so were not permitted to take full vows. Like me, they wore a plain dark dress, an apron and heavy clogs, their hair covered with a white cap with a veil hanging down the back. They did most of the work, though the nuns each had their chores to do as well.

Not even serving women were allowed in the convent. Nanette had offered to join the community as a lay sister, so that she could serve me, but Sœur Theresa had told her that novices were not permitted to have servants and she would be put to work scrubbing out the pigsty or some such nonsense. So Nanette went back to the Château de Cazeneuve, prepared to beg my sister to ask her husband, the Marquis de Théobon, to intercede on my behalf with the King. I knew it was no use. Théobon was too fat and lazy to bother to travel to Versailles, and the King never granted favours to noblemen who chose to stay on their estates instead of joining the whirligig of life at court. 'I do not know him,' he would say, and flick the letter away.

I had been allowed to see Nanette before she left, though we were separated by an iron grille so thick that we could not touch more than a fingertip.

'They will not let me stay with you,' she wept. 'Me, who has looked after you since you were no more than a tiny flea.'

'Don't cry, Nanette,' I told her. 'You don't want to be locked up in here with me, I promise you. The food is dreadful.'

'Oh, Bon-bon, I don't like to leave you here.'

'You must,' I said. 'You'll do more good nagging my brother-in-law to get off his fat arse and help me than scrubbing out pigsties, I assure you.'

I had heard nothing since she left. Nuns were not permitted to receive letters, Sœur Emmanuelle took great pleasure in informing me.

The only break from dreary routine was the monthly arrival of the priest to take confession and give mass. And you cannot count that as seeing a man. Even if you consider a priest a man — which I don't — I never actually saw him. He was just a shadow and a sweaty smell and a mumble and a grumble. And what did I have to confess, locked away here with all these old women? Wishing the food was better? Wishing I had a man in my bed to keep me warm? Confessing that I had woken up more than once with my body twisting with desire, my dreams filled with images of Charles . . .

'What I wouldn't give to see a man,' I exclaimed one morning as the other novices and I swept and dusted the dormitory. 'A young comely one, preferably, but I swear any man would do.'

The other novices giggled nervously.

'Oh, you mustn't say such things.' Sœur Irene looked over her shoulder.

'The butcher comes in autumn to slaughter the pigs,' Sœur Juliette said. 'But we all have to stay in our cells till he's gone. It's horrible — all we can hear are the pigs screaming. We hate it when he comes.'

'Sometimes, the bishop sends a handyman to fix anything that's broken,' said Sœur Paula, a novice with a freckled face and gingery eyebrows. 'But he only comes when we're all in church and must be finished by the time we return. The portress rings the bell so we know not to enter the cloister.'

'It's been a long time since anything's been repaired here,' said Sœur Olivia, a lovely young woman with the smooth oval face of a saint in a painting. She might have gone on to say more if Sœur Emmanuelle had not then entered the room and given us all penances for speaking without cause.

There were only a handful of novices, ranging from Sœur Olivia, who must have been approaching eighteen, to little Sœur Mildred, who was only twelve. We all slept together in one long dormitory, with canvas hung up to divide our rooms into the semblance of cells. With the sound of the midnight bell dying away, I could hear the girls next to me stretching and yawning, and Sœur Emmanuelle's knees creaking as she clambered to her feet.

I dressed quickly, wrapping my heavy cloak about me. My nose felt like an icicle. My hands were mottled blue. Sœur Emmanuelle looked past my curtain, frowning and beckoning. I moved instantly to join her, knowing that the slightest sign of insubordination would result in yet another humiliating punishment.

Beyond my curtain, the other novices were already lined up, their eyes lowered, their hands tucked into their sleeves for warmth. I hastened to fall into line with them. Together, we glided down the length of the corridor and down the night stairs to the church. There was no sound but the shuffle of slippers on the stone floor and the occasional chink of rosary beads. All was black and sombre, the only light coming from the small lantern that burned at one end of the dormitory. It illuminated each black robe and white veil briefly, before each novitiate passed back into shadow.

My thoughts turned, as always, to the court. If I was in Versailles, I'd be drinking champagne as I strolled through the gardens under the light of rose-coloured paper lanterns, listening to an orchestra play as it floated past on a gondola. I'd be leaning on a gentleman's satin-clad shoulder, rattling dice in a cup, promising him some of my Gascon luck. Perhaps I'd even be dancing.

I must have displeased the King greatly for him to have banished me to this bleak place. Perhaps the Noëls had been the last drop of water that caused the jug to overflow. Perhaps the King had been enraged with me for some time. I wondered if I had offended him with the novel I had written about Queen Margot, his grandfather's scandalous first wife, the previous summer. It had been published anonymously, but I should have guessed the King would know I had written it. Thanks to his spies, the King knew everything.

I had always been fascinated with Queen Margot, having heard lots of stories about her at the Château de Cazeneuve, where I'd been born and where she had once lived. Perhaps it had not been wise to choose her as the subject of one of my secret histories. After all, she had made the King's grandfather, Henri of Navarre, look like a cuckold and a fool.

But it was such a great story, too good to resist. Queen Margot had had many lovers, including, some said, her own brother, Henri, who would in time become king himself. She was accused of insatiable sexual desires, murder and treason, and left a wake of broken hearts and scandal everywhere she went. It was said that her parties in the Rue de Seine were so noisy that no one in the Palais du Louvre was able to sleep.

At the age of nineteen, poor Margot had been forced to marry Henri of Navarre, a Huguenot, even though she was said to be in love with Henri de Guise, head of one of the most powerful Catholic families in France. She refused to say 'I do' during the ceremony and so her brother, King Charles IX, had taken her skull in his hands and nodded it up and down for her.

Six days later, on St Bartholomew's Day, King Charles had signed the order for the slaughter of thousands of Huguenots. It was whispered that the whole wedding had been a trick designed to lure the noble Huguenots to Paris. Margot's mother, Catherine de' Medici, was said to have already murdered Jeanne of Navarre, Margot's mother-in-law, with a gift of poisoned gloves; the slaughter of another fifty thousand Huguenot dissenters was not such a stretch for her, surely?

No one knows for sure how many died. The Duc de Sully, who escaped the massacre by carrying a Book of Hours under his arm, said it was closer to seventy thousand. My own grandfather said simply that everyone he knew had died: his father, his brother, his uncle, his cousins, his servants . . .

Margot had saved her husband's life by hiding him in her room and refusing to admit the assassins, which had included her lover, Henri de Guise. It had still been an unhappy marriage, though, with infidelity on both sides. As is often the way, the men in Margot's life had been determined to break her. Poor Margot was kept imprisoned in the Louvre by her brother after the massacre, and then later — after rebelling against her husband — was imprisoned by him in various chateaux, including that of my family, for eighteen long years. At last, their marriage was annulled and she was allowed to settle in Paris, running a literary salon where poets and philosophers, courtiers and courtesans all rubbed elbows together.

I admired her immensely, for her boldness and her wit and her refusal to be broken. Besides, it was far too delicious a tale not to tell. I had collected every anecdote I could find about her, and studied Margot's own memoirs and read between their lines, and woven the most exciting story I could manage. Published in six volumes in Paris and Amsterdam, my secret history of her life had taken the court by storm, rather to my surprise. For a while, my novel was all anyone could talk about, and it was all I could do to hide my surprise and delight. I should have remembered what Queen Margot herself had said: 'The more hidden the venom, the more dangerous it is.'

The King had said nothing, just smiled his placid inscrutable smile and continued with his day: rising from his bed; saying his prayers; sitting immobile while he was shaved and bewigged; rising to his feet as the First Valet passed the royal shirt to the Grand Master of the Wardrobe, who passed it to the Dauphin, who passed it to the King, who put it on. Every moment of the King's day was ruled by etiquette, even the hour in which he would visit his mistresses and his dogs, until at last he retired again to bed, the First Valet being permitted to unclasp the garter on his right leg and the Second Valet the garter on his left. Really, the routine of the abbey was not so different from the routine of the court, except that here it was work and prayer, work and prayer, and so much harder on the knees.

I looked about me. All I could see were rows of black-clad backs, bowing before a gilded and embossed reliquary in which was meant to reside a scrap of St Bartholomew's skin. The chest gleamed in the light of hundreds of candles, which trembled in the draughts that crept about our ankles like hungry rats. Far, far above, at the summit of towering pillars of stone, graceful arches held up the high vaulted ceiling. I wondered how those long-ago stonemasons had ever built the place. Surely it defied the laws of nature? Surely the whole edifice should come crashing down upon our heads? I felt as small and insignificant as an ant under all that mighty weight of stone. *Wasn't that the whole idea?* I thought. All those soaring spaces, those immense windows in gorgeous jewelled hues, the babble of rite and ritual, was it not all designed to make us feel small?

I knelt when I was meant to kneel, rose when I was meant to rise, crossed myself and murmured 'Amen' as I ought, feeling numb all through as if even my soul was deadened with cold. All the while, my mind slipped free. I remembered warm golden days when my sister and I had run wild in the chateau's parkland, riding horses, sailing boats on the millpond, exploring the caves and cellars under the chateau, and building fairy bowers in the park. I remembered swinging all one long afternoon, higher and higher into the sky, legs pumping hard, then slowly drifting down till I could draw in the dust with the toe of my slipper. I remembered my first days at court, dazzled and afraid, and how the

King's mistress, Athénaïs, had taught me to talk with my fan, and where to place my patches. I remembered the first time I met Charles, my lover, my husband, my doom . . .

La Puissance D'Amour

Palais du Luxembourg, Paris, France —
July 1685
'Paugh! I could not stand another second in Versailles. The stench, the heat, the people. I swear I'd have gone stark staring mad if I'd been forced to stay another moment. Give me the sweet air of Paris any time,' I cried.

Everyone laughed. Paris smelt far worse than Versailles. Travelling to the capital from Versailles, you could smell the city before you could see it. We all wore perfumed gloves, and carried pomanders attached to our girdles with ribbons to hold to our noses whenever we had to step outside. They all knew that I meant the rank stench of sycophancy and corruption that followed the King wherever he went.

'Well, we are glad you managed to tear yourself away from Versailles to grace us with your presence,' Madeleine de Scudéry smiled. She was a short stocky woman, badly dressed, with pockmarked skin. Nonetheless, she

74

moved in the highest circles. Able to converse as easily in Latin as in French, she was rumoured to be the true author of the most popular novels of the century, *Artamène* and *Clélie,* though they had been published under her brother's name. I certainly believed the rumours. No man could write with such passion and sensitivity about the landscape of a woman's heart.

I had just entered the Salle du Livre d'Or, a gilded jewellery box of a room at the Palais du Luxembourg, the home of Anne-Marie-Louise d'Orléans, the Duchesse de Montpensier. The room was so crowded I could barely see the famous painted walls, the mouldings and frames heavily encrusted with gold. In one corner, the courtesan Ninon de Lenclos was arguing with Jean Racine, the playwright, and his saturnine friend, Nicolas Boileau, who had recently written a poem that cruelly mocked women. Ninon de Lenclos was not pleased with him, you could tell at a glance. The Abbé de Choisy fluttered his lace fan nearby, dressed as usual in a gorgeous gown that any woman there would have been happy to have hanging in her wardrobe. Jean de la Fontaine, an elderly poet famous for his fables and his vagueness, was deep in conversation with Charles Perrault, whose lined face was more haggard than ever under his heavy wig. Once the King's court-appointed writer, producing glowing biographies of the King's favourite artist and mistress, Perrault had lost his position and his pension, though not his taste for finery, by the look of his silver-encrusted satin coat. Standing quietly beside him was his plain and clever niece, Marie-Jeanne L'Héritier. She flashed me a quick smile and caught me by the elbow. 'Charlotte-Rose! I have not seen you in an age. Have you written anything new for us?'

'A frippery, no more,' I answered. 'Who has time to write at court? It's all very well for you, you're a woman of independent means. I have to earn my living.'

'By going to balls every night,' she teased.

'Life as a maid of honour is not all dancing and partying, I'll have you know. I have to advise the Marquise on what jewels to wear and the best place to stick her patches. An inch too low and she'll be signalling that she is discreet instead of coquettish. Just think of the scandal.'

Marie-Jeanne laughed, but my mistress, Athénaïs, the Marquise de Montespan, beckoned me impatiently and I had to go. Athénaïs was dressed in a gown of gold lace — shockingly expensive, I knew — which barely covered her capacious bosom. Her hair was dressed in a thousand dancing yellow ringlets. 'You must not speak so of Versailles,' she scolded me. 'It is the most magnificent place on earth, a fitting symbol of the King's glory.'

'Far too many courtiers and not enough latrines for me,' I responded. 'Living in a bandbox and having to take my own chamber pot to parties is *not* my idea of magnificence.'

Anne-Marie-Louise, the Duchesse de Montpensier, smiled up at me from her low gilded couch. As the King's cousin, she was the only one in the room permitted to sit. 'Mademoiselle de la Force, you are simply too wicked. Do you have a story for us?'

'Throw me a line. Anything!'

'Well, then . . .' Anne-Marie-Louise tapped one finger on her chin, thinking.

'Something about love,' a young man called out.

I glanced his way. He was young and wore claret-red velvet with lace spilling at his throat and over his wrist. I unfurled my fan and waved it before me. 'All my stories are about love.'

'Tell us a story about a man who falls in love with a woman the first time he sees her. A *coup de foudre*,' the young man said.

'As if shot by an arrow from Cupid's bow,' I replied.

'Exactly.' He pressed his hands to his chest, pretending that I had shot such an arrow straight through his heart. I smiled and looked away, aware of a quickening of my blood.

'Sssh, everyone. Mademoiselle de la Force has a story for us,' Anne-Marie-Louise called. Gradually, everyone quietened, turning their eyes to me. I took a deep breath, feeling a familiar surge of vitality as I faced the crowd.

'Once upon a time, in enchanted Arabia, there was a prince called . . .' I looked the young man up and down, and then said, 'Panpan.'

There was a ripple of amusement through the crowd. *Panpan* was baby-talk for spanking and, in more sophisticated circles, a metaphor for *faire l'amour.*

'Although his father was an enchanter, Prince Panpan had never bothered to learn his magical arts as he sailed through life on the back of his beauty and charms. One day, Cupid decided to tame his capricious heart and caused his path to cross that of the Princess Lantine.' I felt the young man's eyes intent on my face and looked away, trying to calm the slow mount of blood to my cheeks and the acceleration of my pulse.

'To see her and to love her were one and the same thing. But how Panpan's heart was changed! His soul was on fire, his whole being filled with light. He knew that he loved the princess, ardently and truly, and that he had always loved her. But that is not the only miracle of the Power of Love. At that moment, Lantine too was pierced by the arrow of love . . .'

On I went, inventing problems to throw in my lovers' way and obstacles to be overcome. At last, Panpan succeeded in rescuing his princess and marrying her, though both realised that the flames of love could burn as well as arouse. I gave a mock-curtsey to indicate I was done, and a round of applause broke out.

'Marvellous,' Anne-Marie-Louise cried. 'Ah, I wish I lived in one of your stories, *mademoiselle*!'

'Most touching,' Athénaïs said, toying with one of the ringlets coiled on her breast. 'I must get you to write it down for me so I can read it to the King.'

'Of course,' I said with a smile, even though I knew the King's interest had passed on and Athénaïs was no longer his *maîtresse en titre*. He still visited her, though, nearly every day. If Athénaïs did read him one of my stories, and he liked it, perhaps the King would pay me a pension as he did other writers at court. My spirit soared at the thought.

'Another story!' Madame de Scudéry clapped her hands. 'Anyone wish to try and outdo Mademoiselle de la Force?'

A young poet quickly took up the challenge and began reading a long poem entitled 'To the Pearl Trembling in Her Ear'. I sipped my wine and listened critically. The poem was well-written enough but he would lose points for reading from a scroll of paper. The idea was to be tossed a topic and spin a tale from it on the spot, with as much inventiveness and sophistication as possible. That is not to say that I didn't spend days writing and polishing my stories in advance and learning them by heart so I could toss one off at will, with absolute assurance and a great many double entendres.

The young man in claret velvet was still gazing at me admiringly. Although I knew I'd never be a beauty, at the court of the Sun King I had learnt to make the most of what I had. I could not make my mouth small so I painted it crimson and put a patch just by its left corner — *la baiseuse,* as it was called. I padded my bodice and plucked my eyebrows till they were an arch of perpetual disdain. I wore riding dress whenever I could, for I knew it suited me, and, when I could not, I made sure I wore rich vivid colours of gold and crimson and emerald green, quite unlike the frothy dishabille Athénaïs was fond of lounging about in. I wore the highest heels permitted to me by the sumptuary laws, near as high as the King's thanks to my noble blood. My collection of fans was famous, and I made sure I was never seen carrying the same fan more than once in a season. Tonight, I carried one of gold silk and ebony, painted with dancing figures. I furled it and lifted it to tap gently just under my right eye, then glanced at the delicious young man to see if he was paying attention. He was. Within a few moments, he was at my side and bowing over my hand.

'I enjoyed your story, *mademoiselle.*'

'Indeed?' I let my eyes run over him. He was young, barely into his twenties, with smooth olive skin and a strong jaw. His eyes were black, like mine, and spoke of the hot lands of the south. His coat was cut by a master tailor, and the long wig and foaming lace at his throat and cuffs spoke of easy wealth. His heels were nearly as tall as mine; he was a nobleman.

'Yes, very much. You are so quick. How can you think of such drolleries off the cuff like that?'

I shrugged my shoulders. '*La,* it is easy. Can you not?'

'No, I'm afraid I can't. But then I have other talents.' He spoke in a low husky voice, leaning close to me so I could feel his warm breath on my ear.

I unfurled my fan and waved it lazily, allowing my eyes to meet his. 'I'm sure you do,' I answered, then looked away as if searching for more interesting company elsewhere in the hot and overcrowded room.

'Like dancing.' He seized my hand. 'Do you like to dance?'

'I do,' I answered, smiling despite myself.

'They are dancing in the other room. Shall we?'

'If you like,' I said, but he was already towing me through the crowd, his grip strong and sure on my hand. I tried to repress the smile on my face, but it kept creeping back. His enthusiasm was charming, even though it made him seem very young to me.

The next moment, his hand was on my waist and he was leading me into a *gavotte*. He smiled at me, and my heart gave a distinct lurch. I looked away, concentrating on the steps.

'I like your dress,' he said. 'That colour makes you glow like a candle.'

'Why, thank you, kind sir,' I answered mockingly. 'I like your coat too. I do love a man in velvet.' I lifted one hand to stroke his sleeve and was surprised — and pleased — to feel the swell of hard muscle beneath.

'I love a woman who can look me in the eye,' he said, swinging me around so swiftly I was brought up hard against him.

I glanced up, to see him smiling down at me. He was a few inches taller than me, which I must admit pleased me. I was tall for a woman. My sister always used to call me 'beanpole' and ask me if it was cold all the way up there. 'It's a nice change not to have to look down on a man.'

'In all meanings of the phrase,' he replied.

I lifted one eyebrow. 'You may be taller than me in height, but have you not already admitted that you cannot match me in quickness of wit?'

'Is that what I said? I must admit I was so stupefied by your beauty I hardly know what words came out of my mouth.'

I laughed, quite without meaning to. 'If the sight of *my* beauty leaves you lost for words, you shall be struck quite dumb once you get to court.'

'I've been to court and somehow managed to retain my senses. I guess the usual style of court lady is not to my taste.'

'Well, you show some sense at least,' I replied. 'The court is full of empty-headed fools who have been taught to do nothing but sing and dance and sew a fine seam.' The resentment in my voice surprised me. I shut my teeth and looked away over his shoulder.

'Well, you dance better than most of them,' he said, smiling.

'I love to dance.' At the touch of his hand, I turned and glided away from him. He glided with me and then, at the exact same moment, we both gave the little hop called for by the beat. Our eyes met. We laughed. Around us, other couples were trying to coordinate their sidesteps. We did not have to try. His hand was on my waist. He turned me, and then together we glided and hopped effortlessly once more.

'I love to dance with a woman who moves so well,' he said, bending his head to speak close to my ear once again.

'I love a man who doesn't trample all over my feet.'

'You must have loved many men then, or is the reputation of the King's courtiers as fine dancers all a lie?'

'Perhaps we should say merely an exaggeration?'

His eyes were intent on my face. I could feel the scorch of his hand even through the layers of silk. Once again, he bent his head close to mine. 'You certainly seem an experienced . . . dancer.'

Colour rose in my cheeks. I raised my chin and looked him in the eye. 'And you, sir, certainly seem an experienced flirt.'

'I never flirt,' he answered.

'No?'

'Never.'

'I see.' For once, I could think of nothing to say. My breath was coming more quickly than was usual when dancing the *gavotte*. I tilted my head and glanced at him from the corner of my eye. 'What a shame, *monsieur*. You will never do well at court. It is de rigueur to understand the art of gallantry.'

'Perhaps you will teach me. I have had dancing-masters and fencing-masters but never a flirting-master . . . or mistress.'

'Well, you seem to need no instruction in the art,' I said. 'You are doing very well all on your own.'

'No, no, *mademoiselle*. I am just a novice, a mere apprentice. Will you not teach me the art? I promise I will be a willing student.' He was laughing at me, his eyes on my bare shoulders and décolletage.

Haughtily, I drew myself away, unfurling my fan with a quick turn of my wrist. 'I'm sorry, I'm afraid I have no time to be a wet-nurse for a bantling.'

To my surprise, he did not flush or draw away in embarrassment. He grinned and winked at me, as if to say I could suckle him any time, and to my horror I felt myself grow red.

The song had come to an end; the lines of couples were all bowing to their partners. I gave the barest hint of a curtsey and went to turn away. He stepped forward and seized my wrist, as the musicians began to play a lively *bourrée*. 'Don't be angry with me. Come dance with me again.'

'I'd best not,' I replied, all too aware of the avid eyes in the crowd, the fans lifted to hide malicious whispers.

'You cannot condemn me to dance with someone else. All the other girls will seem so heavy of foot, so devoid of grace after you.'

'And he says he has no knowledge of the art of gallantry,' I said to the air over his shoulder.

'I told you I was a quick learner,' he replied at once. I could not help but laugh.

'*Encore plus belle,*' he said, and I raised one eyebrow, not sure what he meant.

'Your eyes,' he explained. 'Their light pierces my heart.'

I rapped him across the knuckles. 'You are a trifler.'

'Not at all,' he protested. 'I mean every word.'

I could think of nothing to say, so I just flashed him a look, half laughing, half in warning, as the steps of the dance took me away from him. I could not help but look for him as I turned. He too was looking for me. Our eyes met in a single, long, charged glance. Once again, I felt my heart give that treacherous lurch. I scolded myself silently. He was only a boy, barely out of short trousers. I was a mature woman in my thirties, and one who could afford no more scandal.

Yet, when he caught my hand and drew me out of the drawing room and down the hall, I went without demur. The roar of conversation fell behind us. He opened a door at random and led me into the dark room beyond. As soon as I was inside the room, he slammed the door shut and pressed me back against it. I laughed. When he bent his head to kiss me, I rose eagerly to meet his mouth. Without hesitation, his tongue tangled with mine in a sweet familiar dance. I felt his hand searching for the shape of my bottom through the layers of my skirts, his other caressing the curve of my breast through the stiff boned fabric of my bodice. I gasped and arched my back, and at once his mouth was on my neck, his body pressing me hard against the door. All I could do was cling to him, close to swooning, as he rucked up my mantua and underskirts. When his eager hand found my bare skin, he groaned aloud. I had to stiffen my legs to keep from falling. His fingers slid higher, plunging into the slick wetness between my legs. *'Mon Dieu,'* he gasped.

I gripped his head with both hands and pulled his mouth down to mine again. He fumbled at his satin breeches. Laughing, I helped him, my skirts crumpled about me like the petals of an overblown rose. In seconds, his breeches were undone, and he lifted me against the door and drove hard into me. It was all I could do not to cry out with the intense pleasure of it. His big hands were cupping my bottom, his mouth was on my throat, my ear. Suddenly, I felt a golden explosion deep inside me. I gasped and clung to him. He shuddered. For a while longer, we rocked together, unable to bear the thought of parting, then slowly he eased himself away.

'Mon Dieu,' he whispered again, letting me slide down his body so I was again standing on my own two feet. He did not let me go, though, which was a good thing as I was not at all sure I could stand. I buried my face in

his shoulder. He lifted my chin so he could kiss me tenderly.

'I don't even know your name,' I said, when I could speak.

'I am Charles de Briou,' he answered. I almost groaned. The son of the president of the Treasury courts. His father was a powerful and ruthless man, I had heard. Not a man to cross.

'My name is . . .' I began, but he bent and pressed his mouth against mine again, taking all my breath away.

'I know who you are. I saw you ride to the hounds with the King yesterday. I've never seen a woman ride like that. You were as much a daredevil as any young blood. I wanted you then, more than I've ever wanted any woman. I asked someone your name. They told me who you were and said that you could ride a Barbary stallion with nothing but a silken ribbon from your hair to control it. Is that true?'

I smiled and shrugged. 'An exaggeration, perhaps. I've never attempted such a thing. I'm prepared to try, though.'

'They also told me you've had many lovers, including acrobats and lion-tamers.'

I laughed. 'Now that is definitely an exaggeration.'

'I watched you all night. I watched you dance and laugh and tease the Dauphin. You were at home in all company. You even mocked the King, which no one else dares to do.'

'It's bad for him to be too indulged. He begins to believe his own myth.' I lifted my hands to tidy my hair, making sure my *fontanges* was straight, and then tugged up my bodice again, hardly able to believe I had allowed myself to be seduced only a few feet away from the worst gossips in the world.

'I thought about you all night long. I rose this morning determined to make your acquaintance but I could not find you anywhere. Someone said you had gone to Paris. So *voilà,* I too came to Paris.'

'You followed me here, to Paris?'

He nodded and kissed me again, so passionately I felt my body stir again.

'When can I see you again?' he asked urgently. 'Where do you stay?'

'At the Louvre, of course.' As maid of honour to Athénaïs, the Marquise de Montespan, I had a closet of a room at the royal palace for my own use, close to her own luxurious suite.

'Good. I'm there too. I will come to you tonight, yes? Have you privacy?' As he spoke, he was rapidly tying up his breeches again, straightening his coat and his wig, shaking out his crushed lace.

I nodded.

He stroked one finger down my cheek. I leant into his hand. 'Where are your quarters?' he murmured.

I told him, even though my heart was pounding with fear as much as with desire. What was I doing, entering into an affair like this? Had anyone seen us leave the ballroom? Were my lips as red and bruised as they felt? Had the nip of his teeth left marks on my throat and breast? How badly was my dress crushed?

He bent his head and kissed me, and I felt the ground sway under my feet, my soul leave my body. 'Till tonight,' he whispered, then he parted the curtain and was gone.

DEVIL'S SEEDS

The Abbey of Gercy-en-Brie, France —
April 1697

I seemed to be falling, down into an oubliette.

It was such a vivid sensation that I put out my hands and gripped the back of the pew in front of me. I felt as if I did not know myself any more. This plain old woman in a novice's black gown was not me, not Charlotte-Rose de la Force. The salon had nicknamed me 'Dunamis', which meant 'Strength', for my force of character as much as for my name, but now I felt as weak and helpless as a dragonfly caught in a gale. Above me was the vast weight of the dark vaults, below me nothing but a pit of despair.

I had thought I could bend the world to my will. I had thought I could break free of society's narrow grooves, forging a life of my own desire. I had thought I was the navigator of my soul's journey. I had been wrong.

At last, the bell rang. Wearily, I rose, all too aware of my red swollen eyes. Just one more black-clad figure in a long line of black-clad figures, I filed out of the church, passing from shadow to light and back to shadow as I shuffled past the thick stone pillars. *Is this my life from now on? Day after day, each the same, until I die?*

Sœur Emmanuelle's cane caught me a sharp crack across the shoulder as I moved out of line. I was too miserable to care.

One by one, we filed into the refectory, taking our place at the long wooden table, ready to break our fast, if not our silence. No one was permitted to speak at meals, as I had discovered to my cost on my first morning at the abbey. Tired, rumpled, chilled to the bone, I had spooned up a blob of the cold congealing gruel and said sardonically to my neighbour, 'Surely we're not meant to eat this? It looks like pigswill.'

My punishment had been to scrub the floor of the lavatorium till it gleamed.

One of the sisters mounted a small pulpit, where she proceeded to read aloud a depressing tale of some saint or another, martyred by having both her breasts cut off — a charming vocal accompaniment to our meal.

Sœur Olivia made a stirring motion with one downward-pointing finger, and obediently I passed her the cauldron of gruel, first ladling myself some. It was thin and grey and tasteless. I glanced at Sœur Emmanuelle and laid one finger on my tongue, the signal to pass the honey. She met my eye, smiled maliciously and passed the honey down the table, away from me. I sighed and stirred the mess with my wooden spoon, unable to bear the thought of putting it to my mouth. I imagined I was at Versailles, eating fresh-baked sweet rolls with plum jam and a cup of steaming chocolate . . .

Someone nudged my hand with the pot of honey. I looked up and saw Sœur Seraphina nodding her head at me, her thin brows drawn together in concern. I jerked my head in thanks and ladled some honey onto a slice of rough brown bread, but my throat was too dry, my chest too tightly constricted with misery, for me to eat. After a few nibbles, I let it lie on my plate. The littlest novice, Sœur Mildred, had scraped her bowl clean and picked up all the crumbs left on her plate with one small moistened finger. Now, she eyed my untouched food longingly. I passed her my plate and she devoured the bread and honey in seconds.

Sœur Seraphina frowned. She caught the eye of one of the lay sisters and rhythmically stroked her right forefinger and thumb up and down her left finger, as if milking a cow. The lay sister brought her a jug of milk and poured it into a cup, which Sœur Seraphina then passed to me with an emphatic nod. I scowled at her but drank a mouthful, not wanting to suffer any more punishments for disobedience. I was too tired and too heart-sick to bear any more.

The milk was frothy and warm. I drank the cup down and felt better for it. Sœur Sera-phina nodded, pleased. The bell rang — how I hated the sound of that bell — and we rose as one, the bench loudly scraping over the paving stones as we pushed it away from the table with the backs of our knees. One by one, we filed away from the refectory, our steps ringing hollowly on the stone, to the chapterhouse. Vaulted and pillared, the chapter room was hung with heavy tapestries to try to keep out the cold. I had to sit with the novices on a hard wooden pew at the back of the room, though I was so much older than them all. Sœur Emmanuelle sat with us, her cane in her hand in case any of us dared to whisper or fidget or cough or fart.

I did not really listen, fixing my eyes on the nearest tapestry, which showed a white unicorn sitting with its front hooves in the lap of a fair-haired maiden in a gorgeous medieval gown. The embroidered grass was studded with flowers, and the two overarch-ing trees were hung with pomegranates. Small beasts — rabbits and squirrels and badgers — watched from the shelter of the forest, not noticing the hunters creeping closer with their dogs and their spears. I stared at this tapestry for an hour every day and still I found new things in it — a nest of baby birds, a hunter who looked sad, a ladybird on a leaf. As usual, I let my thoughts drift away . . . to Charles, always to Charles.

I thought of that time at Fontainebleau when I had crept away from the ballroom to meet with Charles in the moonlit garden. He had seized me from behind and whirled me under a tree, flinging me down on the warm grass and rucking up my skirts before I had time to catch my breath.

'It's been so long . . .' he had whispered in my ear.

'What, four hours?' I had laughed . . .

My attention was jerked back to the present by the sound of my own name — or at least the name that I had been given upon my induction in the novitiate a week after my arrival. Sœur Charité. Subtle.

'Sœur Charité rolled her eyes during the reading of St Lawrence's martyrdom at prandium last night,' a meek little voice was saying. This was Sœur Irene, who sought to win favour by constantly telling tales on the other novices. Normally, I would have impaled her with a glance and then scandalised the other nuns by saying, 'Well, it just seems unlikely to me that a man being roasted alive would have told his torturers to turn him over so he could be cooked on the other side.'

Instead, I just shrugged and said, *'Mea culpa.'*

'And she spoke during the Great Silence,'

Sœur Irene said.

'What did she say, *ma fille*?' Mère Notre asked.

'Oh, I cannot possibly repeat it,' Sœur Irene said.

'You must,' Sœur Emmanuelle said. 'How else can we judge the depth of her infraction?'

'Oh, sister, I cannot. Such foul words! Such blasphemy!' Sœur Irene pressed both hands to her flat chest.

'I said *"sacré cochon"*,' I said. 'I dropped my clothes-chest on my toe. I'm sorry, it just slipped out. *Mea maxima culpa.*'

'We know you are having difficulty adjusting to our life here in the abbey, *ma fille*,' Mère Notre said. 'However, this is a serious infraction. Is it not said that "Death and life are in the power of the tongue"? Proverbs eighteen, twenty-one. St Benedict is clear on this point. He says, in chapter six of the rule, "But as for coarse jests and idle words that move to laughter, these we condemn everywhere with a perpetual ban, and for such conversation we do not permit a disciple to open her mouth." '

'Yes, I know, Mère Notre. I'm sorry.'

'Sœur Emmanuelle, it is up to you to discipline our postulant. May I suggest long hours spent in prayer and reflection?'

'A good whipping would serve her better,' Sœur Emmanuelle said.

'Another night spent in prostration before

the cross?' Sœur Theresa suggested.

My heart sank right down into the toes of my ugly sabots. Anything other than that! I'd rather scrub a thousand potatoes. I'd even rather be whipped. At least it'd be over quickly.

'Mère Notre, may I voice a need of my own?' Sœur Seraphina said.

'You may speak, *ma fille.*'

'Today is the first day that the earth has been warm enough for turning. I have much to do in the garden in spring. The garden beds must be hoed, the compost turned, the bees unswaddled, the first seeds sown. It is heavy dirty work, hard on the back and on the knees and on the hands. I am not as young as I once was. May I ask for the assistance of one of our young novices? She will need to be strong and used to rough work, though.'

'Of course,' Mère Notre said. She turned to Sœur Emmanuelle. 'Who would you recommend?'

There was a malicious gleam in Sœur Emmanuelle's dark eyes. 'Why not our newest novice, *ma mère*? What better penance for breaking the Great Silence and blaspheming the Lord's name than working for his greater glory in the dirt?'

She glanced at me and suppressed a smile at the look of dismay on my face.

'Very well,' Mère Notre said. 'Sœur Charité,

97

you will go and work with Sœur Seraphina in the garden till such a time as she no longer requires your help.'

I closed my eyes in silent anguish, then looked down at my soft white hands. I was the daughter of the Marquis de Castelmoron and the Baronne de Cazeneuve. The closest I'd ever come to working in the garden was helping my mother pick roses for our drawing room. I could not help casting Sœur Seraphina an angry resentful glance. She smiled at me.

As soon as chapter was finished, I followed Sœur Seraphina past the abbess's rooms and through a stone tunnel in the high wall. As she opened the heavy oak door at the end of the passage, the sun slanted across her face and I saw her skin was finely webbed with lines, deepening into cracks at the corners of her eyes and mouth.

Despite her age, she moved gracefully, leading me through to a peaceful garden, with bare trees espaliered against the walls and long beds of dank straw sheltering the bases of what looked like twigs sticking out of the soil. There was a small stone hut against one wall, with a quaint thatched roof that almost touched the ground.

'We'll find some hoes and spades in there.' Sœur Seraphina gave me a look of laughing sympathy. 'Come on, don't look so sour. It's a beautiful day. Surely you'd rather be out

here in the sunshine than being whipped by
Sœur Emmanuelle?'

'I suppose so.' I lifted my face to the
warmth of the sun, took a deep breath and
felt some of the weight of misery fall away.

Sœur Seraphina went into the hut and
returned a few moments later, her arms laden with tools. 'Here are some gloves for you,
to save your pretty hands.' She tossed me two
leather gauntlets and a broad-brimmed straw
hat swathed with a veil, like a peasant woman
might wear. 'Put it on. The sun can wreak
havoc with your complexion.'

Gazing at her in some puzzlement, for it
sounded strange to hear a nun speak of pretty
hands and complexions, I pulled on the
gloves and hat, tossing my white cap onto the
windowsill of the hut.

'Let me check my bees first.' Sœur Seraphina led the way across to the south-facing
wall. Recesses had been built in the wall and
stuffed with straw. 'Help me unswaddle the
hives. Take care, you don't want to disturb
the bees.'

She began pulling away handfuls of straw
and clumsily I helped her. A beehive made of
plaited rushes was revealed beneath the straw,
standing on a small round table with a single
leg. 'The straw helps keep the bees warm in
winter,' Sœur Seraphina explained. She
pulled aside a stone shingle set on top of the
beehive and set her ear to the hole. 'Lovely.

Listen to them hum.'

Curiously, I bent my head down. To my delighted surprise, I could indeed hear a low droning sound.

'It was a hard winter. I was afraid I'd lose a few hives,' Sœur Seraphina said as we busied ourselves unswaddling a dozen or so of the round woven skeps. 'The first blossoms are just beginning to show. The worker bees will soon be out and about collecting their nectar. And then the poor old queen will at last escape the hive and fly, for only the second time in her life.'

'Queen? Don't you mean the king?'

She paused in her task. 'There is no king. Only a queen, who spends her life entombed in the hive as surely as we are kept walled up in here.'

I laughed. 'That's not right. Why, it is said that the beehive is the best example of how a kingdom should be run, with all the workers serving the king. And we're always being preached sermons about how His Majesty the King must rule with both sweetness and the sting, just like the king bee.'

'It is in fact a queen bee that rules the hive, not a king. A Dutch scientist proved it more than twenty years ago, when he dissected a queen bee and found her ovaries.'

I gasped, never having heard anyone speak quite so frankly, and then began to laugh. Gusts of merriment shook me, so much that

I had to lean my hand against the wall to stop myself from falling to the ground.

'*Zut alors.* To think how I adorned myself in a dress embroidered with bees to do homage to the King . . . Would he know, do you think? He only sits and smiles whenever anyone calls him the King Bee.'

'I don't know . . . he's interested in the sciences, isn't he? Didn't he establish the Académie?'

I looked at Sœur Seraphina in surprise. She was knowledgeable for an old nun. 'Well, yes,' I replied, 'though to my knowledge he's never been. I've never even seen the King read a book, let alone go to a salon or a meeting of the Académie. *Sacré bleu.* What a joke. I must write to the Princesses and tell them. They would love to style themselves the queen bees of the court.'

With that last comment, my laughter died, as I remembered that I was no longer the confidante of the King's daughters, nor even permitted to write letters. I felt my misery return.

'I will call you when it comes time for the bees to swarm,' Sœur Seraphina said. 'It truly is a magnificent sight. Magnificent and terrifying.'

'Rather like the court,' I answered, trying to smile.

'Indeed. Maybe the beehive is a true symbol of the court after all. If so, perhaps you are better away from it. It can be as much a prison for the soul as a convent, you know.'

This was true. I looked at her in interest. She was an intriguing woman, this nun, with her brilliant, honey-coloured eyes and her worldly wise conversation. Not at all what I had expected of an apothecary in a small poverty-stricken convent in the depths of the country.

'When it comes time for the queen to lead the swarm, you must help me catch them. I do not want to lose any of my bees,' the old nun said. 'Come, let us light a fire and boil a kettle for some tea before we begin to dig and hoe. I don't know about you, but the food they serve here never seems to truly fill the hole.'

Since I had had nothing but a cup of milk for hours, I gladly helped Sœur Seraphina kindle a fire in the hearth of the little hut, and then looked about me with interest.

Herbs hung from the beams, and the shelves were laden with jars filled with dried leaves and flowers and curious powders of red and sulphur yellow and chestnut brown. There was a scarred wooden table and two stools in the middle of the hut, and, against the back wall, a small bed covered neatly with a crazy patchwork counterpane, the most colourful and chaotic thing I had seen since coming to Gercy-en-Brie. A heavy marble mortar and pestle stood on a bench, its interior stained dark brown.

'Let me see, what tea shall I make us today? St John's wort to make us happy; rosehips and elderflowers to make us healthy; mother-wort to make us wise; and a spoonful of honey to make us sweet.' Sœur Seraphina scooped dried leaves and flowers from vari-ous jars and added them to a squat clay teapot, then poured in boiling water from the kettle.

'Nothing to make us wealthy?' I asked.

'What need do we have of money?' she answered, her hazel-golden eyes bright with humour. She poured the pale fragrant brew into two earthenware cups and spooned in some honey.

'If I had money, I could buy my freedom. I wouldn't have to be locked up here at the whim of the King. I could go wherever I wanted and fear nothing.'

Sœur Seraphina filled up the kettle again from the barrel of rainwater outside the door and put it back on the fire, before replying gravely, 'Yes, I can see that it would make a difference to you. Me, I've been wealthy, and I can promise you it does not lead to happiness.'

'Neither does poverty.'

She passed me one of the cups. 'No, that is true, of course. Come, let's go out into the sunshine and drink our tea. Would you carry my basket for me?'

Carrying the steaming kettle in her other hand, she led the way out into the garden again. We perched side by side on one of the low walls, and tentatively I sipped my tea. It was quite delicious and warmed me through.

'Look, the bees are already foraging.' She pointed to a few golden striped insects busy in the pale-blue rosemary flowers. 'They're glad spring is here too.'

I smiled and drank my tea, and ate a small sticky ball made from honey and nuts and fruit that Sœur Seraphina passed me from a jar. With the sun on my back, the bees humming and the hot cup in my hands, I felt comfortable and at peace for the first time in months.

'Now the danger of frost has passed, we can plant the first seeds.' Sœur Seraphina rummaged in her basket. 'Cabbage and leeks, broad beans and peas, parsley and borage and thyme. Let us do the parsley first — it takes the longest to germinate. You know they call parsley "the devil's seeds"?' She pulled out a small calico bag with *'prezzemolo'* scrawled on it.

'No, why?' I asked, putting down my empty cup.

'I'm not sure why. There's a legend that parsley first grew where the blood of some Greek hero was spilt. And so the Greeks used to put bunches of it on graveyards, and sprinkle it onto corpses.'

'Why? To hide the stench? I didn't think parsley had a strong smell.'

'It probably had more to do with its symbolic meaning: parsley self-seeds, which means it can spring up again from where the mother plant died. Though it takes a while to germinate, like I said. When I was a child, people said that's because the seeds travelled to hell and back seven times before sprouting.'

As she spoke, Sœur Seraphina was raking aside the half-rotten straw and making shallow grooves in the dark soil beneath. She then sprinkled tiny black seeds into the grooves. 'It could just be because they are the very devil to strike,' she said. 'Would you pass me the kettle?'

I did as she asked, wrapping the handle in my apron so I did not burn my hand. Sœur Seraphina then poured a stream of boiling water from the kettle over the seeds. 'They like it hot,' she said with a broad grin. 'Here, you have a go now.'

Kneeling beside her, I copied her movements. The fresh spring air smelt wonderful, of sunshine on new leaves and the first sweet blossoms. It took me back to my childhood, for my mother could be found in the small walled garden at the chateau in her rare moments of repose. In her simple grey gown, she would walk along the brick pathways, scissors in one hand and a basket over her arm. She would pick flowers for the chateau and healing herbs for her simples room.

'Here, Bon-bon, smell this,' she would say, picking a pale purple spike of lavender. 'It is the best thing for headaches. You soak two handfuls of the flowers in boiling water and a few drops of lavender oil, and then let it cool. Then all you need to do is soak your handkerchief in it and lay it on your brow.'

Many times, I would limp to her, weeping, with a grazed knee or bruised shin after falling from my pony or being knocked down by my dog. She would sit on the carved wooden bench and draw me into her lap, examining the bruise with grave attention. 'Never mind, my Bon-bon. I have some ointment made from wolf's bane that will soon fix that. Do you remember which one is wolf's bane? Yes, that's right, the yellow flower there, like a little sunflower. It'll draw all the pain away, just like the sun draws away the clouds. By tomorrow, you won't be able to tell where you hurt yourself.'

Looking about the convent's walled garden, I saw that buds were about to burst open on the apple trees and a few tender green shoots were just nudging aside the straw. Pale hellebores swayed on their delicate stems under the trees, and the white-spotted heart-shaped leaves of lungwort were bursting out all around the mossy base of the well.

I took a deep breath and said impulsively

to Sœur Seraphina, 'I'm so glad I'm out here in the garden with you.'

'I thought some fresh air and exercise would do you good. You were looking rather pale,' Sœur Seraphina replied.

'I felt as if the walls were closing in on me.'

'I was counting on Sœur Emmanuelle viewing gardening as a punishment, not an escape. She comes from a noble family, and she found the rule that we all must work difficult to obey. To her, grubbing about in a garden is peasant's work, and so she hoped to humiliate you. She does not understand that it is a joy to work in God's garden, and the best cure for any ill of the body or soul.'

'It's certainly better than emptying chamber pots, which is what she normally tells me to do. I'll have to pretend that I hated it, so she'll allow me to come out again.'

'I had another card up my sleeve if I needed it. Only married women or widows are meant to plant parsley seeds. Any virgin who does so risks being impregnated by Lucifer.' Sœur Seraphina laughed. 'So, you see, they'd have had to let you come and help me. There's not another woman in the place who is not still *virgo intacta.*'

I laughed too. I could not help it. Her amusement was so infectious. And once I started laughing, I could not stop. I could just imagine Sœur Seraphina in chapter, her hands piously folded in her sleeves, solemnly telling Mère Notre that only a known *cocotte* like me could possibly help her plant parsley seeds. Sœur Seraphina laughed as well. With her hat pushed back on her brow, showing tendrils of pale reddish-grey hair, and her mud-stained apron and gloves, it was possible to forget that she was a nun and I was incarcerated in a convent, and imagine myself just a normal woman, laughing in a garden with a friend.

'So . . . does that mean that you too . . .' I faltered, not knowing how to frame my question without being offensive.

'Have had lovers? Oh, yes, my dear, many. I have not always lived in a convent, you know. Like you, I came to the cloisters later in life. I think sometimes it is better that way. So many of the women here have never tasted life. They feel sick with longings they do not understand, and so it is hard for them to find peace. I came to the shelter of the abbey after a long life of joy and sorrow and many, many sins, I fear, and so I am content here with my garden and my bees.'

I looked down at my muddy leather gloves. 'I don't think I'll find peace here.'

'Not at first, but perhaps with time you will. Time heals what reason cannot.'

'I don't think so.' My voice was harsh.

She was silent for a long moment. 'I know you find your banishment from court hard, but, believe me, it could be much, much worse. This is not a true prison. You can come out here to the garden and see the sky and listen to the birds singing and the bees humming in the flowers. You can work with your own two hands and see things you have planted grow and bring beauty to the world. You can eat what you have grown, and that is a joy too. Then there is the music and the singing, which is a balm to the soul, and the convent itself is filled with beauty, the soaring pillars and the windows glowing like jewels and the embroidered tapestries. And you will make friends too. You are not alone. Trust me, it is much harder to endure such things if you are alone.'

I shrugged one shoulder, not willing to believe her. She sat back on her heels, looking down at the bag of parsley seeds she held in her hands. 'I knew a girl once who was kept locked away for years, all by herself. It's a wonder she didn't go mad.'

I leant forward, eager for a story as always. 'But why? Who locked her up?'

'Her parents had sold her to a sorceress for a handful of bitter greens.' Sœur Seraphina ran one hand through the tiny black seeds in the bag. 'Parsley, wintercress and rapunzel. When she was twelve, the sorceress shut the girl up in a high tower built far away in a forest, in a room without a door or stair. The tower had only one narrow window, with its shutters locked tight so she could not see the sky . . .'

CANTATA

All my childhood I heard about love
but I thought only witches could grow it
in gardens behind walls too high to climb.

'The Prince'
Gwen Strauss

A Sprig of Parsley

The Rock of Manerba, Lake Garda, Italy —
May 1599

These three things were true:

Her name was Margherita.

Her parents had loved her.

One day, she would escape.

At the worst times, when the walls of the tower seemed to press upon her ribcage, Margherita would repeat these three things over and over again, like sorrowful mysteries muttered over a rosary.

She had been locked away in this one small stone room at the age of twelve. Fifty-one full moons had passed since then, shown by the scars on her wrists. If she did not escape soon, surely she would die.

Venice, Italy — April 1590

Margherita first met the sorceress on the day she turned seven.

Ordinarily, on the way home from market, Margherita would have been skipping along, singing at the top of her voice, or walking precariously along the narrow edge of the canal, arms spread wide. Today, though, she walked slowly, her tongue curled sideways and set in the gap where her front teeth used to be — a sign of intense concentration. Margherita was carrying a small, warm, precious cake in her hands. It smelt fragrantly of cinnamon and sugar. She lifted it to her nose, then quickly licked the edge of the cake. The taste was an explosion of sweetness and richness in her mouth.

It was hard not to cram the whole cake into her mouth, but Margherita's mother had trusted her with its purchase and safe return. Last year, Margherita's birthday had been in the middle of Lent, and she had not been allowed to eat any meat, or milk, or eggs, or anything delicious at all. This year, her birthday fell on the day after Easter Sunday, so her mother, Pascalina, had decided to hold a special feast for her birthday. Margherita resisted temptation, revelling in the warmth between her hands and the fragrance in her nostrils.

The canal beside her was murky green, its undulating skin glinting like scales of silver, reflecting ripples of light all over the stone walls on either side. Far above the flapping lines of washing, the narrow slice of sky was misty blue.

As Margherita turned into the narrow *calle*

that led to her father's studio and shop, a woman stepped out of a shadowy doorway in front of her. She seemed to shine in the gloom like a candle. Her dress and cape were of cloth of gold, worn over a sheer chemise with a high ruffled collar that framed her face like a saint's halo. She was tall, taller than Margherita's father, taller than any woman Margherita had ever seen before.

'Good morning, Margherita,' the woman said, smiling down at her. 'Happy birthday.'

Margherita stared up at her in surprise. She was sure she had never seen this woman before. It was not a face that would be easily forgotten. The woman had skin as smooth and pale as cream, and her hair was almost as red as Margherita's. She wore it hanging loose like a maiden's, though so artfully curled and coiled and plaited it must have taken an hour to create. On the back of her head was a small cap of golden satin, sewn with jewels and edged with gilt ribbon. Her eyes were exactly the same colour as her hair. *Like a lion's,* Margherita thought. Lions were everywhere in Venice, standing proud on pillars, carved in bas-relief around doors, or painted on the walls of churches. Lions with hungry golden eyes, just like this woman who knew Margherita's name.

'I have a present for you,' the woman said. As she bent towards Margherita, her heavy perfume overwhelmed the fragrance of the little cake. It seemed to smell of hot exotic lands. Margherita took a step away, suddenly afraid, but the woman only smiled and slipped something about Margherita's neck. She saw a flash of gold, then felt an unfamiliar weight on her chest. She squinted downwards and saw that a golden pendant was now lying upon the rough brown fabric of her dress.

'But . . . who are you? How d'you know my name?'

The woman smiled. 'Why, I'm your god-mother, Margherita. Has your mother not told you about me?'

Margherita shook her head. The woman touched her nose affectionately. 'Well, we shall soon be getting to know each other much better. Give your mother my regards, and tell her to remember her promise.'

'*Si,*' Margherita answered, though it came out sounding like '*Thi*' because of the gap where she had lost her two front teeth.

'Run along home now. I will see you again very soon,' the woman said.

Margherita obeyed, breaking into a run in her eagerness to get home and show her mother her present. She looked back over her shoulder as she went and saw a huge man in a dark robe step out of the shadowy doorway. He held out his arm to the mysterious woman in cloth of gold, and she laid her own hand on it, accepting his help to negotiate her way over the uneven cobblestones, her other hand lifting her wide skirts so that Margherita had a quick glimpse of the extremely high *chopines* she wore.

For a moment, the man and woman were silhouetted against the light at the end of the alley. The man was dark and massive, head and shoulders taller than the woman. *He must be a giant,* she thought with a painful jerk of her heart, and her steps quickened. The next moment, she tripped and fell. The cake flew from her hands and smashed on the cobblestones. Margherita began to cry. She bent to pick up the pieces of cake, trying to squash them back together again. She cast a look of appeal back towards the end of the *calle,* but the woman and the giant were gone. There was only the dazzle of the sun on the canal, and the high walls of stone, punctuated by doorways and window frames and shutters. Margherita was alone.

She stumbled home, all her happiness in her birthday cake gone.

Her father was a mask-maker, and the downstairs room of their home was his shop and studio. The shutters stood open, giving a glimpse into a cave of glittering treasures. Masks hung from hooks all about the window and covered every wall — plain white masks with inscrutable eye slits and veils, harlequin masks in gold and red, weeping masks and laughing masks, masks fringed with peacock feathers, masks edged with precious jewels,

116

masks framed with golden rays like a rising sun, and white masks with sinister beaks like a sacred ibis, worn during times of plague.

Margherita's father sat on his wooden stool, a papier-mâché mask held in one hand, the other holding a fine-pointed brush. He was painting delicate golden swirls and curlicues all over the mask, his touch deft and sure. He turned as Margherita came limping in, laying down the mask and brush so he could open his arms to her. 'What is it, *chiacchere*? What on earth is the matter?'

'I broke my cake,' she sobbed, as he lifted her onto his lap. 'I was being careful, I truly was, but then I tripped . . .'

'Ah, well, never mind. Accidents happen. Look, it's broken into three pieces. One for your papa, one for your mama and one for you. We would have cut the cake so anyway. All you've done is leave a few crumbs for the poor hungry mice and birds.'

Margherita's father was a handsome man, with heavy dark eyebrows, a large noble nose and a neat dark beard. When he laughed, his teeth flashed white against his brown skin. Margherita loved it when he lifted her high and threw her over his shoulder. While she squirmed and shrieked with delight, he'd rotate about, pretending to be puzzled, saying, 'Where has Margherita gone? Has anyone seen my *chiacchere*? She was here just a moment ago.'

'I'm here, Papa,' Margherita would shriek, kicking her legs against his chest and banging his back with her fists.

'I can hear a mosquito buzzing in my ear, but not my *chiacchere*.' Her papa called her *chiacchere* because he said she chattered away all day, just like a magpie. He had all sorts of funny names for her: *fiorellina*, my little flower; *abelie*, which meant honey-suckle; and *topolina*, my sweet little mouse. Margherita's mother only called her *picco-lina*, my little one, or *mia cara Margherita*, my darling daisy.

Papa picked up his painting rag from the bench and found a clean corner so he could wipe away Margherita's tears. It was then he saw the golden pendant about her neck. He stiffened. 'Where did you get that?'

Margherita touched it. 'Oh, I'd forgotten. A lady gave it to me. For my birthday.'

Margherita's father dropped her on the floor and twisted her about so he could stare at the pendant. 'Pascalina,' he shouted.

Margherita was frightened. Her father hardly ever called her mother by her real name but by nicknames such as *bellissima, cara mia* and *pascadozzia*.

Pascalina came running, wiping her hands on her apron. 'What is it? What's wrong?'

Her mother was the most beautiful woman in the world, Margherita had always thought.

118

Her hair was the colour of new bronze, her eyes were periwinkle blue, her skin was fair and softly freckled, and her figure was soft and plump and comfortable. Pascalina sang all the time: as she rolled out dough, as she swept the floor, as she washed the dirty clothes in the tub, and as she tucked Margherita up in bed at night.

Oh, veni, sonnu, di la muntanedda, she would sing. *Lu lupu si mangiau la picuredda, oi nini ninna vò fa.* Oh, come, sleep from the little mountain. The wolf's devoured the little sheep, and oh, my child wants to sleep.

Pascalina looked white and sick when she saw the necklace. She gripped Margherita by the arms. 'Who gave it to you?'

'A lady. She said it was for my birthday.' Tears sprang to Margherita's eyes.

'What did she look like?'

'What did she say?'

Margherita looked from her father's stern face to her mother's anguished one. She did not know who to answer first. 'A beautiful lady,' she faltered. 'Dressed all in gold like a queen. She said she was my godmother. She said to give you her regards, Mama, and that you were to remember your promise.'

A groan burst from Mama's white lips. 'Alessandro, no. What are we to do?'

Alessandro put his arms about his wife and daughter, drawing them close. 'I don't know. Perhaps, if we pleaded with her . . .'

'That's no use. She has no mercy. No, we must go. We must flee from here.'

'Where?' Alessandro asked. 'I'm a mask-maker, Pascalina. It is all I know how to do. Where else in the world could I make a living? They don't have Carnevale in Bologna or Genova. For all I know, they may not even have the *commedia dell'arte.* I'd be a man without a craft. We'd starve in a month.'

'But we cannot stay. If she should accuse you . . . you cannot make masks without your hands, Alessandro.'

All this time, Margherita had been crying and begging her parents to tell her what they meant. 'Who is she? What do you mean?' At this final comment of her mother's, she gave a little scream of terror. 'Papa!'

Her father remembered her and squeezed her close. 'Never fear, *topolina,* don't cry. All is well.'

'Your hands, Papa. What did Mama mean?'

'Nothing. All is well.'

'But who was she, Papa? Who was the lady? Why is Mama crying?'

'She's a witch. And a whore!'

'Alessandro!'

Margherita stopped crying out of sheer amazement to hear her father say such things.

'It's true. What else am I meant to call her?' Papa took a deep breath. 'I'll talk to her. She has everything, we have nothing but our own little treasure. Surely she could not be so cruel?'

'She could,' Pascalina replied with absolute certainty.

'Come on.' Alessandro stood up. 'It's our girl's birthday. Let's go eat this delicious cake and give Margherita her presents.'

He took Margherita's hand and led her through the door and up the steps to the *portego*. This was a long narrow room with windows at either end, one set overlooking the *calle,* the other overlooking the little canal. The *portego* was sparsely furnished, for Margherita's parents were poor, but Mama had embroidered some cushions to soften the hard bench, and a rather shabby carpet was hung over the table, its red fringe faded to a soft pink. On one wall was a wonderful tapestry, showing ships in a harbour. On one ship, a party of people in gorgeous robes of blue and crimson and orange was sitting down to a feast of fruit and roast fowl and wine in strangely shaped jugs; another ship was being loaded with barrels and boxes; yet another was setting off to sea, its unfurled sails billowing with wind. Margherita had always loved this tapestry and liked to imagine that she too would one day set sail to faraway lands, where she would see extraordinary things and have marvellous adventures.

Rich customers would sit here in the *por-*

tego and drink wine while Alessandro showed them fabric and feathers and jewels, and a display of masks he had made. As his customers described the mask of their dreams, Alessandro would sketch it in charcoal, the mask bursting into life on the parchment, sometimes beautiful, sometimes grotesque.

Margherita's father always said a person only truly revealed themselves when in disguise.

Margherita was not allowed to play in the *portego,* for one never knew when a customer would come, and the room must always be clean and tidy and respectable. It was only ever used by the family on special occasions, and so Margherita's eyes widened when she saw that her mother had spread the table with a spotless white cloth and the best pewter bowls and mugs. A small bunch of *margherita* daisies was in a fat blue jug, and three sweet oranges sat in an earthenware bowl. Coarse brown bread stood ready on a wooden board, next to a bowl of soft white cheese floating in golden oil and thyme sprigs. Soup made with fish and clams and fennel and scattered with sprigs of fresh parsley steamed in a big clay pot.

'Come and eat, *topolina.*' Alessandro lifted Margherita up to sit in the only chair, a heavy throne made of dark carved wood with a back and armrests, and softened with cushions. If this had happened three hours ago, Margherita would have been thrilled. She always thought the chair belonged to a princess in a story, and loved the way it had claws for feet and griffin faces on the armrests. Now, though, she felt only miserable and uneasy. She did not understand why her parents were so upset.

As her parents began to serve the food, Margherita picked up the golden pendant in her hand and examined it for the first time. It was a delicate golden sprig of parsley, hanging on a fine gold chain. It was so realistic, it looked as if someone had plucked a parsley leaf from the garden and dipped it in gold. Margherita thought the pendant one of the prettiest things she had ever seen.

Her mother looked up and saw what Margherita was doing. 'Take it off.' She dropped the soup ladle with a clatter, spraying brown droplets all over the white tablecloth. She dragged the necklace over Margherita's head and hurled it out the open window. A few seconds later, Margherita heard the faint sound of a splash as it fell into the canal below.

'My necklace!'

'Pascalina, that was stupid. What if she asks us for her gift back?'

'I won't have my Margherita wearing anything from that woman.'

'Pascalina, it looked expensive . . .'

'I don't care.'

'My necklace! You threw it out the window.'

'I'm sorry, *mia cara*. I'll get you another necklace, a much prettier one, I promise. You didn't want that awful thing, did you?'

'It wasn't awful. I liked it. I want my necklace back.' Margherita began to cry and pushed her mother away when she dropped on her knees beside her. Pascalina began to cry too, gasping sobs that frightened Margherita and silenced her. She put out a tentative hand and stroked her mother's face, and Pascalina flung her arms about her and cried into her hair. For a moment, mother and daughter clung together, then Pascalina wiped her face with the corner of her apron and stood up. 'I'm sorry, my daisy, but you don't want anything that woman gave you. It's true what your father says. She's a sorceress. Her gifts always have strings attached. Your father and I will buy you something pretty next time we go to the market. Come, eat up your soup, it'll be getting cold.'

Trying to smile, Pascalina served the soup, and Alessandro cut the bread and passed it around, giving Margherita a large dollop of soft cheese and olive oil. She could not eat, laying down her spoon and putting her left thumb in her mouth.

'And look, we have oranges for you. We know you love them. And I've made you a new dress.' Pascalina unfolded a simply made frock of dark green wool, with a sash of copper-coloured ribbon, exactly the shade of Margherita's hair. It would have been cut down from a gown bought at the second-hand dealer's stall in the market and carefully sewn together to hide any stains or darns, but Pascalina must have been working on it for weeks in secret. 'And Papa has made you a mask of your own. Look, it's just like a daisy's face.'

Margherita stared at the mask. It was painted bright yellow and marked with little copper-coloured circles to suggest florets. White petals streaked with gold radiated out in all directions. Long golden eyelashes fringed the eye slits, and the mouth was painted as a big happy smile. *'La sua bella,'* she whispered, her lisp more pronounced than ever.

'You'll be able to wear it to the Festival of Ascension in a few weeks' time, *topolina,'* Alessandro said.

Once, Margherita would have danced about in joy, wearing the new dress and the mask, singing jubilantly. Now, she said, 'Thank you,' in a subdued voice.

'Don't you like them?' her mother asked anxiously.

Margherita nodded and conjured a smile, as much a mask as the constructions of papier mâché down in her father's studio.

THE SORCERESS

Venice, Italy — April 1590

The next day, Margherita saw the sorceress again.

The woman with the eyes like a lion's looked in through the shutters of the shop and spoke to Margherita as she sat sorting beads and feathers at her father's bench.

'Good morning, Margherita.'

Margherita did not answer, though her hand jerked and silver beads spilt across the wooden benchtop.

'You must be ready to come to me.'

Margherita shook her head.

The sorceress frowned. 'What do you mean? Has your mother forgotten her promise?'

'I . . . I didn't tell her,' Margherita lied instinctively, her face growing hot.

'Well, tell your mother I've not forgotten her promise and neither can she. I expect her to honour it.'

Putting her thumb in her mouth, Margherita nodded. As soon as the sorceress had walked away, she ran to find her parents. She heard the angry sound of their voices as she hurried up the stairs.

'She'll never agree.' Pascalina was crying.

'I have to try. Surely she cannot have a heart of stone?'

'A heart of ice!'

'It's worth a try. What can she want with a little girl? In seven years, *chiacchere* will be practically a woman grown. I'll go and find a letter-writer in the market. He'll know all the best phrases . . .'

'A letter? Madonna have mercy, as if a letter would sway that cold heart. Alessandro, I beg you! We must get away from here.'

'She will find us wherever we go.' Alessandro's voice was sharp and angry. 'She's a witch, remember. We cannot hide from her eyes.'

'But we cannot give her our *piccolina*.'

'Mama, what do you mean?' Margherita ran into the kitchen and to her mother's side, throwing her arms about her legs.

For a moment, a strained silence. Then Pascalina bent and embraced her. 'Do not fear, my darling, my daisy. Papa will make everything all right, won't you? Alessandro?'

Margherita's father looked at her with eyes filled with grief and something else. To her dismay, she saw it was fear. She did not tell her parents that she had seen the sorceress again, but put her thumb in her mouth and leant against her mother, her hand gripping a twist of Pascalina's skirt.

Alessandro squared his shoulders and stood up. 'I'll go now.' He took off his leather jerkin and shrugged on his embroidered doublet, hanging behind the door. For a moment, he stopped, his hand on Margherita's copper-coloured head. 'Don't worry, *topolina,* all will be well.' Then he was gone.

After dinner, Pascalina took Margherita and tucked her up in her bed, a small ragged piece of pale-green material in her hand, the only surviving remnant of Margherita's baby blanket. Pascalina had sewn the sage-green wool with white satin stars before Margherita was born, but only one star was left, framed by a halo of ragged fabric. Margherita called it Bella-Stella and had only recently been persuaded not to carry it with her everywhere in case it was lost.

With her thumb in her mouth, Margherita lay curled like a baby dormouse, while her mother sang her lullabies until Margherita's tight grip on her mother's hand relaxed, and she let herself slip towards sleep.

The next day passed slowly. Her father paced the floor, unable to work, his face haggard. Her mother sat with her sewing on her lap, her hands clenched, crushing the fine linen. No one spoke very much.

As the afternoon lengthened, Alessandro

got to his feet. 'She's had plenty of time to read the letter. I'll go and speak to her.'

'Oh, my darling, be careful,' Pascalina said. 'Don't lose your temper, don't enrage her. Beg her . . . beg her to be merciful.'

Alessandro put on his best doublet and went out. Pascalina sat as if in a trance, till Margherita came and climbed into her lap, twining her arms about her neck. 'Mama, why . . .'

Her mother stirred and stood up, putting Margherita down. 'How about we bake a special pie for your father, just you and I? He'll . . . he'll be back soon. We'll make him something delicious for when he gets home.'

Yet, when they went down to the cellar, it was to find that rats had been at the flour. Pascalina sat on the bottom step and drew Margherita onto her lap. Together, they stared at the spoilt sack. 'Today of all days,' Pascalina murmured. 'Oh well, we'll need to go to the market after all . . .'

'No, please. Let's not go.'

Pascalina chewed her lip. Her freckled face looked pale and weary. 'I need to go. I cannot make bread, or a pie, or even soup without flour.' She stood up.

'I don't want to go.' Margherita clung to her mother's leg, tears welling up in her eyes. Pascalina was silent for a moment, as if contemplating trying to go to market with a weeping girl clinging to her leg every step of the way, then said with a sigh, 'Very well, you stay here, my daisy. I'll go to the market by myself. I won't be long. Don't open the door to anyone.'

Margherita went up to her room, to play with her doll. Her room was small, with a low slanted roof. It had a little window, with a lovely view across the narrow alleyway into the garden on the far side of the wall. The garden was the most beautiful place Margherita had ever seen. In spring, it was a sea of delicate blossom. In summer, it was green and fruitful. In autumn, the trees blazed gold and red and orange, as vivid as Margherita's hair. Even in winter, it was beautiful, with bare branches against the old stone walls and green hedges in curves and curlicues about beds of winter-flowering herbs and flowers.

Margherita's mother never liked to look down into the garden. She always kept the shutters closed, so Margherita's room was dim all day long. Margherita needed more light to see her doll, though, so she opened her shutters and looked down into the garden.

The sorceress was sitting under a blossom tree, drinking from a jewelled goblet, her skirts spread out like the petals of a blue flower, her torrents of golden-red hair shining in the sunshine. She looked up and smiled at Margherita and beckoned. Margherita slammed her shutter closed and jumped into bed. Her heart was pounding against her ribs.

A little while later, someone banged on the door. The visitor banged and banged, and kept on banging. Margherita tried to ignore it, but it was too loud. She imagined the neighbours hearing it and wondering what was wrong. She imagined an accident to her father, some catastrophe in the marketplace that had injured her mother. She could not bear the suspense. She got up and crept down the stairs to the shop, the masks grinning and winking at her in the gloom, and opened the door, just a crack.

A huge man stood there, dressed all in black, his face as round as the moon.

'What is it? What's wrong?'

'La Strega Bella wants you.' The man shoved the door open, even though Margherita was pressing all her weight against it.

The sorceress stepped into the doorway. 'Margherita. I'm disappointed in you.'

Margherita was too afraid to speak, her legs feeling weak beneath her.

'Did you tell your mother what I said?'

Margherita shook her head.

'But why? Are you afraid? You shouldn't be afraid of me. I've been waiting for you a long time.'

Margherita frowned. She felt she had been rude but did not want to apologise.

'Hold out your hand,' the sorceress said.

131

Obediently, Margherita held out her hand. For a moment, she wondered if the sorceress meant to give her another necklace, and her heart lifted in anticipation. Then she thought perhaps the sorceress would whip her across the hand with a willow switch, like the priest whipped the boys at school, and she began to take her hand away.

But the sorceress had smiled and bent down, taking Margherita's hand in both of her own, soft, white and perfumed. She lifted Margherita's hand to her mouth and bit off the tip of her left ring finger. Margherita screamed.

The sorceress spat out the ragged little piece of flesh. Blood stained her mouth. She dabbed it with a handkerchief, which she pulled from her sleeve. 'Tell your mother to remember her promise or I will eat you all up,' the sorceress said sweetly and stepped out of the doorway.

Margherita kicked the door shut and flung herself against it. Blood was running down her left hand. She wound it in her apron. In moments, the linen was stained red. Margherita sobbed out loud. She slid down the door and sat with her knees pressed against her chest, her hand throbbing with pain.

She did not know what to do.

Soon, she heard a key in the lock. She crawled away as the door opened. Her mother came in, carrying a basket of food. Margherita lifted her tear-swollen eyes to her mother's face and held up her injured hand, still wrapped in the bloodstained apron. Pascalina dropped the basket. 'Oh sweet mother of Jesus. What happened?'

'She . . . she came . . . she bit off my finger . . . she said . . . she said she'd eat me all up . . . if you forget your promise.'

With a hoarse cry, her mother was on her knees beside Margherita. She opened the bloody apron, to see the ragged wound at the tip of her daughter's left ring finger. 'It's not so bad. It's not the whole finger. It's not even the whole tip. It'll heal. It'll heal, my darling. Don't cry. Here, let me bandage you up. Oh, my poor darling. Didn't I say don't open the door?'

'She said she would eat me all up.' Margherita felt as if she was two people. One was crying and shaking, holding out a hand that ran with crimson streaks. The other stood outside the first, cold and stiff.

Pascalina carefully bound up Margherita's finger and warmed up some soup for her. She spooned it into her mouth as if Margherita was a baby again, and Margherita swallowed obediently. Then Pascalina sat, rocking her daughter on her lap, singing her a lullaby. '*Farfallina, bella e bianca, vola vola, mai si stanca, gira qua, e gira la — poi si resta sopra un fiore, e poi si resta sopra un fiore . . .* Butterfly, beautiful and white, fly and fly, never get tired, turn here and turn there — she rests upon a flower . . . and she rests upon a flower.'

Alessandro came home long after dusk. 'I'm sorry. She kept me waiting a long time,' he explained wearily. 'Is *chiacchere* asleep?'

Margherita kept her eyes closed, her face pressed against her mother's breast.

'While you were kicking your heels at her palace, La Strega Bella came here and bit off the top of Margherita's finger.'

'What!' Alessandro bent and picked up Margherita's hand, examining the bandaged finger. 'Is she mad?'

'It's a warning.'

'My hands.' Alessandro sat down heavily. 'If we don't give her Margherita, she'll have me charged with theft, and both my hands will be cut off. How will we survive then?'

'Did you see her?' Pascalina said after a while.

Alessandro shook his head. 'She would not see me. That castrato servant of hers came, after a long while. It was strange to hear such a high squeaky voice coming from such a gi-ant of a man. He said . . .'

'She'll have no mercy.' Pascalina spoke in the same flat dreary voice, after Alessandro was unable to go on.

'No. She won't relent. She says I stole from her, and I must pay the penalty. God knows, it was only a handful of leaves, not worth much at all, but she could say anything and the judges will believe her. She sleeps with most of them.'

Margherita could feel her mother's chest heaving under her head. 'My little girl.'

'She's seven now.' Alessandro's voice cracked. 'Old enough to go to the convent, or into service. If we had a litter of little ones, we'd be happy to see her well settled.'

'But she's our only one, she's our precious little girl. We can't give her into the hands of that woman. Imagine what she would do to her.'

'The castrato said Signorina Leonelli will treat Margherita like her own daughter. She'll go to school and have everything she needs.'

'But what does she want with her? Does she intend . . .' Pascalina's voice broke.

'He swore to me that Signora Leonelli would not . . . train our girl up in her own profession. He says she promises to keep her safe.'

'Will I . . . will I be allowed to see her?'

Silence.

'I don't think so,' Alessandro said finally.

Pascalina was crying, clutching Margherita so close to her that she could scarcely breathe. She struggled to sit up. 'Mama?'

Pascalina hugged her close again. 'Oh, my little darling, I'm so sorry, I'm so sorry.'

Margherita could not speak. She felt a lurch in her stomach, as if walking downstairs in the dark and suddenly finding no step beneath her foot.

'Come on up to bed, my darling. Come, let's get you all tucked up. It's all right, all will be well, all will be well.' Pascalina tucked Margherita into her bed, her bandaged hand carefully laid on the bedclothes. She sat beside Margherita, smoothing back her hair from her brow, curling a ringlet around and around her finger.

Grasping her tattered blanket against her chest, Margherita looked up at her mother's face, white and tense in the candlelight. 'Mama, why?' she whispered. 'Why does that woman want me? Why did she bite off the top of my finger? What does she mean when she says you promised to give me to her?'

HE LOVES ME,
HE LOVES ME NOT

Castelrotto, Italy — November 1580

All my family died of a terrible fever, Pascalina said, tracing gentle circles on Margherita's brow.

Where I came from, we called it *blitzkatarrh,* for it hit with the power and suddenness of a lightning bolt. One day, my mother complained of a sore throat and a headache. A few days later, she was dead, and my whole family was tossing and burning with fever. I did my best, I really did, but I was sick myself and only fourteen. And I had no one to help me. Soon, they were all dead: my parents, my grandparents, my little sister and my baby brother.

I cannot tell you how terrible it was. I did not know what to do. The corpse-bearers came and dragged their bodies away and flung them in the death-pit outside the town, but I was nailed up in my house and left there alone for forty days and forty nights. I think I went a little mad. I had nothing to do but pace our little house and pray, and sing myself lullabies. The days passed, and I marked them off on the hearth with a stick of charcoal. On the fortieth day, no one came to set me free. I smashed my way out through the attic window, to find the street deserted. Nearly everybody had died.

I foraged for food, stealing from the empty houses. In one house, there was a dead woman with a dead baby beside her. No one had come to take them to the death-pit. I left them there and took some coins off the mantelpiece.

I didn't know where to go or what to do. I walked to the main road and followed it downhill because it seemed the easiest way to go. I walked and walked, begging for food or work as I went. Sometimes, people were kind to me. Sometimes, they were cruel. Nowhere did I find happiness or tranquillity. My family's deaths haunted me.

Two years after my family died, I came to Venice. It seemed like a magical city, floating on the lagoon as if conjured by an enchanter's wand. I sat in the meadow and stared at it, picking meadow flowers from around my feet — clover and daisies and wild garlic — and making myself a wreath. I walked down to the shore, and a boy in a boat gave me a lift across the lagoon in return for a kiss.

By that time, I was dressed only in rags. My feet were bare, and I was so hungry I felt as if I was made of thistledown. But it was summer, and the paving stones of the squares were cool under my feet. I wandered through the city, going wherever my feet led me. I came to an ornate bridge, rising above its wide stone arch like a little city built on a rainbow. I climbed the steps till I reached the seventh archway, with its cocked stone hat, and there I stopped, leaning over the handrail. Far below, I saw my rippling reflection in the water and wondered who that girl was now . . . that thin-faced girl with a wreath of weeds on her fiery hair. She looked nothing like the Pascalina I knew. I think I began to weep. Suddenly, a face appeared beside mine in the water, the face of a young man.

'Why do you weep?' he asked.

I almost said that I was lonely, but then I was afraid he would misunderstand me, so I told him I was hungry.

He was quiet for a moment, then said, 'Will you sell me the flowers in your hair? We rarely see such pretty flowers here.'

I nodded, and pulled the wreath off my head and gave it to him. In return, he gave me a small coin and told me where I could find the markets. I thanked him, and then waited till he was out of sight before creeping after him. I saw where he lived, in a shop hung with the most beautiful and strange things I had ever seen, masks that glittered with jewels and gilt and bright paint. It was a treasure trove. Above the shop was a window, with flowers and herbs growing out of a box on the sill, and hanging on a line strung above my head was a fine carpet, which a kind-looking woman was beating with her broom. I could smell soup and freshly baked bread. It was such a homely picture that I began to weep again. I longed with all my heart for a home like that.

Still clutching the coin in my hand, I crept a little closer, wanting to peep in the window. I heard laughter and the sound of a teasing voice. Then the young man who had given me the coin replied, right above my head, 'Very well, then, I admit it, she was pretty. She had the most beautiful red hair. That's not why I bought the flowers, though. She looked so sad . . .'

I did not wait to hear more, afraid I would be caught eavesdropping under his window. I crept away down the alley, looking back to make sure no one saw me. When I turned to go, it was to find a woman was watching me from the end of the alleyway. She was very beautiful. She wore a dress like nothing I'd ever seen before, sewn with so many jewels that she glittered as she moved. Her hair was golden-red like mine, and she wore it hanging down her back like a young girl. Her eyes were exactly the same colour as her hair.

She smiled at me. 'Are you hungry?'

I nodded, and she pulled open a doorway

in the wall. Beyond was the most wonderful garden you could imagine, stretching cool and green and beautiful, towards a grand palace at the far end. There were orange trees in tubs, and all sorts of herbs and vegetables and flowers, all grown within green hedges clipped in the shapes of flowers themselves. More fruit trees were standing against the high stone walls. I saw apricots and plums and pomegranates and figs. The smell made my mouth water.

'Help yourself,' she said.

I did not rush heedlessly into that garden, I promise. I had grown wary over the past few years. I looked at her suspiciously. 'What would you want in return?'

'Just to talk to you.'

I looked longingly at the garden again, but I dared not cross the threshold. The walls were high, too high to climb over, and the door she held open was made of heavy wood as thick as my clenched fist, and crossed with ornate iron bands. A heavy iron key was in the lock. It would take her only a moment to turn it and lock me inside.

'We can talk here,' I said.

She smiled at me and stretched her hand through the doorway, plucking a fruit from a tree and passing it to me. It was a fig. Its skin was the colour of a twilight sky. I thought about how it would taste on my tongue, how its juice would trickle down my parched throat. For a moment longer, I resisted, then I remembered the coin in my hand. I offered it to her.

She was surprised and then amused. 'You're right. There's a cost for everything. For that coin, you can have some bread and wine as well. Come in.'

The smell of fresh-baked bread was a torture to me. When she took my coin and went through the doorway, I followed her, cramming the fig into my mouth. She led me through the garden to the terrace, where a table stood under some grapevines. There was a decanter of wine there. She poured me a glass and rang a bell, and soon servants came with trays of food. I ate my fill, for the first time since my family had died. As I ate, she asked me questions.

'What is your name?'

'Pascalina.'

'How old are you, Pascalina?'

'Seventeen,' I lied.

'Are you still a maiden?'

I blushed and hung my head. I have told you not everyone was kind to me when I was begging on the road. Well, that is all you need to know. I think she may have guessed what had happened, for she was quiet for a while.

'My name is Selena Leonelli.' She poured me more wine. 'I am a courtesan. All you see here — my house, my garden, my dress, my jewels, my servants — I have it all because I sell my body.'

I must have flinched back. I had heard stories of women who tricked or forced young girls into prostitution, and I was suddenly sure that was why she had enticed me into her garden.

'Don't be afraid,' Signorina Leonelli said. 'I am a courtesan because my mother died when I was just a child. I was forced to take up her profession or starve to death. I would never force anyone to do the same against their will. You're lovely — you would do well if that's what you wanted — but I think by your face that's not what you want.'

I shook my head.

'What do you want, Pascalina?'

I thought of the kind young man who had given me the coin, and his house in the alleyway with the flowerpots on the sill and the carpet on the washing line, and the glimpse I had seen of a shop like a treasure trove. 'I want a home. And a man to love me and only me.'

'I can help you,' Signorina Leonelli said. 'But you must promise to pay the cost when the time comes.'

A week later, I waited on the Rialto Bridge with a bunch of meadow daisies in my hand. I had washed my face and my hair in the well in the centre of the *campo,* and it hung down my back in soft red curls. A few other men

143

approached me, thinking I wanted to sell my body, but I spurned them angrily. I was waiting for the young man who had given me the coin.

He came at last. He was tall and handsome, with dark curls and a noble nose, dressed in a fine red doublet. I went forward shyly, holding out my flowers. 'Buy my daisies, kind sir?'

His eyes crinkled in amusement. 'What is your name?' he asked me as he fished in his pocket for a coin.

'Pascalina.'

'An Easter child, are you?'

I nodded, though my eyes stung with sudden tears as I thought of my parents, who had loved me and named me, now gnawed bones lying tumbled in a death-pit.

'You're a very vision of springtime beauty,' he said gently as he gave me the coin.

As I passed him the flowers, my fingers brushed his. I jumped, feeling a spark arc between us like the static I get when I brush my hair.

He looked at me intently. 'Where do you live?'

'Nowhere.'

'But you must live somewhere.'

'Wherever I can sleep. Inside a church, or in a doorway, or under a bridge.'

'Have you no family?'

'They're all dead.'

144

'You poor thing.' He sounded genuinely sorry.

'God must have had his reasons. I can't think what they could be, but I have to believe this else I'd hate him. For taking them, I mean.'

He nodded, looking grave.

'I wish I'd died too,' I said with passion.

'Don't say that. It's better to be alive, isn't it?'

I shook my head and looked away.

'I'm sorry. I hope . . . I'm sure things will get better.'

I shrugged. After a while, he walked away, leaving me clutching his coin.

A week later, I waited for him again, another bunch of daisies in my hand. This time, he came towards me eagerly, saying, 'Pascalina, I've been worried about you. Is all well with you?'

My heart was warmed. I smiled at him and nodded.

'That's the first time I've seen you smile.'

'It's the first time I've felt like smiling. Will you buy my flowers?'

'I'd love to.'

We stood talking a while, of the weather, and the flowers, and what I planned to buy with my coin, and then he said, 'I must go, I'll be late. Will you . . . will you be here again?'

I nodded. As he walked away, he glanced

back over his shoulder and our eyes met. He smiled, and I smiled back.

A week later, it was Midsummer's Eve. I went to the meadows and picked as big a bunch of daisies as I could find, then I waited for him on the bridge. He came hurrying towards me, smiling eagerly.

'I was wondering,' I said, after we had talked for a while, 'if you would like to see where I live.'

He stepped back, frowning.

I drew myself up proudly. 'I was not wanting to . . . to sell you my body, if that's what you think. Would I be here on the streets, selling meadow flowers, if that was my game? I'd be living in a fine house, dressed in silk and eating larks' tongues. I could make a fortune as a courtesan. I know, one told me so. Yet here I am, in rags, and barefoot, eating scraps from the gutter.' My eyes full of tears, I turned to go.

He caught my arm. 'I'm sorry. I didn't mean to insult you.'

'You've been kind,' I said, not looking at him. 'You didn't need to buy my flowers. I wanted to thank you.'

He let go of my arm and bowed. 'I'm sorry. Of course I'll come with you.'

As we walked down the bridge, I said shyly, 'I don't know your name.'

He smiled at me. 'It's Alessandro.'

'That's nice. I like it.'

'It was my father's father's name,' Alessandro said. 'And probably his father's father's name too.'

'Come to the market with me. I'll show you what I do with the coin that you give me.'

I bought fresh bread, a head of garlic, a small pat of butter in muslin and a fish from the fishmonger. He carried this for me, and I smiled to see him with a bunch of daisies in one hand and a fish dangling from the other. He smiled back, then laughed, and almost, almost, I laughed too.

I took him to the little nest I had made for myself in a disused porch of an old church. The doorway was locked, with dusty cobwebs swaddling the keyhole. I had dragged an old door to cover the entrance, and other old bits of timber and slate so it looked just like a rubbish pile. Alessandro had to crawl inside on his hands and knees. He stood up, dusting off his hose, and looked about him, a strange expression on his face.

I had done my best to clean the porch, making a broom from twigs and finding an old bucket to fill with water at the well in the square. To one side, I had made a hearth from a circle of old stones, and there I had laid a fire. On the other side was a bed of old curtains and cushions, as clean as I could contrive. There was a bunch of flowers in an old jar on the window alcove above the bed — daisies, yarrow, fennel, lovage and wild roses — which I had gathered in the woods and meadows of the mainland. All were flowers of love and longing, the courtesan had told me. She had also given me a squat red candle, and some myrtle and rose oil to rub into it.

'You've made a proper little home here.'

I nodded. 'I'm afraid someone will find it and will throw me out. Each day I come back, expecting to find it cleared away.'

'It'll be cold in winter.'

'Not as cold as sleeping on the streets.'

I lit the candle with my flint and steel, and used the candle to light the fire. Then I nestled a little iron pot in the coals. Inside were two handfuls of fresh parsley from the courtesan's garden, which had been steeping there for the past two hours. While the water came to the boil, I cut up the fish on an old board and then tossed it and a little minced garlic and some melted butter in my battered old frying pan, one of many things I had found in the rubbish tip. When the fish was properly sautéed, I scraped it into the water and parsley, and put the pot back on the fire to simmer.

Soon, a fragrant smell filled my little house. Alessandro had spread his cloak to sit on the tiles. I crouched on my little bed. He asked me gentle questions about my home and family. I answered them, in a voice that cracked with pain. Once, he held out his hand to me.

148

I took it, and he cradled my hand in his.

I had only one bowl and one spoon, so we took turns to eat, dipping our bread in the clear green broth and scooping out small pieces of sweet white fish. It grew dark, and the light of the red candle and the small fire flickered over the planes of his face. I thought he was the most handsome man I had ever seen. My heart swelled with painful tenderness. I thought that if I could just make him love me, I'd be happy for ever after. When our soup was gone, I drew his face to mine and kissed him.

Oh, my darling *piccolina,* I loved him truly. Maybe you think I should not have asked the courtesan's help to make him love me. Maybe he would have loved me anyway, without the parsley I picked from her garden, without the red candle she gave me. But how could I know? I was a beggar girl, dressed in rags. It was Midsummer's Eve, so it was warm enough to sleep on the streets. But soon winter would come, and I'd have frozen to death. I needed him to love me.

I think you were conceived that night, my darling girl, my daisy. I would not know that for a while yet, though. What I do know is that Alessandro and I lay together on that little pile of rags, and we loved each other as totally and as truly as any man and woman have ever loved each other. And when we rested in each other's arms, I laughingly pulled a daisy from the bunch we had put in the bucket and tucked one behind his ear.

'Where I come from, we call daisies "he loves me, he loves me not",' I said.

'Do you? That seems a strange name.'

'You are such a city boy. Don't you know what you do?' I laid my head on his chest and took another daisy. I pulled one petal off and chanted, 'He loves me.' I pulled another petal and chanted, 'He loves me not.' One by one, each of the small white petals fluttered down to the ground till there was only one left. I pulled it off, saying triumphantly, 'He loves me.'

'I do,' Alessandro said and bent his head to kiss me.

BITTER GREENS

Venice, Italy — January 1583

We should have been happy. We very nearly were.

When we were married, you were still a little mouse in my tummy. No one but me and your father knew that you were there, though I think your *nonna* may have guessed.

She insisted we have this house, and she went and moved in with your Zia Donna, who had just had the twins. Nonna left everything for us, the shop, all the masks, the moulds and the paint and the feathers and the crystals, most of the furniture, even her own bed. I had everything I had dreamt of, even the carpet that needed to be beaten clean on the line over the street.

Yet every time I stood at my window and looked down on the courtesan's garden, I felt a squirming feeling of shame in my stomach.

We weren't rich, not like she was, with her grand house and her own gondola and her gowns and servants. Yet, a few months after

Alessandro and I were married, I took to her door all the housekeeping money I had managed to save, and I tried to give it to her. 'There's a cost for everything,' she had said.

She only looked at me coldly. 'I have no need of money,' she said.

'I just wanted to thank you.'

'I have no need of thanks.'

'You helped me, please let me thank you.'

'There'll come a time when I want something, and you'll be able to help me.' Her eyes caressed the curve of my stomach. Instinctively, I drew my shawl closer about me. 'Keep your money. You'll be needing it all too soon.'

It was after that visit to the courtesan that I began to long for green things. Venice no longer seemed an enchanted city to me, but a place of cold barren stone. It was winter, and the domes and spires were wrapped in grey mist, muffling the sound of the bells and the warning cries of the gondoliers. A cruel wind from the sea struck through every crevice, and the *calli* were awash with icy water so that my shoes and the hem of my skirt were always damp. I could not get warm.

I wanted to rest my eyes on green meadows. I wanted to sit on green grass under the shade of a green tree. I wanted to eat cool green salads. I longed for arugula tossed with olive oil and parmesan, for asparagus tips dripping with melted butter, for a salad of

152

sweet and bitter green leaves. Most of all, I longed for fish and parsley soup.

When I first moved into the house above the mask shop, I kept the shutters of my bedroom closed so I could not see the courtesan's garden. Now, I sat there all day long, staring down at the evergreen rosemary hedges, surrounding garden beds that still flourished, despite the cold, with hellebore and self-heal, wintercress and field garlic, wintersweet and witch-hazel. How I wanted to devour that wintercress. Snow blew in on me, but I sat there, shivering, in my woolly brown shawl, gazing at the courtesan's garden. Alessandro would come and beg me to go to bed, but I'd stay until darkness closed in and only then would I let him draw me up and help me away from the window. He would tuck me up in bed, a stone bottle filled with hot water at my feet, the faded old carpet-rug laid over me, but still I could not get warm.

And nothing could tempt me to eat.

The midwife clucked her tongue and talked with my husband in low voices in the next room. 'The baby will not grow properly if she doesn't eat,' she said. So Alessandro searched the markets for food he hoped would appeal to me. But it was winter, and times were lean. I grew thin and pale.

Lent had never seemed so long. Alessandro said a mouse would have eaten more. He even bought me meat, going to a butcher in the ghetto, risking being paraded around the square with a leg of lamb strung about his neck. He almost wept when I turned my face away and refused to eat it.

Spring came, and the courtesan's gardeners shovelled away the snow and unswaddled the trees from their sacking. I lifted my head to watch. Over the next few days, seeds were sown, and soon a fine mist of green floated over the beds of freshly turned earth. I watched, sick with longing. Each day, green sprang to life in the courtesan's garden. I recognised parsley, chives, wintercress, nasturtium leaves, dandelions — a strange plant for a rich woman to grow, I thought — and the pretty bellflower my mother always called rapunzel, which made a delicious salad.

'I must eat some or I shall die,' I told Alessandro.

He chewed his lip and clenched his fists, and when the midwife came to see me — for my baby was late and she was worried — he told her what I had said.

'You must let her eat what she wants,' the midwife said. 'Don't you know that it will harm the baby if you let her cravings go unsatisfied? You must never frighten or upset a pregnant woman for the child will be misshapen by her imaginings. If she longs for milk, and does not drink it, her child will be born with white hair. If a hare jumps across her path, the baby will be born with a harelip. If you do not give her parsley, your child will be born with a parsley-shaped birthmark disfiguring his face, mark my words.'

I lay in my bed, listening to the rain beat against the shutters, my hands cradling the warm bulge of my stomach. *Who are you? I thought. What little life flutters in there? Have I cursed you by using magic to make your father love me?*

The door banged open. Alessandro stood there, dripping wet, his eyes exultant. His hands were full of fresh green leaves. 'I picked them for you. The door to the garden was ajar. Someone must have forgotten to close it. I sneaked in and grabbed these, and ran.'

I leant on my elbow, raising myself with difficulty. I had not realised how weak I had grown.

'Wait, I'll dress them for you. Some oil, some lemon, some salt. It'll be delicious.'

It was. I ate with intense pleasure, loving the crunch in my mouth, the sudden unexpected bitterness. Then Alessandro brought me fish soup, made with handfuls of parsley. I ate it all, then, smiling, I slept.

Later that night, I felt sharp stabbing pains in my groin. I cried out, raised myself, bent over my bulging stomach. The pains faded, came again, faded, came again, each time coming faster, stronger, more intense. The day came, but I barely noticed. Alessandro did all he could to help me, but something was wrong. My baby — you, my *piccolina* — did not want to be born.

Daylight faded into a fig-coloured dusk. The midwife came and tried to help me. I felt as if I was drowning, black waves of pain crashing over me. Around midnight, I clutched Alessandro's hand. 'I'm dying. Help me.'

'What can I do?' Alessandro begged.

'I need . . .'

'What?'

'More . . .'

'More salad? More parsley?'

'Parsley is said to ease the difficulties of childbirth.' The midwife bathed my anguished face with rose water. 'But where could we get some at this time of night?'

Alessandro ran down the stairs. I hardly noticed he was gone. I was lost in a hell of fire and pain. Sometime later, he came back, clutching a handful of greens in his hand. 'I've got it!'

The midwife boiled up the green leaves on the little stove and soon had a cup of dark green liquid for me. Alessandro lifted me up to drink. It tasted bitter, so bitter, but I swallowed it down. You were soon born, my darling, my daisy. You slid into the world and gulped a breath, and screamed, and I wept and laughed together, unable to believe the miracle I had wrought in my own body.

When the midwife washed you, we found a head of fiery curls. 'Just like your mother's,' Alessandro said, cradling you in his big hands.

'And look, a little birthmark shaped just like a sprig of parsley.' The midwife pointed to a small red stain on the skin of your chest, just above your heart. 'If you hadn't brought that bunch of parsley for her, it would have been all over the babe's sweet face, for sure.'

She held out her hand for her money, packed up her things and went home. Alessandro lay on the bed, cradling you and me in his arms. *'Pascadozzia,'* he said tentatively, as dawn began to blush in the sky above the city. 'She was waiting for me in the garden. I'm so sorry.'

I was dazed and exhausted. 'Who?' I asked.

'The woman . . . the whore they call La Strega Bella. I stole the leaves from her garden the night before last, when you said you would die . . . and then I went back there again last night, to steal some more. She was waiting for me.'

Cold dread filled me. I sat up, wincing with pain, and looked into his face. 'What . . . what happened?'

'She said I was a thief. She said she would have me charged, and that I'd be lucky not to hang. I pleaded with her. I said you were dying and that the child would die with you. She said that words were nothing but wind and that the best I could hope for was to have my hands chopped off. I was in despair. I fell to my knees before her and begged for mercy. She said . . .'

He stopped, and there was a long silence. All I could hear was the wind, and the little nuzzling sounds you made at my breast. 'What?' I asked.

'She said she would let me go if I promised her the baby.'

'The baby?' I looked down at your precious little head, covered with the most adorable little red curls, and clutched you closer.

Alessandro nodded. 'I'm so sorry. I didn't know what else to do. You were dying. If you died, the baby would die, and I'd be dead too, or maimed horribly, unable to work or keep myself or you. So . . .' Again, he was silent. I did not speak, waiting, tears already sliding down my cheeks. 'So I agreed,' he said in a flat tone. 'She let me take the handful of leaves I had grabbed, and she let me come back here to you. And she said . . . oh, *Pascadozzia,* I do not understand it, but she said that everything has a cost, and the time had come for you to pay. What did she mean?'

I could only weep and clutch you close to me.

Selena Leonelli came the next day to take you away, but I would not let you go. I begged her, 'Just let me have her a little while, please, please. I'll do anything.'

She caressed your shining curls with one

finger. 'You may have her for seven years, but you must promise me to give her up then. I'll be like a mother to her. I'll guard her and keep her safe, don't you fear.'

Seven years seemed like a long time. Anything could happen in seven years. So I agreed. And now the seven years have gone by, and she has come for you . . .

Venice, Italy — April 1590

Pascalina bent and laid her head next to her daughter's on the pillow. Their russet curls interwove, their soft breath mingled. Margherita was asleep, her thumb still in her mouth.

'My darling, my daisy,' Pascalina whispered. 'I can't lose you. I can't.'

She wept for a while, then rose and went to the window. It was a clear moonlit night. The courtesan's garden and palace seemed forged in curlicues of wrought iron and silver. Pascalina looked down upon them, wishing with all her heart she had the power to summon fire to incinerate what she hated. Yet smoke did not begin to cloud the luminous sky. Flames did not bring gaudy colour to that monochromatic view. All was still and quiet.

I must save my daughter, she thought.

Weakness suddenly overwhelmed her. She had to lean forward, gripping the windowsill with both hands, her head hanging down. When the dizziness passed, Pascalina lifted her head and saw the white bell-shape of a woman standing in the moonlit garden, looking up at her. La Strega. The whore. The witch.

She slammed the shutters closed, but it was too late. The witch had seen her.

Pascalina stood, unmoving. Moonlight struck through the shutters, striping her face and body with bars of black and white. She felt that if she stood still, not even breathing, she could freeze time. Margherita would sleep peacefully forever, her thumb tucked in her mouth. Alessandro would lie waiting for her in their bed, forever. Their home would float in a little enchanted bubble, outside time, safe from harm.

Then the bells of the city rang out, marking the midnight hour. Pascalina gasped a breath. The earth seemed to tilt under her feet. She groped out blindly, took a stumbling step forward. Time ratcheted forward.

Pascalina fell on her knees by her daughter's bed. There was just enough light for her to see the curve of Margherita's face, eyelashes fanned against her cheek, her russet-coloured hair strewn over the pillow. Pascalina bent her head to kiss Margherita's soft little hand.

Blood had seeped through the white bandage, causing a stain on the tip of Margherita's finger like a wayward flower. Or a sprig of parsley.

PIETÀ

Venice, Italy — April 1590

'Margherita, wake up, darling. Wake up.'

Margherita stirred sleepily and opened her eyes. Her mother knelt by the bed, shading a candlestick so its light did not pierce her eyes too cruelly. The room was otherwise dark.

'You need to get up. Come on, my darling daisy-girl. That's right. Sit up. Here, I'll put your dress on for you. Lift up your arms.'

When Margherita was dressed, her mother bundled her up in her cloak, pulling down the hood to hide her hair.

'You'll want Bella-Stella.' Pascalina caught up the beloved little rag and pressed it into her hand.

'But, Mama, it's night. What's happening? Where are we going?'

'Sssh, *piccolina*. We're going on an adventure. But we must be quiet. Can you walk downstairs in the dark?'

Margherita nodded. Her mother blew out the candle, leaving a question mark of smoke

161

in the air. They went down the stairs, feeling their way. Pascalina kept a tight hold on Margherita's hand.

Alessandro was waiting for them in the courtyard where he baked his papier-mâché masks. Mist was swirling through the bars of the water-gate, which Alessandro held open. Faint splashing sounds came from the canal outside. 'The boat's here. Come quickly. We don't want anyone to see us leave.'

Peering through the darkness, Margherita recognised the long curved shape of a gondola bobbing up and down on the canal, with somebody standing towards the back, bending over a long oar. The gondolier turned and smiled at Margherita. It was Zio Eduardo. Margherita smiled back at him, though she was troubled. Why was her uncle here in the middle of the night? Were they going to visit her *nonna*?

Pascalina climbed in, then lifted Margherita in. 'Quiet, *mia cara.*'

Alessandro lowered the water-gate and locked it, the key grating loudly in the lock. He winced and whispered, 'I've been meaning to oil that for months.'

'Sssh,' Pascalina hissed back.

Slowly, the gondola glided forward, carving apart the mist. 'Will we ever be able to come home?' Alessandro stared back at the little house where he had been born.

'Not while La Strega lives,' Pascalina answered.

'Mama, where are we going?'

'I don't know.'

The dark walls on either side fell away, and the gondola nosed into the Grand Canal. Margherita could see the faint shape of domes and spires, dark against the night sky, and hear the gentle lapping of water against stone.

Suddenly, a beam of light was shone right into her eyes. Margherita shrank back. Pascalina gasped and wrapped her arms tightly around her. Alessandro swore. 'Go, go!' Zio Eduardo thrust the boat forward.

But dark figures crowded on either side of the gondola, seizing the prow and dragging the boat close to the pavement. A high-pitched voice squeaked, 'Get the child.'

'No!' Pascalina hugged Margherita as close as she could, but hands were on her, wresting her away. Grunts and cries. A thud. A splash. Her mother screamed.

'Keep it quiet!' the squeaky voice ordered. 'We want no scandal.'

The gondola rocked wildly as the giant stepped onboard, shoving Pascalina away with one hand and seizing Margherita with the other. Pascalina screamed and lunged for her. Margherita punched and flailed and kicked with all her might, but it was as if she was punching a mattress stuffed with wool.

None of her thumps had any impact at all, and the giant with the moon-face seemed not to notice. He threw Margherita over his shoulder and stepped out of the gondola.

'Margherita!' Pascalina desperately tried to move the drifting gondola back towards the shore, scooping with both hands, sobbing and gasping.

'Mama! Papa!'

The giant shoved something into her mouth, cutting off her screams. 'You be quiet now, else I'll knock you to kingdom come.'

Margherita whimpered behind her gag and beat the giant's back with her fists. He slapped her across the bottom. 'Keep still.'

Margherita strained her neck, trying to see as the giant strode away. Nothing but stone walls, stone ground, stone sky, a never-ending maze of stone.

Some time later, the giant dragged away the gag and made her drink some nasty-tasting liquid. Margherita coughed and tried to spit it out, but the giant held her mouth shut with his enormous hands and she had to swallow. The liquid seared her throat and gullet but warmed her stomach. She was put into a gondola and some dark cloth flung over her face. She lay still, sick with fear and the endless rocking of the waves, as the world she knew slipped away from her.

Hours seemed to pass as Margherita bobbed in and out of sleep, her sleeping and waking moments filled with nightmares. Each time she woke, choking, to darkness and despair, she would try to scuttle back into oblivion.

Eventually, Margherita came to full consciousness. Her head ached, and she felt sick. 'Mama,' she whimpered, but the gag was tight in her mouth, her tongue was dry and swollen, and she made barely a sound. The boat was still rocking, but the motion was different. The cloth over her had slipped sideways, and Margherita managed to lift her hand and draw it away so she could breathe more easily. Light stabbed her eyes. It was daylight. She raised herself and looked over the edge of the gondola. Grey water stretched away, as far as she could see. She gave a little sob and shrank back. She had never seen so much water. She must have travelled across the sea, she thought, far, far away from her own home. Terror filled her.

She heard voices.

'Are you sure she cannot know which way you came, Magli?' a woman said. Margherita caught her breath at the sweet familiar tones of the woman her father had called a witch and a whore. La Strega.

'She couldn't possibly know,' the giant replied in his squeaky voice. 'But hush, she's stirring. Let's take her in before she wakes.'

The cloth was drawn away from her, and the giant lifted her up and set her on the jetty.

Margherita had a dazzled impression of a wide stone square, with the dim shape of domes and spires and roofs looming out of the mist behind. Water lapped, lapped, lapped at the stone wall.

La Strega bent over, gently taking the gag from her mouth. 'There, is that better?'

Margherita shrank back fearfully.

'Don't be afraid, I won't hurt you. Would you like a drink?'

Margherita nodded. The giant gave her a silver flask and Margherita drank a mouthful. It was the same liquid as before, and she choked and almost spat it out. Her mouth and throat were so dry, though, and the giant's round moon-face was so forbidding that Margherita swallowed it down.

'Good girl,' La Strega said. She was dressed in a sombre gown of midnight-blue satin, a stiff, wired lace collar framing her face and fanning out behind her head. Her hair was hidden behind a white coif and she wore a jewelled crucifix hanging about her neck. Nothing could be seen of her skin but her heart-shaped face. Only her golden eyes remained to remind Margherita of the woman who had bitten off the top of her finger.

'Where's my mama?' she blurted out.

'Why, I'm your mother now,' La Strega said.

Margherita shook her head, as much in bewilderment as in denial. She felt strange, as if the mist had drifted inside her ears and eyes and nostrils, filling her head with cloudy numbness.

'One day, I will come and claim you as my daughter, and take you somewhere beautiful, where you will be safe from the world,' La Strega said. 'But you are still too young. So I have found somewhere for you to live till then. They will be kind to you and keep you safe. Come.' She held out her hand, and after a moment's hesitation Margherita took it. *Safe,* she thought dazedly. Then, with a sudden spurt of terror, *But where's my real mama?*

La Strega gripped her hand more tightly. 'Do not dare defy me,' she whispered, bending so her mouth was near Margherita's ear. 'If you do as you're told, I will be kind to you, but if you resist, my fury will have no bounds.'

Margherita looked down at the blood-stained bandage wrapped around her wounded finger and shivered. 'But . . . what about my own mama and papa?'

'They don't want you any more.'

The words cut Margherita cruelly. Tears welled up in her eyes. 'That's not true.'

La Strega bent and kissed her, stroking away a lock of Margherita's hair. 'I'm so sorry. I know it hurts. But it's better to know, isn't it, than to always be wondering? They'd have lied to you, of course — people do. But the sooner you realise that you can never rely on other people, the better. Come on. Here we are.'

As they had been talking, La Strega had been inexorably drawing Margherita across the square to a large, square, grey building with many small windows. A heavy wooden door was set into a low portico, with a bell hung beside it. At the base of the door was a small opening, just large enough to squeeze a large parcel through.

La Strega rang the bell peremptorily.

A wooden door grated open. A shadow fell upon Margherita's face.

She looked up and saw a figure all in black. A soft old face was framed in a white veil. 'Can I help you, my daughter?' she asked in a shaky old voice.

'I have brought you an abandoned child. She has nowhere else to go.'

'Oh, the poor child, the poor blessed child. Bring her in. I'll call Suòra Eugenia.'

Margherita was feeling sick and dizzy and afraid. She did not want to go through that heavy wooden door, with its iron bolt and lock. La Strega bent and whispered in her ear, 'Remember what I said. Defy me and you will suffer. Do as I say and all will be well.'

Trembling, Margherita obeyed the sharp tug on her hand and stepped forward through the door. The old nun closed it behind them, folded her hands in her sleeves and led them down a long cold corridor. Somewhere close by, a bell rang out. The nun opened a door and led them into a small room. An iron cot was set against the wall and a low fire burned in the grate. La Strega lifted Margherita and set her on the bed. 'You're weary, *bambina*. Why don't you lie down?'

Margherita obeyed. She felt strange, as if she was shrinking. The fog inside her head filled her whole body now. She shut her eyes. *Where's my mama? I want my mama.* Tears seeped out from beneath her eyelids.

A cool hand was laid on her brow. 'Her family does not want her?' a new voice said. Margherita opened her eyes and saw a tall figure in black, her face as still as if carved from pale stone. 'She seems whole and unmarred. What is wrong with her that they choose to give her up?'

'They are poor,' the sorceress said. 'And she is a wild unmanageable child, much given to fancies and temper tantrums.'

Margherita thought dazedly, *Who are they talking about? Not me?* She struggled to sit up, to shake the mist from her brain.

The nun frowned. 'That does not seem reason enough to give away your own child.'

'The father died, and the mother is all alone. She is struggling to make enough to even feed the child. You can see how thin and pale the child is.'

The nun bent and circled Margherita's

wrist with her finger and thumb. 'She is thin.'

'I'm made that way,' Margherita cried. 'It's not because my mama doesn't feed me.'

She remembered how her mother would shake her head as she piled another serving on Margherita's plate. 'It's so unfair,' Pascalina would say. 'I only have to look at a plate of pasta and beans and I get fat, while my daisy-girl eats platefuls of it and stays as skinny as a stick. Where do you put it, *piccolina*?'

She gasped with pain. 'Where's my mama? I want my mama.'

'She refuses to believe her mother doesn't want her any more,' La Strega said. 'If it wasn't for me, the poor child would be out on the streets. Her mother was offered a job on the mainland, but her new employer didn't want her if she had a child, so she simply packed and left, leaving the child to fend for herself.'

'She did not. That's not true.' Margherita found the strength to sit up, but the two women discussing her at the end of the bed did not even glance her way. The old nun sitting beside her smiled at her sadly and stroked back her hair with one gnarled hand.

'I thought that if you would take her for the next five or six years, I would offer her a job in my household,' La Strega said. 'She is too young now and too unruly. But I have great faith in your ability to tame the wildest of girls, Suòra Eugenia.'

'You are too kind, Signorina Leonelli,' the tall nun replied, rather drily.

'I'm not wild. I'm not. Please, I shouldn't be here! She took me . . . I want my mama.'

'Poor child,' the old nun said.

Suòra Eugenia did not even glance her way. 'What's her name?'

La Strega tilted her head to one side. 'Mmmm. I believe it is Petrosinella.'

'Little Parsley? The child is named Little Parsley?' The old nun's voice was sharp with incredulity.

'Children are named after rosemary and angelica and clover, why not after parsley?' There was a rich undercurrent of amusement in La Strega's voice. 'Besides, she has a birthmark shaped like a sprig of parsley on her left breast. No doubt she was named after that.'

Margherita's hand crept to her chest in bewildered surprise. How did the sorceress know about the birthmark? She tried to argue, but suddenly bile rose in her throat, sharp and sour. She leant over the side of the bed and vomited on the floor.

The old nun jumped back, raising her black skirts. 'Poor *piccolina.*'

At the sound of her mother's pet name in this stranger's mouth, Margherita began to cry even more desperately. Sobs shook her body, making her retch again. 'Suòra Gratiosa, will you tend to Petrosinella?' Suòra Eugenia said. 'Let us talk outside,' she said to the sorceress.

'Hush, hush, little one, all will be well,' the old nun said, bringing a damp cloth to wash Margherita's face. Margherita pushed her away, straining to listen to the quiet conversation in the hall, but all she caught were fragments.

'She has been ill . . . you must pay no heed to her ravings . . . poor little thing doesn't understand . . . not a florin to her name . . .'

'She is not infectious?'

'No, no, just under-nourished and ill-treated . . .'

'She is thin, it is true, but I can see no signs of ill-treatment.'

'Not all cruelty can be seen by the eyes.'

'That is true, God knows. Yet surely she has other family that could take her in?'

'Not a soul.'

Not Nonna? Margherita thought in numb misery. *Not Zia Donna and Zio Eduardo? Does no one want me?*

'I know I can trust you to keep her safe.'

'We maintain strict enclosure at the Ospedale della Pietà . . .'

'I do not want her hair cut . . . I'm prepared to make a generous donation . . .' Margherita heard the faint chink of coins.

'May God's blessing be upon you.'

'I will return for her in five years' time . . .

172

I expect her to be well versed in menial tasks . . .'

The voices faded, as if they were walking away down the corridor. Margherita scrambled to her feet, meaning to try to escape, but the room spun into starry blackness. She reached out and grasped the bed, not understanding why her legs felt so weak.

'Come, back into bed, Petrosinella,' Suòra Gratiosa said.

'That's not my name. I'm Margherita!' she sobbed.

'You need to rest, Petrosinella. You're not well. Back into bed.'

'I want my mama,' Margherita wept. 'Where is she? Where's Papa?'

'I'm so sorry, little one, they're gone.'

'No!' Margherita tried to run for the door, but the nun caught her and held her tightly. 'I want my mama and papa. Where are they? That bad man hurt them. Oh, please, let me go. I need to find them . . . let me go.'

The nun lifted her into the cold hard bed and Margherita began to weep heartbrokenly, calling for her parents. The nun soothed her as best she could, bringing her some medicine on a spoon. Margherita swallowed it, hardly noticing what she did. 'Where's Bella-Stella? I want Bella-Stella,' she wept, curling herself up into a ball. But her beloved little rag had been lost.

Far away, the ethereal sound of singing

rose. Tears wet on her face, Margherita listened. It sounded like angels. 'Who is that singing?' she asked.

'It is the *figlie di coro,*' Suòra Gratiosa answered, dabbing away her tears. 'If you're a good girl, maybe one day you'll learn to sing just like them.'

The music cast its enchantment on her. Her body no longer racked by sobs, Margherita's thumb found its way into her mouth. Her other hand crept up and found a tendril of hair, and she began to wind it about her fingers. Gradually, she drifted away into a troubled sleep.

SUNSHINE AND SHADOW

Ospedale della Pietà, Venice, Italy —
1590 to 1595

Her days were ruled by bells and prayers. Margherita rose at dawn, with all the other girls in the long grey dormitory, prayed, dressed, went to chapel, prayed again, sat to learn her letters and numbers with all the other girls in the long grey classroom, prayed again. After a grey lunch, she sat and sewed with all the other girls, prayed again, then was sent to the kitchen to help peel turnips and chop onions. After she ate, she helped scrub pots and wash bowls and mugs in water that was soon as grey as everything else about her. Then she prayed again, and went to bed again.

So the long grey days passed.

Margherita tried to escape a few times but was unable to find a way out. High walls enclosed the Ospedale, and the doors were kept securely locked. The windows were all covered with an iron grille, and the girls were marched everywhere in lines of two and never left alone for a moment, not even to go to the toilet. On her second night, Margherita waited till all were asleep and then got up and tiptoed out of the dormitory, but she was found only a few steps down the hallway and taken back to her bed. Another time, she managed to creep away halfway through the church service but could not find her way to the front door. She was found banging hopelessly against a locked side door, and made to do penance and threatened with a whipping if she dared miss church again.

In all this time, Margherita barely spoke a word to the other girls. She was so hurt and bewildered by her mother's abandonment of her that she could scarcely bear to look anyone in the eye. Besides, many of the girls had been abandoned because of some deformity or defect — some were lame, or had dreadful pox scars, a few were blind or crippled, and one had a dreadful gaping cleft that ran from her top lip into her nose — and Margherita was frightened by the sight of them. She moved through the long grey hours in a daze, weeping silently to herself and daydreaming that it was all a horrible mistake, and that her parents would soon find her and take her home.

But nobody came.

The first gleam of sunshine appeared in her gloomy days as a result of her work in the kitchen. At first, Margherita was set to scrubbing pots in the scullery, but one day the cook called her to come into the kitchen. A kettle sang on the hob, and the air was filled with the delicious scents of bubbling soup and roasting mutton.

The cook was a round red-faced woman, chopping so fast her knife was practically a blur. A few skinny girls laboured at the spit and the oven, their faces pink and damp with perspiration. Another fat old woman sat on a stool, her legs set wide apart, plucking a dead chicken. She pointed at Margherita with one short chubby finger. 'Look, it's another foxy girl.'

'I'm not foxy.' Margherita had had enough of being called 'rusty', and 'carrots' and 'firebox'. Her father had always thought her hair was beautiful, but the other girls at the Pietà said that people with red hair were sly and untrustworthy. One girl said that everyone knew Judas had had red hair, and look what he did to Jesus.

'I like foxes. Foxes smart and pretty.' Round-faced and round-bodied, the old woman had a flattened nose and sleepy brown eyes with heavy eyelids. Her tongue seemed too large for her mouth, so that she lisped, just like Margherita. 'They never cut the hair of the foxy girls. I wish they wouldn't cut my hair. I like long hair.' She pushed back her white cap to show a straggly grey fringe.

'I like long hair too. My mama had long hair.'

The old woman's face mimicked hers, the mouth turning downwards, the bottom lip pouting, the big sad eyes. 'What's wrong? You sad?'

'I've lost my mama and papa. That bad man took me away.'

The old woman nodded. 'Yes. The last foxy girl said that too. A big bad giant and a big bad witch.'

'Yes, that's who did it.' Nobody else had believed her. 'So what happened to the other foxy girls?'

'They went away again.'

'Did their mama and papa come and find them?'

The old woman shrugged. 'I don't know. I don't think so. They were here for a while, and then they went away again.'

'So how many other foxy girls have there been?' Margherita asked.

The old woman put out her fist and slowly released one chubby finger after another, her tongue protruding. She hesitated once all five fingers were splayed and looked at her other hand.

'Petrosinella,' the cook shouted. 'You're not here to gossip. Do you know how to skin and debone salted cod? No? Well, it's time you learnt.'

'That's not my name,' she protested, though

in a rather hopeless way. 'I'm Margherita.'

'Daisy, parsley, what's the difference?' the cook said. 'You can eat them both, if you don't mind your salads a little bitter. Both good for women's complaints, if you make a nice tea of them. Now get to work. You too, Dymphna!'

In bed that night, Margherita thought about the other foxy girls. It was awful to think that the sorceress had brought other red-haired girls here, yet it was also a relief to know that she was not going mad, deluded by fever and sickness, or the devil. Her nightmarish memories of the night she had been taken had been replayed in her mind so often she could no longer be sure it was real. Dymphna's words offered her a safety-line to cling to. It had happened to her, and it had happened to other girls too.

That night, Margherita did not curl into a ball and cry herself to sleep. She thought to herself:

My name is Margherita.
My parents loved me.
One day, I will escape from here.

The next day, she steadfastly faced Suòra Eugenia and told her the same three things. The nun ordered her to be whipped, to drive the demons of deceitfulness from her.

'I'm not lying,' Margherita shouted. 'Ask Dymphna, in the kitchens. She knows. There's been other girls taken as well, redheaded girls like me.'

'Dymphna is feeble-minded,' Suòra Eugenia said coldly. 'She has the intelligence of a small child, though she is an old woman now.'

'She remembers them. She says there's been at least five . . .'

'Dymphna cannot count, you stupid girl.'

'But she did.'

'Do not argue with me. I understand how difficult it must be for you to accept your mother did not want you, but the sooner you admit it, the sooner you will find peace. Hold out your hand.'

The words made Margherita start with terror, the day the sorceress bit off the top of her finger still raw in her memory. She put both hands behind her back, shaking her head. Suòra Eugenia yanked out her right hand, although Margherita fought her as hard as she could. Three sharp strokes of the willow switch across the palm of her hand made her scream in shock.

'Never defy me again. And let me hear no more of this nonsense about being stolen. Signorina Leonelli is one of our most generous benefactresses, and without her you'd be begging on the streets.'

Margherita pushed out her lower lip mutinously but said nothing.

She took comfort in the faint angelic singing she heard several times a day and in the work and companionship she found in the kitchen. The cook, Christina, was brusque and impatient, but not unkind, often giving Margherita extra titbits of food, and the other girls often chattered and sang as they worked.

It was Dymphna who became Margherita's friend, though. Together, they baked clumsy gingerbread men, with big happy smiles made from raisins. Together, they scrubbed pots, salted sides of pork and churned butter, Dymphna's burly arms turning the handle while Margherita caught the buttermilk in a jug, then poured in the cold spring water.

Dymphna found it fascinating that Margherita could curl her tongue. Often, while they peeled vegetables together, Margherita would amuse her by curling it and poking it through the gap in her front teeth. When Dymphna was amused, she would laugh uproariously, her legs apart, hands on her fat knees, her eyes shut. It was absolutely infectious. No one could be around a laughing Dymphna and not laugh too. No one, that is, except Suòra Eugenia, who never smiled at all.

The kitchen was unbearable in the summer heat, and the cook allowed Dymphna and Margherita and the other kitchen girls, Agnese and Sperenza, to take their tubs of vegetables and their paring knives out into the shaded courtyard, where they sat all in a row on a bench, chatting companionably as they peeled.

From the floor above came the exquisite sound of singing voices. One day, the song broke off, and a girl's voice spoke cajolingly, then the song rose again. *Kyrie, eleison! Christe, eleison! Kyrie, eleison!* Margherita began to hum along, then lifted her voice and joined in. She did not understand the words, but the melody was simple and haunting. Above, the song broke off once more, but Margherita sang on, absorbed in her task and the joy of singing.

A voice rang out from above: 'Who's that singing down there?'

'Petrosinella,' the other girls cried in reply. Margherita broke off, embarrassed.

'Don't stop,' the girl called down. 'Better still, come up and join us.'

Margherita looked at the others. Dymphna grinned at her and flapped both hands; Agnese and Speranza nodded and smiled. 'Go on, off you go,' one said.

Margherita put down her bowl and knife and went slowly up the stairs. A girl, about sixteen years old, waited at the top, holding out one hand and smiling. 'Were you the little lark? You sing beautifully. Wouldn't you like to join us?'

'I'm not sure I'm allowed. The turnips —'

'Anyone can peel turnips. Not everyone can sing,' the girl replied with immense conviction. 'What was your name? Petrosinella?'

Margherita gave a little shrug, having given

up trying to make anyone call her by her real name.

'I'm Elena. Won't you sit in for a little while and listen, even if you won't sing? I'll make sure you don't get into trouble.'

Limping awkwardly, Elena led her into the room where the *figlie di coro* all stood in rows. Elena had a club foot, Margherita saw, and pity swelled her heart. No doubt that was why she had been abandoned.

She put Margherita on a stool, and then returned to teaching her class. Margherita watched her with wide eyes. Elena was small and slight, with sherry-brown eyes that lit often with glints of golden amusement. Her white cap was pushed askew, showing a cropped brown head. Her nails were bitten to the quick, bleeding from torn cuticles.

'Alleluia, alleluia,' the girls in the room sang. Elena made gentle suggestions. 'Carmela, why don't you come and stand over here? I think you're trying to sing too high. Listen to me.' Elena sang a single long note and Carmela tried to copy her. Elena sang the note again, and once again Carmela copied her, but this time she hit the note correctly, making a beautiful deep rich sound. 'Perfect,' Elena said. A little burst of spontaneous applause rang out. Carmela blushed and smiled.

'Imelda and Zita, will you try it a little slower? Let each note hover like a bird, before rising a little higher. You'll need a big breath. Let's try it.' Both girls did their best to sound like Elena did, her voice swooping as effortlessly as a hawk in the sky. 'Beautiful! Let's try it once again.'

'Alleluia, alleluia, alleluia,' the girls sang, their voices soaring and falling. Elena listened, her thin hands making swooping movements, one occasionally lifting higher and higher, the other dropping lower in increments. The sound they produced was so beautiful it pierced Margherita with joy. Tears stung her eyes, yet she wanted to laugh out loud. The same rapture transfigured the faces of the girls singing. Then Elena turned to Margherita and made a little gesture with her hand, and before she knew it Margherita had scrambled to her feet and was singing with all of her heart, 'Alleluia, alleluia, alleluia.'

Afterwards, Elena motioned for Margherita to stay. 'You were weeping. Did the music move you so much?'

'Yes, but . . .'

'But what?'

'It's because I miss my parents so.'

Elena nodded. 'I miss mine too. We all do here. Perhaps that is why we sing so well. There's shadow as well as sunshine in our voices.'

Margherita nodded, though she was not sure she fully understood.

'I want you to come and sing with me,'

Elena said. 'Such a pure sound from such a little body. We don't have enough sopranos here, especially ones who can sing with such feeling. What do you say? Would you like to learn to sing?'

'*Si,*' Margherita answered shyly, and blushed to hear herself lisp.

Elena smiled. 'Don't worry, your front teeth will grow in all too soon. It's a shame. You're so sweet without them. Will you come to me then, tomorrow, at this time? You get to miss prayers.'

Margherita nodded, and she ran to join Dymphna downstairs. In her head, she heard the music ring out once more and sang silently to herself, *Alleluia, alleluia, alleluia.*

On Margherita's twelfth birthday, she and her friends gathered in the warmth of the kitchen to share a cinnamon cake that Dymphna had made with her own hands. It was rather lopsided, and burnt along one edge, but nobody minded that.

'I love it when Easter is early.' Margherita licked the delicious crumbs from about her mouth. 'It's awful when my birthday is in the middle of Lent.'

'You're lucky you know your birthday. Most of us don't.' There was no resentment in Elena's voice. She believed it was no use weeping over the past, and, besides, all the girls at the Pietà had been abandoned by their mothers. Many suffered more debilitating deformities than her club foot.

'I wish I knew my birthday,' Dymphna said with uncharacteristic wistfulness.

'You can share mine,' Margherita said. Dymphna's round face creased with pleasure.

'I wish we could give you a birthday gift,' Elena said. 'If I had a fortune, I'd give you your own lute.'

'I'd have liked that.' The lute was Margherita's favourite instrument — able to weep or be joyful, to be played alone or with other instruments, to be high and sweet, or low and intense.

'I'd give you a week off scrubbing pots,' said Sperenza. 'Not a week, a month. A whole month without a single pot.'

'As long as I didn't have to do it instead,' said Agnese, the other kitchen maid.

'I'd give you a different-coloured dress to wear,' Carmela said. A sensitive girl with a gorgeous contralto voice, she longed for beauty and harmony. 'I'd dress you in green, or lilac, or turquoise-blue. Or even grey. Anything but bright red.'

Margherita smiled, but for a moment she felt an inexplicable stab of pain. She remembered a green dress, with a sash the same colour as her hair . . .

'That's not a present for Margherita, that's a present for you,' Zita teased. 'I'd give you a day out on the lagoon on a barge, with a feast and music and dancing. But only if you took all of us with you.'

'At Carnevale time,' Margherita said. 'We could see the fire-eaters and the acrobats and the jesters, and the crowds all dressed up in masks.'

Everyone sighed with longing. It was hard being kept inside four high grey walls all the time.

'I'd give you a horse,' Agnese said. 'A white one, with a silver bridle, like the one in the tapestry in the refectory. Wouldn't you just love to ride through a forest on a horse like that?'

'I'd give you a camel,' Dymphna said.

Everyone fell about laughing. Dymphna laughed too, her mouth wide open, her eyes crinkled into slits.

'But why?' Elena demanded.

'I've always wanted to see one,' Dymphna said. 'I've heard stories about them. You can ride them over the desert and drink their milk and not get thirsty, even if there's no water for miles. And I saw a carving of one once, and it looked a most incredible beast.'

'I'd like to see a camel too,' Margherita said. 'And lions and elephants and monkeys.'

'Me too,' Dymphna said happily.

'I'd like to travel the world,' Margherita said. 'There's so much I'd like to see. Mountains that touch the sky and oceans that pour over the edge of the world.'

'I'd like to travel the world too,' Elena said, 'and sing at the courts of kings and queens, and wear gowns of silk and velvet, with ropes of pearls in my hair.' Her sherry-brown eyes glowed at the vision of herself she saw.

'We can't,' Carmela said. 'We're not permitted to sing in public. Not even once we leave here.'

'If we ever leave here,' Elena said, all her animation quenched. She was now twenty, and there seemed little possibility of her finding a husband or a position in a private household. She would have to stay at the Pietà till she died.

There was a long moment of silence, then Speranza stood up and began to clear away their cups and plates. 'I'd better wash these up before Christina wakes up from her nap.' Agnese got up, rolling up her sleeves and going to the pump to draw some water. Margherita jumped up too, but Speranza shook her head. 'No, let us do it. It's the only gift we can give you.'

'But it doesn't seem fair. I mean, you don't know your birthday . . .'

'You can do all the washing up for us at Christmas,' Speranza said, with a return of her usual sparkling humour.

Margherita groaned. 'But so many pots and pans at Christmas.'

'Ah, well, at least you can have today to relax and enjoy yourself,' Agnese said, carrying a bucket across to the enormous kettle that hung on its hook above the hob.

Dymphna yawned widely and went to check her butter. Margherita went out into the courtyard with Elena, Zita and Carmela, her best friends from the *figlie di coro*. 'You're the one who should be dreaming of singing at court,' Elena said to Margherita in a low passionate voice. 'You have the most beautiful voice of us all, and you have a chance to leave here. It's a crime that you're to be sent to be a scullery maid to that woman. It's such a waste of your talent.'

'You need to be careful,' Zita said, with a thrill of horror in her voice. 'I've heard that she's really a courtesan, and she goes to the *ospedales* looking for pretty young girls to adopt, and then sells their maidenhood to the highest bidder.'

Margherita shuddered. She rubbed her left thumb and ring finger together, feeling the smooth skin of the old, white, scoop-shaped scar there. Had that woman really bitten off the fleshy pad of her finger? Or was that just a dream? Had she really been stolen, or was it just a story she had made up to explain her parents' abandonment of her? Many of the girls there made up such stories and, like Margherita, were always hoping for their parents to find them again. Margherita could hardly remember any life outside the Pietà. It was all faint and blurred, like cloth that had

189

been washed so many times only a shadow of the design remained.

All she knew was that a woman called Signorina Leonelli had sponsored her and would come one day to offer her a job as a housemaid. 'You'll have to do a better job of scouring knives once you're at Signorina Leonelli's house,' the cook would say, watching Margherita cleaning the kitchen utensils with river sand. '*She* won't put up with any laxness like I do.'

When Margherita closed her eyes and thought about Signorina Leonelli, she remembered golden-red hair and eyes like a lion's, and a sweet voice saying, 'I'll eat you all up.'

'Maybe she's forgotten about me. It's been such a long time.'

Elena gave her long braid an affectionate tug. 'She must have paid a fairly substantial amount for you not to have your hair cut, or your heel branded. It offends Suòra Eugenia every time she sees you. I've seen her wince at the sight of you.'

'It's the sight of that orange hair hanging against the red uniform,' Carmela said. 'It makes me wince too.'

'If only I could escape,' Margherita cried. 'I'd run away to Ferrara or Florence, and sing my best as the duke drove past. Didn't Ferdinando de' Medici discover an eleven-year-old girl singing in Rome and take her back to

190

Florence to be trained? I'm twelve and I've already had years of training.'

'There's not a duchy that wouldn't welcome you with open arms,' Elena asserted. 'It's all the rage now, to have a *concerto delle donne.* I heard there's even one in Rome now, despite what the Pope says.'

Elena always knew anything there was to know about music in the world outside their little grey circle; she was taught by the *maestri* who came in three or four times a week to instruct the older girls.

'It'll be much easier to escape from a courtesan's villa than from here,' Zita said. 'You just need to be careful she doesn't sell you off first.'

'But I'm only twelve,' Margherita said.

'The perfect age for some,' Zita said.

'Don't frighten her like that,' Elena reproved her. 'Suòra Eugenia would never allow one of the Pietà girls to end up in a brothel.'

'I bet she would, if enough money was paid,' Zita argued. 'Suòra Eugenia wants to rebuild the church with a new choir. She's insanely jealous of the new church at the Incurabili.'

'Let's not talk about it,' Elena said, slipping her arm about Margherita. 'That woman hasn't been here in five years. I'm sure she's forgotten all about Margherita. Anything could have happened. She could be in the

Ospedale degli Incurabili herself!'

All the girls giggled, for the Ospedale degli Incurabili was a hospital for those suffering from syphilis.

Two weeks later, Margherita was roused from sleep by a firm hand on her shoulder. She woke with a jerk and sat up, clutching her thin blanket to her. Suòra Eugenia stood by her bedside, a tall figure all in black. The frail light of a single candle flickered on the bedside table beside her. 'Get up, my child,' she said in her cool emotionless voice.

Margherita looked about wildly and saw, with a wrench of panic in the pit of her stomach, two immense crooked shadows thrown up against the wall outside the open door, cast by two people waiting out in the corridor. *The witch and the giant!* She opened her mouth to scream.

Suòra Eugenia's hand clapped over her mouth. 'I do not wish any disruption. You must be quiet. If you scream or cry, I will flay the skin from your back. Do you understand?'

Margherita jerked her head up and down. As Suòra Eugenia removed her hand, she took in a deep breath, prepared to scream at the top of her lungs, but Suòra Eugenia deftly tipped a bottle into her open mouth. Margherita choked and spluttered, but the priora slammed Margherita's chin up and clamped her hands over her lips and nose. Involuntarily, Margherita swallowed the liquid. It burnt a trail down her tongue and throat.

The two gigantic shadows made their silent way through the rows of sleeping girls. Margherita struggled. The priora's grip was inexorable. Margherita had time only to see the shadowy faces of her nightmares — one round and pale as a moon, the other beautiful and smiling — then a gag was forced into her mouth, a sack was flung over her head, and she was lifted into the air and dumped over the giant's shoulder. No matter how hard she kicked or punched or flailed, Margherita could make no impression upon his bolster-like figure. She was swept away into darkness.

THE TOWER

Hideous dreams haunted Margherita's sleep.

She dreamt of her mother, reaching out clutching hands to her as she was dragged under a black undertow. She dreamt of Suòra Eugenia standing over her, the bottle in her hand, and tasted again the acrid draught of despair. She dreamt she was riding a camel into a desert at night, her mouth and gullet as dry as dust. She dreamt she was buried in a crypt, skulls staring at her from neat piles of bones. She screamed till her throat was hoarse but made no noise. She fought to be free of the black figure of Death, who carried her over his shoulder, but made no impact. No matter how she screamed, no matter how she fought, she was powerless.

When Margherita next awoke, she was lying in a soft bed. Warm firelight flickered over stone walls. A silken eiderdown covered her, and gentle hands combed her hair. Margherita stirred.

'Ah, you are awake at last,' the sorceress's voice said. 'I was beginning to worry. You must be hungry. Would you like something to eat?'

Margherita raised herself up on her elbow. White powdery rolls, a small roasted bird, a salad of greens and a bowl of figs were set on pewter plates on a round table at the end of the low narrow bed. Saliva rushed into her mouth, but she shook her head, turning away. The motion was difficult. Her head felt heavy and restricted, as if it was bound down with weights. She tried to sit up, looking around.

Her hair flowed down the pillows and along the bed, tumbling down to the floor in waves and ripples like a bolt of golden satin unwinding. Across the floor, the hair spread, filling the small room with silken coils. A white flame of horror coursed through her. 'What're you doing? What's happened to my hair?'

'Isn't it beautiful?' La Strega exulted. 'What a lucky girl you are. Many women would kill to have hair as thick and long and lustrous as yours.'

Margherita stared at the ripples of hair, her breath sharp and uneven, unable to understand how her hair had grown so long so suddenly. Yesterday, it had been long enough for her to sit on. Today, it was so long that twenty little girls could have laid head to toe on it and still not reached the end. Slowly, she began to realise that the hair was not all the same colour. Some of the tresses were more red than gold, some more gold than red. Some hung in tight twists and ringlets, some were smooth and silky, and others formed soft loose curls. Each flowed and coiled into the next, like a river that ran one moment in quick rapids, then fell in a foaming roar, before winding in lazy loops into a tranquil pool.

'Hold still,' the sorceress said. She was kneeling beside the bed, a long curved needle in one hand, threaded with fine golden filaments, a long flow of bronze-coloured hair in the other. Margherita stared with wide frightened eyes as the sorceress deftly sewed the bronze locks into the others.

Each time she bound the hair, she chanted:

By the power of three times three, I bind
    you to me.
Thou may not speak of me, nor raise a
    hand to me
Nor stir from this place where I have cast
    thee.

It was as if her words wrapped chains around Margherita's wrists and ankles and tongue, fettering her. She could not move or speak, though whimpers of terror struggled in her throat. Soon, all the hair was braided into one long thick rope, which snaked around

196

the small shadowy room.

'Now you are mine, sealed and bound,' La Strega chanted, tying off the last knot.

Margherita could not move or speak.

'I will show you how to braid your hair around your head, else you'll never be able to take a step,' La Strega said. 'Then, once a month, when I come to visit you, I will wash it and comb it out for you. We will wash each other's hair. Won't that be nice?'

Still Margherita did not say a word.

'Why don't you eat?' La Strega said. 'You mustn't waste good food.'

This motherly advice seemed so incongruous spoken by a sorceress muttering spells over bundles of purloined hair that Margherita was surprised into laughter. She laughed and howled and sobbed together, rocking to and fro, till La Strega reached forward and slapped her across the face. Margherita fell back, hiding her burning cheek in the pillow, trying to control her gasps. 'Eat, Petrosinella,' La Strega said.

'Don't call me that,' Margherita gasped.

'But it's your name. Names have meaning. You need to know that your parents sold you to me for no more than a bunch of garden weeds. Would they have done that if they truly loved you? A few sprigs of parsley, some wintercress leaves, a spray of rapunzel . . . that is all you were worth to your so-called parents. While I . . . I have kept you safe all these years, Petrosinella, and I'll keep you safe till the day you die.'

'What do you want with me?'

'Just to love you and look after you, like any mother would care for her child.'

'But you stole me. And you left me at the Pietà!'

'So did the mother of every other child there,' La Strega said. 'At least I have come and got you out again.'

Margherita felt so numb and thick-headed she could not think. 'You stole me from my own mother.'

'How dare you,' La Strega cried. 'I didn't steal you, I rescued you. Do you think your father wanted to marry a beggar off the streets? If you hadn't been swelling out her belly, he'd have taken his pleasure and then left her, like all the other men before him. He'd have had you aborted, if he'd dared. And your mother only had you so she could force him to marry her. You think she wanted you whining and clinging to her skirts all the time? She'd have abandoned you on the streets long ago if she wasn't so afraid of what people would say. They were glad you were gone. They never loved you. You were an encumbrance!'

Margherita buried her face in her arms and wept.

'I know it's hard. I hate to have to be the one to disillusion you. But you need to be strong, Petrosinella. So sit up and eat the supper I've prepared for you. It'll be the last fresh food you get for a while.'

Margherita shook her head, her long plait rippling.

'If you don't do what you're told, I'll need to punish you,' La Strega said. 'I don't wish to hurt you, but you must learn.'

'I won't, I won't,' Margherita shrieked.

La Strega grasped her arm and pulled her across to the window, so quickly that Margherita lost all the breath in her lungs. In seconds, she was pushed against the windowsill, the sorceress standing behind her, her hand gripping Margherita's shoulder hard enough to bruise. The drop was dizzying. Margherita gasped.

'Do you wish to die?' the sorceress said.

'No!'

'Then do not defy me.'

Margherita shook her head, both hands gripping the windowsill.

'You cannot escape from here. I have bound you to my will. You are mine, Petrosinella. Do you understand?'

Margherita nodded emphatically. The sorceress turned her away from that vertiginous fall and gave her a little push back towards the table. 'Eat.'

Margherita stumbled forward. The weight of all the hair dragged at her temples, making her head throb.

'Pick up your hair. It'll get dirty. I'll be very angry if I find you not looking after your hair. Pick it up.'

Margherita tried to gather up the hair, but there was too much of it.

'I'm sorry, I didn't mean to shout. I suppose it'll take you some time to get used to it,' La Strega said. 'Come, sit down. Let me bind it up for you, Petrosinella, and then you'll be able to move about more freely.' She made Margherita sit at the table and then, while she ate, began to wind the braid around Margherita's head.

'Here are three gifts for you.' The sorceress showed her a long coil of silver ribbon, an ivory comb decorated with flowers of silver filigree, and a heavy silver snood hung with tiny pearls. 'With these, you'll keep your hair in order. I promise you that you'll come to love it, as I do.'

She then threaded the silver ribbon through her curved needle and began to weave the ribbon in and out of the plaits, securing them in place. While she worked, Margherita made a great effort to eat, pulling apart the roast fowl with her fingers, since no knife or fork had been provided. Once she began, Margherita realised how hungry she was. Soon, the tray was empty of all but crumbs and tiny gnawed bones. A pewter cup was filled with apple cider. Margherita drank thirstily, then realised how much better she felt.

'If you are still thirsty, there is a tap over there,' La Strega said. 'The purest water you'll ever drink, pumped straight from the roots of the mountain. I will bathe in a moment, and you will wash my hair for me. Don't you just love people washing and combing your hair?'

Margherita frowned. She had never much liked it at the Pietà, for the older girls were often impatient and rough, hurting her as they jerked the comb through the knots. La Strega had been gentle, though, and had not hurt her once. But Margherita still did not like the feel of La Strega's hands in her hair. It frightened her, having the sorceress so close.

La Strega looped the remaining braid up and coiled it inside the silver snood. Although the snood weighed heavily on Margherita's neck, she was able to move about without dragging the plait on the floor. 'You will need to take your hair out of the snood at night, but the braids should stay in place,' La Strega said, standing back to admire her handiwork. 'Oh, it looks lovely. You should say, "Thank you, Mama." '

Margherita shook her head, though the motion made her neck muscles ache.

La Strega frowned. 'That is rude, Petrosinella. You must not be so ungrateful.'

'I'm not grateful to you for tying me up with all this hair,' Margherita said in a low shaking voice. 'And you're not my mother.'

'Your own mother didn't want you,' La Strega said angrily. 'If it had been up to her, you'd have starved on the streets.'

'That's not true.'

La Strega looked sorrowful. 'Surely, if your parents really loved you, they would have come and taken you back? But no, they left you at the Ospedale. They didn't come to visit you once. Is that something loving parents would do?'

Tears stung Margherita's eyes. She wanted to argue, saying, *But how would they know where I was?* Her throat had closed over, though.

'You can draw the water for my bath now,' the sorceress ordered.

Margherita had not been able to look around much while she was sitting in her chair, for any movement of her head had caused La Strega to tug her hair and say, 'Be still.'

Now, walking with hesitant steps towards the tap, Margherita was able to look about her for the first time.

The room was square, its walls built of rough grey stone clumsily slapped together with grainy cement. A heavy rug, woven in warm rich colours — green and blue and terracotta-red — covered the entire floor.

In each wall was a shallow alcove. The latrine was in one, half-hidden behind a red and gold brocade curtain. In the alcove opposite was a small copper tap in the shape of an owl, with a wooden bucket set on a wooden tray below it. Cool air gusted in through the narrow slit above it.

In the alcove near the table was a fireplace, with a small fire burning merrily on the hearth. A pot, a skillet and a battered old kettle hung from hooks above it, with dried herbs hanging in bunches on either side. An iron rack of fire tools stood next to the fire, with a poker and a brush and pan. A vase of heavy-headed red roses stood on the mantelpiece, filling the air with sweet fragrance.

Opposite was the narrow window, shutters standing open so she could see out into a starry sky, where a full moon hung. Its cold silvery light streamed through this window, illuminating a deep copper hipbath to one side. Hanging on the wall above the bath was an oil painting of a beautiful woman, her shoulders bare above a loose white chemise. Her golden-red hair hung in ripples down her sleeve, and a bearded man in a rich red doublet held two mirrors, one in front and one behind, so she could see to do her coiffure.

Margherita filled a wooden cup with water and drank deeply. The water was cold and pure and helped calm her.

'It is water from a wild living source,' La Strega said. 'There is no water more powerful, unless it be tears.'

'Where are we?' Margherita whispered.

'This is the only remaining tower of the castle of the Rock of Manerba,' La Strega answered. 'It was built long ago, on the site of a temple to Minerva, the Roman goddess of wisdom. It is said she fled here to escape Typhon, the storm-giant, and found a place of such power that she settled here. The castle is abandoned now and thought to be haunted. No one ever comes here. No one will hear you if you scream.'

Margherita stood still, stricken.

'Time for my bath. You'll need to heat the water on the fire,' La Strega said. Margherita did not respond, and the sorceress said with an edge to her voice, 'Please do not make me ask you again, Petrosinella.'

It was hard work, filling the pot and kettle with bucket after bucket of water, then pouring it into the bath once it had heated. The sorceress did not help her but sat in the other chair, crushing three golden apples in a small apple-press and then mixing the juice with liquid poured from two small bottles. The first smelt sour and vinegary, the second pungent and strong. She then rose, went across to a shelf and took down another wooden pot, ladling honey into her mixture. All the time she stirred and mixed, she watched Margherita trudge back and forth. It made Margherita shiver, feeling those tawny eyes upon her. She kept her own head hunched low, surreptitiously studying the room, looking for some way out.

There was no use trying to escape through the window. No one could survive such a fall. Far, far below, the lake glimmered silver at the base of immense stony mountains, which seemed to rise straight into the air. Margherita could see a few dark columns of cypress trees and, further away, down the valley, the dark mass of a forest. Most frightening of all, there was no door and no stair. The only way in or out was the narrow window, and only an eagle could fly so high.

There must be a way out! Margherita told herself, trying not to panic. *Just wait and watch.*

When the bath was filled with gently steaming water, La Strega poured her potion into a graceful silver goblet and set it on a little table next to the bath. She then unfastened her robe, letting it fall to the ground at her feet. She was naked underneath. Margherita averted her eyes, her heart pitter-pattering. The sorceress showed no self-consciousness, gathering up her own red-gold hair and pinning it loosely at the back of her head. She put her silver goblet on the little table where the candles stood and stepped gracefully into the bath, the moonlit water rippling about her as she sat.

'Light the candles,' she ordered.

Margherita carefully lit the three fat red candles with a wooden splinter. As her taper flared high, it illuminated the oil painting on the wall. Margherita caught her breath, for the beautiful woman painted gazing at herself in her mirror was none other than La Strega herself.

'There is a vial of rose oil there on the shelf. Pass it to me.'

Margherita obeyed, her fingers trembling.

The sorceress let fall three fragrant drops, then passed the vial back to Margherita, who put it away.

'Bring me the jar of dried maidenhair fern next to it.'

When Margherita had brought her the small jar, the sorceress dropped three tiny pinches of dried fern into the bath, turning the water pale green.

'Bring me the roses.'

Margherita brought the flowers, and she watched as the sorceress carefully stripped away the crimson petals and let them drop into her bathwater. A most delicious heady smell filled the small tower room. The candle-light glimmered on the sorceress's red-gold hair and danced on the water's surface, mingling with the silver radiance of the full moon, now high in the sky.

'Here, take the stalks.'

Margherita leant forward to take the bundle of plundered stalks, then suddenly flinched and cried out. The sorceress had purposely slashed one of the cruel rose thorns across the tender skin of her wrist. Blood ran down Margherita's hand and trickled into the water, each drop unfurling like a tiny bud and then spreading tiny stamens, which slowly dissolved, turning the bathwater red. Margherita would have stumbled back, but the sorceress gripped her wrist, forcing her to stand and watch her blood dripping into the water, counting. When nine drops had fallen, she drew Margherita's wrist to her mouth and gently sucked on the wound, stemming the flow. Margherita flinched, snatching her hand away, and the sorceress let her go. Margherita fell to her knees, gripping her bloody wrist, so shocked she could not even cry out.

La Strega lifted the silver goblet to her mouth, her eyes fixed on the portrait of herself hanging at the foot of the bath, and drank a mouthful. 'I shall not pay the apple's price, relinquishing beauty to be wise,' she chanted. Another gulp, and she went on, 'I shall not fade like the petals of the rose, surrendering to the winter's frost.'

With one last mouthful, she drained the goblet dry. 'Bring to me the face I see, so I shall stay as fair as ever.'

For a moment, the sorceress sat still, staring at her painted reflection, a triumphant smile on her lips. Then she turned to Margherita. 'Will you wash my hair for me now, *cara mia*? I do so love to have my hair washed.'

Shaking, tears clogging her throat, Margherita did as she was told. She wiped her bleeding palm on her nightgown, then knelt behind the bath, unpinning the sorceress's mass of fiery curls. Using the empty jug, she carefully poured water over La Strega's head. She massaged the soap in her hands and rubbed the froth through the long red curls. The sorceress sighed with pleasure. 'Can you rub a little harder?' she whispered.

Margherita obeyed, though her heart was beating a wild tattoo in her throat. She dipped the jug in the water, ready to rinse out the soap, but the sorceress shook her head. 'Please, not yet.'

Margherita knelt by the bath, gently massaging La Strega's hair, till her knees throbbed and her back groaned and the water in the bath had cooled. At last, the sorceress sighed and said, 'Very well, enough.' As Margherita was towelling the sorceress's hair dry, a strange ominous shadow darkened the edge of her vision. She looked up and could not help a shriek of pure terror.

The silver disc of the moon was turning blood-red, a dark shadow creeping across its pockmarked face. It looked as if some immense giant had chomped a huge bite out of it. As Margherita watched, incredulous, the stain spread and the moon's face darkened, as if suffused with rage. La Strega was staring up at it with troubled, fascinated eyes. 'What a powerful omen,' she whispered. 'Surely this bodes well for me?'

And ill for me, Margherita thought and covered her eyes with both hands. She did not want to see the moon being eaten alive.

INTERLUDE

Once upon a time
a woman longed for a child, but see how
    one desire easily
replaces the next, see her husband
    climbing the high garden wall
with a handful of rampion, flowering scab
    she's traded for a child.
Look, my mother says, see how the mother
    disappears
as rampion's metallic root splits the tongue
    like a knife
and the daughter spends the rest of the
    story alone.

'Rampion'
Nicole Cooley

WICKED GIRL

The Abbey of Gercy-en-Brie, France —
April 1697

Sitting there on my heels, listening to Sœur Seraphina's tale, I felt such a sharp pang in my heart it was as if someone had reached across the years and driven a rose thorn into my breast.

I too had had my mother stolen from me. I too had been locked away against my will. That girl, Petrosinella, she had been twelve when she was locked away. I had been twelve when my mother was taken.

This garden hidden at the heart of the convent reminded me so much of my mother's garden, hidden at the heart of the chateau where I had been born, the Château de Cazeneuve in Gascony. It was there that I first met the King, which began the chain of events that led me here to the Abbey of Gercy-en-Brie, and Sœur Seraphina's garden.

■ ■ ■ ■

Château de Cazeneuve, Gascony, France —
May 1660

The King came to stay at the Château de Cazeneuve in the spring before my tenth birthday. He and the court were proceeding in a leisurely fashion to Spain, where Louis was to marry the Spanish Infanta, his double first cousin. The Infanta, Marie-Thérèse, was his cousin on both his father's and mother's sides, with Louis' father, Louis XIII, being Marie-Thérèse's uncle, and Marie-Thérèse's father being Louis' uncle.

The court came to Cazeneuve because my mother's grandfather, Raymond de Viçose, was cousin to the King's grandfather, Henri IV, which means my mother is the King's third cousin. The Château de Cazeneuve had been Henri IV's hunting lodge and his favourite residence, and he had given it to his cousin Raymond once he became King of France and moved to Paris.

As boys, Raymond and Henri had hunted boar and courted girls together. As men, they had fought side by side in many a battle, saving each other's lives. Each had survived the St Bartholomew's Day Massacre, which had been sparked by Henri's marriage to Princesse Margot.

Henri's affection for his cousin was so deep

that, after a particularly brutal battle, he had swept off his golden helmet with its long white plume and handed it to Raymond. The white feather then became part of Raymond's coat of arms, and, after Henri gave him the Château de Cazeneuve, he had the royal plume carved over the entrance gate.

The Château de Cazeneuve lies about twenty-five miles south of Bordeaux, on the pilgrim's road that ran from Santiago de Compostela to Vézelay. It was the natural way for the court to travel to Spain and the King's first meeting with the Infanta.

I wonder what the King thought when he first saw the chateau. Cazeneuve was not at all like the graceful symmetrical palaces of Paris, being built for defence, not for beauty. It had thirteen outer walls, all different lengths and angles, and two cone-topped towers overlooking the ravine through which the River Ciron raced. Within the chateau's walls was a sunken courtyard, where my mother had planted her garden, protected from the winds by the high walls. My mother's favourite place at the chateau, it was sweetly scented with the smells of rosemary and lemon balm and thyme. Fruit trees were espaliered all around the walls, and bees hummed in the sweet cicely foaming in the borders.

It was a child's paradise. I had my own fleet chestnut mare, called Garnet, and a long-legged black-and-white-mottled hound called César, who slept on the end of my bed. And, of course, Nanette, who cuddled me and scolded me and brought me a bowl of bread torn up and tossed in warm milk and sprinkled with sugar when I was banished to my room without supper.

Every day, there was a new adventure. I used to love galloping through the park, my eyes closed, my arms held wide, the thunder of my mare's hooves loud and dangerous in my ears. I had a small boat, for rowing on the millpond. (I was not allowed to take my boat onto the river. It was too dangerous, my mother said.) Sometimes, I was allowed to shoot the rapids with the men on the *gabares*, as they took barrels of wine down to the port of Cérons. At harvest time, my sister, Marie, and I would ride home on the top of the hay cart, poppies wound in our hair, singing at the tops of our voices. In winter, we'd go hunting for game for our table and stop somewhere deep in the forest to cook chestnuts on a fire. I remember how they warmed our frozen hands.

Another favourite activity of mine was going down the secret passage to the River Ciron and exploring the caves in the limestone cliffs. Queen Margot was meant to have sneaked down the secret passage to meet her lovers in one of the caves, when she was kept prisoner here by her husband. One day, when

Henri accused her, she replied, 'Is it a crime to be fond of love? Is it right to punish me? Beauty is in the eye of the beholder, and a prison will never be a place of beauty.' To underscore her point, she had had this last line engraved on the mantelpiece in the drawing room. I did like Queen Margot.

Every night, my mother would read to us from one of her many books, my sister and I drawn close to her in an enchanted circle of golden lamplight, the shadows that wavered upon the wall taking the shapes of brave knights and maidens in peril and enchanted beasts. If I could not sleep, my head filled with extraordinary adventures, I would creep down to the library in my nightgown, clutching a candle, which I would light in the embers of the fire. I would curl up in the window seat, the shabby curtains drawn close to hide me, and read further on in the book my mother had laid aside, bending my face to the page to see in the dim uncertain light of my candle.

She read us old poems about nymphs and showers of gold, or tattered accounts of long-ago battles, stories of gods that transformed into swans, heroes that fought one-eyed monsters, and giants that sailed the seas in search of passion and wisdom. I loved them all. But my favourite book, the one that I took down most often and that never failed to divert and delight me, was the heavy il-

215

lustrated edition of *Amadis of Gaul*. And my favourite scene in my favourite book, the one I read over and over to myself in the little circle of candlelight, was the one in the forest when Amadis finally lay down with his one true love, the Princesse Oriana, and there, 'in that green grass, on that cloak, more by the quiet grace of Oriana rather than the bold courage of Amadis, did the most beautiful maiden in the world become a woman'.

I would read until my candle spluttered out in a hot pool of wax, and I would have to creep back to bed through the cold shadowy chateau, heavy-eyed and yawning, my head stuffed full of dreams and visions. If I was caught out of my bed, I'd be shaken and scolded and threatened with a whipping by Nanette, who would then tuck me up with a hot brick wrapped in flannel. 'Wicked girl. If your mother only knew. To bed, to bed!'

I don't remember my father. He died when I was a little girl, and to tell you the truth I never felt his lack. There was Monsieur Alain in the kitchen, always happy to let me help roll dough, and old Victoir in the stables, who taught me to keep my back straight and my head high, and Montgomery, my mother's steward, who could do sums in his head faster than any other man I've met, plus a hundred other grooms and gardeners and footmen to keep an indulgent eye on me.

When the King came, the fields were bright

with cornflowers and poppies and the chestnut trees were in blossom. I had woken early, a fizz of excitement in my stomach, and lay in my canopied bed, thinking of the spectacle ahead. It would be hours before the King and his court arrived, though, and my mother would have us working all morning to prepare.

We had all been kept busy for weeks in preparation for the royal visit. The floors had been scrubbed, the rugs shaken out, and the linen darned and hung over the rosemary bushes to whiten in the sun. Geese had been fattened, hundreds of barrels of wine had been brought up from the cellars, and the huntsmen had ridden in search of wild boar and fat pheasants. It had cost a great fortune, which we could ill afford. Although my mother was the Baronne de Cazeneuve, and my father had been the Marquis de Castelmoron, we were poor. Very poor. All our family's wealth had been lost in the religious wars, before I was born. Normally, we ate cassoulet with white beans and sausage like the peasants, made with a pig's knuckle and some bacon rind for flavour. Our clothes were plain and serviceable, and our only toys were those made for us by the servants: a rag doll, a hoop made from withies, knucklebones saved from the butcher's stall.

My mother had even had new clothes made for us in honour of the King, though as always they were of sober hue and sturdy cloth. Mine was nut-brown, with a plain white collar to match my white linen hood. I'd have liked some lace and ribbons to add some flounce, but my mother did not approve of such things, and besides, as she added truly, I'd only tear it or spill my soup on it.

I gazed at my new dress, with matching slippers of soft lambskin, and then jumped up to run and look out the window. It was only just light. The sky was pale above the mist wreathing from the ground like the steam rising from a weary beast. Birds sang. César put his speckled paws up on the sill beside me and looked at me pleadingly from liquid brown eyes. I grinned.

'Very well, my César. Let's go. We've hours before the King comes.'

I scrambled into an old grey dress, knotting the laces at the back as well as I could. I'm sure girls' dresses were designed to stop us having fun. They were so hard to put on and take off and keep clean.

Along the long gallery I crept, my footsteps muffled by the fine Aubusson carpet. Then I headed down the stairs and along the hallway. César pattered along beside me, his toenails clicking on the old terracotta tiles. I could hear clanging and banging from the kitchen. Monsieur Alain would be busy preparing a fine feast for the court. I went out the side door, into the soft mist of the early morning.

My mare, Garnet, was half-asleep in her stall, her head hanging over the doorway. She whickered at the sight of me and I hushed her, sliding her bridle over her long nose, then taking off her halter. I could not lift the heavy side-saddle onto Garnet's back by myself, so I decided, with a little thrill of rebelliousness, to ride bareback. It felt strange at first, without the pommel to hook my leg over and the planchette in which to rest my foot, but soon Garnet and I were trotting through the mist, César loping behind.

Not wanting to go too far, I went to the pond where the wheel of the mill churned the dark green water into palest emerald. The miller's children were already up, two boys called Jean and Jacques, and a little girl called Mimi. I tied Garnet's reins up and set her free to graze, and then Jean, Jacques, Mimi and I rowed out to the island, where we had built a fort that summer from driftwood and old canvas. We played at Frondeurs for a while, armed with sticks and old rusty pots for helmets, and then busied ourselves making a dam on the shore.

When the King's first outriders came cantering along the road, raising a long plume of dust, I was up to my ankles in mud and water, my dress kilted up above my knees, my arms filled with sticks.

I dropped the sticks. '*Sacré bleu,* the King. He's early. Come on.'

We raced towards the boat. Mimi slipped in the mud and fell. 'Wait for me!' she wailed. I ran back, scooped her up onto my hip and floundered to the boat, which Jean and Jacques held waiting. I dropped Mimi in, then clambered in myself. 'César,' I called and whistled shrilly. My hound bolted from the forest and bounded into the boat, almost capsizing it. Flung to the bottom of the boat, I sat up, only to be knocked down again by my enthusiastic dog trying to wash my face with his tongue.

'Row,' I cried. 'Get me to shore, *tout de suite*!'

In a flurry of splashes, the boat spun in circles as the boys fought over the oars.

'Hurry,' I cried.

Jean dropped one oar. In reaching for it, I almost lurched into the water. Only Jacques' firm grip on my skirts saved me. I seized the oar, jammed it back into its brackets and rowed as fast as I could, feeling blisters springing up on my palm. We reached the shore and I scrambled out, whistling for Garnet. She ambled towards me. I hurried to meet her, my wet muddy skirts flapping against my bare legs.

Garnet sensed my desperation and would not let me catch her reins. At last, I seized hold and cast one agonised glance towards the road. I saw an immense gilded carriage, with outriders streaming before and behind, then a train of smaller carriages, each pulled by a team of fine horses. A woman in a huge hat with a veil wrapped about her face was leaning from the window of the first carriage, one gloved hand gesturing towards me. A young man was cantering alongside on a fine bay gelding. He too was staring at me, and I could clearly see the mocking laughter on his face.

'Sacré cochon,' I cursed, an expression I had heard in the stables that would have earned me a whipping if my mother had heard it on my lips. I scrambled up onto Garnet's back and galloped for home, César loping easily at her heels. The man riding the bay kicked forward his horse, racing me along the length of the field. I felt sick with anxiety. Could that be the King himself? His jacket was so thickly embroidered with gold I could not see the fabric, and he had a fine head of long dark curls, just like the King was said to have. A few other young men whipped up their horses too, beginning a hullabaloo. I was glad when the road curved around to enter through the barbican, and I was able to race across the park to the stables.

'Help me,' I cried as I galloped into the yard. 'The King comes. I'm late! Maman will skin me alive.'

Strong hands lifted me down. 'Run, Bon-bon,' Victoir cried.

I took to my heels, César lolloping gladly

beside me, leaving huge muddy pawprints on the gleaming cobblestones. Cheers and friendly backslappings accompanied me as I raced for the chateau.

Nanette was looking out for me anxiously. 'Wicked girl. Your mother will have your hide! Already, the outriders are here. Look at your dress! Your hair! Your knees! Come, come!'

Together, we raced up the back way, Nanette calling at the maids to bring hot water, soap, a brush, a whip. I was shaken and hugged all at once, the dirty torn dress whisked off me, a wet cloth slapping at my hands and feet and knees, and then my new dress dragged on over my head even while my sister's maid, Agathe, was trying to comb the leaves and twigs out of my hair. Nanette was still tying the ends of my sash as we ran down the corridor and down the grand stairs, just as the front door was flung open for the King and his court.

I slipped in beside my mother as she gracefully curtsied to the ground. I bobbed down too, a few seconds behind my sister and the rest of the household.

'Welcome to Cazeneuve, Your Majesty,' my mother said.

'Thank you, Madame de la Force. We are glad to be here,' an imperious voice replied. I crept forward, eager to have my first look at the King of France.

THE KING OF FRANCE

*Château de Cazeneuve, Gascony, France —
May 1660*

Louis XIV of France was a rather short
young man with long, heavy, dark curls and a
sullen face, his upper lip adorned by a mere
smear of a moustache, which looked as if a
bootboy had pressed his dirty thumbs into
the flesh above his red pouting lips.

There was such a bulk of clothes about him
— lace collars and foaming white sleeves and
a heavy cape embroidered all over with gold
— that he appeared wider than he was tall,
and it seemed impossible that the spindly legs
could actually support the weight. His beady
eyes were sweeping the crowd, noticing
everyone and everything, while he flicked his
whip against his leg in what seemed like a
nervous tic, for an immense lady in black
rustled forward to lay one jewel-laden hand
on his, stilling the movement.

'*Madame,* may I present my mother, the
Queen?'

Once again, everyone on the step bowed or swept down to the ground in a curtsey, and once again I was left bobbing a few seconds behind. The King noticed me. The dark brows twitched together. He saw César pressed against my leg, and recognition flared in his eyes, which flicked at once back up to me, taking in my flushed face, my damp hair and the crooked sash. His eyebrows lifted. His lip twisted in the faintest of sneers. Colour surging into my cheeks, I dropped my eyes, staring resolutely at the ground.

The King's brother, Philippe, the Duc d'Orléans, was introduced. A slim exquisite young man of twenty, he was as painted and rouged as the ladies, and had an earring in one ear. Another sulky young man in lavender silk lounged beside him, a pomander held to his nose, but he was not introduced. In fact, the King seemed to pretend he was not there at all.

Instead, the King's cousin, Anne-Marie-Louise d'Orléans, the Duchesse de Montpensier, was presented. She was a tall lady, in the biggest hat I had ever seen. When she lifted her veil, it was to show a plain-faced woman of about thirty, with a big nose and bright kind eyes. I shrank back behind my sister, for I recognised her as the woman in the coach who had pointed at me, laughing.

Standing close beside the Queen was a tall olive-skinned man dressed in scarlet, with scowling eyebrows and a beautifully groomed moustache with upturning ends. He was introduced as Cardinal Mazarin, the chief minister.

'We thank you for your hospitality, *madame,*' Cardinal Mazarin said, in a deep, accented voice, 'and also for the opportunity to receive your professions of homage and loyalty to His Majesty the King.'

Colour rose in my mother's face. Everyone knew that my parents had fought against the King in the religious wars, but I thought it rather tactless to bring it up at that point and so too did my mother, by the look of her tight-lipped face.

'Of course,' Maman replied. 'But, please, come in. Let us do what we can to welcome you and make you comfortable after your journey.'

The Queen smiled adoringly up at Cardinal Mazarin and took his arm so he could help her up the steps. The King stuck out his sulky lower lip, looking unhappy to have to fall in behind them. His brother, the Duc d'Orléans, sauntered after him, his high heels clacking on the worn old stone. As he came into the great hall, hung with ancient tapestries and my great-grandfather's weapons of war, the Duc d'Orléans said to his friend, 'What a ghastly place. Positively medieval. I am sure, absolutely sure, my dear Philippe, that there must be dungeons here.'

'But of course. With skeletons hanging in chains.' Philippe affected a shudder.

'There aren't any dungeons,' I cried angrily. 'Or any skeletons. There's only cellars and caves, wonderful caves where a hermit used to live.'

The Duc d'Orléans raised one dark eyebrow. '*Saperlipopette!* Cellars. And caves. How thrilling.'

'Perhaps tonight we should go and explore these dark underground caves, *monsieur,*' Philippe said in a strange insinuating way, as if he was making a joke.

'Absolutely,' the Duc d'Orléans replied in the same meaningful way.

I looked from one to the other, not understanding the joke. 'There's a secret passage too,' I said, wanting the King's court to love the Château de Cazeneuve as much as I did.

The two men laughed, but not in a nice way. 'Did you hear, Philippe? A secret passage. Now that we must explore.'

'You must ask my mother's steward for lanterns,' I said. 'It's dark in there.'

They laughed even harder, supporting each other. The Duc d'Orléans pressed his jasmine-scented handkerchief to his eyes. 'And I thought I'd be bored to death in the country. But so many secret passages and caves to discover!'

I backed away, not liking the malice I sensed in their laughter and not understand-

226

ing what amused them so much. I looked for
Maman, who was standing pressed against
the wall, as crowds of people surged past her,
chattering like starlings. Maman's face was
pale and strained.

'I have a gift for you, *madame*,' the King
was saying to her.

'You are too kind, Your Majesty,' she murmured in response.

The King snapped his fingers and my
mother was presented with a small portrait of
himself dressed in ermine fur and blue
brocade, a fleur-de-lys baton in one hand,
the other resting on his crown.

'Thank you,' she said rather stupidly, and I
could tell that she was biting back caustic
words. She stood holding the portrait, looking about her as if wondering what to do with
it. Montgomery came and relieved her of its
weight, and I heard a few muttered words.
'Where shall we put it? And what shall we
do? So many people. Where can they all
sleep? Are there enough oysters? Best open
some more wine!'

Again, I was aware of the King's penetrating stare. I shrank away, my hand on César's
ruff, and found myself caught by my sister,
Marie, and shaken and scolded once more.

'I'm sorry. I forgot,' I cried.

'Forgot the King was coming? How could
you?'

'He was early . . .'

'It was such a fine day, he decided to ride,' Marie said.

'How those poor ladies must've been rattled about, trying to keep up with him,' I said. 'He must've galloped most of the way to be here so early.'

'It's almost noon,' she said. 'You must know Maman is furious. We saw you running from the stables scant seconds before they arrived, looking like some wild child raised by wolves. Imagine if the King had seen you.'

I dared not confess that he had.

The King and his court had a wonderful feast that evening.

Huge tureens of puréed chestnut soup with truffles were carried in and served to each guest, filling the air with a rich earthy smell. Then the servants brought in ballotine of pheasant, served with cold lobster in aspic and deep-sea oysters brought up the river by boat that morning. Our own foie gras on tiny rounds of bread was followed by *margret de canard,* the breast meat of force-fed ducks, roasted with small home-grown pears and Armagnac. There was a white-bean cassoulet with wild hare, a haunch of venison cooked in cinnamon and wine, eel pie, and a salad of leaves and flowers from the garden, dressed with olive oil and lemon.

Queen Anne ate and ate and ate. I had never seen a woman eat so much. No wonder she was so enormous. The King ate nearly as much. Safely ensconced in the window alcove, I had an excellent view of the table through the crack in the heavy curtains. Maman thought me in bed, of course, but I had slipped in while the servants were setting the table and hidden myself. I did not want to miss a moment of the King's visit.

As Queen Anne ate, she talked. 'Ah, *madame*,' she said to my mother, 'I pity you. Two daughters! And no husband. How are you to find dowries for them?'

'I'll just have to do my best,' my mother answered with a polite smile.

'Best send the youngest to the convent,' Cardinal Mazarin said, looking bored.

My mother's smile froze. 'I fear she is not suited for the nunnery.'

'Then the nunnery is just the place for her,' Cardinal Mazarin replied, sipping his wine. 'It'll break her spirit. Maidens should be mild and meek, swift to hear and slow to speak.'

I screwed up my face in disgust, but my mother smiled faintly.

'It costs as much to marry a girl to Christ as it does to marry her to a man these days,' the Duc d'Orléans said with a sneer. The King's brother wore rose-pink satin, his sleeves slashed and beribboned, the lace falling from above his elbow to cover his fingers. He wore an enormous pink diamond in his ear, and another on his finger. His friend,

Philippe, who I had learnt was the Chevalier de Lorraine, was as exquisite in a short flared coat of puce satin. Both wore extraordinary baggy breeches that made them look as if they were wearing skirts, with loops of ribbons at the waist and knee.

'Poor girl,' said Anne-Marie-Louise, the Duchesse de Montpensier, laying down her fork. 'Why must she marry? Surely she can be of service to her family without having to marry?'

'So you say,' the Duc d'Orléans said cuttingly, 'as an excuse to cover the fact that nobody wants you. The richest heiress in all of Christendom and you still can't find a husband.'

Anne-Marie-Louise flushed scarlet and looked down at her plate.

'The Grande Mademoiselle could have had any number of husbands,' Queen Anne said coldly. 'But King Charles of England was too ugly, and King Alfonso of Portugal not fit enough . . .'

'He was half-paralysed,' Anne-Marie-Louise protested. 'And a halfwit.'

'And the Duke of Savoy was too young . . .' Queen Anne continued.

'He's seventeen years younger than me. And he still lets his mother rule for him.'

There was an awful moment of silence. The King thrust out his jaw and his mother the Queen looked embarrassed. She had been

Regent of France for so many years, she still thought of herself in that role. She tossed back a goblet of wine, then, fortified, returned to the attack. 'Well, what about the Emperor Ferdinand? You wouldn't have him either.'

'He was twenty years older than me.'

'I suppose that was your reason for turning down my brother as well,' the Queen said.

'He was a cardinal!'

'Pfff! A small worry. He was never ordained a priest, being an Infante of Spain. Something could have been arranged.' The Queen shook out her napkin, looking most displeased.

Anne-Marie-Louise bit her lip, looking down at her plate. 'They all just wanted me for my money. I . . . I want someone to want me for myself.' Her voice shook.

'Now you are talking like a milkmaid,' the King said in a voice sharp with contempt. 'You are a granddaughter of France. Your marriage is a matter of alliance, to bring power and riches to the throne.'

'So I am to be sold like a cow to the highest bidder?' Anne-Marie-Louise answered, her hands gripped together.

'If I so ordain it,' he answered. 'There is no other use for you.'

There was a long tense silence. Anne-Marie-Louise was clearly fighting back tears.

'Surely France has wealth and power enough?' my mother said. She smiled at the King. 'All Europe talks of the brilliance of

231

the Sun King's court.'

His face was impassive. 'Yet such brilliance comes at a price. And it is in the marriage market that it is paid.'

'Yet, if *mademoiselle* does not wish to marry,' my mother went on, sympathy in her voice, 'surely it is not necessary?'

'It is not a matter of choice. It is a matter of duty and propriety,' the King answered.

'Besides, a woman needs a man to command and protect her,' Queen Anne said. 'My husband the King died nearly twenty years ago, and I do not know what I would have done without the guidance of my dear Jules.' She smiled fondly at Cardinal Mazarin, who was leaning back in his chair, his brows raised, his eyes on my mother's face.

'Yet you were the King's Regent for so many years,' Maman said. 'You have raised two sons on your own, just as I have raised my daughters since my husband died.'

'Yes, indeed,' Queen Anne agreed. 'That is very true.'

Cardinal Mazarin frowned. The Queen hastened to add, 'Though I had the very best of all advisors.'

Maman continued eagerly, 'And although I miss my husband greatly, I hold my estates and titles in my own right, and it was always my responsibility to run them wisely. My husband had his own affairs to manage. The Château de Cazeneuve is mine, and it shall

232

be my daughter's after me.'

Anne-Marie-Louise was gazing at her with bright curious eyes. 'So, *madame,* you think it possible for a woman to have her own little corner of the world and be mistress of it?'

'Of course,' my mother answered her. 'Women have been saints and soldiers and mothers. They are more than capable of managing their own affairs.' They shared a warm complicit smile.

'Do you not know that women are defective and misbegotten, a male gone awry?' Cardinal Mazarin said with scathing contempt. 'St Clement spoke truly when he said that all women should be overwhelmed with shame at the very thought that she is a woman.'

The women all looked down at their plates. The Duc d'Orléans smirked at his friend. I was angry. Why didn't Maman speak up? Why didn't she say to him, as she said to her daughters, 'Why did God give us a brain if he didn't want us to use it?' I looked at her doubtfully. Her back was straight, her face was flushed and there was a deep line between her brows. She was angry, but she did not speak.

'I see only one of your daughters here tonight,' the King remarked. 'Where's the one I saw riding as if the devil was on her tail?'

'I am not sure who you mean, Your Majesty,' my mother replied coolly.

'You mean that wild little creature we saw today?' Anne-Marie-Louise said. 'Surely she was just a peasant girl?'

'The little girl with the great dog.' The King watched my mother over the rim of his goblet.

'We have many small girls here and many hunting dogs, Your Majesty.' My mother's voice was curt.

'A tall blue-grey one, mottled all over with dark spots and a high noble nose,' the King probed. 'Is that not your daughter's dog?'

'If you are fond of dogs, Your Majesty, you must visit our kennels tomorrow.' My mother made a signal to Montgomery, and he ordered the empty dishes removed and the servants to bring in pewter bowls of apple and Armagnac croustade with cream.

'I would like that.' The King smiled unpleasantly. 'But where is your youngest daughter, *madame*?'

'She will have retired for the night, Your Majesty, being only a child and too young for such revelries.'

'Two daughters and no son,' Queen Anne said through a mouthful of honeyed cream. 'What a shame. We must have one to court, Louis. The eldest one is passably pretty. Let us have her to court and find her a husband.'

Sitting further down the table, Marie blushed and looked down at her plate. I glared at the Queen. How dare she call Marie only passably pretty? I thought her the prettiest girl I'd ever seen. It was true her dark eyes and warm olive skin were not fashionable at the moment, but she at least had not inherited my father's strong nose like I unfortunately had.

'She will need one if she is to inherit,' the King said. 'It seems a prosperous enough estate. She will need someone to manage it for her.' He gave my mother a sideways glance.

My mother made a quick impatient movement. 'I have managed these estates well enough without a man, Your Majesty, and Marie has been trained for the role since birth. She is quite capable.'

'A woman in charge of a great estate is against the natural order of things,' Cardinal Mazarin said. 'A man is made to lead; a woman is born to obey. A family cannot have two masters. It would be like having two suns in the sky.'

'It would be like the servant ordering the master about,' Queen Anne agreed.

'Or letting the horse ride the man,' the Duc d'Orléans said with a giggle.

Cardinal Mazarin gave him a pained glance. 'Women, after all, were never made for strength. They were made from Adam's rib, remember, so are frail, weak things, easily bent.'

My mother gripped her hands together. 'Your Excellency, that is something I have

235

never understood, and would be most grateful to you if you could clarify for me. If women were truly made from Adam's rib, should men not have one less rib than women? Yet all my observations have shown me that men and women have the same number of ribs on either side.'

'You are mistaken,' Cardinal Mazarin replied, frowning. 'Men have one less rib.'

'Have you ever counted your ribs? I can tell you that I have twelve ribs on each side, and so too did my dear husband.'

The Cardinal showed his teeth in what was meant to be a smile. 'I'm afraid you must've miscounted, *madame.*'

My mother opened her mouth angrily but then shut it again, visibly swallowing her words. Two bright spots of colour burnt high on her cheeks.

'You'll have to count your ribs tonight, Your Excellency,' the Duc d'Orléans said in a teasing voice. 'And then find some woman willing to allow you to count hers. Perhaps . . .' He turned towards his mother, who coloured and began to rapidly stir the Armagnac sauce into her cream. 'But no, that shan't do. Think of the scandal if the Cardinal was caught counting the Queen's ribs!' He glanced now at his brother, who was listening with a slight frown on his face. 'I know, Louis. You are soon to be married. I charge you with the task of counting your new bride's ribs. You must let us know what you discover. That is, if you can find your lady love's ribs. By all accounts, she's a plump little pigeon. I'd wager you have trouble locating them.'

'How you do rattle on,' Queen Anne protested, rather breathlessly. 'I beg you, Louis, take no notice of Philippe.'

'I never do.' The King turned his dark penetrating glance to my mother, who was sitting bolt upright, her hands clenched. 'Do you deny the Scriptures, *madame*? For is it not said that a woman should be silent and have no authority over man?'

'Of course I do not deny the Scriptures, Your Majesty.'

'Yet you are one of these *réformés,* are you not?'

She met the King's gaze. 'I am, Your Majesty. But we do not deny the Scriptures. We believe they contain all that is necessary for the service of God and our own salvation.'

He frowned. 'Yet you argue against the one true Church, is that not so?'

She picked her words with care. 'The one true Church is made up of those faithful who agree to follow the word of God.'

The King thrust out his lower lip. His frown had deepened, so that he looked like a sulky child who was deciding whether or not to have a tantrum.

'And what of the intercession of the holy saints?' Cardinal Mazarin demanded. 'What

237

do you think of the confessional, and the sacrifice of the mass?'

'I think these are weighty matters for a meal designed to celebrate the honour of His Majesty's visit to our home,' my mother said, smiling a little stiffly. 'And certainly not ones that I, a mere frail woman, would dare discuss with the anointed leaders of state and church.' She gave a small bow to the King and the Cardinal, before adding, with a more natural smile, 'I will only say that if one was to gather up all the pieces of the True Cross in the world, we'd have enough timber to build a ship.'

A laugh broke out, but Cardinal Mazarin looked displeased and the King's frown did not lift.

'I beg your indulgence, Your Majesty,' my mother said. 'I didn't mean to offend you. Are we all not free to worship according to our conscience, under your grandfather's wise law? Come, let us talk instead of what we can do to amuse you during your stay here with us. Would Your Majesty care to hunt?'

The King's eyes brightened. 'Indeed I would. Your forests look good and thick. What game is there?'

'The forest of Cazeneuve is famous for its deer, and there are also plenty of bear and wild boar and wolves, if you would care for some rougher sport.'

'The rougher the better,' the Duc

238

D'Orleans said, with that strange insinuating note in his voice, which made his mother blush and the King slap him lightly with his gloves.

THE HUNT

Château de Cazeneuve, Gascony, France —
May 1660
The hunters gathered in the courtyard in the
quiet chill before dawn, the horses stamping
on the cobblestones. The pack of hounds
tugged at their leashes, impatient to be off.

The King sat astride his big bay gelding,
dressed all in velvet and lace. His cousin,
Anne-Marie-Louise, rode side-saddle beside
him, a long whip in one gloved hand. She
wore her big hat with the veil lowered to
protect her skin. She was one of the few
women to have risen early. I was a little disappointed; I'd been looking forward to seeing
the dowager-queen heaved into the saddle. It
would have taken about ten men, I thought,
and a very sturdy mount.

The huntsmen were all in the saddle, their
great horns coiled about their arms, many
taking a quick swig of Armagnac from their
silver flasks to warm the blood.

In the stables, my sister and I were being

lifted onto our ponies, Victoir beside us on an old sway-backed mare. César stood beside me as always, his black-patched head near my stirrup.

'You'll keep an eye on the girls for me, won't you, Victoir,' my mother said with a weary smile. She looked as if she had not slept well.

'Of course, *madame,*' he answered, lifting his hat.

I bounced up and down in my saddle with excitement. 'If he can keep up with us on that old hack. He looks like he's riding an armchair!'

'I am sorry, Victoir,' my mother said. 'So many lords in the King's retinue who did not bring their own hunters.'

'I understand, *madame.* Old Misty will do me well enough.'

'I'll need to trust you girls to be on your best behaviour,' my mother said to us. 'Don't lead poor old Victoir on a wild-goose chase.'

'I wish you were coming with us, Maman,' Marie said.

Maman smiled at her. 'I only wish I could. But there is too much to do. We can rest and enjoy ourselves once the King has gone.'

We heard the horns call, and the dogs barked in excitement. The familiar elation raced through my veins. I loved to hunt. The exhilaration of the chase, the sense of wild freedom and escape, the pitting of one's wits against a noble adversary, all combined to make the *chasse à courre* one of my absolute favourite things to do. I did not like the killing of the stag so much, though I enjoyed eating the roasted meat at the end of a long hard day in the saddle. The captain of the hunt, however, had said that I must watch. 'It is best you know what it is you do,' he said. 'The stag, he dies so that we may live.'

Chattering gaily, Marie and I rode out into the courtyard, Maman at the head of my pony.

'You do not ride, *madame*?' the King called.

'Not I, Your Majesty, but I look forward to eating roast venison tonight,' she called back.

The King sneered at the sight of me. 'Why, if it isn't the littlest one. Surely she's too young to ride to the hunt.'

'Charlotte-Rose rides very well, Your Majesty. The girls are accustomed to hunting through our woods.'

'I'll show you the way, Your Majesty,' I cried, making the crowd of courtiers laugh.

My mother tugged on my skirt so I bent my head to hers. 'Be quiet and respectful, Bon-bon. I fear His Majesty is quick to take offence.'

I raised my chin. My blood was up. I'd show the King that I could ride.

'Bon-bon,' my mother warned.

'Very well then, Maman,' I replied, shrugging. She released my skirt.

In another moment, we were off, the horses galloping across the parkland in a long train, the bright velvet coats of the lords gaudy against the misty sky. The dogs led the way, silent now and casting about for a scent. Along the edge of the gorge we went, and over the little bridge across the river and into the dark moss-hung forest on the far side. At once, the pace slowed. The horses made their way carefully through the undergrowth, falling into single file when the path narrowed. Birds sang in the branches and I saw a stealthy fox slip away under some brambles. Green catkins were hanging from the chestnut trees, and here and there a wild plum showed a haze of white flowers against the great stands of oak and beech. The air was clear and sharp, and smelt of leaf and water and moss and blossom.

The captain of the hunt dismounted, looking for signs of velvet rubbed from the stags' antlers against the trees. The dogs snuffled about his feet, searching for scent.

César lifted his muzzle and gave his deep sonorous howl. Then he began to run, his nose to a trail. The other dogs loped after him, bellowing with joy. As the captain vaulted back into the saddle, we all broke into a canter. Away through the trees we raced, swerving in and out and occasionally jumping a fallen log. Although Garnet was small, she was quick, and soon I was near the front. I saw a stag racing ahead, his antlers held high. I gave a wild ululating cry and kicked Garnet on faster.

Hooves pounded against the ground, and the dogs were giving voice, the call of the horns adding a triumphant bugle to the music of the hunt. The stag swerved and bounded to the top of a great fallen tree, scrabbling there for a moment before dropping down the other side and out of sight. The King reined his bay. 'Go round, go round,' he cried, making a wide gesture with his arm. 'It's too high to jump.'

I kicked Garnet towards the giant mossy bole. I knew this forest well and had hurdled that fallen tree before. I knew it was a clear landing on the far side.

'Go round,' the King called again.

'It's not so high.' Whipping off my hat to shake it triumphantly in the air, I took Garnet over the trunk with a few inches to spare. Neatly, she landed on the far side, and she raced off in pursuit of the stag, the dogs and huntsmen pouring over the log to follow me. In moments, the stag was held at bay by the dogs, tossing his antlers and threatening to charge as the dogs barked and nipped and held him still.

A short while later, the King and the rest of the court joined us at the kill. The King's face was dark and furious. He shot me a look of intense dislike, then ignored me, though a few of the lords cried out, 'Fine riding, *mademoiselle.'*

'You silly girl,' Marie hissed at me. 'Don't you know better than to ride in front of the King like that? You've shown him up in front of his court, and I swear he'll want a piece of your hide.'

Tears rushed to my eyes. I had not meant to humiliate the King, just to show him what a clever rider I was. I had to wipe my eyes on the cuff of my glove.

The captain of the hunt stood back to let the King dismount and draw his dagger. The King strode forward and slashed the stag's throat. Blood spurted down the beast's pale breast. He bellowed and tossed his wide rack of antlers, then fell onto his front knees, bellowing again. The dogs all howled and lunged forward, fighting to get to the beast.

I forced myself to watch, remembering what I had been taught. 'You must watch and remember the kill,' the captain had told me, 'and be grateful to the stag for giving up his life so that we have meat to eat. Without meat, we would be weak and hungry. Yet remember we do not deal death just for death's sake. A man that does that is black and rotten inside, and someone to be feared. Beware a man who takes pleasure in the kill.'

It seemed to me, watching the King as he hacked off the stag's forefoot and held it high, staring triumphantly around at the clapping cheering courtiers, that he was someone who took pleasure in the kill.

Château de Cazeneuve, Gascony, France —
October 1662
Two years later, when I had almost forgotten that day in the forest, I remembered the dark fury of the King's face and the way he had held up the bleeding stump of the stag's hoof.

Cardinal Mazarin died at half past two in the morning on 9th March 1661. As soon as he heard the news, the twenty-two-year-old king locked himself in his study. When he emerged many hours later, it was to declare himself the absolute monarch, with no need for any more councillors. 'I am the State,' he told his startled ministers, who departed grumbling and expecting him to call them back within the week. He never did.

His other, undeclared, ambition was *'une foi, un loi, un roi'.* One faith, one law, one king. Although it would take many years before Louis XIV finally emptied France of the Huguenots — hundreds of thousands of them slaughtered, sold into slavery or driven into exile — he began early, with my mother.

At first, when the Marquis de Maulévrier arrived at Cazeneuve in October 1662 with a troop of dragoons and the order that my mother was to be imprisoned in a convent, none of us could believe it. It seemed like a horrible joke.

'But . . . I am the Baronne de Caze-neuve . . . and I am a *réformée,*' Maman said blankly.

'It is the King's order, *madame,*' the Marquis de Maulévrier replied. He was dressed in black velvet, with a heavy jewelled cross hanging about his neck, his narrow beard jutting out over a collar of white lace.

'But . . . this cannot be . . . he knows I am of a different faith.'

'You are to be converted to the one true faith, *madame.* You will be incarcerated in the convent of Annonciades until the abbess is sure that your conversion is honest. Your dowry and all your expenses must be borne by this estate. There is no need to pack. Nuns are not permitted any personal belongings.'

My mother's face was white. 'Let me see this order from the King.'

The Marquis de Maulévrier held out the *lettre du cachet.* My mother read it, one hand at her throat. 'My daughters . . .' she choked.

'The King, in his infinite wisdom and mercy, has appointed your daughters wards of the court and me their guardian until suitable marriages can be arranged for them. You need have no concerns for their safety.'

The *lettre du cachet* fluttered to the ground. Maman swayed and would have fallen if one of the soldiers had not stepped forward to catch her. She was put into a small cart, while my sister and I wept and screamed and called for help. As Montgomery came running, the soldiers thrust forward their halberds, almost impaling him. The lurch of the cart woke my mother from her swoon. She dragged herself onto her knees, holding out her arms to us, tears running down her stricken face.

'*Mes fifilles! Mes fifilles!*'

That was the last I saw of her. We heard some time later that she managed to escape on her way to the convent, with the help of her cousin, who had heard of the King's intention. His Majesty sent troops against her at Castelnaud, though, and she was taken under guard to the nunnery. And there she stayed till she died.

Palais du Louvre, Paris, France — June 1666
Four years later, when I had just turned sixteen, I was summoned to court, where the King nodded his massive curly head at me and said with a cruel smile, 'Ah yes, I remember you. Do you still ride, *mademoiselle*?'

'Of course,' I replied. 'Do you?'

REVERIE

And yet — but I am growing old,
For want of love my heart is cold,
Years pass, the while I loose and fold
The fathoms of my hair.

'Rapunzel'
William Morris

A Kind of Madness

The Rock of Manerba, Lake Garda, Italy —
April 1595

The day after the eclipse of the moon, La Strega showed Margherita why she now had such a long braid of hair.

She uncoiled the plait from Margherita's snood, wound it about a hook at the side of the window, then threw the end over the windowsill. It unfurled like a rope of living gold, reaching to the bottom of the tower a hundred feet below. Low thorny bushes crowded about the base, starred with tiny white flowers. Below were sharp rocks, the beginning of a precipitous stairway cut into the stone, and beyond, nothing but air. The tower was built on the edge of a cliff, and far below, distant as a dream, lay a blue lake, cradled in forest at the base of towering snow-capped mountains.

'You see, there's no point trying to escape,' La Strega whispered in Margherita's ear, one hand on her shoulder. 'You would be broken on those rocks if you were stupid enough to jump. To make sure you don't try, I'll lock the shutters behind me.'

'Please don't. Please.'

The previous night, Margherita had thought it was impossible to feel any more fear or misery. She had longed to be just left alone. Yet, now that the sorceress was leaving her, new depths of terror opened below her. Margherita could not bear the thought of being on her own.

'Don't worry,' La Strega murmured and stroked away a tendril of hair. 'I'll be back soon. A month is not so very long.' She climbed up onto the windowsill, holding the plait between both hands. For a giddy moment, Margherita thought of pushing her out. La Strega smiled down at her. 'I'll be back in a month. Take care. Remember that if I fall and die, or if you damage your hair somehow, so you cannot throw it out to me, you'll starve to death up here. No one knows you are here. No one can help you. If you are good, I will bring you a present on my return. But if I find you have been naughty, you will have nothing to eat but dry bread and water.'

'Please don't leave me,' Margherita begged, but it was no use. The sorceress slammed the shutters and padlocked them closed, first lifting the braid so it ran through the heart-shaped hole. Margherita was locked inside.

Then the sorceress began to climb down

the side of the tower. The pull of her weight on Margherita's hair was almost unbearable, even with the help of the hook. Sobbing, Margherita braced herself against the wall. Eventually, the jerking stopped. A distant voice called, 'I'll be back when the moon is full once more.'

Then silence.

Margherita pulled up the braid, hand over hand over hand, until it lay coiled about her, then stepped to the ground and looked around.

One small room. A tap. An empty bath. A large basket of firewood. A bed with rumpled pillows and silken coverlet.

No door, no stair, no open window, no air, no light, no sound.

A kind of madness possessed her. She ran about the room, looking for a way out. She shook the shutters with all her strength and battered her fists upon them. She put her mouth to the heart carving and screamed for help. She stared down the stinking hole in the latrine. She went back to the window and screamed again. She sat on the floor and sobbed into her hands. She wrenched at the plait, seeking to tear it out by the roots. She paced the floor, dragging the plait behind her. She shouted and called and cried and begged, till her throat was raw and her voice hoarse. She went back to the latrine. She stared down its narrow chute. She dropped a pine cone down it and waited till she heard the faint clatter as it hit stone, a long way down. She sat on the edge and dangled her legs down the hole. Gingerly, she lowered her body down but got stuck straightaway. When she managed to wrench herself free, her hip was grazed and bleeding, and her nightgown was stained and filthy. Tears blinded her. *No way out, no way out, no way out.*

Eventually, with the spout of her kettle and the poker, she managed to prise one of the shutters off the window, so that it hung crookedly. Margherita leant both hands on the windowsill and took great gulps of air. A panorama of clouds spread across the darkening sky, rose and peach and saffron, limned with liquid gold. She imagined leaping from the windowsill and being caught by soft misty arms. High on the clouds' shoulders she'd be carried, over the mountains and far away, rain darkening the sky behind her, a lightning bolt sizzling in her hand. Back to Venice she'd be carried, that city of stone lace and shadowy canals, seeming at times to drift among clouds. Down she'd bound, sure-footed and fleet, outside a window opening into a treasure trove of masks and sequins and feathers. The door would spring open, her parents would rush out, arms flung wide, and she'd cry, 'I'm home.'

The clouds rolled on without her, the glorious colours fading to violet and grey. Far below her, the lake grew dark. Rain lashed the stony cliffs.

Margherita took a deep breath and wiped her wet face on the sleeve of her nightgown. She turned and sat down, hiding her face in her arm. There was no way out. Not unless she grew wings and flew.

If I could cut off my plait, Margherita thought, *perhaps I could tie it to the hook somehow and climb down it like the sorceress did.*

But there was no knife and no scissors, not even something made of glass that she could have broken, using the sharp edge to saw through the hair.

Maybe I could just tie the end of my plait to the hook and climb down it while it's still attached to my head, she thought. *Once I'm down on the ground, I'll be able to cut my hair somehow.* She thought of the bushes below and imagined slicing through her hair with sharp thorns. Surely it could be done. She tried not to think of the dizzying drop and what would happen to her if she fell. *If the sorceress can climb down, so can I.*

So she took the end of her plait and wound it round and round the hook and tied it in a knot, as tightly as she could. But every time she pulled on it, testing her weight, the slippery hair simply unwound itself and she fell to the floor. Nothing worked. Her hair unravelled each time.

By now, Margherita was utterly disheartened. She curled up in the plaited coils of her hair and wept. When she woke, much later, it was dark. She started up in terror, afraid that she had somehow been buried alive in the crypt of her dreams, but then she saw the narrow arch of the window, glowing with silvery starlight. She managed to grope her way to her bed and climb into its softness. Soon, she was asleep again.

The next day, Margherita sat in her bed and looked around hopelessly. She felt the weight of the invisible fetters on her wrists and ankles and tongue. Only her need to use the latrine gave her the will to get out of bed and walk across the tiny room. Three paces to the latrine. Ten paces to the fire, to poke it into sullen life once more. Six paces to the pantry, to look for something to eat.

Hanging from the top of the little cupboard were a sheaf of dried cod, a string of salami and a small leg of salt-cured ham, the hoof still attached. On the top shelf were a row of wooden spice boxes with salt, pepper, ginger, saffron, and other spices that Margherita did not recognise, and a wooden lidded bowl filled with dried fruit and nuts. Small sacks of turnips, onions, cabbages, beets, parsnips, dried peas and beans, and limp purple carrots were piled on the bottom shelf. On the shelf above were sacks of rice, flour, yeast and semolina, a bowl of apples, a tub of honey and a large ceramic jar of olives in oil.

Somehow, this cornucopia of ingredients only made Margherita even more miserable. Although she had helped in the kitchen at the Pietà since she was seven years old, she had only ever assisted the cook, and she was overwhelmed by the thought of preparing and cooking all her own food, with only a few basic tools. And no knife. How could she slice the ham, or peel and cut up the turnips, without a knife?

She ate an apple and a handful of nuts and dried fruit, then sighed and began to mix flour and salt and yeast together with water. She cooked it on the griddle. The smell of baking bread brought her new courage. She washed her face and hands and tidied her hair as best she could. Once she had eaten her flat bread with some honey and tidied up, there was nothing left to do but try once again to escape.

She tried tying the end of her plait to the hook with ribbons; she tried weighting it with her iron pot; she tried tying it to the stool. It always unravelled. And her hair became messier and messier, which frightened her terribly. She did her best with the comb La Strega had given her, but soon her arms were aching and she had to stop. She tried to stuff it all into the snood, but somehow there seemed so much more of it, and the snood became all entangled in her hair. *Why is it I cannot tie my hair in a knot when I want to, yet it gets all snarled up when I don't want it to?* she thought, struggling to unravel the snood. In the end, she just yanked the snood loose and plaited the great mass of the hair again, knots and all. Then there was nothing to do but pace the floor, the plait trailing behind her, her hands clenched white-knuckled.

What if something happens to the sorceress? she thought. *What if she catches the plague? No one knows where I am. I'll die of starvation.*

Margherita sank onto her bed, overwhelmed by panic.

Surely she'd have thought of that. Surely she'd have left a letter. Then Margherita remembered the giant, Magli, with his high shrill voice and imperturbable face. He knew. He'd carried her here. Surely he'd not leave her here to die. Surely.

What does she want with me? Why am I here? Was it magic she was doing last night? Is it my blood that she wants? Old stories of bloodsucking ghouls came back to her, chilling her blood. She looked down at the thin red cut across her wrist. It was a little puffy and sore but was already healing.

Such panic filled her that she could no longer be still. Once again, she stood at the window, screaming for help. Once again, she ran around the room, searching for a chink in the stone, a rope, a knife. Once again, she wept. Eventually, she had no more tears in her body. She lay in a daze, retreating from the horror of the present and the dark uncertainty of the future into a daydream of the past.

The beam of sunlight through the broken shutter faded and retreated. Soon, it would be dark. And Margherita was hungry once more. She stood and stared at her pantry, then took a deep breath and began to make a rudimentary meal.

The dried cod had to be soaked overnight before it could be cooked, so she put some in a bowl of water and set it aside on the dresser, then made some more bread dough and this time set it to rise. She then filled her iron pot with water and a selection of vegetables, throwing them in whole with a pinch of salt. Then she examined the ham longingly. The skin had been expertly cut at one end and she was able to peel it away, revealing the dark crimson flesh beneath. After a while, she lowered her mouth to it and bit into it. Her mouth was filled with an explosion of flavour. She was so hungry that she gnawed off a few more mouthfuls, then bit off chunks and spat them into her soup. She then smoothed down the skin to protect the ravaged flesh beneath, a little worried by how much of the ham she had already devoured.

Everything has to last me a month . . . She looked in some dismay at her shelves, and what had seemed a cornucopia now seemed dangerously paltry.

The silence of the small room bothered her. She was used to the low murmur of chanting, the soft sound of singing or the playing of musical instruments, the constant ringing of the church bells, the scrape of chairs and boot leather on stone, the rustle of cloth, the small farts and burps and squeaks of a dormitory of girls. High in her tower room, there was no sound but the wind and the occasional high cry of a hawk.

So Margherita hummed as she worked, then broke into song. The sound of her own voice steadied her. The smell of soup and bread helped her even more. She ate a meal by the low light of the fire, washed up her pots and dishes, then curled up in her bed, taking comfort in her favourite daydream. Tomorrow, the door would burst in, and her parents would rush in, calling her name. 'Margherita, we've found you at last.' All three would embrace, weeping, and then her father would lift her onto his shoulders and they'd march out triumphantly.

Except there was no door. No door and no stair.

There must be a stair, she thought. La Strega and the giant could not have brought the bed and the table and the chairs and the pantry and the bath and everything in through that narrow window. *Under the car-*

pet, she thought.

She sat up in bed and stared at the floor, covered by the beautifully woven rug. For a moment, she wanted to fling herself out of bed and set to work shifting all the furniture, but it was dark and cold and she was tired. *Tomorrow,* she told herself. She lay down and sang herself lullabies till she slept.

The next day, she jumped out of bed eagerly. The first thing she did was take down the portrait of the sorceress and turn it to face the wall. The sight of that perfect oval face unnerved her. Then she set to work moving the table and chairs and the bath. This took a while and a great deal of effort, for they were heavy and she was only twelve and all alone, but eventually all the furniture was shoved together on one side of the room. Margherita folded back the carpet and sat back on her heels.

A trapdoor was set in the flagstones.

It was made of stone and was as long as a pace on all four sides.

It had no handle.

It took Margherita eleven days to prise it open, with the help of the poker and the iron hooks.

At first, urgency drove her. Using the skillet as a hammer, pounding on the end of the poker, she chipped at the stone around the trapdoor. Her arms and shoulders ached, her back throbbed, but she kept pounding away as long as she could, only stopping to eat and drink and rest. The masses of her hair were a terrible encumbrance, constantly slipping undone from her snood and getting entangled.

It was such hard work, though, and all her efforts seemed to have so little result that gradually she grew discouraged. One day, she did not even get out of bed but lay still, staring at the flagstone, surrounded by its halo of chipped stone. The silence and her loneliness were impossible to bear. She curled in a ball, gazing at the crack of light revealed by the broken shutter, twisting a loose lock of hair about her finger, her thoughts slipping back to the past. She sang to herself in a monotone, *Oh, come, sleep from the little mountain. The wolf's devoured the little sheep, and oh, my child wants to sleep.* Tears began to seep from under her swollen eyelids again and she buried her head in her pillow, wishing with all her heart for someone to come and rescue her.

But nobody came.

That night, Margherita stood on the chair and stared out through the broken shutter, looking for the moon. *I'll be back when the moon is full once more,* the sorceress had said. It was now waning, dwindling away to a tiny sliver. Soon, it would begin to swell again.

Panic stole her breath. She half-fell from

the chair, knocking it over. She crawled to the trapdoor and took up her tools once more, chipping and chipping and chipping away at the stone, working more by touch than by sight, for her little room was filled with shadows. She only stopped when her arms screamed with pain and her hands bled.

In the morning, Margherita began her work once more. She found that, if she held the poker at a certain angle, she was able to knock away larger fragments of stone. She began to concentrate all her efforts just on one point. By evening time, she had gouged away enough stone to lever the trapdoor up just a few inches, but it was too heavy and crashed back down, almost crushing her hand. She levered it up again and wedged it open with the iron skillet.

A foetid smell rolled up into her face. She gagged and moved away, staring at the black slit in trepidation.

For a moment, her spirit quailed. She dared not try to lift it any higher. Old childhood stories of ghosts and goblins came into her mind; she thought of rats and spiders and snakes. It was growing dark. Margherita could not bear the thought of exploring the tower at night, even though it would surely be just as dark down there in daylight. But neither could she bear the thought of going to sleep with that black slit staring at her. After a while, she pulled the iron skillet away and let it slam shut again.

At first light, she was awake. She had not slept very much. All night, her brain had whirled with schemes and worries and fears. It would be best, Margherita thought, if she prepared herself as if expecting to find a way out. She was dressed in nothing but a soiled nightgown. Her feet were bare. She would need food and fire and other necessities if she was to survive out in the forest. So she made herself some breakfast, then emptied a sack and filled it with supplies. She took the eiderdown off the bed and wrapped it over her shoulders like a cape, then took up a candle in a holder with one shaking hand.

Then she levered up the heavy trapdoor again, opening it as wide as she could. A flight of steep steps spiralled down into darkness. Margherita wedged the trapdoor open with the iron spit, so it would not crash down and trap her below, then gathered up her courage and tiptoed down the steps. Her hair trailed behind her, dragging a clean path through the dust and cobwebs.

Margherita's candle flame trembled. The air was dank and heavy. She would have liked to clap her hand over her nose, but since her hands were full she could only breathe shallowly through her mouth. Here and there, the wall was pierced with arrow slits. She put her mouth to each of these and breathed in the fresh spring air, and then looked out. All she could see was sky.

Step by step by timid step, she went down, till the staircase opened out into the lowest floor — a dark echoing place with heavy beams on the ceiling and a base of hard-packed earth. It was so lightless down there, it could well have been midnight instead of noon.

Margherita lifted up her candle and then, with a jerk and a scream, dropped it. Darkness snuffed her. She fell to her knees, her hands covering her face. Her breath came in sharp uneven gasps.

The cellar was filled with skeletons.

WATCHING THE MOON

*The Rock of Manerba, Lake Garda, Italy —
April 1595*
Margherita crouched motionless, her heart
thundering, listening with all her might.

Silence.

After a long time, she fumbled for the
candle, fitted it back into its holder and then
felt through her sack for her tinderbox. She
tried to strike a spark, but her hands were
shaking too much. She remembered the
breathing exercises Elena had taught her, to
calm her nerves before singing with the *figlie
di coro.* After a few deep breaths, filling her
lungs from the bottom to the top, Margherita
felt calm enough to try once again to light
the candle.

By its wavering light, she saw eight skeletons
laid out on the floor. Heads to the wall, feet
facing each other, each laid out like radius
lines in a circle. Their bony arms were crossed
on the empty cage of their ribs, their leg
bones stretched out neatly. Beneath them lay

the rotting remains of fine velvets and brocades, much like the eiderdown Margherita
clutched about her shoulders. Their empty
eye sockets gazed serenely at the ceiling.

A heavy oaken door was on the far side of
the room, beyond the skeletons. Margherita
struggled to control her breath. She could
not bear the idea of walking across the room,
stepping over those bones. Yet it was the only
way out. Holding her breath, walking as
gingerly as if stepping over sleeping guards,
she tiptoed forward. Her eyes moved from
skeleton to skeleton. One was small, about
the same height as her. She had, weirdly, a
thick hank of filthy matted hair coiling in the
cavity below her ribs. The others were taller.
A few were heavily shrouded in cobwebs and
dust. The skeletons closest to her were only
lightly draped, as if they had been lying here
in this room for a lot less time than those
against the far wall.

Margherita gathered up her long plait of
hair, which dragged along behind her like a
fine lady's train, sick with trepidation at the
idea of it disturbing the bones. It was hard to
carry her sack, and her candle, and thirty
yards of hair, but by moving slowly and carefully she was able to manage it. It was a relief
to reach the other side and be able to drop
her plait once more.

The door was ancient, made of thick dark
wood, and banded and studded with iron.

Margherita tried the handle but it would not open. She bent and peered through the keyhole but could see nothing but blackness. She groped in her bag and pulled out her spoon, inserting the handle into the hole. Her heart sank when the spoon hit something hard just on the other side of the door. She poked again and heard iron ring on stone.

Rocks had been piled against the door. Even if Margherita found some way to break down the door, she would not be able to get out.

She slid down and sat on the filthy floor, her head bowed to rest on her knees. It had all been no use. She could not get out.

It was hard to tiptoe past the skeletons once more, but Margherita had no real choice. As she carried her burden of hair over the bones, she wondered who they were. Other girls locked away by the witch? Had they lived in the tower long? Had she cut their wrists with rose thorns and bathed in their blood? How had they died? Had they died by accident or old age or sickness? Had they killed themselves, throwing themselves from the tower height? Had they starved slowly to death? Or had the witch murdered them?

There was no answer to such questions.

When she was finally safe in her tower room once more, Margherita stood in the window frame, looking out. It was late afternoon. The lake shone like burnished gold, and the mountains floated in a violet mist, looking as if they stretched away forever. Cypress trees marked the edge of the lake like a dark knotted fringe, casting long shadows across the water. Margherita took her plait in her hand and wrapped it around the hook three times, and then she climbed up onto the window ledge. She leant out into the wind, till the plait was stretched taut and she was tilted out over the abyss, like a flying figurehead. She looked down.

At the base of the tower was an immense pile of rocks, some of the boulders larger than she was. Margherita heaved a sigh and pulled herself back up with her plait. Her arms shook with the strain, her legs trembled. She sat on the floor, the plait still wrapped about her wrist, and rested her forehead on her knees.

There was no hope. She was trapped in this tower forever.

I must be strong, she told herself. *I must not let myself go mad. Don't think about the skeletons. Don't think about falling.*

She watched the moon rise, wafer-thin, then crept into her bed and pulled the coverlet over her head. She felt as if she wanted to stay in that dark cave forever.

Yet morning came, and with it hunger. Margherita ate, and then slowly set about trying to hide the evidence of her attempts to escape. First, she filled in the gouges around the trapdoor with the rubble she had dug out. Yet she could feel the unevenness beneath her feet as she walked across the carpet. So she mixed flour and water together to make a paste, which held all the rubble in place and smoothed the edges of the trapdoor again. It set hard, like cement, but Margherita knew she could soon hack through it again if she needed to.

Making the flour paste gave her a sweet kind of pain. Margherita had often helped her father prepare papier mâché this way in his mask-making studio. She wondered where her parents were, and if they missed her, and if they had ever looked for her. She did not have much memory of the night she had been snatched. Only the mist, and her mother's white face, and being carried through a labyrinth of dark alleys. It could have been a dream. Only the constant repetition of her three truths helped her believe it had been real. She ran the words through her mind as she worked, taking comfort from them:

My name is Margherita.
My parents loved me.
One day, I will escape.

Margherita let herself drift away on her favourite daydream. She imagined her mother frantically knocking on doors, saying, 'Have you seen a red-haired girl? With eyes as blue as the rapunzel flower?' She imagined her father asking at every wharf and jetty, 'Have you seen my little girl? She'd be twelve now.' And one day, perhaps, they'd hear the *figlie di coro* at the Pietà and say to each other, 'Our little girl used to sing like that.' And perhaps their longing to hear little girls singing would take them up to the grille, and they'd ask, in trembling voices, 'Have you seen a girl with hair as red as fire and eyes like the twilight sky who can sing sweet as any angel?' and Elena would say, 'Why, yes. I have.' And so her parents would track her down, and come to the tower with the tallest ladders in the world, and free her.

By the time she had laid the carpet down again, her hair was filthy and knotted. Drearily, she set to work filling up the bath and washing away the dust and cobwebs she had collected on her trip down the stairs. She began at the bottom and washed it in lengths, having to empty the bath and refill it over and over again. Her arms and back ached, and soon the carpet was wet through. But she persevered, dreading the thought of the sorceress coming and finding her hair in such a mess.

As she washed and combed and twisted the hair dry, Margherita realised there were eight different colours and textures, all somehow sewn into one extraordinary mane of hair.

Eight tresses of hair.

Eight skeletons.

Her hair had come from those dead bodies laid out in the room below her.

Margherita crouched very still, leaning over the bath, her wet purloined hair flowing around her. She met her own reflection in the water. Her eyes were dark and hollow, her skin very pale, her face thin and angular. She looked different. Older. Margherita slowly stretched out one finger. The girl in the water reached out hers in response. Their fingers touched and dissolved into each other.

One day, I'll not be a little girl any more, she thought. *One day, I'll find the way to get away from here. All I need to do until then is survive.*

Day by day, the supplies on the shelves dwindled. The bowl of dried fruit and nuts was empty, the ham bone had been boiled to make soup, the flour sack had been shaken till not a speck of dust remained. Hunger became a hot presence in the room, a companion that never let her be.

Every evening, Margherita sat on the windowsill, watching the moon rise. It grew fatter and redder as the month slipped past. Sometimes, it filled her with dread. At least, while she was alone, she could sing to herself and spend the hours daydreaming of the things she would do once she was free. She could believe her parents really had loved her and that they were searching for her every day. She could hope that they would find her soon.

The coming of the sorceress would shake all the precarious peace she had found, turn it all inside out and upside down. It would reawaken the terror that she had steadfastly buried under the trapdoor. Margherita was afraid the sorceress meant to murder her, leaving her bones to be shrouded with cobwebs along with the other eight dead girls, her hair to be plaited into a rope and sewn onto some other girl's head.

Yet Margherita was hungry and lonely. The sorceress would bring food. She would be company of sorts. And perhaps, if Margherita was very good, she would bring her something to play with. Margherita daydreamt a lot about what she would ask for.

The day came when the moon rose at the same moment that the sun set. It was huge, as big as Margherita's fist, and the same colour as her hair. Margherita picked up the painting of the woman looking into a mirror and hung it on the wall again.

'Petrosinella, let down your hair so I may climb the golden stair.'

At the distant call of the sorceress's voice, Margherita stood and began to unwind her plait from the snood. She wrapped it about the hook three times then let the hair ladder tumble down to the ground. She felt the yank as La Strega took hold of it, the heavy drag as she began to climb. Margherita imagined her grasping the knots of silver ribbon to stop her hands from slipping, imagined her walking up the side of the tower. She must be strong and fearless. If Margherita wanted to escape her, she would have to be strong and fearless too.

At long last, the sorceress stood framed in the window. She looked at the shutters, wrenched off their hinges and pushed to one side, then looked at Margherita. 'Well, you have been a naughty girl while I've been away,' she said in a voice of mock-scolding. 'No comfits for you.'

'I'm sorry,' Margherita said meekly. 'I wanted to see the sun and the sky. I couldn't breathe with it all shut up.'

'You'll be sorry when winter comes,' La Strega answered. 'Or a big rainstorm.'

'If you'll bring me some tools, I'll do my best to fix it,' Margherita replied.

La Strega pressed her lips together, regarding her steadily. 'So, what else have you been doing, apart from wrecking the shutters?'

'There is not much to do,' Margherita said. 'I cooked and cleaned and tried to keep my hair tidy. I almost went mad with boredom, though.' She took a deep breath. 'You said you'd bring me a gift if I was a good girl. Well, I've been good. Look how neat my room is. Look how well I've combed my hair. Will you not bring me something to play with?'

La Strega's tawny eyes lit with amusement.

'What would you like?'

'A lute,' Margherita said at once. 'Some music. An orange. Some books to read. Something else to wear. I'm not a baby to spend all day in my nightgown.'

La Strega laughed. 'You'll have to be very good for all that.'

'I will, I promise,' Margherita said.

TALLY MARKS

*The Rock of Manerba, Lake Garda, Italy —
March to April 1596*

Margherita often dreamt of the eight dead girls.

She knew their hair intimately, and imagined faces and personalities to match. The girl with the fiery-red ringlets would be hot-tempered and wild. The girl with the wheaten sheaves would be a comely country girl, smiling and peaceful. The one with the soft strawberry-blonde hair was a shy little girl. She was the one who had found it hardest being locked up in this one small room. Hers was the littlest skeleton in the cellar.

One girl at least had leapt to her death — Margherita was sure of it. She too had felt the allure of the drop. Probably the fiery redhead. Another girl had had waves of bright bronze hair, just like Margherita's own. Margherita called her Rosa — a name she had always liked — and the little strawberry-blonde girl was named Peony. She named the other girls Celandine, Alyssum, Hyacintha, Magnolia, Jasmine and Viola. It seemed fitting that they all had flower names, like Margherita herself.

'Tell me your stories,' she would whisper sometimes, late at night. 'Were you stolen too? How old were you when you died?'

Margherita imagined at least one of them living on for years. She had found marks on the wall behind her bed one day, hundreds and hundreds of tiny regular scratches, marking away days and weeks and months and years. Decades, even. She could not tell if it was just one other girl who had made the marks or a few of them. Some scores were small and neat, others straggly and wild, some deep and measured, others just a faint scratch. Did the girl or girls making those cuts in the stone mark off each day, or only the coming of the full moon, and, with it, the call of the sorceress: 'Let down your hair so I might climb the golden stair.'

The scratches fascinated her. She often rubbed them with her finger, thinking about the girls who had made them. She decided to make her own scratches. Yet, when she crouched before the wall, the iron spit in one hand and the griddle as a hammer in the other, she was frozen with sudden panic. How many days had she been here? How many months? She counted up the presents that the witch had brought her on each of her visits.

A muslin bag of comfits, which she had not been allowed to eat, as punishment for breaking the shutters.

Some screws, to fix the shutter, along with a screwdriver, which the sorceress had taken away as soon as the job was done. At least La Strega did not make Margherita screw the shutters shut. She was to be allowed to keep them open, to let some air into the stuffy little tower room. 'Even if you did try to signal, no one would see you,' the sorceress said. 'There is no one for miles.'

A dress of turquoise green and silver brocade, and two clean chemises.

No present the next month, for tearing up her new chemises and tying the rags together to make a rope. No ham either.

A lute and some songbooks. How delighted she had been at those. Margherita loved to sing so much, but the tunes had begun to evade her. Now, she was able to spend much of her day playing her lute and learning new songs. It made the long days seem much less empty.

An illustrated atlas, with maps stretching from the Land of Silk to the Great Gulf, and the fables of Aesop, illustrated with beautiful woodcuts.

A fur blanket, some fur-lined boots and a thick shawl. It was cold in the tower.

A basket full of delicacies to celebrate

Christmas, a chess set and a book called *Repetition of Love and the Art of Playing Chess.* La Strega loved this exotic new game, with its queen that could rampage all over the board while the king cowered in his corner. She taught Margherita to play as best she could.

No present the next month, to punish Margherita for having a temper tantrum and knocking over the board. No apples, honey or dried fruit either.

An illustrated volume of poetry by Ovid, filled with stories of gods and magic and disguises. Margherita was fascinated by Minerva, the Roman goddess of wisdom, for the tower had been built on a shrine to her. Margherita read the pages where she appeared over and over again.

No present the next month, to punish Margherita for quoting Ovid's Minerva: 'Not everything of old age should be shunned: wisdom comes with the years.' Very little food either.

Eleven months had passed. Margherita stared at the little marks she had just made on the wall in horror. Almost a whole year. She would be thirteen in a month. She lay for the rest of the day on her bed, watching the sun creeping across the rug, her pulse fluttering with panic.

Eleven months of filling the dreary hours as best she could.

Eleven months of watching every mouthful she ate, in case her food ran out.

Eleven months of watching for the moon, half dreading its fullness, half longing for it.

Eleven months of submitting to the sorceress.

Eleven months of offering her wrist to be slashed with rose thorns.

Margherita glanced down at her wrists and realised she had her own tally marks engraved upon her skin. Eleven thin scars, crossing and criss-crossing.

She sighed heavily and looked back at the wall. Her eleven marks looked no different from the thousands crowding above them. She got up, her long braid dragging at her scalp, and chipped a scraggly 'M' above her scratches. *M for Margherita.*

That night, she lay in her bed and looked out at one faint star glimmering in the arch of the window. *Help me,* Margherita whispered, thinking of the ancient goddess of wisdom, with her owl and her distaff, who had once been worshipped at this rock. *If any power remains to you, help me.*

Far away, she heard the hoot of an owl, as she often did at night. It seemed like an answer, though, and so, comforted, Margherita turned her cheek into her pillow and slept.

The days passed in their usual way. Margherita combed and plaited her hair, cooked and ate breakfast, made her room tidy, walked swiftly around it three hundred times, played her lute and sang, played chess against herself, read Ovid aloud for the pleasure of hearing her own voice, lifted sacks of onions and potatoes to make her arms strong, cooked and ate dinner, and then sat watching the sun set over the lake, singing to herself. Every day, the view was different: sometimes, the lake was placid and blue; sometimes, it lay concealed under mist; sometimes, it was tossed in a tempest; sometimes, it was smeared with flame and gold as if God himself had drawn his fingers across the sky.

During the early winter, the mountains were grey and the lake like a pewter mirror. Then the snow would come, swirling around the tower, hiding everything. With the snow came the beast-wind, howling from the north, tearing at the tower with claws and fangs, finding every crack and hole to hiss and spit through. All Margherita could do then was huddle under her eiderdown, her face hidden in her hands, hoping the beast would not tear the tower apart.

Despite the cold and the darkness, she had to be careful with her candles and her kindling. She was terrified of running out and having no fire or light at all. So she lay in her bed, as snug as she could make herself, and imagined herself out in the world, having all kinds of grand adventures: fighting giants;

defeating witches; finding treasure; sailing the seven seas; singing at the courts of kings. Soon, Margherita had spun herself a tale almost as epic in scale as Ovid's.

As spring came, Margherita began to scatter crumbs on her windowsill in the hope that birds would fly down and befriend her. She was delighted when a little brown bird came fluttering down to her sill to feast and later brought its mate. Margherita saved some of her own bread for them, though she had little to spare, and soon the birds came every day, growing tame enough to land on the sill even when she was standing there. Margherita watched, entranced, as they built a nest of mud under the arch, lining it with grass and soft ash-brown feathers. Soon, three small eggs were laid inside, white with brown blotches. It gave Margherita great delight to watch the mother sit in the nest, guarding her eggs, while the father brought her insects to eat. Once the eggs had hatched, three hungry beaks screeched all day, demanding food, which the two parent birds did their best to supply.

The moon fattened every day. When it was almost full, Margherita, as always, began to clean more frenetically, comb and braid her hair more carefully, and make sure her room was tidy, the bed back in its place, the portrait hanging on the wall. She was terrified that the sorceress would come early one month and discover the tower room out of order.

The day came when the moon was round and as golden as a sequin, sewn to the silk of the sky, and the sorceress's voice called from the base of the tower. Margherita let down her hair and braced herself as the sorceress clambered up the immense height. Her approach agitated the little birds, and they swooped about her head, shrieking. La Strega ducked her head, then, as she pulled herself up onto the windowsill, reached up and knocked the nest away. It tumbled down, spilling the baby birds. Although they flapped their tiny wings, squawking in terror, the baby birds could not fly, and they plummeted down into the blue abyss. The parent birds darted after them, their distraught cries filling the air.

'No!' Margherita cried, both hands flung up as if hoping to catch the falling birds. Her impetuous forward motion was halted by the cruel wrench of her hair, looped three times around the hook. She watched the nest and its precious cargo disappear, tears flooding her eyes.

'What on earth is the matter?' La Strega was genuinely puzzled.

'The nest . . . the baby birds . . .'

'It was in my way,' she said, stepping down into the tower room. 'Come now, don't cry over a silly nest. The birds will build another one.'

'It wasn't a silly nest. It was their home. You shouldn't have knocked it down.'

'You shouldn't be so rude. You don't wish me to cut your rations again, do you?'

'No!' Margherita cried. 'I'm sorry. I don't mean to be rude. I was just sad about the baby birds.'

'You must learn not to be so tender-hearted,' La Strega said. She took the heavy coil of rope she had carried over her shoulder, tying one end to the hook and tossing the other down so her servant Magli could tie the first of many sacks to it. 'The world is a cruel place, Petrosinella, and it wounds the weak.'

'Yes, I know. I'm sorry.'

'Wait till you see what I've brought you,' she said, helping Margherita pull up the heavily weighted rope. 'You'll be so surprised.'

Let it be a puppy, Margherita wished, crossing the fingers on both hands. *Please, let it be a puppy.*

But the sorceress's birthday present for Margherita was nine small terracotta pots, a sack of soil and some small calico sacks of seeds: parsley, basil, oregano, rosemary, thyme, chives, sage, wintercress and the little rampion bellflower that Margherita's mother had always called rapunzel.

A harvest of bitter greens for Margherita's thirteenth birthday.

■ ■ ■ ■

The Abbey of Gercy-en-Brie, France — April 1697

The bell rang, signalling the beginning of sext.

I looked towards the convent irritably, not wanting to return to the vast gloomy church for yet another hour on my aching knees. But Sœur Seraphina was brushing the earth off her tools and laying them in her basket, drawing off her gloves, rising to her feet. 'I'll have to finish my story tomorrow. Hasn't the morning flown? We've almost finished planting out the whole bed.'

'Why? Why lock a little girl away like that? It seems . . . it seems so cruel,' I burst out.

I was remembering the times that my guardian, the Marquis de Maulévrier, had locked me in the hermit's cave at the Château de Cazeneuve. I'd crouch in the bitter-cold darkness, my body bruised and aching from his birch rod, hating him with all my might. 'I hope you're smitten with boils all over,' I'd rave. 'I hope you'll be plagued with gnats, and flies, and locusts, and cockroaches. I hope you'll be trampled by a herd of stampeding pigs, and kicked by an incontinent camel. I . . . I'll make you sorry. I'll put scorpions in your bed. I'll spit in your soup.'

Eventually, I would run out of curses and

threats, and sit rocking in the darkness, furious with my mother for allowing herself to be taken away, furious with myself for caring so much. Then the tears would come, a gale of sorrows. I'd still be crying when Nanette would unlock the door and creep in, bringing me a handkerchief — I had always lost my own — and a warm shawl, and some wild-boar *saucisson*. 'Don't cry, Bon-bon, it's all right. The Marquis is praying. He'll be on his knees for hours. You run through the secret passage and play in the caves, but listen out for the bell. M'sieur Alain will ring it when the Marquis comes down. I'll make sure you're locked up tight when the bastard comes looking for you.'

'Thank you,' I'd sniffle and wind my arms about Nanette's neck to kiss her cheek, and then I'd be off, running wild in the caves and the forest.

What must it have been like to have been locked in one small room for years and years? What must it have been like to find the skeletons of other girls in the tower's cellar and to know that their hair was bound to yours? The very thought made me feel queasy.

I had never forgiven the Marquis de Maulévrier for his cruelty, nor had I ever understood what demons drove him to treat my sister and me so. How much more mysterious were the motives of that long-ago sorceress.

'Why would she do such a thing?' I said more softly.

A troubled expression crossed Sœur Seraphina's face. 'I think . . . I think she was afraid.'

'Afraid? Afraid of what?'

'Afraid of time,' Sœur Seraphina answered quietly.

LAMENT

. . . so hold me,
my young dear, hold me.
Put your pale arms around my neck.
Let me hold your heart like a flower
lest it bloom and collapse.
Give me your skin
as sheer as a cobweb,
let me open it up
and listen in and scoop out the dark.
Give me your nether lips
all puffy with their art
and I will give you angel fire in return.

'Rapunzel'
Anne Sexton

THE WHORE'S BRAT

Venice, Italy — August 1504

My true name is not, of course, Selena Leonelli. Nor is it La Strega Bella, though it pleases me to be called that.

I was baptised Maria, like most little girls born in Venice in the year 1496. I had no last name, unless it was Maria the Whore's Brat, Maria the Little Bastard.

It is true that my mother was a whore. Not one of those poxy streetwalkers that plied their trade around the Bridge of Tits. She was a *cortigiana onesta,* a courtesan as much sought after for her wit and charm and cleverness as for her sexual allure. She was paid to sing and play music, to compose poetry, to dance, and to delight with her conversation. And for sex, of course.

Sex paid for our palazzo on the Grand Canal. Sex paid for the cook and the footmen and the gondolier, who piloted my mother to parties in our own glossy black gondola. Sex paid for the maids, who silently picked up my mother's fallen silk stockings and who changed the stained sheets every day.

I was dressed like a little princess, in white satin sewn with pearls. I had a chest full of nothing but shoes. Red velvet mules. Boots of purple silk embroidered with flowers. Slippers sewn all over with silver sequins so my feet sparkled as I danced.

When men came to visit my mother, I was always taken to my own rooms by my nursemaid. This made me angry. I'd scream and throw things at my nursemaid till my mother rustled in to console me. 'You must not be angry,' she'd say, smoothing back my golden-red hair gently. 'They're nothing to me. You're the one that I love. No man will ever be able to come between us.'

The man who came most often was tall and lean with a pointed beard, a thin flourishing moustache and curly hair perfumed with precious oils. His name was Zusto da Grittoni. I hated him. As soon as his gondola drew up at our water-gates, a servant would come running to hustle me away. I was always glad to go. I did not like the way he looked at me. His eyes reminded me of a cobra I had once seen swaying to the tune of a snake charmer at the Piazza San Marco.

My mother was always restless and uneasy when he was there. I would hear her shrill laugh and the clunking of her *chopines* on the marble as she hurried back and forth, offering him food, pouring him wine, strumming her lute and launching into song. 'Enough,' he would snap. 'I don't come here for your voice. Come to bed.'

Her steps would slow as they climbed the stairs to her bedroom. Slower and slower she would climb, and he would tell her to hurry up. Then I would hear her door open and shut. At that point, my nursemaid would put her fingers in her ears, but I would always listen. Deep guttural grunts from him. The occasional sharp cry from her. Afterwards, my mother would stay in bed for hours. I would crawl in beside her and we'd lie in silence, my mother trying not to let me see her wiping away tears with the corner of her silken sheet.

My mother was very beautiful. Her name was Bianca. It suited her well for her hair was silver-gilt, that rare colour so prized by the Venetians. Most of each day was spent maintaining her beauty. Bianca washed herself in white wine in which snakeskins had been boiled, rubbed crushed lily bulbs on her face to make her skin paler and burnt away her hairline with caustic lime, to make her forehead look higher.

Most sunny afternoons, she and I would sit on the roof terrace of our palazzo, wearing broad-brimmed straw hats woven without a crown, so we could pull our hair through the hole and spread it out across the straw brim, hanging down the backs of our chairs. My mother would anoint her hair with a paste made from lemon juice, urine and sulphur; it made her hair shine like the palest of golden silks.

It made my hair frizzy and brassy. So my mother made up a mixture of carrot and mangelwurzel juice and soaked my hair in that, coaxing me out of my fit of temper by promising it would make my hair shine like new copper. It did.

My mother knew all sorts of strange things like that. She had grown up in the country with her grandfather, in a garden filled with fruit trees, vegetables and herbs. Chickens scratched in the straw, there was a dovecote filled with plump birds, and a goat that kept the turf in the orchard smooth, so fallen quinces were easy to find. Six beehives sat on trestles under a pomegranate tree, and her grandfather would bid them good morning each day on his way to collect the eggs.

'Oh, I miss my *nonno*'s garden,' Bianca told me. 'From dawn to dusk, we were out working in the fresh air. He always said that is why my hair was so fair, because of the sunshine I soaked up as a child. He knew everything there was to know about the earth and the seasons and animals and plants.'

'I wish we could go there.' I was allowed outside so rarely, and I always had to keep

291

close to my mother, holding her hand so I wouldn't get lost in the crowds. I had never seen a tree, or a lawn of soft velvety grass, or a bank of sweet-smelling flowers. Venice was a city of stone and water, the only green the slime that grew where one sank into the other.

'So do I.' She gazed over the jumble of red roofs and pale domes and towers.

'Why can't we go?'

'My *nonno* is dead. He died before you were born.' Bianca got to her feet as she spoke, holding out her hand to me. 'Come on, it's time to go in, Maria.'

'But it's still sunny.'

'I am attending a party at the Doge's tonight. I must get ready.'

The maids poured hot scented water into my mother's hipbath, and we sat in it together, naked, washing the paste out of each other's hair. 'Your hair is so beautiful,' she said. 'Like cloth of gold. If only we could weave it, we'd make a fortune.'

'I wish I had fair hair like yours.'

'Everyone in Venice has blonde hair,' she replied with a laugh, 'even if they weren't born with it. Yours is as rare and precious as amber.'

She rose, cascading water over me, and the maids dried her and dressed her and anointed her with perfume. I sat forgotten in the cooling water as they braided her hair with pearls and silver ribbons.

I asked her again about my grandfather the next day, as we lay in her bed together. To my surprise, my mother answered me.

'Nonno was a *benandante*.' Her voice was full of pain.

'But what does that mean? A good walker? Do you mean . . . a gypsy? A vagabond?'

'No, no. It means . . . someone who travelled away in their dreams. It's hard to explain. You see, Nonno was born with a caul over his face. It's a thin veil of skin that the midwife must cut away carefully if the baby is to live. He had a scar on his face from where she tore it away. He used to carry his caul in a little bag about his neck. Sometimes, he showed it to me. It was like a crumpled piece of translucent silk, like a partlet.' She had turned to face me, her face a pale oval in the dimness. Her fair hair was strewn all over the pillow. I nestled my own face closer to my mother's, the copper strands of my hair mingling with hers.

'It was considered a great blessing to be born with a caul,' my mother said. 'It was said that caul-bearers would never drown and had a special affinity with water. Caul-bearers could travel away from their bodies at night, while they were sleeping, and so they could battle the forces of evil in the world and keep the rest of the village safe from harm. That is why they were called the good walkers, because four times a year, on the Ember

Nights, they would leave their bodies behind and go to fight the *malandanti,* the evil walkers.'

'What does that mean, the Ember Nights?'

She hesitated, her breath warm on my cheek. 'They were the days when saints and martyrs used to fast and do penance, and the *benandanti* would fast too, and eat nothing but bitter herbs and drink nothing but pure water. Four times a year, at the changing of the seasons. Autumn into winter was called Shadowfest, and was the night to predict the future and communicate with the dead. Winter into spring was called the Feast of the Wolf, and was a time to celebrate and make love. Spring into summer was called Lady's Day, and was a time to be handfasted and to dance about the maypole. Summer into autumn was called Cornucopia, when we celebrated the harvest and enjoyed the fruits of the earth. They were days when the powers of magic, both good and evil, would be at their peak. My grandfather would fast and pray and then sleep, and his soul would leave his body and go forth in the shape of a wolf to do battle with the forces of darkness.'

I stared at my mother, eyes wide, and repeated the words in my head. *Ember Nights. Shadowfest. The Feast of the Wolf. Lady's Day. Cornucopia. The shape of a wolf. Battle with the forces of darkness.* Every phrase was a charm filled with magic and danger.

'Who did your *nonno* fight with?'

'Strega e stregone.'

Witches and warlocks. I shivered at the thought, half thrilled, half terrified.

'If the *benandanti* won, the harvest would be safe, and we would all eat well and be prosperous for the year. If the *malandanti* won, there would be famine and plague. My parents and my grandmother died one year when the good walkers lost. I don't think my grandfather ever forgave himself.'

There was a long silence. I was seething with questions, but my mother was quietly weeping and I did not know what to do. I would have liked to have comforted her, but I was afraid that she would turn away from me and I'd have lost my chance to know more. After a long while, I said, 'So what happened?'

'That same year, the Pope . . . the Pope passed a law. He set the Inquisition to hunt down witches.' My mother's voice failed, and she took a deep breath. 'I suppose many people were angry that the plague had come again. Fingers were pointed, wild accusations made. My *nonno* . . . oh, Maria, he was the world's gentlest man. If you could only have seen him delivering a kid or binding up a bird's broken wing.'

'They arrested him?'

She nodded. 'I was wild with fear and grief.

I went to everyone I knew, begging for help. The problem was . . . he did not know any of his other *benandanti* . . . he only ever met them in the spirit. He said their leader was a red-haired man who ran in the shape of a lion . . . so I went searching for any red-haired man I could find . . . that was how I met your father.'

'My father?' I sat up, staring at her. My mother had never once mentioned my father before. It was as if I had been an immaculate conception. Any time I had dared ask her, she would only droop and shake her head and tell me that he was long gone, and it was no use breaking my heart over him, as she had done.

My mother sighed. 'Yes. He promised to help me but it was too late. They had tortured my poor *nonno*. Despite all they did to him, he refused to admit that he had any pact with the devil, or ever stole a child and ate it, or any of the other terrible things they accused him of. He was a good walker, he told them, working for the powers of light. They let him go in the end, so at least he did not burn at the stake, but his health was broken. He died a few weeks later.'

'What did you do to the men who tortured him?'

My mother looked at me in surprise. 'Why, nothing. What could I do?'

'I would have cursed them,' I said. 'Or

changed shape into a wolf, like my grandfather did, and hunted them down.'

'I cannot change shape,' she said. 'Only those born with a caul can do that. And it was a power to be used for good, not for hunting down men who work in the service of the Pope.'

'But they killed your *nonno.*'

'I know. But what could I do? I was only sixteen, and although I didn't know it yet, I was growing you inside my belly. Oh, I was sick. And so sad. And I didn't have a home any more. After my grandfather was accused, the local lord confiscated our house. I was driven from the door.'

'But what about my father? Couldn't he help you?'

'He had gone to sail the seven seas,' she told me. 'It was not safe for men like him to stay when the Inquisition was in town.'

'My father . . . he was a *benandante* too?'

She gave a derisive snort. 'So he said. I do not believe it though. No, the spell he laid on me did nothing but harm. If he was a walker of the night, he was a *malandante,* that I assure you.'

THE ROYAL THIRTY-NINE

Venice, Italy — May 1508

The sun sparkled on the lagoon, and waves rippled under our gondola. Laughter and music filled the air. I leant forward from under the *felze,* taking a deep breath of the briny air. Everywhere I looked were boats hung with brightly coloured flags — *batellas* and *caorlinas* and, ahead, the Doge's massive *bucentaur,* with its purple velvet canopy to shield Doge Barbarigo's head from the sun. I could just see his thick white beard, and the red hat he wore with its peak shaped like a horn, and his heavy golden mantle.

'We have a good position,' my mother said. 'It was lucky we came early. I think all of Venice is out on the lagoon today.'

In honour of Serenissima's Marriage of the Sea, Bianca wore a gown of turquoise-green velvet, with long hanging sleeves lined with white satin and trimmed with jewels. I too was dressed in sea-colours, with my long hair caught back in a snood of pearls.

298

'It's such a lovely day,' I said. 'It was raining last year and you wouldn't take me out.'

'Well, who wants to sit in a gondola in the rain?'

Our gondolier manoeuvred our craft closer so that we could see the Doge toss a golden ring into the choppy waters. We were not close enough to hear him, but we all knew what he said: 'We wed thee, sea, in the sign of the true and everlasting Lord.'

'Only in Venice,' my mother said.

Our gondolier then turned our boat around and rowed us slowly back towards the Piazza San Marco. I saw Zusto da Grittoni in his own boat, sitting beside a fat woman with the biggest bosom I had ever seen. It was like she had stuffed a bolster under her purple brocade. Beside them sat a row of shiny-faced children, stepping down in size from a scowling boy with his first soft dark down on his upper lip to a little girl the size of a doll, dressed in a froth of frills and bows. They all looked stiff and unhappy.

Both my mother and I shrank back under the *felze* at the sight of him. If Zusto da Grittoni saw us, he made no sign or gesture.

Our gondolier drew up at the piazza and helped my mother and me to alight. The Fair of the Sensa was in full swing in the piazza, with small wooden stalls selling anything you wanted from anywhere in the world. Jugglers in motley tossed painted balls high in the air, and two men fought each other while balancing on long stilts. We made our way through the stalls, my mother tottering on her cork-heeled *chopines,* I darting from side to side, yanking against her hand, wanting to see everything.

'Bianca, is it you?' a man's voice said.

My mother looked around, then gave a little gasp, her hand to her mouth. A man was standing before us, wearing a rich brown velvet doublet with pale pink billowing sleeves over a tight pair of hose. His face was clean-shaven, but his hair, which hung loosely past his shoulders, was like a cloth-of-gold banner.

'Egidio!' my mother cried. She put out one hand and gripped my shoulder, as if suddenly dizzy.

'It is you. Look at you.' The man she had called Egidio looked her over with a laughing face. 'Don't you look fine?'

Then his eyes fell on me, and his face suddenly sobered. 'What's this? A little girl?'

'I'm not a little girl,' I said at once. 'I'm soon to be twelve.'

'Twelve, eh?' He shot my mother a quick glance. 'And look at you, pretty as a picture.' He reached out and picked up a tendril of my hair, exactly the same colour as his.

'Egidio, what . . . what are you doing here?' My mother's voice was faint.

'Our ship has come in. Oh, Bianca, the

adventures I've had. You'd never believe them. We've seen the edge of the world, and grappled with pirates, and heard the singing of sirens. I've made my fortune and am ready to retire now, to a nice little farm in the country somewhere. I think I'll grow cabbages.'

'You've been away so long.'

'Oh, well, things got rather hot for me in Malegno, you know that. Those damn Inquisitors. Sniffing about and sticking their long noses where they weren't wanted. I wasn't going to risk being burnt at the stake, you know.'

'My grandfather died and his farm was confiscated.' My mother sounded weary, rather than angry or sad.

'No! They didn't burn your *nonno*?' Egidio sounded genuinely shocked.

'They tortured him to death.'

'Bianca, I'm so sorry.' He put one arm around my mother and she leant her face into his shoulder. 'He was the most gentle soul alive. I never thought they'd harm him.'

'You should've been here. You said you'd help me, you promised me.'

'I'm sorry. I heard the Inquisition was coming for me, so I got out as fast as I could. I never thought . . .' He looked back at me, frowning, biting his lip. I stared back at him, wondering, *Is this my father? The man who can change shape into a lion?*

'Is she mine?' he asked in a low voice.

'Can't you tell? She has your hair and your eyes, and, God forgive me, your boldness.'

'This changes everything.'

'Not for me.' Bianca drew herself away from him, looking about her in sudden anxiety.

'I suppose you are happily married now.'

'No, Egidio. I'm not married. I'm a whore.'

He stepped back, his face changing.

'What else was I meant to do? I was alone, destitute, pregnant.' She spoke the last word as if it tasted nasty in her mouth, then at once reached a hand to me and drew me close to her side.

'I didn't know. I'm sorry, Bianca. Surely it's not too late? Let me make amends.' He seized her hand.

'I need to go.' Bianca withdrew her hand and turned and hurried away. For once, I needed to scramble to keep up with her. I turned my head and looked back at my father, feeling such a strange mixture of emotions: curiosity, resentment, fear. He stared after us, his golden-red hair shining in the sun.

My mother was restless and unsettled that night. She paced the floor, pressing her hands together, biting her lip. Zusto da Grittoni's gondola pulled up at the door; she sent a footman to say she was not well. A moment later, she made a quick motion, as if to call the footman back, then she sank into her

302

chair, twisting her handkerchief, her face so white and anxious I wanted to comfort her somehow. I crept over and sat on the footstool at her knee, and reached out to stroke her hair.

She laid her head against the arm of her chair. Encouraged, I gently pulled the pins from her hair, unravelling the complex arrangements of braids and ribbons and jewels. Her hair cascaded down, warm and silky and scented with ambergris. I kept on stroking. Her face was hidden, her breath coming and going unsteadily. I could not tell if she was weeping.

We stayed there by the embers of the fire for a long time, our shoes kicked off. I heard the church bells ring out for compline. I was hungry but did not want to break the spell of tenderness between us. Then a footman came quietly in. 'There is a visitor for you, *signorina*. I told him you were indisposed but he insists on seeing you.'

My mother looked up. 'His name?'

'Egidio, from Malegno, he says.'

A blaze of joy lit up my mother's face. 'He has come!' She rose and ran for the door, heedless of her bare feet and tumbled golden hair. Normally, when my mother had a male visitor, she would put belladonna drops in her eyes to dilate her pupils, chew a clove to make her breath fresh and anoint herself with ambergris so she smelt sweet, but this time she did not even glance at herself in the mirror above the mantelpiece.

I crept towards the half-open door, listening and watching. I heard him cry, 'Bianca!' She leapt into his arms, like an arrow into the gold. They kissed all the way up the stairs and into her bedroom, the door closing behind them with a definite bang.

I ran silently up the stairs to my own room and pressed my ear to the connecting door. I could hear sighs and moans and whispered endearments. Something twisted deep in my stomach. Very slowly, I eased the door open. The room was lit only by the warm glow of the fire. It shone on my father's bare muscled back and on the shining glory of my mother's hair, rippling down her back like a snowmelt in full spate.

I eased the door shut again and went to my own bed. The sheets were cold. I curled my legs to my chest, burying my head in my pillow so I could hear no more.

My mother woke me later. The room was dark. She sat on my bed. 'Maria, wake up.' I sat up, yawning and rubbing my eyes. '*Mia cara*, we're going to go away. Your father wants us to go and live with him.'

'Where?' I asked stupidly.

'Somewhere in the country. Come, sit up. Let me dress you in something comfortable. We won't need any silks or satins there.'

She brought a blue woollen dress from the closet, and my fur-trimmed cloak, and my sturdiest boots. I held up my arms and put forth my feet as commanded, and was soon dressed. She filled a small bag with a few necessities — a clean chemise, a comb, some hair ribbons — and emptied my jewellery box. I caught up my favourite doll, dressed in lavender silk, and clutched her close to my chest. I was conscious of the sharp rapping of my heart against my ribs. *Going away, to live with my father? I thought no man could ever come between us?* The words were rattling against my teeth, wanting to get out, but somehow I could not speak.

'Can you carry your bag? I've got a bag of my own. Come, let us get it and then we'll go meet your father. He has gone to hire a gondola . . . I dare not take mine.'

'Why not?' I followed her through the connecting door into her bedroom. The fire had sunk low. I heard the city bells ring out for the midnight mass.

'Better not . . . this city is full of spies, you know.' She bent and picked up her bag, then crossed the room to her doorway. She put her finger to her lips, then quietly eased the door open. Light struck across her face.

'Going somewhere, Bianca?' Zusto da Grittoni's voice rang out.

My mother fell back a step. Wildly, she gestured to me. *Go! Hide!* I flew across the room and crouched down in the shadows behind her bed, the doll pressed against my chest. Peering around the edge of her bed-curtain, I watched as my mother retreated back into her room.

'My lord! What . . . what are you doing here?'

'I heard reports that you were entertaining. Yet you'd turned *me* away from your door. And now I find you sneaking out in the middle of the night. Where are you going?'

'No . . . nowhere.'

He stalked into the room and she retreated before him, step by slow step. All I could see of my mother was her hair, loosely bound up in one long silvery plait, swaying with each backward step. All I could see of him was his shadow, stretching across the marble. I crouched down, clutching my doll close, the bag squashed uncomfortably below me. My chest was a kettle drum; my heart the hammer.

'No one ever betrays me and escapes unpunished. Do you know what we Venetian men do to whores who have betrayed us?'

'No. Please. I'm sorry, my lord. I didn't mean . . .'

Suddenly, she burst into motion, running for the door. She was caught there by his menservants, dragged back and flung on the bed.

'You may have her when I am finished,'

Zusto da Grittoni said. I heard my mother gasp as her clothes were torn away, then a moist thwacking sound as the bed rocked and squeaked. I shrank back, making myself as small as possible. 'You're all wet and ready for me. Or is that the juices of your lover? Should I thank him for preparing the way for me? I would . . . if he was not already dead.'

My mother gave a guttural cry. The bed rattled as she tried to fight him off. A slap, a cry of pain, and Zusto da Grittoni panted, 'At last! Some life in you. I should've done this . . . long ago.' He slapped her again, calling her terrible names — a hag, a whore, a filthy lying bitch — each word punctuated by a blow. It seemed to go on forever. I buried myself in the velvet bed-curtains, my hands over my ears, but the sound could not be blocked out and my body felt each rock and jolt of the bed.

When he had finished, he said, standing up, 'Now you will pleasure my servants, and, after them, yours, as a reward for their faithful service to me. Then, my dear, we have trawled the town for the filthiest, most disease-ridden men we could find. They're all eager for a go at you. But before the entertainment begins . . . where is your daughter, Bianca? A tasty little titbit, I thought last time I saw her. And still, no doubt, a virgin.'

'No! Don't you dare.'

'I would dare,' he answered. 'I've thought

for a while that she would do very nicely, once your beauty began to fade. Which, I'm afraid, my dear, it has. I was beginning to tire of you anyway. Admit it, you're long past your prime. How old are you? Twenty-seven? Twenty-eight? Your daughter, however, is just quivering on the cusp of womanhood. It shall be my very great pleasure to open her up, as it were, to the pleasures of the flesh.'

'No!' My mother's feet hit the floor. She was slapped back down on the bed, and then the menservants came forward in a rush and a clatter of boots. My mother whimpered and sobbed and pleaded, struggling to escape, but the two men only laughed and taunted her, one holding her down while the other climbed onto the bed.

Zusto da Grittoni, meanwhile, went through the door into my bedroom. I saw his embroidered shoe pass by inches from my face. I lay still, the endless *creak, creak, creak, creak, creak* of the bed torturing my ears.

Zusto came back. 'She's not there. Where is she?'

My mother did not answer. Her breath came in short gasps. The man was grunting like an animal.

'WHERE IS SHE?'

'Gone,' my mother said faintly.

That was the last word I heard her say for a very long time.

All night, men came and went in my mother's bedroom.

I could see nothing of them but their feet. Some wore shoes of soft leather, red or forest-green or brown with large buckles. Some wore soldier's boots. One wore a priest's long black cassock. Many were barefoot, the skin filthy, the toenails discoloured.

My mother whimpered and sobbed, but it was the constant *creak, creak, creak* of the bed that most disturbed me. I could do nothing but squeeze my eyes shut and jam my hands over my ears.

Slowly, the darkness ebbed away and grey light began to creep into my mother's bedroom. The parade of feet finally stopped. Zusto da Grittoni, who had watched all night, sitting in the armchair where my mother and I had sat together so many times, got up and came to the bed. I heard him spit on her.

'That, you filthy unfaithful whore, was what we call the royal thirty-nine. I hope you enjoyed yourself. If anyone asks you, tell them this is what happens to those who betray the Grittoni family. And tell that sweet little daughter of yours that she is more than welcome to seek my protection, as long as she better understands her duty to me. Now get out.'

BELLADONNA

Venice, Italy — May to August 1508

Rage gave me the strength to get her away.

Unsurprisingly, she could hardly walk. I half-carried her from that foul house and found us a dark alley in which to hide. She clutched a lock of golden-red hair in one hand. It had been tied at one end with a bloodstained rag of pale pink fabric. I tried to take it from her, but she would not let go. It was my father's hair, I understood that. If only my father had not come back. Indeed, he was a dark walker, the bringer of pain and misfortune.

When dusk fell, I led my mother — halting step by halting step — away from the sound of church bells, deeper and deeper into the alleyways that criss-crossed San Polo. I cannot tell you how I felt. I was cold and numb. My legs were weak, and shivers racked me. All this time, my mother did not speak a word. She clung tight to the hacked-off lock of hair. Her eyes were pale green pebbles in her white bruised face.

We came to a bridge where bare-breasted women hung over the ramparts, hollering down at the gondolas floating serenely along the murky canal below. To one side was a patched and narrow house with a pomegranate tree in a pot by its open front door. A haggard old whore sat in the doorway, cutting a pomegranate open with a knife. It was crowded with seeds glowing like tiny rubies. Without thinking, I pressed both hands together and begged. She looked us over — our fine clothes, my mother's bruised face, her torn bodice and stained skirts — and offered me half of the fruit. I scooped the seeds out with my fingers and thrust them into my mouth. They were delicious.

'Need somewhere to stay?' the whore asked.

I nodded.

'Got any money?'

I rummaged in my mother's bag. It was full of beauty products — a vial of belladonna drops, a tub of white lead powder, a jar of vermilion to redden her lips. I found a pearl necklace, all tangled up with her brush, and showed it to the old whore. She reached out greedily for it, but I held it out of her reach.

'How long can we stay?'

'Saucy little *bimba,* aren't you? You can stay a month, but not a second longer.'

I nodded. I had been afraid she would grab the pearls and tell us only a night.

'And I'll need water, lots of hot water.' I wanted to sit in a hot bath forever. I wanted to scrub myself till my skin bled.

'Anything else, *contessa*?'

'A room with a lock and key.'

Her eyes flickered back to my mother, staring away into nothing. 'Very well. Come with me.' Getting to her feet, the whore drew her shawl to cover her heavy bare breasts.

We climbed a narrow staircase three floors up to a tiny hot room under the roof. The straw mattress was crawling with bed lice, the floor was filthy and the chamber pot crusted with ordure, but at least we could lock ourselves away in there. And there was an escape route out the window and across the rooftops.

First, I washed my mother as best I could. She cringed away from me, trying to hide her body with her hands. 'It's all right,' I crooned. 'We're safe now. Let's just get you clean and then you can rest.'

I washed out the chamber pot, swept the floor and threw the mattress out the window. I scrubbed and rubbed and dusted and scoured, as if I could so easily wash away the images of the previous night. When all was clean, I folded my mother's velvet cloak and laid it on the floorboards, so she could lie down. I bought us some food and fed it to my mother as if she was a child. She lay on her cloak, her legs curled into her chest.

When it grew too dark to clean any more, I tried to cuddle up to her. She jerked herself away. So I lay alone on the hard floorboards and tried not to weep. Eventually, I slept.

The next day, I went out. I told myself I needed to find food, but the truth is I could not bear to stay in that room. First, I took a turquoise brooch to the Jews and exchanged it for a small bag of coins, which I hid in my bodice. Then, I went to market, bargaining with shopkeepers for their leftovers and off-cuts. My coins dwindled alarmingly fast. On my way back to the house with the pomegranate tree, I stole an orange off a table. My heart banged hard against the bones of my chest. It felt good. I felt alive. I stole a shawl off a washing line and a cushion off a chair, and ran all the way home, my lungs compressed with terror and triumph.

My mother lay motionless, her knees to her chin. She did not respond to my chatter, just turned her face away. Looking out the window at the jumble of roofs, I sat on my new cushion, the shawl about my shoulders, and ate my orange slowly, licking the juice from my fingers. Then I went out again.

My days fell into a pattern. I would roam the alleyways, stealing whatever I could, regardless of whether I needed it or not. I wanted to keep my thoughts focused firmly forward. But, every day, something — the creak of an old gate, a smell oozing from a doorway, a flash of something white in the corner of my eye — would stab me like a stiletto through the heart. Then I would scrub our room again, smashing fleas with the back of my scrubbing brush, or I'd beat the rug with a broom out the window till the people below shouted and shook their fists at me.

I don't think my mother ever managed to forget, not even for a moment. She lay on her bed, clutching the lock of red-gold hair to her heart, her eyes wide open and staring at nothing. I tried to coax her to get up, to come and sit in the window and look down at the busy life of the street below, but she always shook her head. I could not coax her to eat much, so she got thinner and paler. She did not even have the energy or the will to weep, though she spoke a few words. 'Thank you' or 'I'm sorry'. Once, she called me *tesorina*. I began to feel a little less afraid.

Summer came. It was so hot in our tiny room that I scarcely slept. Perspiration trickled down my back and prickled my groin and my armpits. Every time I glanced at my mother, she was awake, staring at the wall, her knees tucked up under her chin. 'Go back to sleep,' I'd say. 'Everything's all right.' She'd nod and shut her eyes. It seemed as if I was the mother, and she my little *bambina*.

Sores developed at the corner of her mouth. She felt them with her tongue and turned a piteous face towards me. 'I've the pox,' she said.

I tried to comfort her, but she lifted her skirt and tried to see the red inflamed lips of her vagina. Sores clustered all around it. She felt them with her fingers. 'I wish I was dead,' she whispered. She lay down on her makeshift bed, weeping hopelessly, the lock of my father's hair pressed against her cheek.

I went downstairs and stood for a while in the doorway, leaning my head against the doorframe. It was a hot golden evening and the streets were full of people seeking some movement of air. I looked not at their faces, laughing, glistening with sweat, nor at their swinging skirts or striding legs, bright in multi-coloured hose; I looked at their feet. Feet in soft shoes, in boots, in *chopines.* Bare feet, filthy and black. I felt my rage boiling inside me.

Our landlady came down the hall and stood near me. 'Hot,' she said, waving her hand about her red-painted mouth. She looked at me out of the corner of one black-kohled eye. 'Your month is almost up. Got any more pearls in that bag of yours?'

'No. But don't worry, I'll pay you for the room.'

'How old are you, little *bimba*?'

I crossed my arms. 'Old enough.'

'Old enough for a gentleman friend? I know

315

someone who'd like a pretty little thing like you.'

'If you bring a man anywhere near me, I'll slice off his cock and then I'll shove it up your arse.' I showed her the poniard I had stolen and now carried in my bodice.

She drew back a wary step, then laughed. 'What if I bring more than one?'

'Then I'll kill you.'

She must have realised I meant it, for she called me a little cow, drew her shawl about her raddled bosom and went away down the hall.

I went out into the streets that night, stealing anything that took my fancy, yelling insults up at the whores, dodging the deluge of piss from upturned chamber pots, making rude gestures at anyone who I thought looked at me sideways, throwing stones at cats, kicking over baskets of fruit, anything to make me feel alive and powerful. Though I scored plenty of insults and rude gestures in return, no one chased me or hurt me. I would like to think it was because I radiated waves of red-hot rage, but, truthfully, I think I still looked like a skinny little girl, even though inside I felt I was as world-weary as our landlady.

I came home only when doors began to shut up for the night and the alleys were shrouded in darkness. I carried my poniard in my hand, not at all sure that the old whore, our landlady, wouldn't have men lying in wait

316

for me. All was quiet, though, and I slipped up the stairs to the room I shared with my mother, feeling guilty now for having left her so long.

The first thing I noticed was the smell of vomit.

'Mama?' I peered into the darkness. There was no answer. 'Mama?' I scrabbled to strike a spark with my flint and stone. My hands were shaking with a sudden intense anxiety. A spark lit and died, but in its brief flare I saw my mother lying sprawled on the cushions, her eyes staring at me. My heart beat a staccato. I struck again and again, till I managed to light a taper. I lit a candle and turned slowly to look at her.

She was dead. Her mouth hung open, a streak of dried vomit on her chin. Her eyes bulged horribly. My father's lock of hair lay across one limp palm. The vial of belladonna eye-drops lay fallen from the other. Belladonna was poisonous, I knew. My mother had always warned me not to drink it.

I stood stock still, staring at her. Her eyes seemed to accuse me. Slowly, not taking my eyes off her, I backed across the room and fumbled behind the stove, looking for the drawstring bag full of jewellery I had hidden there. I tied it about my waist, backed out of the room and shut the door. I slid down to the ground, bowed my head into my arms and sat, unable to think or feel, wanting only to disappear into darkness.

I sat there all night. Only the stealthy advance of light into the stairwell roused me from my stupor. I rose stiffly, went downstairs and banged on our landlady's door until she got up and opened the door a crack.

'What do you want?' she croaked.

'I need a witch.'

Curiosity sparked in her dull brown eyes. She tilted her matted head. 'It'll cost you.'

I dug in my pocket for the few *scudi* I carried on me. She examined them carefully, rubbing her thumb over the edges to make sure they had not been clipped, then told me, 'Best witch I know is Wise Sibillia. They say she's a thousand years old and once led a coven of witches in the Appenines, before the Inquisition drove her away. You'd best be careful — if you betray her, she'll tear out your heart and eat it.'

Wise Sibillia sounded perfect.

The witch's eyes were black and inscrutable. Her long flowing hair was as white as an old woman's, though her figure was straight and strong, and her dark olive skin smooth and unlined, except for one deep crease between her brows, angling down from the left. It was her mouth that betrayed her. The lips were sunken and puckered, and, when she opened them to speak, she revealed only a few broken stumps of teeth.

'So, child, what can I do for you?' the witch said.

'I want revenge on someone,' I answered.

'Are you sure you want to dabble in such dark matters? Can you not spit in his soup or put a thistle in his shoe?'

I looked at her scornfully. 'I want him to suffer forever.'

Her lip curled in amusement. 'Powerful black magic, then. You will need to hate him with great intensity.'

'I do.'

'Do you have money?'

I did not trouble with the few battered *scudis* I carried in my pocket. I lifted my skirt and unknotted a ruby ring I had tied in the hem of my petticoat. It was the most valuable piece of jewellery my mother had owned. I lifted it against the light to show Sibillia. She raised her left eyebrow, deepening the line at its corner so I knew how it had been carved into her flesh.

'You must hate him very much.'

'I do,' I repeated.

'What is your name, child?' Sibillia asked.

I bit my lip and looked away. We were sitting in her garden at dusk. The air was heavy with perfume from a white hanging flower like an angel's trumpet. Giant moths beat against the lanterns strung along the archways of her patio. A thin crescent moon was pinned to the sky above the crooked tilted roofs of

319

San Polo.

I remembered an old story my nursemaid had once told me about the moon and witches. 'Selena,' I answered.

'A most intriguing name. Much more interesting than Maria.'

I tried hard not to react. How had she known my name was Maria? *Most girls in Venice were called that,* I told myself, and raised my chin.

'Do you have a last name, Selena?' the witch asked.

The whore's brat. The bastard. And now a new one: the orphan. I shook my head.

'So when is your birthday?'

I told her, and she said, 'Born under the sign of the lion — most suitable, given your hair and eyes. You should call yourself Selena Leonelli. That's a name with power.'

Selena Leonelli. It rolled around my mouth like the sweetest of jujubes. I smiled at her, and the unfamiliar movement of the muscles around my mouth seemed to tug up my heart from the black pit into which it had fallen. A new name seemed to signal the possibility of a new life.

'And how do you come to have such a fine ruby, Selena?'

'It was my mother's.'

'Your mother is dead now.' Sibillia said it as a statement of truth, not as a question. I nodded. 'And you wish revenge on the man who caused her death.'

I nodded again.

'Very well, I'll help you, but if you are caught and charged with witchcraft you must not mention my name.'

'I won't,' I promised.

But she gave me that quizzical lift of her eyebrow again and said, 'No, Selena, you will not, for I shall bind your tongue so that you cannot speak my name, no matter how much you wish you could.'

So that was the first spell I ever learnt: the binding of a tongue, the binding of another's will.

The second spell I learnt was how to drive a man mad by disturbing his sleep with nightmares. This is how you do it.

Take a long black candle and a sharp pin. Write your enemy's name along the candle with the pin, driving the letters in good and deep. Bind the candle in the spiny brambles of a blackberry vine. Wrap it in a square of black cloth, along with a handful of grave dirt (I used dirt from the communal pauper's grave my mother's body was tossed into). Sew it closed with black thread. On the first night of the full moon, smash the candle as hard as you can with a hammer, while chanting:

Wake with a scream, haunted by dreams,
never rest, never sleep,
clawed from the deep.

Do this for the next three days. Then take the bag, now filled with smashed candle powder, and bury it in your victim's garden, preferably under his bedroom window.

Zusto da Grittoni did not have a garden but I buried it in a topiary pot on his balcony. I took to lurking outside his villa, watching him pacing back and forth across his window when all the rest of Venice slept. By the end of winter, when the streets of Venice were flooded with icy water, Zusto da Grittoni had hanged himself from his bedposts. He would have gone straight to the deepest level of hell, I know, and there he would suffer for all eternity.

And I went to live with Wise Sibillia to learn her craft.

LOVE AND HATRED

Venice, Italy — 1508 to 1510

Love and hatred were the witch's currency.

Her garden was an aphrodisiac garden and a poison garden. Roses and myrtle and passionflowers grew entwined with hemlock and foxgloves, mandrake and nightshade, the heavy-headed, bell-shaped flowers of dark purplish-red from which was distilled the belladonna eye-drops that had killed my mother.

When I was first shown the small room in which I was to sleep, I felt something under my ribs spring open. It was like I had stepped back into my mother's childhood, or into a daydream. The room was roughly whitewashed, but the sun filtered through jasmine so that shadows of tendrils and blossom coiled and uncoiled across the walls. I was able to step through the narrow doorway and, barefoot, stand on the warm soil, breathing in the heady scent of the garden, filling my lungs and veins with the exhilarating power of life and death.

In return for such beauty, offering Wise Sibillia my wrist to prick and my blood to suck
seemed a small price to pay.

During the day, I assisted Sibillia as she
harvested flowers and leaves, dug up roots,
crushed berries and mixed concoctions. While
she saw clients, I worked for her in her
library, laboriously hand-copying the manuscripts of spells and incantations that she kept
locked away in a stone chest. Venice was then
the centre of the publishing world, printing
presses churning out all kinds of books and
pamphlets every day, yet the books I slowly
copied onto parchment, trying desperately
not to blot, would have sent any printer to
the pyre.

As I finished writing out each difficult
arcane page, I made another secret copy for
myself, which I concealed under my mattress
and dug out again at night to read over and
learn by heart.

Sibillia sold my handwritten manuscripts
for great sums of money, to sorcerers and
philosophers all over Europe, the books
smuggled out in false-bottomed chests filled
with flasks of perfume and rose water, jars of
white lead and vinegar face paint, depilatory
creams made of caustic lime to burn away
eyebrows and the pubic hair, pomanders of
amber and musk, lip salves of vermilion and
cochineal — women's frivolities, which no
customs officer would bother to search

through.

In the afternoons, I filled my basket with love potions and cures, poisons and curses, and delivered them all over Venice. Nearly all of Sibillia's clients were women — whores who wanted revenge on their pimps, nuns wanting to abort a secret child, young women languishing with unrequited love, stout matrons wanting to poison their husbands' young and lovely mistresses.

I came to know the labyrinthine alleys and plazas of Venice as I knew my own body, its snaking canals and crooked bridges, its hidden squares, its round domes and jutting spires, its palaces and hovels, convents and brothels. I was accompanied everywhere by a thickset surly-faced manservant named Sergio, for women did not walk the streets of Venice alone, not even whores.

As I walked the stony streets, basket over my arm, I examined the feet of the men who passed me, looking always for shoes that I knew. I listened to gossip, asked questions and set street kids to spy for me, till — one by one — I tracked down the men who had raped my mother. Our old servants were the first I found. I made wax figures of them all, dressing them in little outfits I made from old clothes I paid to have stolen from their chests. I also paid to have the hair plucked from their brushes or nail clippings gathered from under their beds. I stuck the hair on the

little poppets' heads and sewed the nail clippings inside, then amused myself in the
evenings by sticking pins in them, into their
heads and their feet, and especially at the soft
juncture of their legs. Eventually, I'd hold the
poppets over my candle flame till they had
melted into grotesque shapes, and then I'd
bury them in the garden.

After our servants, I tracked down Zusto
da Grittoni's. Then, when they too had died
or gone mad, I began to search for those
other men, the ones in soldier's boots and a
priest's long cassock, those filthy tramps with
their yellow curling toenails. I used every ma-
leficent spell I learnt from Sibillia's books —
pulling a parsley root from the earth while
crying out my enemy's name, burying the
decomposing heart of a dead rat in their
garden, sprinkling food they were to eat with
dirt gathered from my mother's grave —
experimenting to see which spell worked fast-
est or had the most dire effects. I watched
my enemies, enjoying their slow torment,
relishing their eventual breakdown and death.

As they dwindled, I grew plump and sleek,
my hair growing in ripples of fiery red-gold,
down past my waist. I became aware of the
glances of men in the street, and occasionally
a young blood in striped hose and slashed
sleeves would call out to me, begging me for
a smile, a kiss, a fuck. I always shook my head
and hurried away, glad of the bulk of Sergio

behind me.

One day, in the spring before my fifteenth birthday, I was coming down the stairs of a grand house on the Campo San Samuele when one of these young bloods came bouncing up. He was dressed in salmon-pink and indigo velvet, one leg striped pink and purple, the other pink and grey. His codpiece bulged out, pushing aside the folds of his doublet.

'Here's a pretty sweetmeat,' he said, pausing at the sight of me. 'I'm feeling a trifle peckish. Let me have a taste of you.' He pushed me into the wall, one hand squeezing my breast, his wet tongue swirling inside my mouth like a child trying to lick out a bowl. Revulsion filled me. I whipped out my dagger and pricked him in the side.

He jerked away with a curse and touched his side. His fingers came away bloody. 'You cut me, you little cow.'

'Touch me again and I'll curse you so your cock falls off.'

'You've torn my doublet. Do you know how much it cost?'

'Do you think I care?' With my dagger held out threateningly, I went backward down the steps.

As I reached the floor below, he suddenly called out, 'Witch.'

Smiling, I made the sign of the horns with my left hand, pointing my extended forefinger and little finger straight at him. Horrified, he grabbed his left testicle with his right hand. I laughed and went out to where Sergio was waiting for me. He frowned at the sight of me, and I wondered if my face showed the sting of the young man's beard. I glanced down at my dress and saw that my bodice was disordered. Surreptitiously, I straightened it.

A few days later, Carnevale began with an explosion of fireworks and continued in a wild hurly-burly of feasts and masquerades and parties. With a hood over my distinctive hair and a mask hiding my face, I accompanied Sibillia as she wandered the crowded noisy streets or glided in her gondola down the crowded canals, the surface fizzing with the reflection of flaming torches and shooting stars of pink and orange and purple and silver, the air thick with acrid smoke, which stung my nostrils. Everyone was filled with frenetic gaiety, as if Venice sought to forget the humiliation of the last few years, when we had lost our Dry Land Dominion in the west and our trade routes in the east. Our diplomats had been forced to kneel before the Pope and confess their sins and accept the ritual scourging rods. At least the Pope had not forced them to wear halters about their necks as he had threatened.

Sibillia had told me that the Venetian coffers were rattling like a beggar's after the disastrous war, but there was no sign of poverty on the canals and *campi* of La Serenissima. Everywhere I looked were billowing gowns of satin trimmed with fur, embroidered *chopines* as thick as a Bible, velvet cloaks and flashing jewels. Music and the deep thrum of conversation floated from every window, lit by the light of a thousand tall white candles, and from dark alleyways I heard soft laughter and the occasional grunt and moan of pleasure.

I had stopped to watch a troupe of acrobats in the square as they walked on their hands and turned neat backflips and cartwheels. One was spinning wheels of fire in his bare hands, throwing flaming torches up in the air then catching them again. As I tilted back my head to watch the whirl of bright flame, my hood fell back. A man behind me exclaimed, 'How beautiful.'

I half-turned and saw a young man reaching out his hand to me. He was dark and swarthy, in his early twenties, with a shabby cloak and broad peasant hands speckled with paint. He picked up a tendril of my hair and twined it about his fingers. 'Look, Francesco, is this not the most gorgeous colour? How could I capture this on canvas?'

Another young man, a little taller and a little older, stared dispassionately at me and said, 'Vermilion?'

'It darkens too much. She'd be a brunette by the end of the year. I'd want her to flame from my canvas for centuries.'

Francesco snorted. 'You always were an ambitious brute, Tiziano.'

'Is it ambitious to know you have talent and want to use it? Surely you don't want your little brother to waste his God-given gift instead of making our fortune with it?'

The young painter still had a firm grip on a lock of my hair. I said coldly, 'Excuse me,' and tried to jerk my head free. He grinned at me and used the long tendril of hair as a leash to draw me closer. He smelt of earth and crushed herbs, as if he had been rolling in a garden. 'Red and yellow ochre for your hair and the yolk of a town hen for your pearly skin,' he said. 'And I'd pay a fortune for some cochineal to capture the red of your mouth.' As he spoke, he suddenly bent his head and kissed me. His mouth was soft and gentle. I could not move, as if he had cast a binding spell upon me. I gave no thought at all to my dagger, but only to the feel of his mouth on mine, his hands in my hair, drawing me ever closer so I felt as if I could swoon in his arms and he would catch me.

He drew his mouth away and smiled at me. 'Come to my studio and I'll paint you,' he whispered in my ear. 'My name is Tiziano Vecellio. What's yours?'

At the same moment, we became aware of the hulking presence of Sibillia's bodyguard, Sergio, looming over us. Tiziano said 'Uh-oh' under his breath, gave my hair one last affectionate tug and melted away into the crowd, followed quickly by his frowning brother. I followed him with my gaze, then realised Sibillia was watching me from the shadows, her dark stare inscrutable as ever. I shrugged and gave a quick smile and hurried to join her, saying, 'Carnevale time, it goes to everyone's heads. It must be the masks.'

I was quiet and preoccupied for the rest of the evening, though, very aware of the heaviness of my breasts and the tingling of my blood. *Tiziano,* I said to myself, and wished I dared ask Sibillia what she knew of him.

The next morning, Sibillia called me to her sitting room. I came in smoothly, sank into a graceful curtsey and offered her my arm, wrist upwards, even though I knew the moon was not full and she would not take blood from me in the full glare of the day. It was a gesture of submission and placation, false as my smile.

She shook her head, her gaze calculating. 'Not today, Selena. Come, sit down. I want to talk to you.'

Thoughts of my hoard of secretly copied manuscripts flashed into my head. I pushed them away at once, afraid Sibillia would read my mind. I bowed my head and sat down on a stool before her, smoothing my skirt over my knees. Truth be told, I was afraid of Sibillia. I wanted her power, her wealth, her strength, but I dared not let her know it. She was ruthless, and I was not yet fifteen. Despite all my watching and listening and stealthy copying, I was just beginning to dimly grasp the knowledge she had spent centuries acquiring.

'Selena, you are a woman now. Your blood has begun to flow.'

I bit my lip. I had washed my rags in secret, revolted and disturbed by my own traitorous body. I did not want to be a woman, at the mercy of men and time — I wanted to stay immaculate and inviolate forever.

Sibillia's eyes were gentle with understanding. 'You cannot stop the passing of time, Selena. Believe me, I have tried with all my strength. The world turns, seasons pass, everything changes. You were a child, and now you are a woman and so no use to me any more.'

I had not been expecting this. I stared at her, eyes wide with shock. 'But . . . I . . .'

'I need the blood of a virgin,' she said.

'I'm still a virgin.'

'But for how much longer?' Her left eyebrow rose in that characteristic quizzical expression of hers.

'Forever,' I cried.

She smiled wryly. 'You plan to take the veil and be a nun?'

I was taken aback. 'No . . .'

'Then you shall soon lose your maidenhood, whether willingly or not.'

'I'd rather die.'

'You'd rather die than surrender to the pleasures of the flesh? I did not think you were a fool, Selena. Or so devout you believe all the blather of bishops and popes, who mouth sanctimonious words from the pulpit while their mistresses and bastards jostle in the pews below. Do you not realise that sex is a sacred force of nature, filled with power and passion and life and laughter? You cannot be a witch unless you master that force.'

I was silent, my stomach cramping. All I could think of was my mother's soft animalistic grunts of pain.

'You are very beautiful, Selena, as I'm sure you know. You must understand that your beauty is as much a curse as a blessing. It will give you power, if you use it wisely. But it does mean that you must choose your sphere of influence. There are only three choices for women in this world that we live in. You can be a nun, or a wife, or a whore. Which will you choose?'

'I want to be a witch like you.'

'Then you must be a whore.'

For a moment, I could not speak, my ears and eyes filled with memories like maggots.

Then I realised Sibillia was right. A nun was locked away behind high walls, never to step foot outside again. Even if the tales of nuns tunnelling through the walls to let in their lovers were true, the fact remained that they were bound in service to their god and had little freedom or power in their lives. And, in Venice, wives were kept almost as close as nuns. At Carnevale time, men took their mistresses out to see the festivities while their wives stayed at home with their children. They went out only to church, or to visit family in their private homes, their hair tucked under demure caps, their bodies encased in armour of farthingales and petticoats. I could not bear such a life.

'I must warn you, without a dowry, you'll have little chance of a good marriage,' Sibillia said. 'You'll maybe win a shopkeeper willing to take you on as a pretty face to lure customers in. You'll be expected to work hard, and heaven help you when your beauty fades.'

'Is that not true of a whore as well?'

'Indeed, though there are ways to help preserve your beauty longer if the only work you have to do is lie on your back and let men spill their seed into you. At least your hands stay white and your back unbowed. And a good courtesan can earn as much as a ship's captain and twice as much as a master tradesman.'

That was something to think about. I never wanted to be poor again. But I remembered my mother and father in bed, panting, moaning. I screwed up my mouth in distaste. 'I don't want men slobbering all over me.'

Sibillia was amused. 'It's not so bad. You may even come to enjoy it.'

'I don't think so.'

'Then you had best become a nun, because it's the only way to escape it. A wife sells her body just as surely as any whore, though the coin is different.'

'Can I not just stay here with you?' I asked in my most childish voice.

'Not unless you are of some use to me. Even if you were to retain your maidenhead for some while yet, your blood loses some of its potency once you begin to menstruate. I need to find some other girl on the cusp of womanhood. Sergio is out searching the streets right now, though it seems to be harder and harder to find a virgin in Venice these days. We might need to entice one out of a convent.'

'And how would I be of use to you if I turn whore?'

'You would be bringing in some money,' Sibillia pointed out. 'Times are hard, and I am getting old. No man would pay to taste my flesh any more. You, however, are as sweet and ripe as a peach. Any man would pay dearly for the chance to pluck you.'

'You'd turn procuress?'

Sibillia smiled. 'Not I. There are enough of those in Venice already without adding to them. No, I'd simply allow you to pay for the privilege of copying all my secrets.'

Heat rushed into my cheeks. I dropped my eyes, pretending not to understand what she meant, while I considered what she had said. Nun, or wife, or whore. It seemed I really had no choice at all.

So it was done. My maidenhead was sold to an elderly man whose sagging folds of hairy skin and sour smell made me feel sick to my stomach. It was all over quickly, though, and I was able to give Sibillia a fat purse, and still buy myself velvet gowns and ropes of pearls and fine perfumes from Arabia. Sergio found Sibillia a skinny little virgin from the docks, glad enough to offer up her wrist to the witch to suck in return for a warm bed and a meal every day. I became Sibillia's apprentice by day and a courtesan by night.

One I loved and the other I hated. A good training ground for a witch.

THE LAZZARETTO

Venice, Italy — July 1510

Plague came to Venice in the summer of 1510, like a hail of poisoned arrows.

Our little virgin was the first in our household to fall ill. At first, she felt just a little unwell and refused her bowl of *spezzatino di manzo* for the first time ever. Then her fever began to climb, and our cook — a chubby man named Bassi — called for Sibillia. She gathered together an infusion of ground willow bark, feverfew and lavender water, and shook together dried linden and elderflowers to make a fever-cooling tea.

'Come with me and I'll show you what needs to be done,' she told me. 'You must be careful not to give her too much of the willow-bark infusion. It could make her sick in the stomach.'

I followed, though I had no real interest in the girl, being jealous that she had replaced me as the source of blood for Sibillia's spell against ageing, and having always been more interested in knowing what plants could kill than what plants could heal (strangely, they were often the same plant in different strengths). I knew, however, that as much of a witch's income came from healing as from curses and cantrips, and I should learn what I could.

The girl, Fabricia, lay on her pallet, her head moving restlessly, her face sweaty and red. Sibillia gave her some willow-bark infusion to drink, instructing me to make up the linden tea. I swung the kettle back over the fire and was getting a cup down from the dresser when Sibillia said, in a high strained voice, 'Selena, you had best get out of here. Bassi, you too.'

I swung around. Sibillia had pulled down the girl's blanket and lifted her nightgown to examine her. I saw large, red, inflamed swellings in her groin, just inside the hairless juncture of her legs.

'What's wrong?' I asked.

'It's the plague. Selena, I want you to go to my room and gather up everything that the Inquisition would find of interest and lock it in my stone chest. If you are wise, you'll hide your own secret hoard in there too. Bassi, you and Sergio must bury my chest under the compost heap. Go. Hurry, all of you.'

We did as she said. I put everything into the stone chest, all the books of magical lore, all my secret copies, the different-coloured candles, the seashells and stones, the wand and dagger and cauldron, the broom of elder twigs, the silver cimaruta amulet with its symbols of fish and key and hand and moon and blossom. I closed and locked the chest, and the two big men dragged it out into the garden and buried it deep.

'We must try and hide Fabricia's body,' Sibillia said when I returned to the kitchen, standing just outside the door.

'Is she dead?' I asked fearfully.

'Not yet. It won't be long, though. If the Health Officers discover we have plague in the house, we'll be put in quarantine and they'll be burning all I own in the square. If we can keep it quiet, there's a fortune to be made here.'

'Magic cures?' I guessed.

Sibillia nodded. 'Last time we had the plague here in Venice, the Council of Ten had to pass an ordinance limiting pharmacies and apothecaries to one every hundred paces. The city was seething with them like maggots on a dead dog. I'll need to collect some frogs, as many as we can get hold of. And I'll make a batch of my special Venice honey . . .' She stopped suddenly, lifting one hand to her head.

'What's wrong?'

'Nothing. I'm fine. It's hot in here.' There was a long fraught silence, then suddenly Sibillia sat down. 'I drank her blood three nights ago, when the moon was full. Do you think . . . ?'

I could not speak. I feared Wise Sibillia, but I also revered her.

'Bring me parchment and a quill.' For the first time, hunched over in fear, the lines around her mouth driven deep, she looked like an old woman. Silently, I obeyed. Sibillia wrote out a will leaving the house and the garden and all her worldly goods to me. 'Witch lore is passed from mother to daughter. You have no mother and I have no daughter. It is fitting that we should have found each other in time.'

Fabricia died before dawn. Sibillia wrapped her body in a sheet and the two men carried her out to the gondola. 'Drop her in a canal or in the lagoon, somewhere away from here,' Sibillia instructed. 'Be careful.'

The hours passed, and the men did not return. Bells pealed out all over the city, and several times we heard wailing and sobbing from somewhere nearby and, once, the anguished yowling of a cat. Sibillia and I busied ourselves hiding our jewels and most precious belongings. Soon, however, the witch was too weak to stand and she lay down, shivering with fever. I did not want to tend her, but neither did I want to go out into the streets, filled now with shouting and screaming. It all seemed to have happened so quickly. Bassi had come back from the market only the day

340

before to say there were rumours the plague had come again. Sibillia had told me not to make my deliveries that morning and to stay home from the brothel. I had been glad to obey her, for the heat had been stifling and I was happy to spend an evening in my bedroom, studying my books. Now, the skinny virgin was dead and Sibillia herself was sick. How was it possible? Did she not have spells to cast the plague away?

'Water . . . please . . .' Sibillia croaked. I brought her a cup but kept a fold of my sleeve across my mouth. 'Help me . . .' She struggled to sit up. I did not want to touch her. Strange black spots were disfiguring her face and I could see purple swellings on her neck, under her ear. I held the cup to her lips and she managed to drink a sip, before beginning to cough violently. I stumbled back, averting my face.

'Angelica in wine . . . and chew some garlic,' she said when the coughing stopped. 'Are they not back yet?'

I shook my head and backed away. She sighed and lay down again. I went into the garden and sat in the hot sunshine, crushing herbs in my hands and smelling them, listening to the bells clamouring. I was weeping with fear. I did not want to die.

The sun was directly overhead when someone began to bang at our front door. The maids had all fled during the night, and there was no one left in the house but me and the dying witch. Reluctantly, I went to open the door.

Outside, a plague doctor loomed, knocking on the door with the end of a long hooked stick. He wore a black waxed coat falling over high leather boots, a wide-brimmed hat, and a white mask with a long hooked beak and glass eyepieces that flashed in the sun. Behind him were two filthy men, rags tied about their mouths, pulling a cart filled with dead bodies, buzzing with flies. The bodies were naked, a jumble of protruding arms and legs and backs and buttocks. A man with an enormous hairy belly lay on the very top. As I watched, he groaned and tried to lift his head, and one of the corpse-bearers knocked him back with a cudgel.

The fat man was Bassi, our cook. I stared in horror, seeing the swelling of buboes at his neck and groin and armpits, the dark marks like bruises on his swollen belly.

'You've plague in the house,' the doctor said, his voice muffled by the mask. 'Bring out your dead.'

'No. There's no plague here. Go away!'

'Two of your servants have been found with plague marks. All bedding and clothing must be burnt and the house shut up. You and anyone else living here will be taken to the Lazzaretto for forty days and forty nights. If you survive, you'll be allowed back to Venice.'

'But not many ever come back,' one of the corpse-bearers sniggered.

I tried to stop him, but the doctor shoved me aside and went into the house. The corpse-bearers followed him, dragging down priceless tapestries and curtains, gathering up cushions and bedclothes and throwing them out into the street. I wept as my new velvet dresses and fine lawn chemises were tossed out the window. Then the doctor found Sibillia, sweating and moaning in her bed. He called sharply to the corpse-bearers and they came to carry her downstairs.

'It's not the plague,' I argued. 'She just has an ague. She'll be better tomorrow.'

The doctor did not bother to reply. He watched, inscrutable behind his beaked mask, as all our bedding and clothes were set on fire. Gasping, I ran back inside and caught up Sibillia's purse and shawl and a loaf of bread from the kitchen. It was all I had time for, the corpse-bearers coming to manhandle me away. Sibillia was tossed on top of the dead bodies, her cook, Bassi, groaning beside her, and planks were nailed across our door. I had to walk, stumbling and weeping, behind the cart as it made its way through the narrow alleyways and over arched bridges towards the lagoon. Every house and inn was shut up, every shopfront shuttered. Fires smouldered in every square, and the air was orange with smoke. The corpse-bearers rang

343

a handbell, shouting, *'Corpi morti, corpi morti!'*

Each narrow *calle* ran with the same cry and the tuneless clanging of countless handbells.

In Piazza San Marco, a great bonfire was burning. Amidst the cloth and trade goods, I saw the small shapes of skinned cats and dogs impaled on sticks. Black smoke billowed everywhere, smelling nauseatingly of cooking flesh. Corpses lay in piles. People wailed, on their knees, hands lifted imploringly to heaven. A priest in a black cassock chanted incomprehensible prayers.

The clock on the Torre dell'Orologio began to toll out.

One.

Two.

Three.

Four.

Five.

Six.

Seven.

Eight.

Nine.

Ten.

Eleven.

Twelve.

Each toll a second of my life unravelling, each toll a moment gone forever. I felt as if I was falling down into a great pit of blackness and madness and despair. The smoke choked me. I could not breathe. My heart clamoured in my ears.

A young man lurched at me out of the haze. His fine velvet clothes were torn and disordered, his handsome face streaked with tear-tracks through the char of smoke. He saw me. Eyes widened in recognition.

'You! You did this! You cursed me. Witch! Whore!' The young man launched himself at me, knocked me to the ground. He punched me in the face, so blood poured from my nose. I could taste its strange metallic richness on my tongue. He punched me again, and I felt a tooth crack.

No one came to my rescue. He could have sat astride me and pummelled me into a pulp, if Sibillia had not somehow found the strength to slip from the cart, falling to her knees beside it. She struggled up and stumbled towards me, her hands held out. With her white hair straggling about her pain-contorted face, her eyes wild with fever, she looked exactly like the evil witch of fairy tale.

The young man moaned in terror and rolled away from me. Sibillia pointed one hand at him, two fingers extended in the sign of the devil's horns, and chanted some words in a strange language. Terrified, the young man fled across the square, almost falling over a pile of dead bodies. I scrambled to my feet and ran to Sibillia, both hands catching her when she would have fallen. All around us, people were staring and pointing. 'It's

345

Wise Sibillia,' someone cried. 'And her witch apprentice.'

'He said she'd cursed us.'

'Plague-carrier.'

'Devil.'

I put my arm around her back and supported her, obeying the plague doctor's emphatic gesture towards the docks. As we stumbled past him, he drew away and made a quick sign of the cross. Sibillia's legs almost gave way beneath her, and only my arm kept her from falling. An angry mutter rose from the crowd.

We were put together in a small boat, tied by a long cable to another boat, where a cloaked and hooded man waited. The plague doctor bent and whispered something in his ear, and he turned his terrifying white-beaked mask towards us, eye-holes staring blankly. I saw his hand clench on the handle of the long oar he was holding. His fingernails were black and cracked and rotten. He made the quick sign of the cross and spat at us.

Bassi and the dead bodies on the cart were tipped into a barge. I watched, shaking, as more bodies were flung on top. Soon, Bassi's chubby form was hidden from sight. A few more people were ushered onto our boat — a distraught woman with a weeping child, a haggard young man, an old man in a night-gown and bare feet. They had evidently seen Sibillia cursing the young man, for they huddled at the other end of the boat, too frightened to look at us.

Then the hooded oarsmen rowed away across the lagoon, dragging our smaller boat behind theirs. Sibillia coughed hoarsely. I wrapped her shawl about her and wished I had thought to bring something to drink. Smoke drifted through the air, stinging my eyes. The water did not glitter as it usually did but heaved up and down, grey and lustreless as the scales of a dead fish, occasionally gleaming with lurid reddish light. I peered ahead.

We passed a low-lying swampy island. Ancient black galleons were moored about it, their bare masts creaking as they rocked on the swell. People crowded the decks, holding out imploring hands to us, calling in thin cracked voices. On the muddy shores were piles of dead bodies, some naked, some wrapped in shrouds. Men were digging graves nearby.

Our boat was dragged past, heading towards another swampy island, the Isola del Lazzaretto Nuovo. Set right at the mouth of the lagoon, it was the place where ships had to go and unload their cargoes of spices and silks to be decontaminated with smoking herbs before being allowed into Venice. I had heard of it before — I did not know when. It seemed now it had been turned into a place where those suspected of having the plague were to be quarantined.

We were left on the beach, Sibillia leaning heavily against my arm. A man in a leather coat and breeches came to meet us, a kerchief tied around his mouth. We picked our way past open graves, where corpses in their hundreds lay tumbled. I saw one with maggots seething in the eye socket, another who sat upright, arms held out stiffly, leering at me. The stench made me retch. I was glad when we finally reached the long building in the centre of the island. Graceful arches all along one side led into a cavernous and shadowy space within.

It was worse inside, though. Straw pallets had been set up on the floor, with up to four people crowded on top. Others lay on the bare stone or sat against the walls, their heads hanging low. The sounds of retching and coughing and moaning filled the air. The smell was unbearable.

Men in plague-doctor masks walked about with incense censers filled with smoking herbs. Mostly, they did not touch the sick, just prodded them with their long sticks. One doctor nearby lanced the angry boils covering a young woman. Putrid black liquid oozed out. 'She should be at the Old Lazzaretto,' he said to a colleague. 'Those who come here without the plague will soon catch it.'

'There's no more room at the Old Lazzaretto. As fast as people die, more get sick,' the other replied. 'At this rate, half of Venice shall die.'

I remembered the hot filthy little room where my mother had died and how I had ordered water for washing and smashed the cockroaches and fleas with the back of my scrubbing brush. There was no hot water here, and no scrubbing brush. I had sworn I would never live like that again, but the Lazzaretto was far, far worse.

'I'm in hell,' I whispered.

'This is not hell,' the doctor replied wryly. 'This is purgatory.'

'Is there not a bed where I can lay her down? Is there no medicine, no food?' I held out my hands to him.

'Have you money?'

'Some.'

'Find a Jew. They'll sell you a mattress and something to eat.'

So I looked for the distinctive yellow scarf the Jews all had to wear and paid an outrageous amount for a filthy vermin-ridden pallet and a cup of thin soup.

Sibillia suffered all through the night, coughing till I feared she would retch up her insides. As the sky began to lighten, a jet of black blood gushed from her mouth. I ran, looking for help. Everyone was just as sick. I found a wooden hut with smoke trickling from a makeshift chimney. A man stood outside, a shovel in one hand. As I hurried towards him, he lifted his arm to press his wrist against his mouth and nose.

'Help me, please . . . she's dying.'

'I know you, you're the witch. Filthy witches and Jews, you're what's brought the wrath of God down upon us.' He made the sign of the cross, with a hand whose nails were black and rotten, then went inside the hut and shut the door in my face.

I went back to Sibillia and sat with her head cradled in my lap, stroking back her white hair, until she coughed and wheezed no more. Soon, the corpse-bearers came, calling through their white-beaked masks, *'Corpi morti! Corpi morti!'*

One of them was the man who had spat at my feet. I recognised him by his blackened nails. He and his partner picked Sibillia's body up by the arms and the feet and flung her into the cart. Then the man picked up a broken brick from the cart, wrenched open Sibillia's jaws and jammed the brick inside her mouth. I cried out in protest.

'She's a witch,' he said. 'She'll be chewing her way out of her shroud if we don't jam her jaws.'

'She's dead,' I wept.

'Shroud-eaters feast on the flesh of the dead, then rise from the ground to infect us all. If we don't jam her jaws, we'll have to dig her up later and burn her heart and liver.

We've got enough to do digging graves here without having to open them up again later.'

His partner leant in so close that I gagged on the foul gust of his breath. 'You can hear the shroud-eaters down in the ground, chewing away. First, they eat their way free of the shroud, then they gnaw off their own fingers, then they start on the bodies of the other dead. You can hear them grunting and snuffling and chomping away down there.'

'They'll eat their way out eventually, and then come looking for living flesh to gnaw,' the man with the black fingernails said.

His partner leant in even closer, fondling my waist. 'Don't worry, *bella,* if you're afraid you can cuddle up with me tonight. I'll keep you safe.'

'Don't touch me.' I shoved him away.

He laughed, and together they trundled the cart away down to the warehouse, stopping to collect other dead bodies, and I stood, my fists clenched, wanting to scream and rage at them. If I'd had a sword to hand, I would have run them through with pleasure, enjoying the spurt of their crimson life-blood. It was only then that I realised I had come to love Sibillia. She had indeed been a second mother to me.

I went down to the beach and waded into the lagoon, and I scrubbed the smell of that foul place off me, using handfuls of sand to scour my skin. As I scrubbed, I wept, and as

I wept, I planned what I would do to that rotten-fingered man. I'd curse him till his fingers and toes all dropped off. I'd fill his sleep with nightmares. I'd raise Sibillia from the plague-pit and send her to haunt him till he gouged out his own eyes and tore off his own ears.

And then I would go and read every word of every book of Sibillia's, till I found the spell to make sure I never grew old and died.

Touch Me Not

Venice, Italy — March 1512

I knew curses and charms and cantrips aplenty, spells to bind and to banish, spells to enthral and to enfeeble.

Yet the one thing I could not banish was boredom. Not one of the men who crowded around my velvet chaise longue every night aroused even the faintest flicker of interest in me.

Until I met again the young artist who had kissed me during Carnevale so long ago. He appeared at the brothel one spring night, almost two years after Sibillia's death. He came in, shabbier than ever, paint on his hands, his dark curls in wild disarray.

'Look, it's Tiziano Vecellio,' a fat merchant said. 'He must have returned from Padua.'

'He's probably looking for a new model,' another man said. 'No respectable woman would ever let him paint her.'

I stood up and moved towards him, smiling. He saw me through the crowd and came eagerly towards me. 'It's you, my beautiful redhead from Carnevale.' A shadow flicked across his face. 'I didn't realise you were . . .'

'I was not when I first saw you.' For some reason, this seemed important for him to know.

'You were certainly well guarded then,' he answered with a quick wry grin. 'What happened?'

'The plague.'

At once, his eyes flashed to mine. 'I'm sorry. I lost friends in the plague too.'

'There are few in Venice who did not.' I gestured to a servant for some more wine, then raised high my goblet. 'To life.'

'And beauty.' His face was sombre. I was glutted with compliments, yet these words of his pleased me. I smiled. He picked up a lock of my hair, coiling it around his finger. 'It is the colour of fire, of passion, of life itself. It's a colour to warm the soul.'

My heart quickened, heat in my cheeks and in my loins. I wanted him to kiss me again — me, Selena Leonelli, who hated to be kissed. I let my clients slobber all over my body, but never, ever, on the mouth. My desire astonished me.

'Can you stand very still?' he asked me.

Once again, his words surprised me. I thought of how often I stood, cold as a statue, as I was looked over by prospective clients. The other girls flirted and giggled and wriggled their hips. Yet there was always someone who wanted me.

I nodded.

'Would you let me paint you? I cannot pay much.'

I thought of some of the great paintings I had seen in churches and salons in Venice, the women in them immortalised, their beauty untouched by worms and maggots.

'Yes,' I answered. 'When?'

'I need you to kneel here,' Tiziano said, pushing me down onto a cushion on the floor. His hand was hot through the thin fabric of my chemise. 'Lean forward, like so.'

I obeyed, bracing one hand on the floor, looking up at him.

'Here, put your hand on this pot.' He passed me a small round jar with a lid. When I leant my weight on it, it cut into my hand.

'I was painting my neighbour's daughter but she could not stand having to hold the pose so long and began to cry,' he told me. 'The tears were just what I wanted. My Mary needs to be weeping and in despair, but then transfigured at seeing the resurrected body of the man she loves. It was wonderful when she began to weep. I got the first glimmer of how the painting should be. But then, when I finally let her go home, her mother said she could not come any more, that I was cruel to her. Cruel. Did she not realise I am trying to make a masterpiece?'

'Do you wish me to weep?' I was not pleased by the idea. I had not wept since Sibillia died, and I was determined to never do so again. Tears undermined your strength the way the sea washes away a sandcastle.

'I want you to look up at me and realise that your beloved is not dead after all but alive,' he said.

I remembered how my mother had looked when my father had come to the palazzo, how she had run barefoot across the hall and leapt into his arms. I reached up one hand to Tiziano.

'Yes,' Tiziano cried and bent over me, catching my hand. 'That's it! Don't move.'

He hurried to his easel and swirled the paintbrush in paint. He looked at the painting, then at me, then bent his attention to the canvas again. Soon, my back was aching, my knees crying out in torment, but I did not move. I fixed my eyes on the ceiling and thought of my mother's face, illuminated with joy. In all the horror of what had come after, I had forgotten how she looked then, how much she had loved my father.

'I have been thinking of death a great deal since the plague,' Tiziano said in a low voice, dabbing at the canvas with a brush loaded with red paint. 'My friend Zorzi died, you see. Giorgione Barbarelli was his real name. He was a great artist. Almost as great as me.'

He cast me an impish grin. 'I decided I wanted to paint the scene just before the Ascension, the moment when Mary Magdalene sees the Saviour risen from the cross and realises the gift of his sacrifice, that one day we too shall follow him and experience our own resurrection.'

My shoulders sagged. I had thought I sensed a wildness in him, a sensuality, a longing for freedom that matched my own. Yet here he was, mouthing the same empty platitudes I heard from the church pulpit. Then, once again, Tiziano surprised me.

'I want to show how Mary loved Jesus as a woman loves a man, with all the force of her ardent nature, and how he too yearns towards her. He wants to touch her, he wants to feel the press of her flesh against his, yet he must not. It is time for him to leave such longings behind. Yet she is so beautiful and loves him so much, and he cannot bear to hurt her. And so he says to her, "Don't touch me," but it is a plea as much as a command.'

His words had been so soft I could hardly hear him. Unconsciously, I had turned my face towards him, to watch his face. He felt my gaze and looked up again. 'Don't move.'

I smiled at him.

He smiled back involuntarily. 'Why are you smiling?'

'I don't know. I'm sorry. I'm supposed to be weeping, aren't I?'

'I think I like smiling better than weeping.'

'May I get up? I'm not used to spending so much time on my knees.' I spoke with soft innuendo, but Tiziano only sighed and looked at his painting.

He answered courteously enough, 'Of course. Get up, move around. I think I have you anyway.'

I straightened my back with a groan, then tried to get up, but my knees were so stiff that I staggered. Tiziano hurried forward to offer me his hand. It was so large and broad that my own disappeared inside it. He lifted me up effortlessly and held me steady till my legs were able to hold me up. Then he went back to examine his painting again with a cool frowning glance. I walked around, looking at other paintings stacked up against the wall, a little disconcerted. Any other man would have tried to kiss me, or made a lewd comment about what else I could do while on my knees, but Tiziano seemed utterly absorbed in his painting.

'May I see it?' I asked.

'I suppose so. It's not any good. The figure of Mary is beautiful enough, and I think I've caught some of your expression, but the rest is all wrong.'

I stood beside him and stared at the canvas. 'I like the countryside.'

'I tried to capture the view as it looks from the village where I grew up: Pieve di Cadore, near Belluno. The ground falls away into blue infinity, and you think you can see forever.'

'You grew up in the country? Did you have a garden?'

'The whole of the valley was our garden. You've never seen such flowers. When I was ten, I painted a Madonna and Child, with a little boy-angel, from juice squeezed from wildflowers and berries, on the walls of the Casa Sampieri. My family were so amazed that they sent me here to Venice, so I could be apprenticed to Zuccato, who made mosaics. It was not long before I realised it was painting I wanted to do, though, so I convinced the Bellini brothers to take me on and teach me.'

He scowled at the painting. 'I want to be even better than they were, though. I want to be the greatest painter ever. Yet it never comes out how I see it in my head. Something's wrong. The balance. Or the shape.'

'Why is Jesus wearing a hat?' I asked.

He glanced at me in surprise. 'Well, it's a gardener's hat. When Mary first sees him in the garden of Gethsemane, she thinks he's a gardener. See, he has a hoe too.'

'I can see he might catch up a hoe to lean on, if he was as stiff and sore as I was when I first got up. But why a hat?'

'Why indeed?' he asked himself, under his breath, and laid one finger over Jesus' head, hiding the hat, then drew it away.

I gazed at the depiction of myself. I was only a small presence in the painting, my face in profile, my figure concealed beneath flowing white sleeves. To me, the single tree that struck across the top half of the painting seemed to grab the eye much more than my figure, crouching at its base. And the figure of Jesus, rather than being tempted by my beauty, seemed to be fleeing away from it. I said as much, trying to conceal my pique beneath a note of warm teasing.

Tiziano just stared at the painting. 'Would you kneel again, just as you were before?'

I did as he asked, with a flounce of my red skirt. I tossed back my hair, braced my hand painfully on the jar and fixed my gaze upwards again. Tiziano called one of his apprentices, busy grinding powders at the far end of the studio, and ordered him to come and stand before me, dressed in nothing but a sheet knotted loosely about his loins. The apprentice was only young, a year or so older than me. He flushed at the sight of me kneeling at his feet and bent towards me, no doubt trying to peek down my bodice.

'Yes,' Tiziano whispered, and he began to paint furiously, sometimes throwing down his brush and smearing paint with his fingers. The apprentice stood frozen in place, holding his arm in front of him as if trying to hide his erection.

Soon, my knees were screaming with pain

again. The ache in my lower back spread slowly up towards my awkwardly braced shoulders, but I did not move or speak. It was as if I was having a silent battle of wills with Tiziano. *Notice me. Notice I'm in pain. Notice that it's dark outside, and I've been here for hours, and you've not even offered me a drink.*

At last, his apprentice gave a kind of moan and turned away from me. 'I . . . I need to . . .' he said and hurried away towards the door.

'Poor boy. Do you think he needed to pee? He must've been holding it in for hours.'

Tiziano lifted his head and glanced at me, as if surprised I was still there. 'Has it been hours?'

'Hours and hours,' I responded. 'May I be permitted to straighten my back? Though I am not at all sure that I can.'

He lifted me to my feet. 'I'm so sorry. Look, it's dark. I had no idea it was so late. You should've said something.'

'And interrupted the genius at work? I wouldn't dare.'

'You should have spoken earlier, reminded me what time it was.'

'You seemed absorbed. I did not want to break your concentration.' Despite myself, my voice had softened a little. The feel of his warm hands tingling on my shoulder and back, the earthy, outdoorsy smell of him, combined to allay my displeasure.

'Thank you,' he said. 'Not just for being so patient for so long. Come and see the painting.'

This time, I stood and stared in silence. The changes were small, but somehow the whole feeling of the painting had changed. The scarlet turmoil of my skirts showed I had flung myself down in some strong emotion. The brilliant splash of colour drew the eye irresistibly to me. My hair was disordered, as if I had just risen from a restless sleep. And now the figure of Jesus bent towards me, as though he longed to reach down and catch my hand, drawing me up against his almost naked body. Instead, though, he drew away the folds of his shroud, afraid that the merest touch of my fingers would unman him. The hat was gone, and the face looking down at me with such tenderness was that of Tiziano himself.

EARTHLY LOVE

Venice, Italy — 1512 to 1516
Yet Tiziano did not try to seduce me, even as
the year rolled towards autumn and he
painted me once again.

I didn't understand why. I could tell he
desired me. Sometimes, he stared at me with
such intensity that I felt my loins clench. But
no matter how I tempted him — brushing
my thigh against his, crossing my arms so my
cleavage deepened — he only frowned and
looked away. He wanted me yet would not
touch me.

Instead, he ran his fingertips through the
colours squeezed onto his palette, then
caressed my painted form on the canvas. He
wanted to capture me binding up my loosened hair, as if I had just risen from my
lover's bed. I stood there, my *camìcia* slipping off my shoulders, for days, pretending I
did not feel the scorch of his gaze on my bare
throat and shoulders. He would not let me
see the painting, not till the last day when he

363

was adding the last few touches with a brush as thin as the tip of a lock of my hair. I demanded to see what he had created. He refused. I threatened to never sit for him again. Reluctantly, he stood aside and let me see.

I looked dreamy, satiated. My skin was illuminated with warm candlelight, my river of loose crinkled hair glowing like newly polished bronze. The vivid blue of the robe draped in the lower corner of the portrait only made me look more luminous. It took me a moment to notice I was not alone at my toilette. A man — Tiziano — stood behind me in the shadows, almost invisible. He gazed at me with such troubled longing, as if wishing he dared bend and press a kiss against my bare shoulder. In the mirror behind me was my dim reflection, a block of light angled above my head like a crooked halo.

I stood still before this painting of me, filled with a most unusual sense of humility. I had seen my own face and form in a mirror before. I knew I was beautiful. Yet somehow, in Tiziano's painting, I realised what Sibillia had meant when she said beauty was both a gift and a curse.

I looked up at him. 'In the painting, you look as though you desire me.' There was no reproach in my voice, only a wish to understand.

'I do . . .' Tiziano cleared his throat. 'I do

desire you. Very much.'

'Then why do you not take me to bed? You must know that you can.'

'I cannot pay for love. It is something that should be given freely between a man and a woman.' He looked away, his swarthy cheeks darkening. 'Besides, I could not afford you.'

'If you give me this painting, you may have me in return,' I said.

Tiziano glanced at me quickly. 'You love it so much?'

I nodded.

He frowned. 'I need it. I must make a sale if I am to afford to keep on painting, and this is the best work I have ever done.'

'Could you not make me a copy? To have for my own? I will keep it in my private rooms where no one will ever see it.' I leant towards him so that he could see the pale curve of my breast and smell the warm scent of my body, anointed that morning with jasmine and rose for the sole purpose of arousing him. I cannot tell you why I wanted him to want me so much, when I was sick and weary with being wanted. It is not enough to think that it was simply because he made no move towards me. The reasons were more complex than that. I think now it was because I understood that he was the only man who could truly immortalise me, capturing me in all my fresh beauty on the canvas.

'I could paint another one,' he said slowly.

'So we have an agreement?' I was puzzled as to why he did not look at me, let alone seize me in his arms and devour my mouth with his. Sexual tension crackled between us, as it had done from our very first meeting. Yet still he stared away from me, his whole body rigid with unhappiness.

'What is wrong?' I asked.

'I do not think I can share you with anyone else. You're a whore, Selena. You sell your body to men. I cannot bear to think of those fat rich men pawing at you. How can I make love to you when I know you have come to me from another man and will go from me to yet another?'

I took a deep breath, feeling my ribs hurt. For a second, tears stung my eyes.

'I have no choice,' I said. 'How else am I to live? My parents are both dead. My father was murdered, and his killers raped my mother. She poisoned herself and left me all alone. I was little more than a child. Tell me what else I could do?'

Tiziano stared at me, eyes wide and shocked. Then his mouth twisted and he reached for me. I went into his arms and pressed my face against his strong shoulder. I may even have wept a little. Just a little. Then I lifted my face and blindly sought his mouth. For a moment longer, he resisted me, but I pressed myself against him, moulding my body against his, kissing his cheek, his throat, his mouth until at last he took a deep uneven breath and bent me back over his arm, his mouth frantically seeking mine. Although I had had sex till I was weary of it, I had never kissed before. I had never been able to bear it. Now, though, my mouth opened wide for him. I sucked his tongue deeper. My whole body melted. We fell to the floor, Tiziano tearing at the sash of my dress. The bare floorboards were below me, my skirt was rucked above my knees and he was wildly dragging at his hose, his urgent desire near bursting his seams. I laughed out loud and pressed my mouth to the pulse in the hollow of his throat. I felt gloriously, powerfully alive. Invincible.

Our love affair was tempestuous. We made love, quarrelled, threw wine glasses, banged doors, swore never to see each other again, only to meet at a party and make love against the wall in the stinking alley outside. He sold his painting of me for a large sum, and we celebrated by getting drunk and spending the night dancing, kissing, gambling and making love in my gondola as the silver dawn turned Venice into a fairy-tale city of towers and domes wreathed in mist. Far to the north, the violet-blue shape of the Dolomites bulged above the panoply of clouds. Half-naked, Tiziano lay in my arms and gazed at their mysterious heights.

'I was born there, you know. One day, I will

buy a house that looks upon the mountains.'

'You do not wish to go back, to live there again?' I asked, drawing circles on his smooth back. My breast looked very white against his warm olive skin.

He cast me a scornful look. 'I would if I could. But there are no patrons in Cadore, no one to buy my paintings. If I am to make a living from my art, I must be here in Venice, or go to Rome or Florence or Mantua.'

'But surely your art is something that you should give freely to the world?' I mocked him. 'God forbid that you should be paid for your labour.'

He scowled. 'It's different. I'm a man. I need to support myself and my family.'

'While I, being a woman, should be nothing but a man's decorative possession, my life spent bound to another's will.'

It was an old argument, one with no solution. Tiziano wanted to marry me and keep me under his hand, with nothing better to do than sweep his filthy floor and shop in the markets for bread and cheese and wine, or whatever it is that housekeepers buy. I relished my freedom, however. I relished my palazzo and my witch's garden, my stone chest full of books of magical lore, my own bed with clean crisp sheets that no one but me ever slept in, the cool rooms kept in perfect order by my housekeeper, a whiskery old woman who lived to sweep away cobwebs and polish silver.

No man was ever permitted to step inside my high stone walls. Not even Tiziano. Some whores held court at their own house, their bills paid by a rich patron, other men knocking on their door at any time of day or night. Not I. My address was kept secret, as were my true name and my history. My gondolier came at dusk every evening and ferried me to the salon of my procuress, Angela, where men paid for the honour of my company for an hour. I sang and played the lute, and argued about art and nature and religion and politics, and occasionally allowed a man to clasp me in his arms and dance with me around the ballroom. No man was ever permitted to think he had a right to my time and my company, let alone my body. Sometimes, I allowed a man to take me to one of the bedrooms in Angela's palazzo. More often, I refused, no matter how heavy the bag of coins dangled before my eyes. I was cruel and scornful and capricious, which only made me more eagerly sought after.

It was a dangerous game, though, and I needed a bodyguard. I wanted a woman but soon realised that men held women in contempt, regardless of their size and strength. No woman would ever be able to give me that aura of invincibility that I needed.

One day, I was searching through the Jewish quarter for old books when a giant of a man dressed in little more than rags came in to pawn a battered old cittern. As soon as he spoke, I was struck by his high shrill tone, the voice of a boy inside the body of an oversized man. I also saw the way his fists clenched and his brow lowered as he was mocked by the young bloods jostling to pawn their jewels. *Rascaglione,* they called him. Eunuch.

I followed the eunuch out into the street. *'Signor,'* I called.

He turned, glowering. 'What do you want?'

'I'm looking for a singer, a musician, to play at my parties.'

'I can sing no longer.' As he spoke the word 'sing', his voice suddenly changed, growing deeper and more melodious.

I raised one eyebrow, and he added gruffly, 'The wind was in the wrong quarter when they took my manhood. I lost my voice.' Again, the timbre of his voice shifted, squeaking like an old wheel.

I considered him. He was huge, his fists as big as cobblestones. 'I need a bodyguard. You must understand, though, that I demand utter loyalty.'

He looked me over. 'How much?'

I named a sum, plus food and board. His face lit up. He glanced back at the pawnshop. 'Can I have some in advance? To get back my cittern?'

'You have no need of that,' I said. 'Your

voice is gone and will never come back. It is no use dreaming of what can never be.'

As his shoulders slumped and he fell into step behind me, I thought what I must do to make this true. Music was a jealous mistress, and I wanted no rival for his loyalties.

Over the years, I found out most of Magli's story. It was simple enough. A sweet singer as a child, his parents had sold him to the Pope's men, who took him to a butcher in a back street to be castrated like a calf. They poured opium-laced brandy down his throat, put him in a cold bath and held him down while the butcher chopped away his small soft penis and left him with a mess of scars and a wounded soul. The butcher had botched the job, or it had been too late and Magli's voice was already beginning to break, or he had been too shocked by his betrayal. Who knows? His soprano did not survive the knife, so he was abandoned by the Pope's men and left to beg in the streets. He was the perfect body-guard, hating all men who had what he did not, and loving the woman who gave him a home and a purpose.

Soon, I was as famous for my eunuch as I was for my beauty and my devilish temper. I bought myself a lynx and a small black girl to carry my train, and I wore dresses that were cut as low as my navel and left my long red-gold hair flowing freely like a banner of war. So I became the most expensive and eagerly sought-after courtesan in Venice.

Poor Tiziano. I think he wished to murder me sometimes, and other times to lock me away with a key, to keep me all for his own. He adored me and hated me in equal measure. I could have married him, and won his heart forever, but that I would not do. No man shall have dominion over me, I declared. Ever.

But Tiziano could not do without me. My face was making him his fortune. He painted me as Flora, with my *camìcia* slipping so low off my shoulder that the eye naturally sought a glimpse of my nipple. He painted me as Salome, cradling John the Baptist's head on a silver platter like a haunch of roast pork. He painted me as a naked nymph in a sylvan landscape, listening to two musicians play, oblivious to my voluptuous presence. He painted me as the Virgin Mary, surrounded by adoring cherubs and angels, aloft on a cloud above a world of saints and sinners.

I was now eighteen. I was beginning to fear the loss of my beauty and, with it, my power. Tiziano had found another model, a pretty enough little milksop called Violante, who began to appear in a number of paintings as a sweet blonde with a yearning face. I knew Tiziano well. He could not see so clearly into her soul without having slept with her. I accused him. He denied it. I slapped him and kicked him, and swore I would kill her. He was frightened and told me to leave her alone. 'Just tell me the truth,' I demanded. 'It's cowardly to lie. I hate cowards.'

'Very well,' he admitted. 'I slept with her. Why shouldn't I? You sleep with ten men a night.'

'I do not. How dare you? I'm no street whore, fucking ten men a night in a back alley. I'm a courtesan of honour.'

'So sorry. Such a difference, fucking strangers in the street or in a silk-hung bed. You're still a whore.'

'I'm a courtesan, that's how I make my living. Just like you paint endless paintings of cherubs and saints, when what you really want to do is paint real people doing real things. You prostitute yourself to make a living. You just do it with a brush and I do it with my body.'

So once again we had a parting of ways. I went back to my white immaculate house and sat in my white immaculate bedroom and wept. Tears of rage, nothing more. Would I grieve for a peasant painter with hands like a market gardener? I think not. Let him have his pretty little powder puff. Let him see how much her paintings brought. He would crawl back to me in the end.

In the morning, I woke, my face stiff with dried tears. I staggered to my dressing table, to splash water on my face. I saw myself in the mirror, haggard, with swollen eyes and blotchy skin. My breath snagged in my throat. I looked old and worn and weary. I looked from my mirror to the painting of myself looking into a mirror, and I was frightened. I spent all of that day and the next and the next and the next reading through Sibillia's stone chest. When a bill needed to be paid, I plastered my face with white lead and went to Angela's salon, where I fucked whoever had the fattest money roll. I drank too much and ate too much and laughed too much, and spent all day searching for the secret to eternal youth. Sibillia had never been beautiful; she had only wanted to trick time into allowing her to live longer than the natural span of years. I wanted more. I wanted to stay beautiful forever.

I found one clue in a fragment of scorched parchment, and another in a rambling philosophical treatise in Ancient Greek (it took me a while to learn to translate that one). An old spell in a scroll, combined with notes scribbled in Sibillia's own secret code (which was harder to crack than the Ancient Greek), and I began to have an inkling to the secret. Blood. It was always blood.

Sibillia was right when she said it was hard to find a virgin in Venice. All the little girls were locked up either in convents or behind the high walls of their families' homes, or were already whoring on the streets. And I wanted someone clean, uncorrupted, with skin as white as lilies and hair as red as flame. I wanted someone who looked like me, before that dreadful night had charred my soul.

I found her eventually, a foundling child living at the Ospedale della Pietà. Her name was Abundantia. I adopted her and brought her back to my home. At first, she was gloriously happy, her grey eyes starry, her thin face lit up with joy. But though I was kind enough to her and she had plenty to eat, all the light died out of her once I began to bathe in her blood. It was only nine drops; it hardly hurt her at all. I cannot understand why she hated it so much. I had been happy enough to let Sibillia suck on my wrist. And it was only once a month. The rest of the time, she was free to do as she pleased, as long as she did not go outside my walls. I knew what men were like; it wasn't worth the risk. The silly girl did not see it that way, however. She kept trying to escape. Once, she even got so far as the Calle Tiepolo before Magli found her and brought her home.

My spell worked, however. I had never been more beautiful. I often saw Tiziano in the streets and salons, and although I ignored him I was always at my most brilliant and amusing when he was present.

In the spring of the year 1514, Tiziano came to see me at Angela's salon and dropped to his knees before me. 'Selena, I need you.'

I arched one eyebrow (an art that took me

a long time and a great deal of practice in the mirror to achieve). 'Indeed? Bored of Violante?'

'She never meant a thing to me. She was just . . . a consolation.'

'Really? I heard she got the pox and is sadly disfigured.'

A shadow crossed Tiziano's face. He looked away, his broad chest rising and falling rapidly as if he fought some strong emotion.

'So, what do you want of me?' I spoke coolly.

'Selena, I've been offered a commission . . . it's incredibly important. I need the most beautiful woman in the world to sit for me.' His intense gaze was fixed on my face, his rough peasant hand grasping mine tightly.

I laughed. 'And I am the most beautiful woman in the world to you now, am I? I thought simpering little blondes were more to your taste.'

He shook his head. 'Please, Selena, no one else will do.'

The painting was to commemorate the marriage of Niccolò Aurealio, secretary for the Council of Ten, to the young widow Laura Bagarotto. Signor Aurealio did not just want a painting of exquisite beauty, which celebrated love; he also wanted a painting that would subtly restore the reputation of his bride. For Laura was the daughter of the traitor Bertuccio Bagarotto, who had been hanged between the columns in the piazza five years earlier, before the eyes of his wife and children. Laura had lost her dowry and her status; her husband-to-be wanted both reinstated.

So Tiziano painted me twice. Once, clothed and demure, my hair bound up with myrtle like a new bride's, with one red sleeve to symbolise my hidden sensuality. The second time, on the opposite half of the canvas, he painted me naked except for a tiny wisp of white cloth, red draperies billowing behind me. Once as Earthly Love, once as Heavenly Love. Once as Innocence, once as Experience. Once as Virgin, once as Wife. The possible interpretations were endless. Tiziano was nothing if not clever. Perhaps that was why he was the only man to make my pulse beat faster, the only man I ever met with the wit to match me.

We were lovers again, our passion deeper and more desperate than ever. I even made excuses to my procuress, going to her salon only when I had to, and making up the deficit in my income from love spells and curses, grinding up roots and berries in my stillroom, the memory of Wise Sibillia always etched in acid before my mind's eye.

It was a dangerous time to make a living as a witch. The Roman Inquisition had sent Dominican friars out into the countryside, searching for heretics and sorcerers. More than sixty so-called witches were burnt to death in Brescia, and many hundreds more were investigated. I don't think many had any real power, though I managed to buy a few tattered old handwritten manuscripts, passed down through generations of some of the families who died. The Grand Inquisitor had even prevailed upon the Council of Ten to lock up all the Jews of Venice on a dirty little island, called Ghetto Nuova as it had once been used as a foundry. No Jew was permitted to leave the island without wearing a red hat to mark their race, and all had to be back within the high walls of their island by nightfall.

Mindful of my own safety, I cultivated the Grand Inquisitor as a client, though I disliked the stench of smoke that hung around his hair and clothes, and his cold bony hands on my body. He took pleasure from pain and always left red marks on my neck and breasts, and bruises between my thighs. I did not mind the pain so much — pain is proof that you're alive — but the smell was unendurable. He was one of those men who think sanctity is found in dirt.

Giovanni Bellini, Tiziano's teacher, died in the winter of 1516 and was buried in the Basilica di san Giovanni e Paolo, where the doges were always buried. This plunged Tiziano into melancholy for weeks. He did not paint, he did not drink and he did not want to make love. The signing of a treaty with the Holy Roman Empire, which brought to an end two decades of war and sent La Serenissima into a delirium of relieved decadence, hardly lightened his mood. He was a man who felt things deeply, my lover Tiziano. Misery and despair; passion and exultation: there was no fulcrum between the two. He was afraid he would die before achieving anything great, that he would be snuffed out like a candle, leaving nothing but a frail wraith of smoke that soon drifted away into darkness. I understood this terror. It shadowed my life as it shadowed his.

One night, when the moon was full, I went to him naked under my velvet cloak, with a vial of Abundantia's blood hanging between my breasts. In my basket, I carried a leather bottle of freshly pressed apple juice, mixed with apple cider at the peak of its strength, and apple brandy, mellowed and old. I ordered a bath to be poured for us both, then banished his brother and all his apprentices and servants — I never could understand why he must always have such a crowd around him. Then, by the light of the full moon, I carefully dripped nine drops of red blood into the warm water in which we wallowed, and I spoke the words of the spell, and I made him drink.

I had never had to rouse him to make love before, but that night he was shrivelled and limp. I worked as hard as I ever had for the oldest and most impotent of my clients, and at last brought him to climax, the bloodied waves of the bath surging about us.

I will keep you safe, we shall both live forever, together, I exulted.

I woke in the morning, stretching like a cat, fulfilled and content. Normally, I didn't stay, unable to bear the dirt and chaos and noise of Tiziano's studio. I had wanted to stay that night, though, bound close to my lover by blood magic.

The bed beside me was empty. Sleepily, I looked around. Tiziano was painting, bent over his canvas like a miser over a chest of jewels. I got up, wrapping the sheet about me, and padded silently over to the canvas.

He had been working on another portrait of me looking into a mirror, because demands for one like the original kept pouring in from all the duchies of Italy. In the painting, I was dressed in the same loose green gown and white *camìcia* as before, my hair bound back with a translucent scarf. Tiziano had not included himself in this painting, however. I stood alone, holding my own mirror.

I stood close beside Tiziano, leaning my head against his broad shoulder, and gazed at the painting. My eyes swept the canvas with sleepy pleasure. Then they widened, my pupils dilating, my heart surging into a rapid staccato beat. For a moment, I could not

380

breathe, I could not speak, then rage swept through me. I pummelled him with my fists, shrieking, 'Why? Why? Why?'

He had painted an image of a bent old woman in the mirror. Her face was hollowed and wrinkled, her hair grey, and she could only stand with the help of a distaff. In my hand, instead of a pot of perfume, I held an extinguished candle, smoke wreathing upwards.

'I shall call it "Vanity",' Tiziano told me, his face graven with deep lines, his eyes bloodshot. He looked as if he had not slept.

'Do you seek to curse me?' I cried. 'Change it. Change it, or I will curse you!'

His mouth set in a stubborn line I knew all too well.

'Change it, or I'll curse you,' I said, in a low steadfast voice.

Slowly, he raised his brush and swept it across the haggard old woman, extinguishing her. With a few deft daubs, he painted in a spill of coins and jewellery where her face had been. He did not look at me.

I wrapped myself in my cloak, gathered up my empty vial and went towards the door.

His voice stopped me. 'I am going to Ferrara. The Duc d'Este wants me to paint pictures for his Camerino d'Alabastro. He wants it to be the talk of all of Christendom. I don't know how long I'll be away.' He did not look at me as he spoke, all his attention

381

on gilding the coins on the canvas.
I laughed and went on my way.
He was afraid of me, the coward.
He should be.

TIZIANO AND HIS MISTRESS

Venice, Italy — 1516 to 1582
There was no escaping time in Venice.

Every square had its church, with bells that tolled out the passing of the hours.

At the clock tower in Piazza San Marco, the Moors swung their hammers at the great bell every hour, and a gilded ball showed the waxing and waning of the moon. I went to the Piazza San Marco only when I had to. The clanging of that bell made me feel dizzy and sick. My heartbeat accelerated, as if I had run up all the stairs to the top of the clock tower, when I was only standing in its shadow. I wanted to get away, but my legs trembled so much I could scarcely walk.

One day, the Grand Inquisitor brought his new toy to show me. Of all the men who bought my favours, the Grand Inquisitor was one I never dared to turn away, even though he was in Venice only under sufferance from the Council of Ten, who had told him dryly that they thought the poor peasants of the

Veneto — suffering greatly under the scourge of the Roman Inquisition — were in need of a good preaching rather than persecution. The Grand Inquisitor was a tall spare man with a pale ascetic face, who relished the heavy dark robes of his Dominican order since they hid any erection the sight of a young devout girl in church might bring. His new toy was a portable clock, an incredibly tiny mechanism no larger than the size of my clenched fist, which he wore on a chain around his neck. It ticked loudly the whole time he jerked in and out of me, each brutal thrust marking off the seconds of my life. I could not breathe, my lungs cramping with panic. I could not pretend to enjoy what was happening. Indeed, I cringed and flinched and whimpered and bit back sobs, wishing I could seize that little clock and smash it to the floor and stamp on it and stamp on it and stamp on it till nothing was left but bent metal, mangled cogs and wheels, and smith-ereens of glass. And silence.

The Grand Inquisitor seemed to like my whimpers. He finished sooner than usual but came back the next day, and the next, so a new torture was added to my life: the caustic tick-tock of a clock.

Tiziano came back to Venice but did not seek me out. In fact, he must have gone to some pains to avoid me. I soon heard that he had taken his housekeeper — a conniving young woman called Cecilia — as his mistress. She was the daughter of the village barber from Tiziano's home town of Cadore, come to Venice for the sole purpose of serving him. I never met her, though I soon knew her face, for Tiziano painted her as he had once painted me, with single-minded obsession. She was pretty enough, I suppose, though nothing could disguise her thick peasant neck and ankles. She must have been disgustingly healthy too, for she delivered him up two strapping baby boys in the next few years and did not seem to suffer from any of my ill-wishing. All that happened was she got sick and almost died, and Tiziano hurriedly married her to legitimise his sons. It made me grind my teeth in annoyance. I could not cast a stronger curse without being able to get hold of some of her hair or fingernails, but it seemed the barber's daughter from Cadore was an efficient housekeeper, if nothing else.

I told myself I did not care, and, indeed, I truly believed I did not. I luxuriated in a life of semen-stained silken sheets, priceless perfumes, rare delicacies, glittering jewels and, in defiance of the sumptuary laws, the most luxurious clothes Venice could produce. I surrounded myself with the most vicious and depraved rakes in Venice, all eager to buy what I could sell. Apart from maintaining my perfect never-ageing body, I concocted all kinds of spells from the plants in my witch's garden. Tea made from mandrake roots, powders ground from angel's trumpet, potions made from nightshade and black hellebore, wine made from juniper berries and fennel, anything that would bring delirium and desire. I bought opium from sailors returned from the East China coast, wild mushrooms plucked from the Black Forest, strange-tasting powders carried to Venice along the Silk Road, and tobacco brought back from the New World by Spanish soldiers. Angela's salon became renowned for being the wildest, the most debauched and most expensive in Venice. Fathers warned young men away from me, which only made them flock to me in greater numbers. I became very rich.

One winter's night, our carousing lasted till dawn. I had dismissed my gondolier hours before, and when I came staggering out of Angela's palazzo it was to find torrents of rain sweeping over the plaza, and not a gondola in sight.

'What's a little rain?' I slurred. 'It'll wash away our sins. Come on, Magli, let's walk.'

My eunuch rarely spoke, hating the sound of his high squeaky voice, so he simply put up the hood of his cloak and offered me his arm. My *chopines* were so dangerously high that I could not walk without assistance. Together, we sloshed through the square, my velvet dress wet to above the knees in moments. Gaunt palazzos loomed above us, shuttered against the driving rain. Damp crept up from their foundations, the stones stained with mould. Water surged from the overflowing canals and poured from the gutters and drainpipes. Venice looked like it was about to sink below the waves, all its palaces and churches and squares drowned beneath the sea. On fine days, people would peer down from boats floating over our heads and point to see fish swimming through the clock tower at Piazza San Marco. They would cup their ears, listening for the tide to rock the great bells, tolling through the shadowy fathoms. Venice would drown and be nothing more than a memory, a myth, a vanished dream. Such sadness overwhelmed me. I felt tears catch in my throat. So I laughed and flung up my arms and danced a few wobbly steps, pretending I felt no fear and no grief. 'Drown me if you can,' I challenged the gloomy sky, and I almost fell. Only Magli's strong hand saved me.

I was giddy with opium smoke and wine. In a few hours, I'd be sick and in pain, my head throbbing cruelly, my body hurting from the pounding it had taken, but just now, in my mingling of sorrow and defiance, I felt completely and utterly alive.

A man hurried past us, his hood drawn over his face. I saw a quick glimpse of a strong hooked nose, a jutting beard, a flash of fierce black eyes.

'Tiziano! Are you on your way home too? You old devil. I had thought you all settled in smug domesticity. What does your dear little wife think of you being out all night?'

He turned on me, rage twisting his face. 'My wife is dead,' he managed to say, his voice raw. 'She died last night.'

I laughed.

In a flash, he struck out at me, but Magli caught his hand and bent his arm back till Tiziano was on his knees before me, the icy water up to his waist. 'Witch! Whore!' Tiziano spat.

'I had nothing to do with your wife's death. You of all people know that death can strike anyone down at any time.'

Tiziano bent his head. Tears were mingling with the rain on his face.

I bent down and took his bearded chin in my hand. 'What will you do now, without your simpering little wife to paint? Will you have to put your brushes away?'

He jerked his face away. 'There are plenty of beautiful women in Venice.'

'Yes, but you know and I know that you cannot paint just anyone. You need to see inside their souls, Tiziano. You need to know every curve of their body, every desire in their hearts, before you can truly bring them to life on the canvas. You need to make love to them, don't you, Tiziano? Yet you are such a prude you cannot make love unless you're *in* love.'

He looked away from me, despair and grief and anger all there on his face for me to see. I knew him so well, you see.

'You know where to find me. When you are ready to paint something truly great.' Then I kissed him full on the mouth. He wrenched his mouth away, but not before I felt his lips quiver in involuntary response. I smiled, gestured to Magli to let him go and went on my way through the deluge, feeling such a fizz and sparkle of excitement in my belly I could have opened my legs to Tiziano then and there, despite my soreness and tiredness. Tiziano stayed kneeling, his face bent down into his hands, rain sweeping over him.

Yet he did not come to me, as I had expected. Tiziano kept away from Venice altogether, travelling about, painting dukes and emperors, cardinals and popes, princes and baby princesses. Sometimes, my rage threatened to overcome me, and I'd roll in my bed, biting my pillows, swearing I'd curse him come morning. But I never did.

Every month, at the full of the moon, I went down to my cellar and took my nine drops from Abundantia's wrist. She no longer tried to escape but spent her days and nights sitting apathetically in her mound of dirty straw. She never permitted Magli to change her straw but cuddled it to her thin chest, growling at us through her teeth if we tried to take it away. She feared the light and screamed if we brought a lantern near her. So we approached her with a shielded candle and gentle words, and she would weep as Magli cut her arm and caught the blood flow in a little bowl. I would then bend to suck at the incision, and she moaned as if I had torn at her arm with fangs instead of licking her most delicately.

One day, as I came out of the cellar with my shielded candle, Abundantia whimpering behind me, I heard a quick frightened gasp of breath and then, almost soundless, the pad of bare feet running away. I hurried to the steps and saw a flash of white at the top as someone fled. Magli locked the cellar securely behind me, then waited for his orders, his face impassive.

'Quick, find out who that was. Check Filomena's room first. I've noticed her peeping and prying as she worked. My guess is it was her.'

Even as we hurried up the stairs, I heard the front door bang shut. 'Too late, she's gone,' I said. We checked her room anyway, and, sure enough, her bed was empty. Her cloak was missing from its peg, though her shoes were still set neatly under her chair. I bit my lip, thinking. Filomena was a new housemaid, brought in to help Old Speranza, who was finding the work keeping my palazzo in perfect order and cleanliness too hard for her now. Filomena had been with us for three months and had outwardly been very meek and demure. Her curiosity had evidently been too much for her, though.

'She will either run home to her mother and tell all she has seen and suspected, or she will keep her mouth shut but post an anonymous letter to the lion's mouth,' I said. 'Either way, we must be ready for a visit from the Inquisition.'

The banging on the door came only three hours later. Magli opened it and bowed deeply, letting in the three inquisitors in their stinking dark robes.

'I will wake Signorina Leonelli,' he squeaked, making the inquisitors smirk with malicious amusement.

I swept into the *portego* in a white silken robe, tied loosely over my nightgown so they had a perfect opportunity to ogle the cleft between my breasts. 'Gentlemen, what an unexpected pleasure. You must know I do not receive guests in my home, but for you, of course, I shall make an exception. Do you wish to take me all at once, or one at a time?'

'We are not here for pleasure, but for business,' the Grand Inquisitor said, though rather regretfully. 'Certain accusations have been made.'

'Indeed? Let me guess. Someone has said I

bathe in the blood of virgins in order to keep my beauty.' I rolled my eyes. 'Or is it something more original? Let me guess. It's that spiteful little cat, Guistina. She's jealous that I have more clients than her.'

'We cannot reveal the sources of our information,' the Grand Inquisitor said.

'Well, gentlemen, feel free to search my house. I can promise you there are no virgins here.' I smiled at the youngest of the inquisitors, who flushed to his ears and tried to tear his eyes away from my cleavage.

They went at once to the cellar, only to find my pet lynx lying curled asleep on a bed of straw, chained to a ring in the wall. She snarled at the sight of the strange men and lunged at them, and the inquisitors backed out of the cellar rapidly.

'You know my lynx, don't you?' I said. 'She can be rather noisy, so we keep her down here at night so I don't disturb my neighbours.'

The Grand Inquisitor frowned but nodded his head. The three Dominicans then made an extremely thorough search, but there was nothing to find. My stone chest was once again buried under the compost heap, all my poisons and spells and books of lore safely locked away inside. Though the youngest inquisitor prodded the compost heap with a pitchfork, Magli had buried the stone chest deep and he did not find it.

Six hours later, they left, though only after

I had let the Grand Inquisitor torture me a little, for his own amusement. When I was sure they were gone, I hurried to my gondola, rocking gently at its berth inside the watergate. Abundantia was hidden under the *felze,* tightly gagged and bound. I unravelled her gag with fingers that shook with fear as much as pain. I had given her opium to keep her quiet, but she had been left alone for a very long time.

I was too late, though. Abundantia was dead.

I wept like a new mother with a murdered child, rocking Abundantia in my arms. I carried her to my bedroom, laid her in my bath and washed her bony limbs and her long fiery hair. It was so beautiful, all the life force that was gone from her pallid face and limp body concentrated there, in the flowing red river of her hair. With my witch's knife, I cut it from her head, shaving as close to the scalp as I could get, and I bound it with a ribbon and climbed into bed, cuddling it under my cheek, tears overwhelming me once again.

I did not sleep at all that night, the pain in my heart far worse than the pain of my burnt arms and breast.

When birds began to tweet and the cuckoo gave its sly cry, I went to my maid Filomena's rooms, wrenched out a handful of hair from her brush and cast the swiftest cruellest curse I knew. No one could be permitted to betray me and get away with it. The next day, her foot slipped while getting off the barge to the mainland, where she no doubt hoped to escape my influence. She was crushed between the barge and the jetty. It took her days to die. It did not assuage my rage, however. So I cursed the Grand Inquisitor as well, and both his henchmen, and took pleasure in watching their slow decline.

Then I found myself another little red-headed girl — named Concetta, bless her. I wanted to take her away from Venice but found I could not leave it for more than a few days at a time. Sibillia had bound me to its stony labyrinth. So I travelled as far as I was able, searching for somewhere safe to hide Concetta.

I found the perfect place. An old watch-tower built on a high rock near the tiny village of Manerba, on the shores of Lake Garda. It was infested with bandits, but Magli and I soon drove them away with spectral sightings, wailings and a few eerie accidents. Concetta was as different as could be from Abundantia. She was glad to be released from the Pietà's dreary round of prayer and domestic chores. She loved food and pretty things, and was happy enough to offer up her arm for me to cut in return for toys and play-things. Her hair was the most beautiful thing I had ever seen, as full of changing colour as a fire of pine cones. She loved me to wash it and stroke it, and we spent many a happy hour combing and braiding each other's hair. Each time I visited her, she would fall asleep snuggling in my arms, the soft touch of her lips on my cheek making me happier than any man's thrusting tongue.

I came closer to loving that little girl than anyone since my mother had died.

Yet she too died. I came one day and found her lying cold in her bed. She must have been dead more than a week, for the room stank of her decay. Weeping, I laid her out in the lowest level of the tower and then I had Magli bury the door behind rocks. I sobbed all the way back to Venice, the first time I had allowed myself to weep since Abundantia had died. I did not go back to my empty immaculate palazzo. I did not go to Angela's and drown my grief in drugged wine. Hardly knowing what I did, I went to Tiziano's studio. He had got the house he wanted, a grand palazzo looking north towards the mountains. One of his apprentices let me in and I walked like a somnambulist towards his studio. Tiziano looked up as I stumbled in. He took one look at my red eyes, my tear-stained face, my disarrayed clothing and jumped up and guided me to a chair. He gave me wine and gently stroked back the hair from my forehead as I wept convulsively. When I was a little calmer, he took up his brush and began to paint me. Exhausted by then, I was content to sit as the daylight hours faded into twilight.

When it became too dark to see, he laid me down on his bed and made exquisite slow love to me. He was no longer a young man. His hair was silvered, he had a soft paunch instead of the hard muscled belly I remembered, and deep lines surrounded his eyes, but he still smelt of earth and pigments, and his broad rough hands still had the power to arouse me.

That painting became his first Mary Magdalene Penitent. It showed me half-naked, my breast peeping through the disorder of my long hair, my tear-wet eyes turned up to heaven. I hated it, hated being shown in all my weakness, but Tiziano loved it. He sold it for a great many ducats and wanted at once to paint another. But I would not let him. 'Paint me looking as beautiful as you can,' I begged. 'Please.'

For I had found a strand of grey in my fiery hair, a faint line scoring between my brows. Without being able to bathe in the blood of a virgin every full moon, my beauty would soon wither. I wanted him to capture me, once and for all, in the full glory of my loveliness.

So he painted me naked except for my tumbling red-gold hair, my hand cupping my pudenda as if about to pleasure myself, my eyes staring straight at the observer, my pupils dilated with desire. A small white dog frolicked at my feet. Behind me, two servant women began to lay out my gown for the evening. I do not think any more beautiful painting had ever been created.

A few months later, I spied a gorgeous redheaded girl skipping along beside her mother, her lustrous hair shining in the sun like a gilded banner. I had to have her. I sent Magli to steal her from her bed. We opened up the tower again and locked her away in the highest room, concealing the trapdoor beneath a rug. I wove Abundantia's and Concetta's hair into hers, so that I would have my dear ones close to me still. Each month, Magli tied a rope to the tail of an arrow and shot it up to the window with a longbow I had bought for him. Bonifacia — for that was her name — tied the rope to the hook so I could climb up to her. Each step I took up the high wall of that tower was made with a fast-beating heart, afraid the knot would slip and I would fall to my death. I began to think of a better way.

Bonifacia gave me many hours of joy, but in the end she too died, and so — weeping — I gave Tiziano another Mary Magdalene Penitent to paint.

When the preaching of the heretical Martin Luther spread like wildfire through Europe, Tiziano's paintings of Mary Magdalene Penitent became his studio's most popular production, as Catholics everywhere found their faith renewed in face of the Protestant uprisings.

Each time a little red-haired girl died in my tower, I would go heartbroken and inconsolable to Tiziano. Seven red-haired girls. Seven paintings of Mary Magdalene.

Let me remember my little loves.

Abundantia, whose body I kept enshrined in my cellar for years, before transferring her to the tower.

Concetta, who seemed to have died by choking on her own hair. When she rotted away, I found a great hank of it in the pit below her ribs, shaped like a gourd. She must, I thought, have been eating her own hair till it clogged her digestive system and killed her.

Bonifacia, my most beloved, whose gentle hands and mouth brought me such peace and comfort. She stopped eating, and no amount of delicacies would tempt her. She died in my arms, and the lines of sorrow carved on my face stayed for months, as I could not bear to replace her.

But then I stole Giovanna, who jumped to her death from the tower height.

Theresa lived the longest, content to spend her days sewing me religious samplers in the hope of saving my soul. I came to dread my visits to her and almost strangled her out of sheer boredom a few times, but her hair was the most magnificent golden colour, so I forgave her stupidity. She eventually died of what had been no more than a little sniffle to me.

Alessandra hanged herself from her bed-head, her first month in the tower.

Vita choked on a piece of apple.

Yoconda died of the plague. Which I took to her from Tiziano, all unknowing. For, in 1576, at the astoundingly old age of eighty-eight, Tiziano died of the plague that chewed through Venice like a pack of rabid rats. He was a bent old skeleton by the end, his sparse hair silver, his teeth all gone, yet still I loved him. One of the very last paintings he ever did was a portrait of us both, me as fresh and young as ever, Tiziano looking like something an owl would spit out. Called 'Tiziano and His Mistress', it was burnt by his son, Orazio, who had always hated me. Only an engraving made by the Flemish artist Anthony van Dyck survived. He had visited Venice just before Tiziano's death and had been so struck by the contrast between the besotted old man and the voluptuous young mistress that he had made a copy.

Tiziano was buried in the Friari church, a great honour for a mere painter. Yoconda was laid out in the crypt of the tower with the other small skeletons, her hair chopped off at the roots and woven into the long braid that I had made from the hair of all my other little loves. And the hair of my father, that pathetic little lock that my mother had died clutching, that was the hair I used to bind all the others.

After Tiziano's death, I stayed in my palazzo for months, staring at myself in the mirror, smelling the whiff of decay in my own mouth, stretching the skin at my eyes, trying to hold back the inexorable sag and crease. I did not weep. My grief made me feel as if a hole had been torn in the fabric of the universe, a hole that could never be mended. All day and night, I heard the tolling of the bells, ringing out the changes in the hour, and there was nothing I could do to hold time back.

My coffers began to empty, so I numbly took up my work again. Many of the men I had once serviced were dead, and it was their sons and even their grandsons who came flocking to the salons of my new procuress, Cecilia. I drank too much, I ate too much and I smoked far too much opium. It was the only thing that seemed to loosen time. Sometimes, in my dreams, I'd be a little girl again, sitting in the bath while my mother washed my hair. Or I'd be in Tiziano's studio, binding him to me with bonds of love instead of black magic. I wondered what life would have been like if we'd aged together and died together. But I had sworn once to never feel regret, so I pushed such weak longings away from me.

One day, I saw a young girl crouching in

the street outside my garden. She wore a tangled wreath of meadow weeds upon her glorious red-gold hair. She was hungry and desperate, but, I'm afraid, no virgin. Still, in all my long life, I had seen that red hair and blue eyes were often passed like heirlooms through the generations. I began to imagine what it would be like to have a girl of my own again, to wash my hair and kiss my cheek, to offer up her delicate blue-veined wrist to me to cut. I looked in my mirror and saw a face I wished not to have. I looked at the painting Tiziano had given me, sixty-four years earlier. I wanted that face again. So I opened my gate and let that red-haired girl in, already plotting how to trap her into giving me her daughter.

For a daughter she would have, if I had to use all my black arts to make it happen.

How was I to know her daughter would be my nemesis?

The one to destroy me and the one to save me.

NOCTURNE

The twelfth prince climbed the tower
on golden tresses he knew were here.
When he penetrated her window,
she turned away to light the fire.
His eyes blinded by hair that mirrored
the leap of flames she stoked,
the prince failed to see the woodpile
of chewed bones at the corner of the
    hearth.

'Rapunzel'
Arlene Ang

Counterfeiting Death

Love can take many strange shapes, I knew
all too well.

As I filed into church with the other novices, my thoughts were full of the story that
Sœur Seraphina had told me. For once, I did
not dwell on my own unhappiness but wondered instead about that poor child locked
away in the tower, and the witch who was
afraid of time. That was a fear I understood.
At the abbey, every hour of every day was ac-
counted for by the ringing of the great bell.
We knelt and rose and ate and slept by its
toll, each stroke taking us closer to our deaths.

I looked down the line of novices, their
heads bowed. Framed by their white wimples,
their faces were so young and smooth and innocent. Sœur Olivia was not yet eighteen, her
face as perfect as a cameo. Her beauty made
my heart ache. She would never feel a man's
mouth on hers, or feel her skin naked against

403

another's, or watch the clock hands creep forward to the time when she could be in his arms again. Did she feel regret for her lack? Was her young body prey to longings and desires, like mine had been at her age?

I slowly became aware that Sœur Emmanuelle was also gazing at the young woman. There was such naked yearning on the novice mistress's face that I had to drop my eyes, in fear she would feel my gaze and know that I had observed her. In that moment, I felt a stir of sympathy for Sœur Emmanuelle that I never would have expected. I, at least, had loved and been loved, even if in the end I had lost it all.

Palais du Louvre, Paris, France — February 1673

My first love affair came about because of a death.

It was dusk in winter, and Paris was covered with a mantle of white snow. All the mounds of garbage were hidden beneath that white cloak, so that the alleyways seemed as immaculate as the domes and spires of the chateaux and cathedrals.

The court was on its way to the Palais-Royal to see a performance of the Troupe de Roi at the Duc d'Orléans' private theatre. I walked from the Louvre, delighting in the crisp cold air and the sight of the golden lanterns strung all along the Rue de Rivoli.

My boots — crimson-dyed and fur-lined — sank deep into the snow, and I kept my hands buried in my muff.

'Mademoiselle de la Force, welcome.'

As I came through the doors into the vast entrance hall, I heard the heavily accented voice of Elizabeth Charlotte, the Duchesse d'Orléans, the new wife of the King's younger brother, Philippe. Nicknamed Liselotte, she was a squat little figure, badly dressed, with a broad nose and a round red face, coarsened from never wearing a veil when she rode to the hunt.

'So you walked, did you? *Gut gemacht.* All these fine ladies who cannot bear to walk more than six paces. No wonder they're all so fat. You know I've been confined to a sedan chair myself? Yes, I'm afraid all the rumours are true and there's a bun in this oven.'

I laughed and offered her my congratulations, stripping off my fur hat and cape to pass to a footman.

'I have to say, it makes me believe in miracles after all,' Liselotte went on in her loud German voice. 'Who could believe my pathetic fop of a husband could be such a man? You know, of course, that he has to drape himself with rosaries and holy medals to get it up at all . . .'

'Sssh,' I said, for the King was only a few paces away, greeting his brother with an inclined head, a mark of highest favour.

405

'Oh, His Majesty knows all about his brother, don't you worry. Who doesn't know?' Liselotte brooded on this for a moment, her thick brows pinched together. I looked at her in some sympathy, because the whole court did of course know that Liselotte was forced to live in a *ménage à trois* with her husband's lover, the beautiful and depraved Philippe, Chevalier de Lorraine.

'Nasty creature, that catamite of my husband's,' Liselotte said. 'Come, sit with me. You know I cannot bear to be near him or my husband, unless I absolutely have to, and I utterly refuse to sit with the King and his whores.'

I stifled a laugh, for the King was settling down in his silver chair with his squat little queen, Marie-Thérèse, beside him, and his two gorgeous blonde mistresses vying to make sure they sat on his other side.

These three women travelled everywhere with the King in his coach, and it was said he usually managed to bed all three at some point during the day. Louise de la Vallière had been his first mistress but had recently fallen out of favour. Her usurper, the voluptuous Athénaïs, the Marquise de Montespan, was now considered the true queen of France, and predictably it was she who won the silent tussle of the chair, sinking down beside the King in a soft explosion of pale silk and speaking to him in such a low voice that he had to bend his ear to her mouth in order to hear.

Athénaïs was, of course, a nickname. Her real name was Françoise, like half the women at court, and the Marquise de Montespan could never bear to be like other women. We all were given nicknames in the Parisian salons in those days, probably to distinguish between all the Louises, Maries, Annes and Françoises. She had adopted the nickname Athénaïs, derived from Athena, the Greek goddess of wisdom. I was called Dunamis, which was the Greek word for strength and so a play on my surname.

'I'm so glad you're here, Mademoiselle de la Force. I like people who laugh at what I say. I am looking forward to the play, aren't you?' Liselotte said.

'All of Paris is!'

'It's a new play tonight,' Liselotte said. 'This is only the fourth time it has been staged. Molière himself is to play the lead role.'

'Oh, that's wonderful. I heard he was unwell.'

Liselotte twinkled at me. 'Consorting with actors again, are we?'

I put my nose in the air. 'What can I say? One comes across all kinds of interesting people in the salons.'

'Including, I have heard, a certain young actor . . .'

'Many actors,' I said firmly, though I felt myself blush. It was true that I had become friendly with one particular young performer, a protégé of Molière's named Michel Baron, who was playing the role of the hero in the play tonight. He was not at all handsome, having a long thin face with a long thin nose, but he was very amusing. Michel could mimic anyone. With a twitch of an imaginary skirt, the wave of an imaginary fan and the lift of a haughty chin, he would become Athénaïs. Or he would droop his eyelids and let his hand flop from the wrist and mince forward a few steps and *voilà*! The Duc d'Orléans.

I had met Michel at the salon of Marguerite de la Sablière, a rich and brilliant woman whose house was always filled with writers and actors, including Jean de la Fontaine, who had written the *Fables* I had so loved as a child. We were among the youngest at the salon, Michel being only twenty and me two years older, and both of us had ambitions to be writers. I introduced him to the court salons, so he could charm and flatter some rich court lady into being his patron, while he took me to the cafés and cabarets of Ménilmontant and Montmartre, two villages outside Paris where wine was exempt from city taxes and so much cheaper for our poor thin purses.

The theatre was filled with the rustling of

silk, the fluttering of fans, the flapping of lace and the nodding of feathers. Six tinkling chandeliers, each holding aloft six tall candles, illuminated the stage while another thirty-four candles were arranged in rows along the front, filling with air with a haze of smoke. Footmen carried about silver goblets of the King's favourite wine, an effervescent rose-coloured concoction from Champagne that was the new craze at court. It was said that the wine-maker Dom Pérignon had cried to his fellow monks, 'Come quickly, I am drinking stars!' True or not, that story alone made me love the sparkling new wine.

The curtains were dragged back and a roar went up, for there sat Molière in a high-backed chair, dressed in a long-tailed green coat. He had a muffler about his neck and a damp cloth held to his brow, and his desk was littered with various bottles of medicines and pills. With the help of an abacus, he was adding up an immensely long bill, which scrolled down his lap and onto the floor.

'Item One, on the 24th, a small, insinuative clyster, preparative and gentle, to soften, moisten, and refresh the bowels of Mr Argan,' he moaned in the plaintive tones of a chronic invalid.

A shout of laughter went up from the men at the word 'bowels', and women pretended to hide their faces behind their fans in shock.

As if encouraged, Molière went on to mention bowels, bile, blood and flatulence several times in the next few moments, until the audience was weeping with laughter.

The play rolled on till the final scene, where the character played by Molière pretended to die so that he could tell who truly loved him: his beautiful daughter or his beautiful second wife. With his green coat torn loose at his throat, Molière sank back on his chair, saying piteously to his maid, 'Is there no danger to counterfeiting death?'

'What danger can there be?' the maid began.

Molière suddenly lurched up, coughing convulsively.

'What an actor,' Liselotte said.

'Brilliant,' the Chevalier murmured. 'I wonder what they put in his maquillage to make him look so grey?'

The actress playing the maid had recoiled, one hand to her mouth, then darted to support Molière. He coughed as if his lungs were wet paper, then suddenly gasped and clasped his handkerchief to his mouth. We were close enough to the stage to see the white cloth suddenly turn red and sodden.

'A vial of pig's blood hidden in the handkerchief?' Liselotte wondered uneasily.

'I think . . . I'm afraid . . .' I started half out of my chair.

The maid turned to the side wings, calling for help. Michel ran onto the stage and supported Molière as he coughed up more blood. The crowd was beginning to stir and murmur. Molière heaved himself upright. 'Enough. On with the play!'

'But, sir . . .' Michel protested.

Molière thrust the bloodstained handkerchief into his hand and waved him away. Reluctantly, Michel withdrew from the stage.

The maid stammered through her next lines: 'Only stretch yourself there, sir. Here is my mistress. Mind you keep still.'

Molière lay out on the couch, looking ghastly, as first his stage wife came in to find him supposedly dead ('Heaven be praised!') and then his stage daughter ('What a misfortune! What a cruel grief!'). The conniving stepmother was banished, the beautiful daughter won her true love (Michel doing his best to look ecstatic while all the time shooting Molière looks of the deepest anxiety). The curtain fell with unusual haste upon the scene, and we were all left to look at each other and marvel and wonder.

'Do you think he is really ill?' Liselotte wondered.

'I fear so,' I answered, close to tears.

The King ordered a servant to go and make enquiries. I waited with Liselotte for news, while the rest of the crowd slowly dispersed, going back to the Louvre or to their own apartments nearby. The two Philippes — the prince and his chevalier — wandered off, and

Athénaïs drew the King down to talk to him, his dark head bent over her golden one.

'I might go back to my room,' Queen Marie-Thérèse said.

'Very well, dear,' her husband the King said vaguely, not looking up.

The Queen hesitated. 'Shall I see you soon?'

The King lifted one hand. 'Later, dear, later.'

Queen Marie-Thérèse waddled out to her sedan chair, accompanied as always by one of her dwarves and a smelly little dog. I should have gone with her — I was one of her ladies-in-waiting and it was my job to make sure she was comfortable and happy — but Marie-Thérèse paid little attention to me, as her French was poor and my Spanish even poorer. I did the absolute minimum of my duties possible, although I always made sure I was around between supper and bedtime. That was when Queen Marie-Thérèse liked to play cards. As she always played for high stakes and always lost, my income was greatly enhanced by this vice of hers. Her latest round of losses had paid for my fur cape and hat.

Truth be told, I could hardly bear the Queen. She spent half her day on her knees mumbling prayers to God to make the King be kind to her and the other half lounging around drinking innumerable cups of hot chocolate, surrounded by her dwarves and her dogs. The latter were far better treated. Her dwarves slept on the floor outside her bedroom door and ate whatever scraps she thought to fling them. Her dogs had their own valets and carriage, and their own room in their palace, and often sat at the table with the Queen and ate from her plate.

If I'd had any choice, I'd have left the Queen's service long ago, but I couldn't afford to. Ladies-in-waiting are not paid very much, and most of my winnings were spent on scented gloves, red-heeled shoes, lace trimmings (exorbitantly expensive) and sedan chairs to get me to the various salons that I slipped out to once the Queen was snoring in her bed. Oh, and on bundles of expensive paper, ink, goose-feather quills and pumice stone. I spent every spare second I had scribbling stories.

I made my excuses, called for my cape and hat, and slipped out behind the Queen. Not to return tamely to the Louvre, but to make my way to Molière's house.

It was not far, being just across from the theatre on Rue de Richelieu, but I was frozen to the bone by the time I got there. The house was full of actors and actresses in the very throes of histrionics, people weeping, sighing, groaning and throwing themselves about. No one paid me any attention at all, so I was able to find my way up the stairs to Molière's bedchamber, where his wife, Armande, and her mother, Margeurite, were chafing his hands, burning feathers under his nose, lifting cordials to his slack mouth and generally trying to make themselves feel useful.

Michel sat by the bed, his head sunk in his hands, his fingers writhing about in his curls. I bent over him and whispered his name.

He looked up, his eyes red-rimmed. 'Oh, Charlotte-Rose, he's dying.'

'Can nothing be done?'

Michel shook his head. 'He has consumption. He caught it in gaol, you know, that time he was imprisoned for debt. He has been ill for years.'

'Why did he go on stage?'

'He needed the money,' Michel said simply.

'Is there anything I can do? A doctor? An apothecary?'

Michel snorted in derision. 'Would they attend him after he ridiculed them so in his play?'

'Surely they would not refuse . . .'

Michel shrugged one thin shoulder. 'People hate to be mocked.'

I nodded in agreement, remembering in one quick flash the King's fury when I had humiliated him in front of his courtiers. I shoved the memory away — it brought nothing but pain — and tried to think what I could do to help. Molière's green coat lay crumpled on the dusty floor. I bent and picked it up, shaking out its folds. Michel shrank back at the sight of it.

'Get rid of it,' he cried. 'It's the devil's colour! Oh, I'll never wear green again.'

I glanced at him quizzically but shoved the coat out of sight nonetheless. Michel was always like this, at the peak of delight or the depths of despair, but it was one of the things that had drawn me to him. I had grown tired of the King's famous impassivity; one was always trying to guess what he was thinking. With Michel, one always knew.

'Have you eaten?' I asked.

'As if I could eat at a time like this.' Michel flung his face down into his arms again.

On the bed, Molière moaned and muttered something. Armande and her mother wept in each other's arms.

'A priest?' I asked hesitantly.

'We've already sent for two, but they will not come. They say the author of *Tartuffe* is no fit person to receive the last consolations.' Michel looked up at me with an agonised face.

'The King will be furious if he hears that. Let me send for the King's own confessor. If he will not come himself, he will at least send someone else.'

I ran downstairs and found a small frightened-looking young actor and gave him some money and told him where to go. I then took some wine up to the gloomy bed-chamber and poured it for Michel and the

415

two weeping ladies. The atmosphere was so oppressive that I must admit I gulped a goblet myself, though it was cheap nasty stuff.

Molière's breath was rasping in and out of his throat. He lay so perfectly still, and his profile was so white, he looked as if he was an effigy carved from marble. Only that dreadful, wet, slow breathing showed he was still a man. Between each exhalation and each inhalation was a long ravine of silence, growing longer each time until we were hanging over him, sure each time that it was his last breath.

The door opened. Two nuns came in, snow still frosting their black veils. They seemed so out of place among this rabble of gaudily dressed actors, still in their stage maquillage, that we all started like guilty children. I thought they had come to give the final rites, ignorant *réformée* that I was, but they shook their heads sadly and said only priests were permitted to do that. Nonetheless, they mumbled some Latin and prayed over him, and it seemed to comfort the two women, and maybe Molière too, for he let out his breath in one long sigh and then did not breathe in again. We listened to the silence for some time before we realised he was gone.

'He was a great man,' Michel said. 'We'll not see another like him again.' I was trembling. I had never seen a man die before. My heart felt as if someone was squeezing it in

416

their fists. I too would die like that one day. People died of consumption all the time, even young women like me. If I were to die tomorrow, what would I have done with my life? Molière at least had written more than thirty plays. He had travelled all of France, and he had had many lovers. I had never even been kissed.

I bent and cupped my hand around the nape of Michel's neck, seeking to comfort him. 'We must arrange his burial.'

'Actors are not permitted to be buried in sacred ground,' Michel said in a shaking voice.

'What? Why?' Incredulity sharpened my voice.

Michel slanted me a wry look. 'Demon spawn,' he explained.

'The King surely would . . .' My voice failed me. 'Bring me some paper. I'll write to him.'

The nuns looked impressed. Even Marguerite, who had played before the King many times, looked impressed. Paper was brought — poor-quality stuff that was brittle and yellow — and I composed a hasty letter and paid more coins to yet another young actor to carry it to the Palais-Royal for me. The reply came swiftly, wrapped around a gold *louis*. Molière could be buried in the cemetery, but it must be at night and in the section reserved for unbaptised infants. The King could do no more.

The church bells were ringing. It was midnight. The nuns were preparing to lay poor Molière out. I bent and whispered to Michel, 'There is nothing more you can do. You must rest. Come.'

He nodded and rose. Catching me by the hand, he led me out of the room and down the corridor, Michel picking up a candlestick from a nearby table.

He opened a door and led me inside. I saw, in one brief glance, that it was a man's bedroom in wild disorder, clothes flung across the chair and spilling onto the floor, a pair of boots lying discarded in the middle of the floor. Then Michel caught me and drew me to him, his mouth coming down on mine.

At first, I froze, startled, but then I kissed him back, urgently, desperately. He fumbled with my bodice. 'I must tell you . . . I want you now . . . more than I've ever wanted anyone,' he said between frantic kisses. 'I'm sorry. Is this wrong?'

'Yes,' I said, helping him rip away the lace. 'So wrong.' I drew his head down to my breast.

And so, willingly, eagerly, I surrendered to him my maidenhead — in the eyes of the world, the only thing of value I owned. Yet I have few regrets. I had never felt so acutely alive, the night I watched a man die and made love for the very first time.

A Mere Bagatelle

Palais du Louvre, Paris, France — March 1674
It was our passion for words and our ardent desire to write that drew me and Michel together, and the same that drove us apart.

Michel wanted to be a great playwright, like his former master Molière. He had high ambitions and scorned what I wrote as frivolous and feminine.

'All these disguises and duels and abductions,' he said contemptuously, one day a year or so after our affair began, slapping down the pile of paper covered with my sprawling handwriting. 'All these desperate love affairs. And you wish me to take you seriously.'

'I like disguises and duels.' I sat bolt upright on the edge of my bed. 'Better than those dreary boring plays you write. At least something happens in my stories.'

'At least my plays are *about* something.'

'My stories are about something too. Just because they aren't boring doesn't mean they aren't worthy.'

'What are they about? Love?' He clasped his hands together near his ear and fluttered his eyelashes.

'Yes, love. What's wrong with writing about love? Everybody longs for love.'

'Aren't there enough love stories in the world without adding to them?'

'Isn't there enough misery and tragedy?'

Michel snorted in contempt.

'What's wrong with wanting to be happy?'

'It's sugary and sentimental.'

'Sugary? I am not sugary.' I was so angry that I hurled my shoe at his head.

He caught it deftly and tossed it into the corner. 'I'll give you that. You're not sweet at all. Too much pepper in the brew. But sentimental. You're definitely sentimental.' As he spoke, he advanced on me, undoing his coat.

'I am not sentimental.' I took off my other shoe and threw it at him, and he caught it and hurled it into the other corner, then flung his coat down on the chair, unbuttoning his cuffs.

'Don't you cry at the end of a play? Don't you sigh when the hero kisses the heroine?' Michel laughed at me and untied his shirt laces.

'That's not being sentimental, that's having a heart.' As he stripped off his shirt and flung it on the floor, I cried, 'Don't do that. We're not making love, we're arguing.'

Michel pushed me back against the bed.

'No,' I protested, leaning up on both elbows. 'I'm talking!'

'You talk too much,' he replied and pressed me down with his weight, stopping my indignant words with his mouth.

And I let him. I was so enchanted with this new game of love that I was in thrall to him. When I was with him, he made me feel as if I was the most important thing in the world. We did not need to speak. All he had to do was lift that black sardonic eyebrow and I knew we were sharing a secret current of amusement at the world.

I had determined long ago not to marry. It seemed to me that marriage was just a way of selling a woman into slavery. A woman could not choose who she married, or protest if her husband beat her with anything thinner than his thumb. It made me angry.

Yet our society did not take kindly to women who wished to live their own lives, to have a small corner of the world in which they could be their own mistress, as the King's cousin Anne-Marie-Louise said to my mother all those years ago.

My poor mother. The very thought of her brought tears to scald my eyes. She had died in that convent, and we had never seen her again. Marie had inherited her title and the chateau, but at the beginning of the year she had been married to a man she had never seen, the Marquis de Théobon, who had cut down a great deal of the oak forests to raise money to pay his gambling debts. I had not seen her since, though we wrote careful letters to each other, trying to read between the lines.

My small corner of the world was to be found in the salons of Paris. There, women ruled and willing men fell at our feet. We created secret societies with passwords and hidden handshakes, where we could discuss politics and religion without fear of being betrayed to the King's spies. In the salons, I met wise and witty women, many of them writers, and there my own secret ambition to write had burst into bloom. Letters, poems, fairy tales and scandalous love stories flowed from my quill. I dreamt of being published, like Marie-Madeleine de la Fayette and Madeleine de Scudéry.

Through these months, my affair with Michel Baron ebbed and flowed, sometimes filled with gaiety and laughter, sometimes a thing of bitter tears. I was of no real use to him, being poor, but I could make him laugh and I could fill him with tenderness, and both these things moved him. He had other, more beautiful, mistresses and many a rich patroness who expected him to dance at her heel, yet somehow we would find ourselves nestled together at the back of some fine lady's drawing room, laughing at a particularly precious line of poetry.

I began to have secret dreams of marriage. I imagined a life spent writing and arguing and making love and going to the theatre. I would no longer need to sit all day with Queen Marie-Thérèse, playing cards and grooming her smelly little dogs and pretending to laugh at the grotesque antics of her dwarves. I would no longer have to smile at people who were not amusing, and flatter people who were not kind, and gossip about people who were not interesting. Michel and I would lie abed in the mornings, drinking hot chocolate and reading, and then we would spend our days writing. I'd write stories of love and magic and adventure that would take Europe by storm; he would write magnificent plays that would make the audience weep and bring carriages of rich patrons to our door. At night, we would go out to dinner or visit the salons or go to the theatre. We'd dance till dawn in Ménilmontant, and then make love till we fell asleep in each other's arms.

One night, I put the idea to him, phrasing it as a spur-of-the-moment notion, a mere bagatelle. We had finished making love and I was tucked into the curve of his arm. Both of us were naked but Michel wore his nightcap, which he had brought rolled up in his coat pocket as a joke, after complaining about how cold my room was. He looked down at me in surprise. 'Get married? But why on earth would we do that?'

I smiled and waved my hand in the air. 'Oh, you know . . . so you didn't have to sneak into my bedroom at midnight with your nightcap rolled up in your pocket.'

'Oh, I don't mind that,' he replied. 'It doesn't take up much room.'

'And you wouldn't have to sneak out before it was light.'

'Oh, well, if that's the price I have to pay to spend the night with you . . .'

'But if we were married, you wouldn't have to sneak about at all. We could have a nice little house in Paris . . .'

'And how would we afford that?'

'Oh, I don't know. If you wrote a hit play . . . if I wrote a bestseller . . .'

'With ifs, Paris could be put into a bottle,' he answered sourly, taking his arms away from me and crossing them over his chest.

'We'd find a patron.'

He huffed out his breath. 'I'm finding it difficult enough to find a patron without being encumbered by a wife.'

I sat up, clutching the bedclothes to my breast. 'I wouldn't be an encumbrance.'

'Don't be a fool, Charlotte-Rose,' he said. 'Women are always encumbrances. You'd want me to stay home and fawn all over you when I should be out keeping my patrons happy. You'd want a squalling baby, women always do . . .'

'I would not,' I cried, though it was true; I had sometimes imagined a sweet rosy-faced baby in my dream house, laughing and holding up chubby arms to me.

'My troupe will need to go out on the road at some point, travelling the provinces. You have no idea how hard life is on the road. You'd never cope.'

'I would so.' Tears were rising quickly in me, and I clenched my fists and gritted my jaw, determined not to start weeping.

'Could you kill a rat with your broom and then skin it and pop it in the pot for dinner?'

I stared at him, biting my lip.

'Could you walk twenty miles in the rain and then sleep in a ditch?'

'If I had to,' I answered gamely.

Michel laughed. 'I don't think so, *duchesse.*'

I had always liked him calling me *'duchesse'* before, as a joking reference to my noble lineage, but it sounded ugly in his voice now. 'I . . . I wouldn't mind . . . rain . . . and rats . . . and things, as long as we were together.' My voice shook revealingly.

Michel gave a sarcastic snort. 'And what use would you be to me on the road anyway? You can't sing, you can't act . . .'

'I can act.'

'Rubbish!'

'I can! Telling stories is like acting. You need

to be able to conjure up different characters, you need to hold your audience and sway them with your voice, you need —'

'You can't act, Charlotte-Rose.'

'But I could learn. I make you laugh with my stories. Why couldn't I make an audience laugh?'

'That's not enough.'

'But why? What do you mean?'

'It's not enough to be funny and clever to succeed on the stage, Charlotte-Rose. You need to be pretty.'

My protests died in my mouth. A flame of humiliation swept over me, scalding my skin.

Michel got out of bed. He pulled on his clothes. 'I'm sorry, *duchesse*. I don't mean to hurt your feelings. But it's true. If I'm to get married, it'll have to be to someone who's rich or someone who's beautiful. Both, preferably. And you, unfortunately, are neither.'

Numbly, I remembered one of my guardian's favourite axioms. 'A poor beauty finds more lovers than husbands,' the Marquis de Maulévrier used to say. So what if you were both poor and plain? I saw my future open up before me, filled with boredom and loneliness and mockery.

Michel dragged on his boots and stamped towards the door.

'Do you intend to wear your nightcap through the palace?' I said icily. 'That'll cause

426

a snicker.'

He threw me a furious look, snatched his nightcap off his head and flung it on the ground. Then, he seized his wig, crammed it on his head and went out, slamming the door behind him.

I curled up into a ball, pressed my face into my pillow and cried.

The next day, I received a visit from Françoise Scarron, a lady of my acquaintance who had only recently come to court but was already causing a great deal of comment because of the King's decided partiality for her company. Yet she was not young. She was not blonde. She was not voluptuous. She was not even vivacious. Françoise Scarron had olive skin and dark eyes, though I am sure, like me, she longed for a *hurluberlu* of pale golden ringlets and cerulean blue eyes like the King's favourite mistress, Athénaïs.

Worst of all, Françoise Scarron was not only low born but also governess to Athénaïs's bastards. The King had housed them all in a secret location, where he could go and visit his children without causing a scandal. A few months earlier, after the birth of Athénaïs's third royal bastard, the King had decided to legitimise his children and bring them to court, and so, of course, their governess had come to court too.

I had been eager to know her, for Françoise

was the granddaughter of the Huguenot writer Agrippa d'Aubigné. Born in Pons, only a hundred miles from the Château de Cazeneuve, he had written one of my favourite childhood books, *Les Aventures du Baron de Faeneste,* about the comic escapades of a Gascon in Paris.

Born in a debtor's prison, Françoise had married the crippled poet Paul Scarron at the age of sixteen. She looked after him till his death eight years later but was then left impoverished. She had seemed the perfect choice to look after Athénaïs's children, leaving Athénaïs free to look after the King.

Except the King seemed to enjoy Françoise's company. She did not flirt, she did not flutter her eyelashes, she did not trill with laughter at his every ponderous witticism. Instead, Françoise talked to him about the children, and whether it was wise for Athénaïs to shower them with sweetmeats and toys. The King was observed seeking out her company more and more, and Athénaïs responded with catty remarks about her dullness and her dowdiness.

When Françoise scratched on my door, I considered shouting 'Go away', but it was not wise to be rude to someone to whom the King was showing favour. I sighed, wrapped a dressing gown around me, and quickly flicked my haresfoot over my face and pinned up my hair, calling for her to enter.

Françoise was not alone. The Duchesse de Guise was with her, a thin, bent, sour-faced woman renowned for her devoutness. The King's first cousin, she would not permit her husband to sit in her presence, since he was only a duke and she had been born a princess. As if in protest, he had died of smallpox only four years after their marriage, leaving her with a small and sickly son. She was greatly committed to good works and spent so much time in prayer that her back was permanently bowed. I had made Michel laugh once by calling her 'pickled with piety', and indeed it was a good description.

'Pardon us for disturbing you, *mademoiselle,*' Françoise said. She was, as always, soberly dressed in a dark grey dress, free of ribbons, lace or puffed sleeves.

'Not at all. It is always a pleasure to see you,' I replied in my sweetest manner, hoping my eyes were not swollen and red. I offered the Duchesse de Guise the chair by the fire and stood in front of my bed, wishing I had thought to straighten the rumpled bedclothes.

Françoise stood before the door, there being nowhere else to stand in my tiny room. 'We have come on a rather delicate matter . . . I do hope you will forgive us.'

'I suppose that depends on the delicate matter,' I replied, smiling. 'Although I cannot imagine you saying anything that could possibly offend me.'

She smiled faintly in response. 'I know how difficult it must be for you here at court, without any family of your own. You have no one to guide or advise you.'

I waited, my smile feeling heavy on my face.

'I do hope you will not mind if I take it upon myself to warn you . . .' Françoise hesitated for a long moment, making my stomach muscles clench in sudden anxiety. I did not know what to fear. The presence of the Duchesse de Guise, tapping her fingers impatiently on the arm of her chair, made me suspect I was once again being pressed to change my faith, yet I was also all too conscious of the rumpled bedclothes beside me and the faint reek of lovemaking rising from the sheets.

I was right on both counts. Françoise expressed sympathy for me, raised like herself as a Huguenot and no doubt wishing to honour my parents' memory by choosing to follow their faith. 'I too felt that way, until I came to see the consolation of the true faith. I would wish for that same consolation for you.'

'Thank you. I am in no need of consolation.'

'You are, however, in need of correction,' the Duchesse de Guise snapped, obviously losing her patience. 'I warn you, it has been noted you do not take Holy Communion or seek penance for your sins. You risk the everlasting fires of hell with your stubbornness.'

My smile was now so stiff it hurt my face. 'I am sorry you think so. I, however, was taught that true repentance consists of looking within my own heart. Luckily, we are both free to worship as we see fit in this country, given the great wisdom of His Majesty the King's grandfather.'

'I warn you, the King will not tolerate such radical views much longer,' the Duchesse sneered. 'They must be purged from the land like a rotten tumour.'

I felt a stab of true fear. I had been brought up on stories of the religious wars, when Huguenots had been cruelly persecuted for their faith. Many had been burnt alive, sometimes whole villages locked inside their plain white chapels while at worship and the church burnt to the ground. Surely, such times could not come again?

After my mother was banished, and the Marquis de Maulévrier was sent by the King to be our guardian, I lost all belief in God. How could God exist, I raged inside my skull, when he let such things happen? My mother had believed that God was our friend, and we could talk to Him whenever we wanted. We did not need to pay the church for His attention. We did not need saints to intercede on our behalf. All we needed was our own pure quiet faith. *Almighty God,* I had prayed, *if you truly exist, you'll save my mother. You'll send a lightning bolt to earth to strike the Marquis dead. You'll turn him into a pile of ashes. You'll send locusts and plague and the pox and all kinds of pestilence until he is dead and my mother is home.*

My mother was not saved. The Marquis was not punished. All I was left with was an aching hollowness where God had once been. In time, I had filled that hollowness with the constant whirl of excitement and entertainment and colour that was life at the royal court. Yet, all through this giddy galliard I had clung to the pure and simple practices of my mother's religion. *Sola Scriptura, Sola Gratia, Sola Fide.* I was indeed honouring her memory in the only way I knew how.

The Duchesse de Guise continued, in her vinegary way, 'The King is contemplating passing a law that will make marriages between Catholics and Huguenots illegal. Any child of such a union will be illegitimate. You are long past the proper age for marriage, Mademoiselle de la Force. If you do not repent soon and abjure your false religion, you'll find yourself left on the shelf.'

I did not know how to answer that. *I am only twenty-three,* I wanted to cry, but I knew she was right. I was indeed long past the usual age of marriage. 'I am poor and ugly, that is why no one will marry me,' I answered.

'Not at all,' Françoise protested. 'You have a most piquant little face, *mademoiselle*. And, perhaps, if you were to abjure . . . the King is eager to reward those who return to the true faith.'

I hardly heard her, the echo of Michel's words ringing in my ears: 'If I'm to marry, it'll have to be someone who's rich or someone who's beautiful. Both, preferably. And you, unfortunately, are neither.'

'No one wants to marry a *cocotte*,' the Duchesse said malevolently.

Blood rushed to my face. 'Indeed? Do I understand you to be implying that I am to be thought of in such terms? I must warn you that I will find such an insinuation impossible to tolerate.'

'It is a small step from *coquette* to *cocotte*,' the Duchesse said with a shrug of one thin hunched shoulder.

'And another small step to garrotte,' I replied, baring my teeth in a counterfeit smile.

The Duchesse frowned, offended without understanding why.

Françoise looked uncomfortable. 'It is not our intention to offend you, *mademoiselle*. It is just that your great love of the theatre has been noted and —'

'What is there not to love?' I interposed rapidly. 'Ah, Racine. Corneille! Indeed, we are blessed to live at such a time.'

'Only a woman of ill repute associates with

playwrights and play-actors.' The Duchesse sounded as if she was saying 'prostitutes' and 'perverts'.

I affected a look of puzzlement. 'But it is all the fashion to offer patronage to men of letters. Didn't the King himself ask Molière to sit with him and have supper?'

'Absolutely not. The King would never do such a thing. That was nothing but gossip.'

'Ah, yes, one must never listen to gossip,' I replied smoothly.

The Duchesse looked taken aback. For a moment, she was at a loss for words, then said angrily, 'We are not here to discuss the King's behaviour, which is of far too elevated a plane for one such as you.'

'But I fear you have forgotten that my mother and the King are kin,' I smiled. 'That is not like you, my lady, to forget the lineage of the great. I had thought you had made a study of it.'

Once again, the Duchesse was at a loss for words. Françoise bit back a smile.

I went on piously, 'I think the love of the theatre must be something that runs in our family. I know my dear cousin . . . I mean, His Majesty . . . is just as much a fan of our playwrights and actors as I am. But enough idle chatter.' I moved towards the door. 'I could spend all day talking about the theatre, having, as you so truly said, such a great love of it, but alas! Duty calls. I do hope you'll excuse me.'

Françoise's eyes were bright with amusement. 'Mademoiselle de la Force, you are indeed right to think us interfering old cats but I must assure you, we have only the noblest of intentions. The King is displeased.'

I caught my breath. 'The King?'

'News of your friendship with the actor Baron has come to his ears. He frowned.'

My heart shrank as if at the touch of winter frost. I took a deep breath. 'I can assure you, *mesdames,* that there is nothing between Monsieur Baron and I but . . . but friendship and the deepest respect.'

'In that case, I must offer my apologies again,' Françoise said. 'I know you are motherless and alone, and that it can be difficult to . . .' she hesitated again, then forged on, 'to keep one's heart and virtue intact at court . . .'

Where everyone has love affairs as easily as cracking a nut, I thought. The difference, of course, was that those women were married and had complaisant husbands who were busy with their own affairs. And, of course, they were rich. My only value in the marriage market was my lineage and my virginity . . . which I had tossed away as eagerly as a child tearing paper from a birthday gift.

'I thank you for your concern,' I replied coolly.

The Duchesse de Guise rose to her feet,

her face looking sourer than ever. 'I should perhaps let you know, *mademoiselle*, that he was seen sneaking from your bedroom *last night.*'

'There is nothing between us,' I retorted angrily, tasting bitter truth.

At that very moment, my bedroom door swung open and Michel sauntered in. I glared at him, trying to indicate with my eyes that he was most unwelcome at that time. 'How dare you? What do you think you are doing, barging into my room like this?'

Michel cocked an eyebrow, surprised to find my room so crowded. 'Pardon, *mademoiselle*,' he replied. 'I merely came to fetch my nightcap.'

All three of us stared at him, unable to find a word to say, as he bowed with an exaggerated flourish, swept up his forgotten nightcap from the floor and retreated out the door. Then the eyes of both women swung back to me. Feeling the heat rush up my face till even the tips of my ears were burning, I shrugged and spread my hands.

'Nothing between you?' the Duchesse de Guise repeated sarcastically.

'No,' I replied, keeping my head high. 'Nothing at all.'

I might have been able to ride out the storm of scandal if Michel had been a nobleman, or even a gentleman. As I was to discover, though, he was neither. He thought it all a great joke and admitted the scene whenever anyone quizzed him about it. Even worse, he thought the whole story too good to keep quiet, and so would tell anyone who listened how I had clung to him in bed, begging him to marry me and offering to go on the stage.

One day, I walked into the salon of Anne-Marie-Louise, the Duchesse de Montpensier, to find Michel surrounded by a crowd of ladies and courtiers, many of whom I had considered my friends, all laughing uproariously. 'I'll write a bestseller,' Michel declared in falsetto, one hand to his brow. 'I can act. I can make a crowd laugh. I'll do anything.'

I stopped mid-step, overcome with mortification. Liselotte, the Duchesse d'Orléans, turned aside, trying to hide her laughter behind her fan. Madame de Scudéry looked at me with pity. Michel had the grace to look a little shamefaced.

'Better to make people laugh than to make them weep,' I replied quietly and turned away.

A COQUETTE

Paris, France — 1676 to 1678

My second lover, I seduced with black magic.

I never meant to dabble in the dark arts. If I had known that I was stumbling into a vast sticky spiderweb of poison, murder and satanism, I would never have gone to the witch La Voisin, and so never have come to the attention of the Chambre Ardente, that grim tribunal that would see thirty-four people burnt at the stake and hundreds more tortured, flung into oubliettes and forced into exile.

I simply wanted a life of my own.

The months after my break-up with Michel were awful. I lost my position as maid of honour to the Queen, who decided that only respectable married women should serve her. I also lost my salary, and my rooms at the Louvre, Fontainebleau, Saint-Germain-en-Laye and the marvellous new chateau the King was building at Versailles. The Duchesse de Guise offered me a position in her household, hoping to bring me into the Catholic fold. I was so desperate to stay at court that I thought I could endure it.

I was wrong. It was intolerable.

The Duchesse de Guise prayed all the time, and I was expected to pray with her. After her son was dropped on his head by his nurse, dying a few horrible days later, it was even worse. Haunted by his death, she could not bear to stay long at the Palais d'Orléans in Paris, where he had died, and so retired to her estate in Normandy, more than a hundred miles away. There, I was preached at and prayed at all day long. She could not bear idleness and was very suspicious if she ever saw me with a quill in my hand, so I could only write late at night, by the tremulous glow of stolen candle stubs. I had to hide my scribblings in case her servants and spies found them, and she made me dress in heavy black, as was usual for those who wait upon royalty. It was no use for me to protest that the Queen had never insisted her ladies dressed like crows; the Duchesse de Guise only sniffed and said dismissively, 'Well, she is Spanish,' in the same tone she might say, 'Well, she is a fool.'

In the summer of 1676, the Queen threw a grand celebration for the King at the Château de Saint-Germain-en-Laye, for he had been away fighting in the Dutch wars for fifteen long months. Being the King's first cousin, the Duchesse de Guise was of course invited, and eagerly I went with her. It was my first visit back to Saint-Germain, the King's principal residence, in over a year.

The Duchesse's carriage rattled through the tall gilded gates and along the driveway towards the chateau. Craning my neck to see out the window, I caught a glimpse of smooth green lawns, clipped topiaries and a sparkling arc of water spouted by a golden god. In the distance, I caught a glimpse of Paris. Tears sprang to my eyes, and I groped for my handkerchief.

'*Mademoiselle,* you are ridiculous,' the Duchesse de Guise said. 'Wipe your eyes and try to act with the decorum expected of one in service to a Daughter of France.'

I sat back, dabbing at my eyes, joy bubbling up inside me. For a week or two, I could dance and listen to music and go to the theatre and talk about something other than my sinful refusal to abjure my parents' religion. Perhaps I'd even be permitted to shed my hated uniform and dress in the spring-like fabrics gracing the shapely forms of the women promenading along the gravel paths. Their gowns were soft, gauzy and romantic, sprigged with embroidered flowers, the sleeves full and caught at the elbow with velvet ribbons. Jewels winked in their ears and in their tight cascading ringlets. I looked down at my own plain black gown and sighed.

'At least we will not have to endure the presence of that woman,' the Duchesse de Guise said, preparing to descend from the carriage as it came to a halt before the chateau. 'She will not dare to show her face at court again.'

I thought this was rather a shame. I liked Athénaïs, who had been shamed by the church into leaving court after nine years as the King's *maîtresse en titre* and the bearing of five royal bastards. When I had first come to court at the age of sixteen to take up my role as maid of honour to the Queen, Athénaïs had been one of her principal ladies. I had been frightened, overwhelmed and homesick, and all too aware of my unfashionable clothes, my gauche manners and my lack of allies.

Athénaïs had taught me to gamble, given me the name of her dressmaker and taught me some of the mysteries of court etiquette. 'You must never knock at a door, you must scratch it with the nail of your little finger. And if you should see the servants bringing the King's dinner along the corridor, you must curtsey right to the very ground, as if it was the King himself. Most importantly, never sit in the presence of the King and Queen, or any of the royal family. Unless you're at the gambling table, of course. I think that's why we all love to gamble so much. It's the only time we're ever allowed to sit down.'

Athénaïs had reigned supreme for so long — all the ladies copying her hairstyles and her clothes, all the men celebrating her wit and lining up to beg her for favours — that I could hardly imagine the court of the Sun King without her.

'I do not understand why that woman is permitted to stay so close to the royal court,' the Duchesse continued, shaking out her skirts. 'She should have been banished to a convent like that other whey-faced whore.'

'I can't imagine Athénaïs allowing her head to be shaved and spending her days on her knees, praying, like poor la Vallière.' I still found it hard to believe that the King's first *maîtresse en titre,* the beautiful and delicate Louise de la Vallière, had truly desired to become Sœur Louise de la Miséricorde of the Carmelite order, one of the most austere of the religious orders. Although Athénaïs had once told me that Louise had been wearing a hair shirt under her silken gowns for years. Certainly, she had looked thin and haggard for some time before her retirement, forced to travel everywhere in the same carriage as the Queen and Athénaïs, who had long ago replaced her in the King's affections.

'Well, at least the Queen no longer has to endure her presence at court. The King should be breeding up new heirs, instead of litters of bastards.' The Duchesse de Guise gestured to me to fall into place behind her, then swept into the marble entrance hall. I followed eagerly, filling my eyes with the magnificence of the royal court once more. Even the air smelt more delicious here than anywhere else on earth, delicately scented with orange blossoms, the King's favourite perfume.

I was standing with a cluster of other ladies-in-waiting when a distant murmur caught my attention. I craned my neck with everyone else to see what the disturbance was. The stir grew louder, and the King looked up, frowning. He disliked any commotion.

Athénaïs swept into the room, hundreds of golden ringlets dancing about her face. Her skin was white, her lips were red and a black patch in the shape of a heart was pressed right at the corner of her mouth, *à la coquette.* She glided up to the King and curtsied to the ground, allowing him — and all of us — an eyeful of her magnificent cleavage.

The King stood and hurried forward to meet her, crying her name, his arms out-stretched. We were all dumbstruck. The King rose for no one. The King embraced no one. The Queen and the royal duchesses all had to rise to their feet at once, their teeth gritted in fury. Athénaïs was smiling, both her hands held captive by the King.

'Thank you for your letters,' the King said.

'They brightened many a dull day.'

'I'm so glad,' Athénaïs answered. 'You know I thought of you every moment.'

I could not help laughing. Her boldness delighted me. It must have been hell for Athénaïs, banished from court for so long, so she was risking all on one final throw. I looked about me. The Queen stood rigid, her hands clenched by the side of her ugly Spanish gown. The Duchesse de Guise looked like she had just drunk a pint of vinegar. Françoise, governess to the royal bastards, had turned an ugly red colour. All the pretty young girls looked chagrined and disappointed; the men were thoughtful or maliciously amused, according to their natures. It was better than a play.

The Duchesse de Guise swept forward. 'What a pleasant surprise, *madame.*' Her voice was stiff with sarcasm. 'You must be thirsty after your drive. Let me procure some champagne for you.' She beckoned a footman forward. Athénaïs cast one mischievous look over her shoulder at the King, before allowing the Duchesse to steer her away.

Françoise stepped forward. 'Sire, I wish to consult you about the Duc du Maine's schooling. Do you not think it is time he began Latin?'

The King replied to her courteously enough, although his eyes followed Athénaïs as she glided away. I eyed Françoise speculatively. I had heard from the other maids of honour that she had ambitions to warm the King's bed herself. Certainly, he had already rewarded her — ostensibly for her loyalty to his illegitimate children — with enough money that she was able to buy herself a lovely little chateau at Maintenon. This meant she was no longer Madame Scarron but Madame de Maintenon, a big step up for a woman who had been born in a prison.

Between them, the devotees — as they were called — were able to keep the King away from Athénaïs all night. Françoise made sure she shared a carriage with her on the journey back to Versailles, dropping Athénaïs at her chateau in Clagny on the way. The damage, however, was done. The next morning, at breakfast, the King remarked to the court (who all stood around the great room watching him eat in solitary splendour): 'I think I may drive out to Clagny today. See what changes Madame de Montespan has made out there.'

'I'll come with you, dear,' the Queen said at once.

'And I,' said the Duchesse de Guise grimly.

'And I, if your royal Majesty will permit,' said Françoise.

By the time the King had been to mass and to council and visited his dogs, half the court had called for their carriages, and a long procession made its way along the hot dusty roads to Clagny. For once, I was glad of my role as maid of honour to the Duchesse de Guise, for I was as eager as anyone else to see the spectacle.

Athénaïs, gorgeously dressed *en déshabillé,* was surprised in her salon, eating strawberries and cream, with a little dog curled by her side.

'Sire! What a lovely surprise.' She rose, the dog nestled against her soft breast.

The King could not take his eyes off the white swell revealed by her loosely laced bodice. 'Yesterday, you surprised me. I thought it was my turn to surprise you,' he answered with ponderous gallantry.

She glanced at the crowd. 'Yes. So nice to see so many old friends.'

She caressed the fur on the dog's chest, and it lifted its throat in pleasure.

'You know that we must only meet in company, *madame.*'

Athénaïs interrupted him, throwing up one hand beseechingly. 'Please, sire, say no more. It is useless to read me a sermon. I understand that my time is over.'

'It is my responsibility to consider my throne and my country above all else.'

She smiled sadly. 'Oh, sire, say no more. You know I wish nothing but your glory . . . and your happiness.'

'A king must think of his duty.'

'Of course. But I am just a woman. All I

446

can think of is my poor heart.'

The King grasped her hand. 'Ah, Athénaïs.'

'Sire, can we . . . can we at least talk in private?'

'Of course,' he said and withdrew with her into a window alcove. She put the little dog down beside her. The King lifted it to the floor so he could take its place. Athénaïs turned her face away. Gently, he took her chin and turned her face back towards him. The Queen left the room, murmuring something about a headache.

'Dear Charlotte-Rose,' Françoise said to me with a strained smile. 'How have you been these past months? It seems an age since I last saw you. Shall we . . . shall we take a turn about the room? Madame de Montespan has some wonderful art.'

'Indeed she does,' I agreed and let Françoise lead me down the great salon, pausing to stare at a painting not very far from where the dark head and the golden head were bent so close to each other in the window alcove. Pretending to gaze at the painting, I strained my ears to listen, conscious that Françoise beside me was doing the same.

'The King must act as he wishes the state to act,' the King said.

'Is the King not a man too, sire?' Athénaïs said.

A murmur too low to hear. A sigh. A giggle.

'Very fine brushwork,' I said, edging closer

447

to the alcove.

'Yes. Um. Lovely colours,' Françoise said.

'You are mad,' Athénaïs sighed. 'Think what you do, sire.'

'Yes, I am mad, since I still love you.' The King stood up, drawing Athénaïs up with him. He bowed to the court, all wide-eyed and gasping with incredulous laughter, and hurried Athénaïs to her bedroom, where the door was shut tight and the curtains emphatically drawn. The little dog ran after them and scratched miserably at the door, whining, until the thump of what sounded like a thrown boot discouraged it and the dog lay down, nose on paws, tail tucked between its hind legs.

Françoise did not speak, her lips pressed hard together.

'Perhaps a stroll in the garden?' I suggested.

She did not respond but gathered up her dark heavy skirts with both hands and went out of the room. I followed, to find Athénaïs's footmen distributing pineapple ices in the garden, where the scent of orange blossom and tuberoses hung heavy in the air.

When the King and Athénaïs came out, flushed and languorous, some hours later, it was as if the past fifteen months' absence had never been. Athénaïs rode back to Versailles in the same carriage as the King and the Queen, and, soon after, a long baggage-train arrived carrying her dresses and jewels and

448

shoes and fans and shawls and maids and pets, Athénaïs taking up her old suite next to the King.

The King was still the King, however. In the summer of 1676, the Princesse de Soubise caught his eye. Soon, she was to be seen hurrying through the dark corridors of the palace to the King's apartments, a carelessly wrapped veil showing shining glints of her famous strawberry-blonde hair.

Unfortunately, the Princesse de Soubise was soon struck down with toothache and had to face the barber-surgeon, who wrenched the offending front tooth out with a pair of pliers. With a black gap in her teeth, the Princesse was not so attractive any more, and the King returned to a radiant and smiling Athénaïs, who soon proved her devotion to him by once again falling pregnant.

Then, in the early months of 1677, when Athénaïs was as big as the elephant in the King's menagerie, His Majesty began a dalliance with one of the Queen's maids of honour, Isabelle de Ludres. Nearly as voluptuous as Athénaïs — and six years younger — she caught the King's attention while dancing the minuet with him, by the simple expedient of pressing close to his body and lifting her blue eyes to his.

Athénaïs was furious. She began a rumour that Isabelle was riddled with sores from the English pox. Isabelle tearfully begged the

King to examine her from head to toe to prove she was free of any sores. An hour later, the King emerged, smiling, declaring her blemish-free. Athénaïs could no nothing but pace the floor and rage. 'That sly, back-stabbing, upstart *putain.* I'll show her! I'll make her wish she'd never been born,' she cried, both hands supporting her huge belly.

'What will you do?' I asked in interest. I was at court at that time with the Duchesse de Guise, who had come for Christmas and had been persuaded to stay a little longer by Françoise, who hoped for her help in break-ing Athénaïs's hold over the King.

Athénaïs cast me an irritated look. 'Just wait till this baby is born. I'll crook my little finger and the King will come crawling back.'

In early June, Athénaïs swept back to court, and Isabelle's power over the King was sud-denly and inexplicably broken. He had eyes only for Athénaïs, who leant her head against his shoulder at the gaming table and ordcred a flurry of new gowns, a pair of dancing bears, orange trees in silver pots and a giant gilded birdcage to keep her turtle doves in.

'He cannot even wait for us to undress her,' Mademoiselle des Oeillets, one of her ladies-in-waiting, told me. 'All she has to do is untie her bodice and he is upon her. He is insatiable.' She looked away, her face harden-ing. 'She knows he'll take his pleasure else-where if she is not here, ready and waiting for him. He'll not be denied by anyone.'

Desperately, Isabelle practised all her flirtatious arts, but it was as if the King did not see her at all. In September, she sent an unhappy message to the King, asking if she might retire to a convent. The King yawned and replied, 'Is she not there already?'

After that, the King dallied with a young girl from the country, who fled back home in tears after a bruising encounter with Athénaïs's wit; an English countess, who declared she found Versailles too stuffy after a week of enduring angry stares from Athénaïs's blue eyes; and my own newly acquired sister-in-law, Mademoiselle de Théobon, who received such a furious letter from her brother that she left the court in some confusion, wondering all the while who had written to let him know.

It was me, of course, writing an account of court gossip to my sister, Marie, with the line, 'Oh, la, have I told you Théobon's sister has caught the King's eye? I'm sure it'll amount to nothing, though *mordieu!* There are more royal bastards littering this place than unwanted kittens now, and the King making no move to legitimise any except for the Torrent's.' (My sister knew that the Torrent was one of Athénaïs's nicknames.)

Some may think it malicious of me to write such a letter, but I knew it would grieve my sister to have her young sister-in-law become

451

the latest of the King's mistresses and, besides, Athénaïs was not someone you wished to become an enemy.

Meanwhile, my own life was unendurable. The Duchesse de Guise would not permit me to leave her side. I spent all day standing on cold marble floors, my legs and feet aching, listening to her sour voice listing the faults of everyone I knew, except for the King, of course. Then all night I was expected to answer her every call, helping her to the chamber pot, rubbing her cold feet, reading to her from the Bible, fetching her a hot posset that she would then refuse to drink, complaining it was too hot or too cold, too spiced or not spiced enough.

Something had to be done. The next time we went to Versailles, for Easter in the year 1678, I went at once to Athénaïs's apartment — a series of twelve rooms, each a symphony of pale blue and gold and rose, filled with the scent of fresh flowers, face powder and expensive perfume.

Athénaïs was lounging on a velvet couch, her swollen feet stuffed into a pair of high-heeled slippers. Her maid of honour, Mademoiselle des Oeillets, was curling her hair with a hot poker (and I'd always thought those ringlets were natural) and she was eating sweetmeats from a violet satin box.

When I had first met Athénaïs, she had been twenty-six and angelically beautiful.

Now, she was thirty-seven and once again pregnant to the King. Her face was round as a wheel of cheese, and her blue eyes seemed to bulge above her plump cheeks. Her belly was so enormous she could have used it as a rather unstable table for four, and her cleavage was so deep she could have kept all the silver cutlery safely stored within.

She raised her eyebrows at the sight of me. 'Charlotte-Rose. What an unexpected pleasure.'

'I need to talk to you!' I clasped both hands near my heart.

'Always so dramatic. What's wrong?'

'I need help. I'm down on my knees and kissing your feet, metaphorically speaking. I will do so literally if you like, as long as you help me.'

'Why, whatever is the matter?'

'I cannot stand it any more. I'm a slave. The King might as well send me to the galleys. I'll be in service to the Duchesse until I'm an old, old woman. My hair and beard will have grown to the floor and I'll be bent in perpetual prayer, my back as bowed as that old hag's. They'll have to bury me kneeling.'

Athénaïs laughed. 'She is rather pious.'

'Pious! What a weak word. She's not pious, she's righteous, punctilious, sanctimonious . . .'

Athénaïs, smiling, held up one hand. 'I get the idea.'

'I will go mad if I'm to work for her any longer. She won't go to the theatre or the ballet, she disapproves of the salons, she prefers Normandy to Paris.'

'Indeed, a fate worse than death. My poor Charlotte-Rose.'

'What am I to do?'

'Well, that's simple enough,' Athénaïs answered. 'You must marry.'

'Who? Who would want me? I'm not beautiful like you, Athénaïs. No one wanted me when I was young and still a maiden. Who would want me now?'

I am twenty-seven years old, and I've already dragged my good name through the mud, I wanted to shriek. Instead, I composed myself and said, 'I have no beauty, no dowry, no land. I have nothing but my father's name, and even that I have disgraced. Who do you suggest I marry?'

She coiled one of her bright ringlets around her finger. 'You may go,' she said to Mademoiselle des Oeillets, who at once rose and backed out of the room. For a moment longer, Athénaïs was silent, her eyes fixed upon me.

'I like you, Charlotte-Rose,' she said at length. 'You never try to steal the King's affections or stab me in the back. Although you are quick and clever, you are not malicious. And your blood is as noble as mine. It makes me furious, seeing so many commoners at

454

court, seeking to creep higher by winning the King's good favour. And you could be useful to me, yes, indeed you could.' She spoke these last words so softly I could hardly hear her.

I stood silently as she gazed at me, coiling her ringlet about her finger. She seemed to come to some kind of decision, for she dropped the curl of hair and leant forward. 'I know someone who can help you, but you must assure me that you'll tell no one about her.'

'Who could possibly help me?'

'There is always a way,' she answered. 'You will need money, but I can help you there, as long as you remember that you owe me loyalty and discretion.'

'Of course.'

'You must have a strong spirit and a strong stomach too,' she warned me.

I thought she must mean the strength to cold-bloodedly marry a man I did not love, probably an older man with a drooping paunch and the whiff of decay in his mouth. I tried to smile. 'Am I not called Dunamis?'

'You must be sure that this is what you want.'

I huffed my breath out. 'I don't know what I want.'

'Of course you do,' Athénaïs answered impatiently. 'A young man of noble blood and good fortune, who knows the way of the court and will turn a blind eye to any affairs you have once you've delivered him an heir or two. Handsome enough that he does not turn your stomach, but not so handsome that he will treat you with contempt. Clever enough that he will not bore you, but not so clever that he will see through you. Rich enough to —'

'Of course I'd like a husband like that. But where am I meant to find him?'

Athénaïs cast me an exasperated look. 'The court is full of men like that, Charlotte-Rose. Take the time to look them over and choose one who you think will do. Pick one who is in favour with the King, if you wish to serve your family well.' She spoke with a faint lift of her lip, for Athénaïs's husband had been out of favour at court and she had had to rely on her own wiles to raise her family's fortunes.

'Oh, yes, a rich beauty like me can choose any man she wants.'

Athénaïs smiled. 'Of course you can. Choose wisely, because once you begin you can't go back.'

Curiosity was rising in me and a certain cold dread.

'When you have chosen the man you want, then you'll need something that belongs to him. A used handkerchief, a lock of his hair, some fingernail parings . . .'

'That sounds like witchcraft.'

Athénaïs sat back, regarding me through half-slitted eyes. 'Not at all. It's just a little love charm. Would you not like to be married, with your own grand house and servants, a carriage and six, and as many gowns as you like? Wouldn't it be sweet revenge, on all those who have mocked and scorned you?'

I hesitated. It would indeed be sweet.

'And your days would be your own. You'd be free to do just as you pleased.'

The temptation was too much. Despite a hard lump of fear in my throat, I nodded. 'Very well, I'll do it.'

A Lock of Hair

For the next week or so, I looked over the
unsuspecting crowd of courtiers for a man I
thought I could marry.

I was fastidious. One man was too corpu-
lent, another too short, yet another ungra-
cious when he lost at cards. One had an
unpleasant odour I could not tolerate, yet
another looked like a sack of potatoes in the
saddle. I could only marry a man who could
outride me.

He had to be clever (no matter what
Athénaïs said), and he had to love dancing,
and he had to make me laugh, and he had to
be kind. My list of desires grew longer and
longer, and the list of possible men soon had
no names on it at all. *Charlotte-Rose, stop being so finicky,* I told myself. *There must be
someone who's to your taste.*

A hunt was organised for the following
morning, the King's huntsmen having spotted a brown bear in the forest. Bear hunting

was considered grand sport at this time of year, when the hunting of most game was banned. Anticipating a grand chase through the forest, I dressed in my most dashing scarlet riding dress with a close-fitting hat of beaver fur. I could not afford my own hunters but was able to borrow a horse for the day — thanks to Athénaïs — a tall strong gelding with rather a wild eye.

'Are you sure you can handle him?' the groom asked as he lifted me into the saddle.

I hitched my knee over the pommel and straightened the folds of my skirt. 'I certainly hope he puts up a good fight,' I answered, touching his flank lightly with my whip. The gelding snorted and pranced. Both the groom and I smiled.

As I trotted out into the courtyard, filled with horses and men and dogs, I felt someone's eyes on me. Glancing around, I saw a square young man with a wig of rather military cut, its long curls tied back with a green ribbon to match his coat. He sat astride a very beautiful roan mare, with a finely bred head and beautiful lines. What I wouldn't have given for a horse like that.

Our eyes met and he smiled. I felt my cheeks warm. I was not the only woman to ride to the hunt, but the others were all either mounted on fat old nags or were seated in a horse-drawn buggy, prepared to follow the hunt as best they could on the country roads.

The King rode out, resplendent as usual in a feathered hat, an elaborately curled wig and a greatcoat embroidered all over with gold and crimson.

The horns sounded. The King led the way, his favourites clustered about him. I waited for them to be well on their way before allowing my impatient horse to follow. The man in green had waited too. His roan mare was close behind me as we rode out, both horses fretting at the bridle, wanting to gallop.

I let the gelding have his head as soon as we reached the road. He was fast and powerful, muscles moving under grey skin like satin. I could have sung with joy as we raced along the avenue of trees, the wind sharp enough to burn my cheeks. I heard hooves hammering fast behind me and half-turned my head. The man in green was close on my heels. I laughed and leant forward, gathering my reins tighter. At once, the gelding lengthened his stride. Clods of earth flew up from his hooves. The parade of poplars flashed past, bright green leaves gilded with sun. I closed my eyes, stretched out my arms and rode blindly, my body rocking easily with the thundering motion of the horse. Against my closed eyelids, warm light and cool shade flickered.

'Do you always ride with your eyes shut?' the man in green asked me, as the horses gathered in a clearing at the outskirts of the forest. The chief huntsman was examining a trace of bear droppings under a tree, the dogs whining and straining at their leash.

'Not always,' I answered. 'Not if I was racing cross-country.'

'You race often?'

'Not as often as I'd like,' I sighed. The Duchesse's idea of exercise was a slow promenade around the rose garden. I had not ridden once since entering her service.

'We should have good sport today,' he said.

I smiled. 'I live in hope,' I answered over my shoulder, turning to join the chase again.

The horns rang out and the dogs were belling. We raced a good course, down a long valley with plenty of fallen trunks to jump, and then a wonderful gallop along the ridge. Ahead, I heard the roar of a cornered bear. I reined in my horse, coming into the clearing carefully.

A shaggy brown bear was held at bay against a stand of beeches by a pack of barking dogs. A row of huntsmen with spears closed in around it. I was surprised that the bear was not bigger. It was only a head taller than me and looked rather cross-eyed. A dog rushed in and closed its jaws upon the bear's flank, and the poor beast yowled in pain.

I turned my face away and saw the King sitting on his black stallion nearby. He was smiling. Spurs glinted on the heels of his boots, and his stallion's satiny sides were torn

461

and bleeding. The bear roared in pain as one of the huntsmen skewered it with the heavy spear, its end braced into the ground. Another spear was thrust into its soft belly, and the bear rocked on its feet. It swiped out, sending another dog flying. Then a third spear was thrust through its throat. The bear fell heavily, blood spraying across the grass. A huntsman ran forward and drove a spear down through its shoulder, pinning the beast to the ground.

The King held up his hand. At once, a servant stepped forward with a mounting block. The King stepped down, fastidiously straightened the embroidered cuffs of his greatcoat, then held out his hand. A carving knife was ceremoniously placed in his palm. He sauntered over to the whimpering bear, dropped to one knee and ritualistically slashed at the bear's throat till the head rolled free. The King then stood, holding high the severed head, careful to hold it away from his body so the dripping blood would not stain his satin breeches. All the courtiers cheered and congratulated him heartily on his skill, his courage, his valour. The King smiled and inclined his head, dropping the bear's head in a sack.

'Would you like a drop of Armagnac?'

I turned to see the man in the green coat holding out a silver flask. I smiled rather mechanically, and took the flask and held it

462

to my lips, tilting back my head so I could drink deeply. The liquor seared a golden path from my lips to my gullet, and then spread a warm haze all through my body.

'Thank you.' I passed the flask back to him.

He made a wry face at the lightness of the container, then swiftly tossed off the remainder. 'I love the chase but have not much time for the kill,' he said. 'And, to be truthful, why kill a bear? It's not as if it tastes particularly good.'

'I cannot see the King wearing the bearskin to court,' I answered, casting an ironic glance at the King in his fine plumed hat and tight satin breeches.

He laughed. 'Perhaps he wants to spread it on his bed,' he said suggestively.

'I can't imagine any of his mistresses enjoying that. Bearskins must stink.'

He raised an eyebrow in surprise at my frankness. I blushed and silently cursed, once again, my wayward tongue. 'Thank you for the Armagnac,' I said and turned my horse's head away.

To my surprise, the young man followed me. 'I've never seen a girl toss back a shot like that before.'

'I'm a Gascon. We invented Armagnac. I'm sure we take it in with our wet-nurses' milk.'

He tilted his head, his gaze quizzical. 'I see. Perhaps that's why we haven't met before. I am Louis de Mailly, the Marquis de Nesle.'

'I am Charlotte-Rose de Caumont de la Force,' I answered proudly, rolling my 'r's with immense gusto. 'Though the reason why I've been absent from court in recent years is that I serve Madame de Guise, who has an inexplicable liking for the provinces.'

'Ah, yes. I know Madame de Guise.'

'She thinks the court is a cesspit of lust and fornication,' I said sadly.

'If only it was,' the Marquis said.

I was startled into a laugh. He grinned back at me. I felt a little jolt of excitement. He brought his horse in close beside mine, so close that the toe of his boot brushed my dress. Companionably, we rode through the trees, following the huntsmen who carried the dead bear swinging on a pole. We talked lightly of the court, and various scandalous affairs, and the new fashion for broad-brimmed hats and other such things.

When I returned my borrowed gelding to the stable, I asked the groom, in an idle sort of way, 'The man in the green coat, the one on that lovely roan . . . who is he?'

'The Marquis de Nesle? He's cousin to the Grand Condé,' the groom answered, understanding that I did not need his name but his lineage.

I bit my lip. The Grand Condé, Louis de Bourbon, was one of the richest and most powerful men at court and second cousin to the King. I would want for nothing if I was

464

to marry into that family. And really, the Marquis de Nesle was very handsome, in a slapdash sort of way. And he had made me laugh.

If I must make a man fall in love with me, it might as well be someone I like, I thought.

But first I had to acquire a lock of his hair or some fingernail parings.

I dared not bribe any of his servants, for I could not risk even the faintest suspicion of witchcraft. Witches were burnt to death, and my noble blood would not be enough to save me. Less than two years earlier, the Marquise de Brinvilliers had been tortured, then beheaded, her body burnt at the stake and her ashes flung into the wind. She had been accused of poisoning her father and two brothers, as well as many other unfortunates who had stood in her way.

The Marquise's death had sent ripples of unease all through the court. Friends and acquaintances of hers had found themselves interrogated, and one of the most important of the King's financial advisors, a man called de Pennautier, had found himself on trial too. He was eventually cleared in July 1677 and returned to court, but no one much liked having to eat with him.

Then, only a few months ago, a well-known Parisian fortune-teller had been arrested, accused of sorcery and murder. No doubt knowing she too faced torture and execution, she had delayed her trial by warning that the King was in danger and that there was a plot afoot to poison him. The King had appointed a royal taster to sample all his food and drink, which took so long it meant that his soup was always cold. At once, cold soup became all the rage.

All the court could talk of was poison and treason and soothsayers and satanic rites. There were rumours that children were being kidnapped off the streets of Paris to make blood baths for some rich noblewoman. The King's police force arrested a gang of alchemists, sorcerers, fortune-tellers and suspected poisoners who, it was said, made a brisk business selling 'inheritance powders' to assist people in getting hold of legacies sooner than expected. In terror, the King's taster employed his own taster, who then employed his own taster, until every meal eaten by the King had to pass through such a chain of tasters that the King received only the barest mouthful. Everyone took to carrying little dogs around with them so they could feed them titbits off their plate, and so make sure their food was free of poison too.

With the court a seething cauldron of suspicion, it was not a good time to draw attention to myself by asking for locks of hair, or fingernail parings, or vials of blood. I would have to be a great deal more subtle.

I prepared myself carefully for my next encounter with the Marquis. I wore my most becoming gown, with a cunningly padded bodice that gave me at least the illusion of a cleavage. I wore low-heeled slippers so I wouldn't tower over him (he was rather short, I must admit), and had Nanette coil my hair about a hot poker till I had a mass of dancing ringlets. I applied my maquillage extremely carefully, choosing a patch in the shape of a galloping horse in subtle reference to our meeting. Only then did I sally forth to the gaming rooms, a little ferment of excitement in the pit of my stomach.

The salons were crowded, the men wearing heavy elaborately curled wigs and long brocade waistcoats, the women with hair dressed in tight cascading ringlets *à la Athénaïs.* The room was hot and hazed with smoke from the candles, and footmen carried about trays of silver goblets filled with champagne.

The Marquis de Nesle was sitting at a basset table, his cravat rumpled and his wig askew. As I approached, he seized his wig and dashed it to the floor, crying, '*Mille diables!* The bank has all the luck tonight.'

'Maybe a new player will break his luck.' I slid into the seat opposite him.

The Marquis' face lit up in recognition but I ignored him, smiling sweetly at the Duc d'Orléans, who sat sideways in his chair, the tails of his salmon-pink satin coat hanging to

467

the floor. He raised a quizzical eyebrow and slurred, 'Ah, the *petite mademoiselle* from Gascony . . . the one who likes poking about in dark corners.'

'Are we here to chit-chat or to play?' I demanded.

'Well said,' the Marquis de Nesle cried, jamming his wig back on again. 'Deal, *monsieur.*'

I bent all my concentration to the game. At first, I played conservatively, taking my measure of the other players and keeping an eye on what cards were turned. In all those long tedious afternoons playing with the Queen and her ladies-in-waiting, I had learnt to memorise what cards were declared so I could calculate which ones remained in the pack and place my bids accordingly. I also found the Marquis ridiculously easy to read, for his broad dark face showed every thought that flitted through his brain. The Duc d'Orléans was not so easy but I observed him carefully and began to notice a few little mannerisms that gave his hand away.

When I had some money in hand, I began to play more recklessly. I laid a tall pile of coins on the Queen of Hearts, crying, 'This is the card for me.'

'A woman after my own heart,' the Marquis cried and pushed forward his own tottering pile of coins. 'Live or die, eh?'

Again I won, and again I left all the money

on the table. There was a little stir around the table, and a few people stopped to watch.

'Bold play, *mademoiselle*,' the Marquis said admiringly.

'Why, thank you, kind sir. It must be the company I'm keeping.'

The game continued. I played nonchalantly, as if I did not much care for the vast sum of money I was gambling. The Duc d'Orléans narrowed his eyes and looked at me unpleasantly. 'Are you sure, *mademoiselle*?'

'Of course, *monsieur*. I do nothing unless I am sure.'

'A woman with force of character,' the Duc d'Orléans sneered.

I smiled at him sweetly. 'You know me so well, *monsieur*.' Then I turned to the Marquis. 'It is my own name that he teases me for, you see. I am Charlotte-Rose de Caumont de la Force.'

'I remember,' he answered.

I tilted my head to one side, tapping one finger against my cheek, affecting a frown of puzzlement. Then I let my expression clear. 'Yes, of course. The man with the very fine roan and the flask of Armagnac.'

'I'm glad you remember my horse,' he said with an expression of mock hurt.

'I remember thinking you were a man of excellent taste,' I responded with a smile.

The Duc snapped out another card and once again I won. Despite myself, sweat prickled down my spine and in my armpits, and I could hear my pulse in my ears. I could not help my hand shaking as I pushed forward another pile of coins. Once again, the crowd stirred and murmured, and more people came to watch.

'You are very confident, *mademoiselle,*' the Duc d'Orléans said through gritted teeth.

'I feel like tonight is my lucky night,' I replied and flickered a wink at the Marquis, who grinned and lifted his goblet to me.

'*Mordieu,* thirty and the go,' the Marquis said. '*Monsieur,* she'll break your bank!'

'I doubt it very much,' the Duc drawled in response. He shook out his laces and prepared to draw another card. The crowd all drew a deep breath and leant forward, then burst into spontaneous applause as I won. The Duc d'Orléans pretended cool nonchalance as he pushed a great pile of shining coins towards me. There were so many of them that I had to tie them up in half a dozen napkins and give them to the waiters to carry away and lock in a strongbox for me. The Marquis de Nesle helped me while the Duc d'Orléans shrugged his narrow shoulders, rose and sauntered away.

'Well, you broke his run of luck. What a game! And you were cool as ice. You didn't even flutter an eyelid.'

'I was quaking inside. Here, feel my pulse. It's racing.' I proffered him my wrist and the

Marquis took it between his finger and thumb.

'It is indeed. I would never have guessed it.'

I bent my head close to him. 'My heart was pounding so hard I feared it would leap right out of my breast.'

He gave my décolletage an appreciative glance. 'Well, I wish I could learn to keep so cool during a game. I'm forever cursing and shouting and getting myself in danger of being called out.'

'Perhaps if we played together,' I suggested, 'we could study each other's techniques.'

His eyebrows shot up. 'What do you like to play?'

'Let's play piquet.' I cast him a smiling look over my shoulder. 'But let's make it interesting, shall we? What shall we wager?'

'How about a kiss?' the Marquis asked, catching me up eagerly.

'Let's take things a little more slowly,' I reproved him. 'How about we play for a lock of hair?'

'Black dust of tomb, venom of toads, powdered mandrake root and dried testicles of a stag,' the witch La Voisin said, grinding a nasty-looking paste in a black marble mortar. 'Did you bring some of your monthlies?'

I nodded, not trusting myself to speak, and passed over a small glass phial containing a sticky sample of menstrual blood.

'Not much here,' the fortune-teller said, holding it up to the flame of the candle. 'I'll add some dove's blood.'

I watched, queasy, as she scraped my menstrual blood into the paste and added a few drops from a bowl containing a meaty lump swimming in a pool of blood. Athénaïs sat next to me, her face wrapped in a veil, her form concealed under a heavy dark cloak. I too was cloaked and veiled, and found it hard to see in the small pavilion where we sat. The only light came from hundreds of candles set on the floor and table. They flickered over La Voisin's broad face, giving her a mysterious, almost demonic look. She wore a long robe of purple velvet embroidered with gold thread, which glittered when she moved. Dark leaves moved restlessly all around the summer house, adding to the sense of unease.

La Voisin took the Marquis' lock of hair and burnt it in a candle, then brushed the ashes into the mortar, grinding it with a few more drops of blood. The acrid smell of burnt hair lingered in the air, making me feel ill.

La Voisin dipped a quill into the mortar and carefully drew a pentagram within a circle on a piece of parchment, using a ruler and a wax seal as her guides. She then inscribed it with mystical symbols. Every now and again, she slugged down a mouthful from a squat bottle, sighing and wiping her mouth with the back of her hand, before refreshing her quill and returning to her task.

From a small jar, she took what looked like toad's feet, then fished out the small meaty lump from the bowl.

'What's that?' I asked, leaning away from the stench.

'A dove's heart.' Deftly, she rolled it all together in a bat's wing and tied it with twine. 'Nothing better for love spells.' She wrapped the noisome bundle up in the parchment and then sealed it shut with black candle wax. 'Tie this up in a pretty bag and give it to him to keep about his person.'

I held it away from me, wrinkling my nose. 'But it stinks.'

'The smell will pass in a day or two. Stuff the bag with herbs and flowers if you like. Jasmine and elderflowers and rose petals are all good for love spells.'

'But what possible reason can I offer him for giving such a gift?'

'Tell him it will give him sweet dreams, or protect him from poison,' Athénaïs suggested.

I dropped the bundle into my big tapestry purse and drew the drawstrings tight. *I'll never get the smell out,* I thought. *My bag will have to go to the rubbish dump.*

When I paid La Voisin, she bit each coin carefully before hiding it away inside an inner pocket. 'The spell won't fail you. Just make sure he never takes the bag off.'

La Voisin led us along a winding path through trees and bushes down the side of a tall house. We emerged in a wide street, lit only by a lantern above La Voisin's gate. Two more carriages were drawn up beside the road, waiting for us to leave. As the coachman handed us up into a carriage, another dark-veiled woman stepped out of the vehicle behind us and hurried up the path after the fortune-teller.

Athénaïs and I sat in silence as our carriage rattled away over the cobblestones. 'So, does it really work?' I whispered after a while.

'It seems to,' Athénaïs responded drily.

I was longing to ask her more. When did you first cast a spell on the King? How many times have you ensorcelled him? Have you ever asked La Voisin for other spells? What and where and when and why?

But I didn't dare ask. The bag seemed to be emanating a dark malignant force. I could feel it pulsating beside me.

'The King is a lustful man,' Athénaïs said, so quietly I could hardly hear her over the rattle of the wheels. 'If I am not in my apartment when he comes, he will fuck one of my maid-servants to kill time while he waits for me. They say it is my temper that makes it hard for me to keep a maid, but the truth is most of them fall pregnant and have to be pensioned off. Mademoiselle des Oeillets has

474

had a daughter by him, but he will not acknowledge it. She is half-mad with anger and despair, though she has sent the child to the countryside and is trying to pretend it was never born.'

I did not speak. Pity and revulsion and fear were knotted together in my heart.

'He used to have Louise in the morning, me after lunch, make a duty visit to his wife and then expect me to be ready for him again, hot and willing, after supper.' Athénaïs's voice was harsh in the darkness. 'We could never be sick, or tired, or, heaven forbid, have a headache. He will not wait for me to recover from giving birth. If I am not ready to bed him, he will simply find another woman. Lord knows, the court is full of them, all panting for him. And if I fail to please him . . . pouf! My chateau, my apartment at court, my jewels, my servants, everything, all gone. He'll simply give it to some other whore, younger and prettier than me.'

'But why . . . why do you stand it?' I whispered.

'But what else am I to do? It is all the power I have, the power to please the King. Without that, I am nothing.'

I shook my head. 'That's not true.'

'Yes, it is. You know it is. Why else are you here, buying love spells?' She gestured towards the bag beside me with one gloved hand.

475

'It's just not right.'

'It's the way things are,' she answered simply.

I knew she spoke the truth. It made me angry and restless. I wished desperately for a world where women were not used as bargaining counters in wars and marriages, a world where they had greater value than as mere brood mares, a world where they could earn their own income, have their own house, choose their own husband, travel where they wished, read and write what they wished, and speak their mind without fear. Such a fever of misery and rage rose up in me that I wanted to hurl the tapestry bag with its terrifying bundle out the window into the night; instead, I clutched it close to me, breathing in its reek of blood and ashes, knowing it could be my only chance to make my mark on the world.

THE DEVIL'S OWN LUCK

Versailles, France — May 1678

'You always have the devil's luck,' the Marquis grumbled, pushing a pile of coins towards me. 'I swear I'll stop playing with you. You're ruining me.'

'Lucky at cards, unlucky at love,' I answered with a shrug.

'Let me win and I'll change that for you,' he said with a wink. 'I've been trying to win a kiss from you for a week now, with no luck at all.'

I thought to myself, *What would Athénaïs say?* I let my lashes drop, looking away from him. 'I fear that I'll end up giving you far more than a kiss.'

'Is that so? Well, then, I fear I will simply need to keep on gambling with you. My luck must turn eventually.'

'I wouldn't bet on that.'

He laughed and tossed a few more coins onto the table. 'I already have.'

I laid down my cards. 'I must admit, sir,

my conscience is troubling me. You say I have the devil's own luck. Well, you see, I have a lucky charm. You know we Gascons are very superstitious and believe in such things. It certainly seems to work.'

He looked up from his cards. 'A lucky charm?'

'Would you like me to show you?'

He grinned. 'Of course.'

I slid my fingers inside my bodice and pulled out the bag of spells that I had hidden there. 'I cannot take the pouch off. It needs to lie against my heart at all times. If I was to take it off, the luck would be broken.' Hastily, I pushed it back inside my bodice.

He stared at my cleavage. 'I'm jealous of that little satin bag.'

I laughed at him. 'Because it lies against my heart, or because you'd like my devil's own luck at cards?'

'Both,' he answered with a grin.

I let my lashes fall. 'I wish . . . but no, such a thing would be impossible.'

'Why?'

I laid my hand over my heart. 'I need my lucky charm because, without my winnings, I cannot afford to stay at court. And if I do not stay at court, I will never find someone to love me. And I long for love.'

He flicked a glance at me, then toyed with his snuffbox. 'I'm sure there are many eager to love you, *mademoiselle.* You are most intriguing.'

'No doubt. But I must have a care for my family's good name.'

He eyed me speculatively, perhaps wondering how much truth there was in the rumours that I had romped about with the actor Michel Baron.

'So, you see why I keep my lucky charm so close.' I slid my hand inside my bodice so I could stroke the satin bag of spells. 'Now, shall we play again?'

Once again, I won. It was easier than I expected, because he was distracted, discarding cards without much thought. He did not ask about my lucky charm again, which surprised and disappointed me. I had been sure he would challenge me to a game, with the bag of spells as the prize. When he rose and bowed and said he would look forward to playing with me again, I felt a spurt of panic. My plan had not worked. He did not want the bag. I only smiled and pretended not to care, however. I was too experienced a gambler to show all my cards at once.

'Perhaps,' I replied. 'Only if we raise the stakes, however. I like a challenge.'

He smiled at me and my heart gave a sudden unexpected hop in my chest. 'Not tomorrow night. I must go to Paris. But the night after? A private game? In my quarters, perhaps.'

'You forget my family's good name.'

'I'm sure we could find a quiet corner somewhere.'

I eyed him quizzically. 'In Versailles? Really?'

He laughed. 'Anything is possible.'

'Very well . . . as long as you don't expect to have your wicked way with me.'

'I live in hope.' He bent to take my hand, turning the palm upwards so he could press a kiss into its soft centre. I felt a sharp stab of desire low in my belly. He must have felt my pulse leap, for his fingers were on my wrist. He gave me a lingering smile and bowed as he left the room.

Two nights later, he led me from the palace to a small grotto in the gardens. Tiny lanterns strung the tree branches. A table had been set up with fine china and silver and a three-branched candelabra glowing with candle-light. Two high-backed chairs with scrolled arms and gold velvet seats were set in place. A fine Persian rug had been spread on the lawn, and set upon it a gilded couch laden with gold velvet cushions.

'I am speechless,' I said, staring around.

He smiled. 'Not a word I usually associate with you.'

I pouted. 'I know, I know. Maidens should be mild and meek, swift to hear and slow to speak. Such a shame I'm not like that, isn't it?'

'A shame you're not mild and meek, or a

shame you're not a maiden?'

I tilted my head. 'That doesn't seem a very gentlemanly question, sir.'

'Won't you call me Louis?'

I gave an internal shudder. I could not bear to call him that. It was the King's name and seemed laden with menace to me. 'That seems a little familiar, don't you think? We've only known each other a few days.'

'It seems like much longer.'

I repressed a smile. 'Is that a compliment or an insult?'

'Oh, absolutely a compliment.'

'Perhaps it could be more prettily phrased?' I suggested.

'I'm sorry. I'll try and do better next time.'

'Perhaps a rondeau to my eyes?'

'I don't even know what a rondeau is. Some sort of poem, I'm guessing.'

'Oh, ignorant man. It's a poem of fifteen lines with a rhyming scheme of two. And "eyes" is so easy to rhyme with. Skies and pies and guise . . .'

'And thighs,' he suggested.

'How about "unwise"?' I returned swiftly.

'How about "tries"?'

'There's always "despise".'

'Or "implies".'

'You're really rather good at this. I fully expect a rondeau to my eyes next time we meet.' I allowed him to pull out my seat for me. The Marquis took a bottle of champagne from a silver ice-bottle and uncorked it with a deft gesture. I raised my eyebrows. 'No servants?'

'I thought I'd serve you myself tonight.'

'Unusual,' I said. 'Did you cook the meal as well?'

'That would be rather too unusual. I don't want to make you ill.'

'It's delicious,' I said, tasting the oyster soup carefully.

'I have a very good chef,' he answered.

I remembered a story about his cousin, the Grand Condé, and his chef. Apparently, the King had once been invited to Chantilly, the Grand Condé's country estate. When the fish had failed to arrive, the chef had killed himself with his filleting knife. His body had been found by a lackey who had rushed to tell him the fish had just arrived.

A little chill ran over me, and the Marquis at once got up and brought me a shawl, draping it around my shoulders. His thumbs lingered on my collarbones, and I shivered again. He tucked the shawl closer about my throat.

'You think of everything,' I said.

'More champagne?'

The oyster soup was followed by a succulent *confit de canard,* served with pear and walnut salad. 'I know how you Gascons like your ducks,' the Marquis said.

'There are more ducks than people in

Gascony,' I said with an exaggerated sigh.

The Marquis poured me another goblet of sparkling wine, then cleared the table by dint of shoving the dirty plates into a large picnic basket. He then brought out a dish of raspberries and cream and two long spoons. At first, I dipped my spoon in the bowl shyly but soon was laughingly duelling him for the last raspberry, our spoons clashing.

'Now, to play,' the Marquis said.

I eyed him quizzically. He laughed and brought out a pack of cards. 'Piquet, I meant. Though I could be persuaded . . .'

'Piquet it is.'

He cut the pack and shuffled quickly. 'You say that you are lucky at cards and unlucky in love. Well, I thought I might give you a chance to change that. How would you like to wager your lucky charm against a perfume that I guarantee will make men fall head over heels in love with you?'

I was intrigued. 'And how do you guarantee such a thing?'

'I'm willing to let you experiment on me.'

I laughed. 'I'll need to smell the perfume first.'

He brought out a beautiful crystal bottle with a glass stopper. 'Give me your wrist.'

Obediently, I held out my wrist. He withdrew the glass stopper and slowly swiped it along my wrist. 'It is made with the oil of roses, for Charlotte-Rose, and rare jasmine and basil and elderflowers and other things I can't remember. It was very costly.'

'It smells divine.' I lifted my wrist to my nostrils and sniffed delicately.

'You must take off the lucky charm, though. This must be a fair game. And if I win, I'll claim not only your lucky charm but a kiss as well, that kiss you've been denying me all week.'

My heart was beating faster. I felt a little giddy. Slowly, I slid my fingers into my bodice and withdrew the satin bag. With a breathless laugh, I tossed it onto the table. He put the perfume vial next to it, and then expertly dealt the cards.

I was determined not to let him win too easily, but to my surprise I found myself fighting to stay in the game at all. The Marquis played with absolute dedication, first taking off his wig and tossing it on the couch. 'Easier to think without my wig,' he explained. His own hair was dark and cropped very short. A short while later, he loosened his cravat. 'Constricts the blood vessels to the brain,' he explained.

'You should try wearing stays,' I said.

'I'd be happy to loosen them for you,' he offered.

'Enough.' I pointed at the cards on the table. 'Focus on your game.'

Rather to my surprise, he won the first round.

'You should play without your wig more often,' I said.

'The King would banish me from court. He did not like my coat last week. He stared at me all evening, then sent a lackey to tell me never to wear it again.'

'Not enough lace?' I asked.

'No lace at all.'

'Well, you know the King makes a great deal of money from the tax paid on lace.'

'It's so infernally uncomfortable. I can't bear the way it flops over my hands all the time.'

'Wear it on your cravat.'

He made a face. 'Must I? I suppose I must. Shall we play again? If I win this round, I'll have won a kiss from you, and I must admit I'm looking forward to it.'

'Don't get too cocksure. I want to win that perfume. I very much like the idea of making men fall madly in love with me.'

'You don't need a perfume for that, Charlotte-Rose.'

'Oh, very pretty. Well said. I'll be hearing a rondeau from you soon.'

'You don't need the perfume, but I think I really do need that kiss. You have the most fascinating mouth I've ever seen.'

'Really? Always in motion, I suppose.'

'Mmm-hmmm,' he replied, staring at it.

I drank down the rest of my champagne, partly to hide my mouth from his intent gaze.

No one had ever called my mouth fascinating before. Too big, too bold, too full-lipped, too red, too loud, too cheeky, too talkative. Never fascinating.

The Marquis cut and dealt the cards deftly, then, smiling, poured us both goblets of Armagnac. I gulped a mouthful, all my attention on the game.

'You intrigue me, *mademoiselle.* You ride like a man, you drink like a man and you play cards like a man. I think you must be utterly without fear.'

I cast him a quick irritated glance. 'What is there to be frightened of?'

'Falling?'

'I haven't fallen off a horse since I was a child. And if I did, I'd just get back up again.'

'That's what I mean.'

'Really, women are not as weak and nervous as you men seem to think. Indeed, if we were allowed to, we could do anything you men can do.'

He was amused. 'Really?'

'Absolutely. We could be great writers, artists or scholars. We could be doctors or scientists or inventors. We could rule a kingdom if we had to.'

'Then why is history not filled with accounts of women doing such things?'

'Because we're not allowed to. Women aren't allowed to study, or go to university, or own their own property. I think men are afraid of what we'd achieve if ever we were allowed to learn.'

The Marquis tilted his head, considering his cards. 'Well, there can only ever be one master, you must admit the truth of that. Are we talking or playing?'

I was so incensed by this that I won the next round by a long lead, which made him frown and bend his attention to his cards once more.

The third round was hard fought. If I had not regained my temper, I may well have won the game. I was, however, more determined than ever to win my independence. That the only way to get free was accepting the shackles of matrimony was an irony I recognised ruefully. However, as the wife of the Marquis de Nesle, my position at court would be assured. I could go to Paris whenever I wanted. I could maybe even find time to write as I so desperately longed to. Perhaps I could even begin my own salon. It would become famous for its wit and brilliance. Poets and philosophers would flock there. I would be famed for my clever tongue, my quick wit and my astounding tales that swept the reader away . . .

'I declare six,' the Marquis said.

I wrenched my attention back to the game and realised that I had stupidly cast away a card that I should have kept. Though I fought back, it was too late. When we added our points, the Marquis had won the round.

He grinned and picked up the small satin bag, tossing it in his hand. Deftly, he slung it about his neck, tucking it inside his shirt. 'Now,' he said, 'for my kiss.'

He rose and came swiftly to my side. I pressed my back into my chair in instinctive denial, but he dropped to one knee, slid his hand round to the back of my neck and drew me forward. I pressed both hands against his chest, but he was too swift for me, pressing his mouth hard against mine. I think I gasped in surprise. He took instant advantage, thrusting his tongue inside my mouth, plundering my mouth ruthlessly.

I felt desire twist in my stomach. One part of me wanted to go down before him like wheat before a thresher; another part resisted. His hand gentled, slid down to cup my shoulder. His mouth followed. For just one moment, I let my body respond. His hand found my breast, squeezing it through the silk. I remembered the padding and pushed his hand away.

'I think a kiss was all you won, *monsieur,*' I said. My voice was unsteady.

'You will not be so cruel,' the Marquis pleaded. 'Surely just one more? A little one?' Even as he spoke, he kissed me on the mouth again. It tasted unbearably sweet. His lips were soft and gentle, his hand slowly caressing the back of my neck. I think I sighed, melting a little in his arms. Once again, he took instant advantage, nudging my lips apart with his tongue, drawing me up so he could caress my waist, sliding his hands down to cup my bottom, pressing his leg between mine, taking me deeper than I had ever intended to go. I felt a surge of desire in my loins, felt the roar of it in my ears.

I tore my mouth away. 'Stop. Please.'

He stared at me hungrily, his breath coming rapidly. 'I'm sorry. It's just . . . I don't think I can resist you. I've never met a girl like you.'

'I'm not that unusual.'

He reached out one finger and traced my mouth. 'One more kiss?'

I shook my head. 'You've already taken much more than we ever wagered.'

He bit his lip, eyeing me, one hand fiddling with the ribbon about his neck. The ribbon the pouch hung on. I wondered if the bag of spells could already be working on him. Perhaps he could smell its faint unpleasant odour. Perhaps it was because it contained the ashes of his hair as well as my own blood.

'Another game?' he suggested.

'What shall we play for?'

He bit his lip. 'Another kiss? Perhaps . . . not only on the mouth. Somewhere else as well.'

'Where?'

He pressed his thumb against my nipple,

which at once hardened against the silk of the gown. I hoped the padding of my bodice would hide it from him, but I fear he felt it nonetheless.

I stepped away, shaking my head. 'No.'

'Then how about . . . here.' He touched the hollow between my collarbones.

'All right . . . but you must wager that bottle of perfume that will make men fall madly in love with me.' I was not really sure what I was doing now. My seduction of the Marquis seemed suddenly fraught with danger. I just knew I was determined not to succumb to him as easily as I had to Michel. All Michel had done was kiss me and tell me that he had wanted me, and I had leapt gladly to my ruin. This time, I was playing for higher stakes.

The first round I won. The Marquis frowned and poured us more Armagnac and squinted at his cards. He won the next round, but only by a few points. The last game was filled with tension. We both played with intense concentration, barely noticing that the candles were guttering in their sockets and the moon was low.

The Marquis won. As he slammed down his cards, his face filled with jubilation. 'Ah-ah! Another kiss. Come here to me, Charlotte-Rose. Come and kiss *me.*'

He flung himself down on the couch and held out his arms to me. I rose and went slowly towards him, searching his face, my stomach fluttering with nerves. His face softened. 'I will not hurt you, *chérie.*' He drew me down so our mouths met and clung.

It was a long, long kiss. Somehow, I found myself lying back on the cushions, the Marquis' body half-covering mine, his hand tangling my hair, one shoulder bared to the cool night air. He lifted his mouth from mine, smiled at me and then shifted his body so that his mouth was at the junction of my collarbones, his tongue tracing lazy circles in the hollow. I sighed. My bones seemed made of honey, my skin dancing with a million tiny stars.

He shifted lower, his tongue finding a winding path towards my cleavage. I pressed both hands into his cropped curls, stopping his slow descent. 'I don't believe that was part of our wager.'

He groaned. 'Charlotte-Rose, you are cruel. Lovely and cruel. Won't you let me . . . just a little taste . . .'

I shook my head.

'Another game?' He hoisted himself up on his elbow so he could play with the dark ringlets coiling over my shoulder.

'I had better not. My family's good name, you know.'

'Just one round? My perfume, wagered against . . .' He paused and drew his hand in a rapid motion down my shoulder to my breast.

I shook my head. He leant closer, kissing my mouth, my cheek, my neck, sucking gently on the lobe of my ear. I tried to turn my head away, but he seized my chin and kissed me again hungrily. For a moment, I let him, surrendering my mouth, taking his tongue into my mouth, sucking it, biting it, letting him slide his knee between mine, arching my back so he felt the whole of my body press against him, my breasts almost spilling from the tight cage of my bodice. Then I thrust him away. 'No.'

He dropped his head onto my shoulder. 'Please, Charlotte-Rose. Just one more game.'

'All right then,' I said. 'One round. If I win, I get the perfume that will make men fall madly in love with me. And then I'll use it to find a man who will love me and care for me and *marry* me. Do you understand?'

He nodded. The candles had all guttered out, so I could only see his face by the faint light of the fairy lanterns strung overhead. I could not tell what he was thinking, but the quick pant of his breath made me hope that I had him where I wanted him.

'Very well, then, this is what you must wager. If I win, I get to see your breasts. I get to see you and I get to touch you.' He ran one finger down my bare skin, towards my cleavage. My body jolted under his touch like

492

a racehorse under a whip. I could scarcely draw oxygen to my lungs.

I managed to shake my head. 'The stakes are too high. I don't believe in this perfume of yours.'

'Trust me, it's working. It's working on me.'

'Really?'

He nodded. 'I promise I'll do nothing you would regret. I'll not . . . take you. I just want to look . . . and touch . . . and maybe . . . taste.'

My body was as hot and soft and malleable as melted wax. If he had wanted to, he could have taken me there and then, and I would have opened to him like a flower to a hungry bee.

'If you win, you can look,' I said harshly. 'But no touching . . . and no . . .' I could not say the word.

He smiled and leant forward to kiss me, confident my mouth would open under his. It did. My head fell back and he sucked gently on my tongue. 'But you taste so good,' he murmured. 'Sweet as honey. I'd like to taste every single part of you.'

'That is not . . . part of the deal,' I managed to say. Somehow, things had got away from me, rather like a carriage drawn by runaway horses.

He smiled. 'Perhaps another game,' he said briskly, lifting himself away from me. 'Shall I cut? Do we need more light? I think we do.

Let me light some more candles. When I win this game, I want to make sure I can see . . . everything.'

I lost the game. It's no wonder, really, drunk as I was on champagne and brandy and love play. The Marquis made me undress for him, removing first my beribboned garter, then my silk stockings, then my outer skirts, then . . . very slowly and shyly . . . I undid my bodice and let it fall, standing before him in only my stays and chemise. He drew a deep shuddering breath.

'You'll have to undo my stays. I cannot unlace myself.'

'It would be my pleasure,' he answered. He drew me down so I sat on the edge of the couch, my back towards him, his thighs on either side of my body. I was so aware of him, it was as if the space between our bodies sizzled and smoked. He lifted the great mass of my hair out of the way, kissing the small bones at the back of my neck one by one. Slowly, he unlaced my stays, kissing my back lower and lower till he reached halfway down my spine. Then he slid his hands forward until he cupped both my breasts, pulling me closer to him so my bottom slipped into the space between his legs. I was instantly aware of the hard bulge between his thighs, pressing against my buttocks.

'I rather think I may need to stop now,' the Marquis said thoughtfully. 'Just let me . . .'

He ran his tongue slowly over my shoulder, then suddenly, so suddenly that I gasped, he lifted me and twisted me, bending me backward over his arm, his mouth finding my breast. He sucked and bit me, so I groaned and writhed, totally unable to stop myself. His hand rucked up my chemise, sliding unerringly for that most secret and feminine part of me. He found it and plunged his finger in, lifting his head to gasp. I moaned and twisted my body away, grasping my untied stays to my breasts.

'I'm sorry. I couldn't help myself. You're just so . . . Charlotte-Rose, please, I need to . . .'

'No.' I gathered up my clothes and tried to tie them around me again.

'I . . . please . . .'

'No.'

He caught me and held me fast, dropping down on his knees before me. 'I think I'm going mad. I must have you. Would it help if I promised to marry you?'

I stared down at him.

'Please . . . I mean what I say.'

'You mean it? You'll marry me?'

'Yes . . . if you'll just let me . . .' He drew down my bundle of clothes so he could caress my bare shoulder. One hand pushed me gently backward, the other slid around to cup my bottom through the crumpled linen of my chemise. His body was against mine, his

weight pressing me down against the cushions, his hand pulling my thighs apart. It
would have been so easy, so easy, just to lie
back, to let him thrust between my thighs, to
let him have his release.

But I pushed him away, shaking my head.
'We must be married first.'

He groaned. 'But it'll take weeks . . . I need
you now.'

I closed my knees. 'When we are married.'

He dropped his head into his hands, his
fingers writhing through the cropped curls.
'Charlotte-Rose, you'll be the death of me.'

'Marry me quickly then,' I said and leant
forward to give his bare shoulder a sharp little
nip with my teeth.

He groaned, lifting up my face so he could
kiss me again. 'We could always make another
wager. Now that I have the devil's own luck
myself.'

One More Game

Versailles, France — June 1678

The news of our engagement caused an absolute sensation at court.

Smilingly, I handed in my resignation to the Duchesse de Guise, and I stayed at Versailles after she went huffing back to Normandy. Athénaïs was amused and told the King she had always liked me, so the King gave the match his approval. I was allowed to keep my stuffy closet of a room, though it seemed smaller than ever now. I could not wait to be married and have my own chateau in Paris and a country estate and a carriage and six. Roans, I thought.

The Marquis' family were livid with rage. 'A Huguenot! Without a dowry! It's a scandal! A disgrace! It must be stopped!'

But the Marquis de Nesle was smitten. *'Je t'aime, je t'adore, tu es mon amante,'* he whispered into my hair. *'Ma belle, ma douce, mon seul amour.'*

It was enough to make me feel giddy. I

began to think I was falling in love with him too. I ran to meet him when he came creeping to my room late at night and laughed breathlessly when he swept me up in his arms. I let him kiss me and fondle my breasts and suck on my earlobe, and once I let him take the glass stopper of his costly perfume and run it slowly down my cleavage, parting my clothes till my breasts were bare to his gaze and he could anoint my burgeoning nipples with the scent of roses and jasmine. He bent then and took my nipple into his mouth, and all I could do was clutch his head and try not to moan too loudly.

It was true that he had the devil's own luck at cards now. Step by slow step, I was persuaded to reveal more of myself to him. We played piquet every night, long past the midnight hour, and every night he won the chance to kiss and touch another part of me.

'Another game?' he would say.

'What's the wager?'

'If you win, I'll give you a necklace of jet to match your wicked black eyes. If I win, you have to sit on my lap.'

'But I'm really perfectly comfortable here in my own chair,' I answered.

'I promise you my lap is very comfortable too.'

'I'm sure it'll be quite hard,' I answered.

He sucked in his breath. '*Mon Dieu*, Charlotte-Rose, you never fail to surprise me.

If I wasn't before, I am now. Please come and sit on me.'

'I'm not sure that's a good idea.'

'I'll take you to the theatre tomorrow night. And give you a ride on my roan. And a necklace of jet.'

'Oh, all right then. But you know it's only because I want to ride your horse.'

He muttered something I didn't catch — but which I am rather sure was a reference to wanting to ride *me* — and cut the cards. And although I won that game and the next, he did eventually win the right to perch me on his lap. He drew me down slowly, spreading his legs, his arm like a vice about my waist, the other sneaking up to cup my breast in its padded bodice, and I could feel that he was, indeed, very hard.

'You are not very comfortable at all,' I told him, pouting.

'No, I'm not. I don't think I've ever been more uncomfortable in my life. Good God, don't wriggle. Stay like that, very still.'

So I sat very still, but he began to rock me, grinding me down against that stiff protuberance underneath me. I broke free, breathless and squirming inside, and fled to the opposite side of the room. 'That was not part of the wager. I shall not play with you again.'

He laughed at me. 'Really? No more piquet? Are you sure?'

'Quite sure,' I answered.

He got up, straightening his waistcoat. 'Very well then.'

'All right, then, one more game. But I won't sit on your lap again.'

'What will you wager? I want your stockings, both of them, and I want to be the one to remove them. What do you want?'

'A kiss?' I said in a small voice, feeling a little like a dazzled child.

'But then I win both ways. All right, let's play.'

He liked winning garments from me, taking first my garter, then one shoe, then the other, then my necklace, then one of my petticoats. He was just as happy to shed his own clothes, but I did not like to see that heavy little pouch hanging about his neck. I could not bear the smell of it, or the feel of it pressing against my skin. He began to lay wagers for me to undress him, but I never let him win those games. Once, we lay together on my bed, the Marquis nearly fully dressed and me nearly fully naked, with him trying to guide my fingers to undo the fastening of his breeches and me resisting with all my strength.

'You're driving me insane, Charlotte-Rose. I want to feel you against my skin.'

'I can't trust you,' I said, and indeed I was right. The Marquis was always pushing me for just a little more. If he won the right to kiss my lips, his hands would be roaming all over my body even as he devoured my mouth. If he won the right to remove my stockings, his hands would slip higher, seeking to touch that secret part of me that so fascinated him. I was always wary, keeping my thigh muscles clenched against him, my knees locked close, and he was always seeking to soften me, making me drunk on Armagnac, inflaming my senses with perfume and delicious foods, inflaming my body with his kisses and his audacious touch.

One night, we kept on playing till I wore nothing but my chemise.

'One more game,' he said. 'Please. I want to see you naked. I'll not touch, I promise. I'll only look.'

I shook my head.

'I'll wager my roan mare. I know you like her.'

I was, I'm ashamed to admit, tempted. But I shook my head. 'No. Else there'll be nothing to look forward to on our wedding night.'

'Please, Charlotte-Rose.'

'No.'

He slammed out of my room in a temper, and I felt sick with worry in case I had lost him. But the next morning he came with flowers and a rondeau to my eyes that must have kept him up composing till dawn. And if there were rather a lot of cries and sighs and thighs in the poem, no one but me was ever going to read it. That night, I let him kiss me till my knees were weak and my head lolling. I did not protest when he untied the ribbons of my bodice. I did not stop him as he kissed me down my body, parting my clothes, freeing my breasts, kissing his way down towards my belly button. I did not make him stop. I only lay back and sighed, and clutched his curly head to me, and wished aloud that we were married *right now*.

'When?' I asked. 'When can we be married?'

'Soon,' he promised. 'I need my cousin's permission.'

'But we have the King's permission.'

He bent his head again and swirled his tongue in my belly button. I lifted his face so he would look at me. 'When?' I asked again.

'Soon, I promise.'

I sat up and pulled my clothes about me again. 'Soon is not soon enough.'

'Set a date,' he said, pulling me against him and kissing my bare shoulder. 'Set a date and I'll make it happen. Just let me touch you . . . down there.'

'Down there?'

With a swift movement, he had me on my back, my skirts rucked up, knees spread so he could kneel between my legs. His hands slid down my bare thighs till his thumbs were just touching the point where my thighs met my pelvis. His touch was like a branding iron.

He smiled at my shocked face. 'Midsummer's Eve,' I answered faintly.

Slowly, slowly, he slid his thumbs inside me. Slowly, slowly, he parted the soft damp lips, then quickly, savagely, he thrust both thumbs as far inside me as he could. I cried out and arched my back. He pulled his hands away and took both my wrists in his, pinning them above my head. For a long moment, he looked down at me, his lips parted, breathing quickly. I twisted, drawing my knees towards my chest, feeling both unbearably aroused and also frightened. His face was so hard, so unreadable. Then he nodded. 'Midsummer's Eve,' he said, and got up and left the room.

During the day, we walked in the gardens, or we rode in the forest and picnicked among the trees. He loved to see my body by day-light. I swear he would have had me out there in the open if I had let him. At night, we danced and drank champagne and went to the theatre. If the lights were low, he would slide his hand under my gown, drawing slow circles on my silk-covered legs, higher and higher, ever higher. I'd have to rap him with my fan, blushing, and hastily straighten my clothes.

One night, playing piquet in my little room, he wanted to brush my hair. I had already lost my garter and my stockings, my pearls and my petticoats and my dress; he had lost his coat and his waistcoat and his cravat and his shoes and stockings. I was languorous and smiling, deep in a haze of alcohol and scented candle smoke and anticipation. Although I could glimpse the bag of spells through his open shirt, I had got used to shutting my mind to it.

'Come sit on the stool,' he said. I obeyed, and he took my hair down from its pins, drawing it through his hands, bending to smell it. I only wore the perfume he had given me now, and the air was heady with its rich enticing smell.

'Where's your brush?'

I gave it to him, and he brushed my hair slowly, sensuously. I sighed and bent my head forward. I felt so dizzy I might fall. He said in my ear, 'Come lie on the bed, *chérie*. I want to see you clad only in your hair.'

'Was that part of the wager?' I answered drowsily. 'I don't think so.'

'Your hair is so long and thick, it's like a cloak,' he said. 'You'll be more modest than if you wore a chastity belt, I promise you.'

I smiled, rather ruefully, but allowed him to draw me up and push me down on the bed. As he unbuttoned my chemise, I raised myself on my elbows. 'Remember . . .'

'I know. Only combing your hair. That's all I'm allowed to do. No kissing.' He leant forward and brushed my lips with his. 'No touching.' He slid his hand inside my chemise and stroked the curve of my breast. 'No tasting.' He put his mouth to my nipple and sucked it briefly through the cotton of my chemise.

I rested my hands on his head. *'Chéri,'* I sighed.

He sat up. 'I know, I know. Here, just let me slide this down. I won't take it all off, I promise.' He slid the chemise off my shoulders so it pooled around my hips, then drew my hair over my shoulders so it hung down over my breasts. He parted it carefully with his fingers, allowing my pink rosebud nipples to poke through. 'There, perfect,' he said. 'That's how I'll expect you to dress at our wedding.'

'Imagine what the Duchesse de Guise would say,' I giggled.

He reached forward and gently touched one nipple. 'I love the way it hardens when I touch it. Won't you touch mine too? Let's see if a man's nipple hardens the way a woman's does.'

Shyly, I reached forward and let my fingers push his shirt open. Avoiding the bag of spells, which hung on its ribbon against his muscled chest, I gently touched his nipple. It immediately hardened into a nub.

'Won't you kiss it?' he asked.

I shook my head, closing the shirt so it covered the bag of spells. He sighed. 'Let me kiss yours then. It's too cruel to let me so close and not let me kiss you.'

So I let him part my hair and take my

nipple in his mouth. He laved it with his tongue, sucking gently, then suddenly bit me so hard I yelped and pushed him away. 'Ouch. That hurts!'

He looked contrite. 'I didn't mean to hurt you. I've never kissed a woman's nipples before. I didn't know they were so sensitive. I know now. I won't hurt you again. Please let me make it up to you. Lie down. I'll be so gentle.'

I lay down on my stomach, and he drew the chemise down over my hips and threw it on the floor. For the first time, I was completely naked before him. I pressed my body down into the bed, feeling vulnerable and a little afraid, but he did as he promised, taking my hair and spreading it over my back like a cloak.

'So beautiful,' he said. I felt my lips lift in a smile. No one had ever called me beautiful before. 'Ravishing. Utterly ravishing.'

Slowly, slowly, the Marquis brushed my hair, from the crown of my head to its curly tip. Slowly, slowly, I relaxed, resting my head on my arms, all my muscles loosening till I was as soft and malleable as clay.

'Your hair's so long,' he whispered. 'Look, it reaches past your bottom.' He took the end of my hair in his hand and began to caress my bare buttocks with its silky tips, as if it was a feather. I sighed and my thighs parted involuntarily. He brushed the tips of my hair

506

down the cleft of my buttock then teased me between the legs. I squirmed.

'Is that brushing?' I asked.

He drew the ends of my hair away, winding it about his wrist and then about his arm. 'It's like a rope,' the Marquis whispered. 'So soft and yet so strong.'

Suddenly, he yanked on my hair, pulling my head back, my back arched like a cat stretching. I cried out.

'I would so love to touch you there,' he murmured, sliding his fingers into the cleft between my buttocks. 'I'd so love to be on top of you. Can I just . . .'

Before I could say a word, he sat astride me, all his weight on the base of my buttocks. Dragging on my hair so tightly my spine was bent like a bow, he pressed himself against me, his other hand seizing my breast. He was naked from the waist up. He must have taken off his shirt without me realising. I felt the bag of spells squashed against my back and tried to break free, repulsed.

'No,' I cried. 'Stop! Enough, enough!'

He would not let me go. Keeping a tight hold on my hair, he let go of my breast and plunged his hand down between my legs, lifting me up and jamming me against his penis, straining against the silk of his breeches. If he had been naked, he would have been inside me. As it was, I could feel my body being wrenched open.

'Stop! You're hurting me. You promised.'

He threw me down on the bed, saying savagely, 'Yes, only your hair, only brushing.' He took the brush, dragging it through my hair so hard it brought tears to my eyes. His hand pushed me down so firmly my face was squashed into the pillows. I could not breathe. I flailed, trying to break free. Then he took the handle of the brush and thrust it between my legs, jabbing it just inside the lips of my vagina. I froze, feeling his hand heavy on my head, the cold hard end of the brush threatening to impale me. For a moment, we rested there, me not daring to move, him panting into my neck. Then he hurled the brush away.

'I'm sorry,' he said. 'You should not tempt me so much.'

I grasped the sheet to my breasts. 'You're right. We should stop.'

'Yes,' he said. 'This must stop.' He got up, drawing his shirt on again.

'Only till our wedding,' I said.

He jerked his head. 'Yes. Till our wedding.'

For three days, he stayed away from me. I was tense with anxiety. What if he had changed his mind? What if the wedding plans had fallen through? Nanette had heard the servants gossiping about how the Marquis' cousin, the Grand Condé, had told him he must end things with me or risk being cast out of the family. I felt I could not bear it if all my plans came to naught, and I wondered if I had miscalculated. Perhaps if I had let him have his way with me . . . *But then why would he marry me,* I told myself, *if he had got what he wanted for nothing.*

I was asleep in bed on the third night when I heard a soft scratching at the door. I scrambled up and ran to open it, dressed only in my nightgown. The Marquis was leaning against the wall, wearing only a shirt and breeches, a candle in one hand.

'I'm sorry,' he said. 'I shouldn't have done it.'

'It's all right. It's my fault. I shouldn't have let it go so far.'

He pushed at the door, stepping in. I stopped him. 'Better not.'

He drew me towards him, his eyes on the slight swell of my unfettered breast beneath my nightgown. 'I cannot stop. I've tried. Don't make me stop.' He kissed me on the mouth, backing me into the room. I pushed both hands against his chest, but I could not stop him. He put the candle down on the table and seized me by the hair, kissing me, grasping my bottom so I was brought up hard against him, feeling his urgent need. 'I love you, you know that. I've told the whole court we are to marry. My God, I've even defied the head of my family. You cannot deny me now.'

'We'll be married soon,' I said desperately.

'No, I want you now. I can't wait any longer.'

'No. Please. No.'

I shouldn't have said 'please', the word he had said to me so often. For he had me back on the bed in seconds, tearing away his shirt, wrenching at the fastening of his breeches, his arm across my throat. He was too strong, too fast. I had only time to gasp a breath before he had ripped my nightgown away.

As he drove into me, again and again and again and again, the satin bag of spells banged against my chest, making me gag with the smell of decay and rotting herbs. The stench filled my nose, my throat, my stomach, as he emptied himself into me. When he collapsed against my breasts, the bag was crushed between us, a heavy stinking lump that seemed to brand my skin, a burning pin to impale me.

BLACK MAGIC

Versailles, France — June 1678
I found it hard to get out of bed the next day.

My body hurt all over. My mouth was puffy and torn, there were dark bruises on my neck and breasts and wrists and thighs, and when I sat on my chamber pot I felt like I was passing acid instead of urine.

It is your own fault, I told myself. *You gave him the bag of spells. You wore the perfume he said would drive men crazy with love. What did you expect?*

Yet tears rolled slowly down my cheeks. I washed myself carefully with my softest flannel, hid my torn nightgown at the bottom of my chest and found myself another one, the softest and most voluminous one I owned. I pulled all the sheets off the bed and thrust them out of sight, then crawled under my eiderdown, too ashamed to ring for Nanette and ask her to remake the bed. I lay there, occasionally sniffing and wiping my eyes with

511

the back of my hand.

It'll be different when we're married. He was only so rough because you teased him so much, I told myself. But I had not forgotten that moment when he had threatened to jam the handle of my brush up inside me. *Perhaps he did not realise how much he hurt me,* I thought. *Perhaps it is the black magic, driving him to be cruel. Perhaps if I get rid of the bag of spells, he will be gentle with me again, and call me* ma belle, *and tell me how much he loves my mouth.*

Nanette soon came scratching at my door, and I told her I was sick. She made up my bed for me with fresh sheets, then brought me broth and well-watered sweet wine to drink, and a cloth soaked in lavender water. She would have combed my hair for me, but I flinched at the touch of her hand. She went away, her face in a knot of worry. I slept for a while. When I woke, she brought me a hip-bath and a train of footmen carrying jugs of hot water, and I sat in the bath, my knees pressed to my chin, until the water was cold. She washed my hair for me, telling me stories about when I was a little girl and the funny things I'd say, and all the naughty things I did. I turned my head and rested my cheek on my knee and almost smiled. She gave me a jar of comfrey salve to dab on my cuts and bruises, and a foul-tasting herbal concoction to drink, and said not a word except, 'There, my Bon-bon, there, my little cabbage, is that better?'

I loved Nanette so much.

When the water was too cold to sit in, I got up and let Nanette towel my hair dry. She would have passed me my nightgown, but I shook my head. 'Court dress, please, Nanette.'

She looked anxious. 'You won't go out?'

'I think I must.'

She helped me dress in one of my new gowns and coiled my hair around the hot poker till it was a mass of long tight ringlets, pinned back above my ears. I painted and powdered my face, carefully concealing the bruises on my neck, then coloured my mouth with carmine. Carefully, I placed a black velvet patch on my chin, to the left. I am discreet, that patch said. Finally, I clasped the jet necklace that the Marquis had given me around my neck. At the end of a string of tiny exquisite jet beads hung a tiny carved rose, black as my hair. 'My dark rose,' he had called me. I picked up my fan of ostrich feathers and rather unsteadily made my way through the corridors to the King's salon.

I felt small and cold and afraid. Worst of all, I felt fragile, as if I could be easily broken. I had always prided myself on my strength. Mademoiselle de la Force. Dunamis.

I came into the Venus Salon and looked for

the Marquis. My lover. My ravisher. He was not there.

The Venus Salon was where the court gathered in the evening and waited for the King to appear. Between heavy pillars of dark veined marble were gilded panels and frescoes. Far above, gods and emperors and ancient heroes gestured and fought among a panoply of clouds and smoke. Even though the King was at that moment signing letters in his cabinet room — his routine being so precise that anyone in France could glance at a clock and know exactly what the King was doing at that moment — a massive statue of Louis XIV brooded over the crowd in the guise of a Roman emperor. Footmen stood stiffly with trays laden with foaming goblets and plates filled with tiny delicacies, such as sautéed scallops, salt cod and caviar on potato pancakes, basil palmiers, and roasted brie with gooseberries. The air was sweet with the scent of tall vases of flowers and bowls piled high with the King's favourite oranges.

I drank a little, ate a little and gazed at the paintings, all the while wondering where the Marquis could be, and what I should say to him when he came. I did not have to wait long to find out.

'*Mademoiselle,* I am so sorry. You must be devastated,' Françoise said.

I turned to her and raised my eyebrows.

'Can it be you do not know? Oh, I'm so

sorry. I do not want to be the one to break the bad news.'

'Bad news?' With an effort, I kept my voice steady.

'The Marquis de Nesle. The Grand Condé has taken him to Chantilly. He says he will not let the Marquis return to court until he has repudiated you.'

I felt a giant hand squeeze my throat so I could not breathe or speak. Sickness roiled in my stomach.

'Are you well?' Françoise asked anxiously. 'You've gone quite white. Here, take a sip.'

I gulped at my silver goblet of champagne. I wanted to faint, or scream, or run, or smash something.

'It is because I am poor,' I said.

She said nothing, though her fine dark brows contracted together.

'What does it matter to them?' I continued. 'They are rich. They are powerful. Why can they not allow me some small measure of happiness? I may not be rich or powerful, but I'm nobly born, I'm clever.'

'Nothing is more clever than irreproachable conduct,' Françoise answered coolly.

I cast her an angry look, even as I acknowledged the truth of what she said. She certainly seemed to have managed her affairs most adroitly, being now the Marquise de Maintenon with her own chateau.

Rumour insisted that the King wanted to

take Françoise as his mistress and she continued to refuse him, which was astounding. I had not managed to hold off the Marquis; how could she possibly hold off the King? The King had only to remark it was a shame that an avenue of ancient trees blocked the view from his window and his host would have every single tree cut down overnight.

What the King wanted, he got. If it was a noblewoman he desired, the King would be discreet, sending a lackey with a note ordering the woman to come to him at an appointed time. If it was a serving-maid, he'd simply ruck up her skirts, have her against the wall and then saunter off, swinging his cane while she tidied her skirts and went back to scrubbing the floor. I could not believe that he would allow Françoise of all people to hold him off — a woman born in a prison, a woman who worked in his household as a governess. Yet neither could I believe the rumours that she was actually a procuress for him, finding him sweet young virgins from the country to deflower. She was too neat, too devout, too cool and calm and collected.

'I am sorry to be the one to tell you,' Françoise said. 'They left this morning. I thought you must have known.'

I shook my head. I could not stay in the overheated salon; I could not bear the glances and murmurs, or Françoise's pitying face. I put down my goblet so abruptly it clanged against the wooden table, splashing wine, and hurried away. I shoved my way through the crowds of laughing ladies in their heavy full-skirted brocades and high-heeled shoes, past knots of men bewigged and beribboned and bejewelled, nearly overturning a footman with a silver tray laden with delicacies. I barged past a group of gawping peasants in wooden sabots and coarse woollen jackets, come to stare at the court, as was their practice every night, and made it through the gilded panelled doors. Down the Ambassador's Stairs I ran, and through the crowded antechamber, where hawkers shouted and thrust their goods into my face: fans, lengths of delicate lace, bowls of ripe purple figs, trays of sugar-dusted marzipan, carved wooden puppets, baskets of mushrooms, coils of bright ribbons, painted snuffboxes, embroidered handkerchiefs, ripe pears, garnet earrings. I thrust my way past them, crying, 'No, no!' and managed to get out through the front doors.

Outside, it was as bright as day. Torches flared smokily at each corner of the courtyard, and people turned to stare at me curiously as, gasping and stumbling, I ran towards the gardens. But there was no place of quiet or darkness even there. People were everywhere, dancing on the lawns, promenading on the walkways, poling gondolas along the canals, pissing in the occasional dim corner. Violinists played, trumpeters blew their horns, and fireworks banged and roared overhead. No matter where I ran, I could find no quiet place to hide and weep and rock with fear, till finally I slipped into the shadowy Grotto de Thétys. I crept behind the statue of Apollo's horses, sinking to my knees and hiding my face in my hands.

Of all the fears and miseries batting their nasty wings inside my skull, the one that banged most insistently was the thought: *Please don't let them look inside the bag of spells.*

A week of unendurable suspense followed. I felt as if every eye was watching me, every flutter of a fan hid a mocking smile, every whisper was of my name.

I had no one I could confess my fear to. Athénaïs had retreated to Clagny in preparation for the birth of her tenth child. Françoise was so holier-than-thou it made me sick to my stomach. Liselotte was too much of a gossip. My sister was too far away. Only Nanette knew, and she was horrified to the depths of her superstitious peasant soul.

'Bon-bon, you naughty wicked girl! How could you do such a thing? No good comes of meddling with witches. The devil will come to take your soul. Oh, that I should live to see you in such disgrace. You'll have to go home to Cazeneuve.'

But that I was determined not to do. Not

even to escape Nanette's scolding.

Then the Marquis de Nesle returned to court from Chantilly, in the train of his cousin Louis de Bourbon, the Grand Condé. I was too afraid and humiliated to leave my rooms, so I sent Nanette to the kitchens to discover what the servants were saying. She dutifully reported back that the Marquis de Nesle was said to be in despair but had promised his cousin to never consort with me again.

'The bag of spells?' I asked anxiously. 'Any word?'

Nanette winced and looked away. 'There is much talk that he was bewitched,' she admitted, 'but that the spell is broken and he is free.'

I paced my rooms, in an agony of indecision and remorse, and, I must admit, humiliation. Soon, I heard the faint sound of music and laughter. There was to be a masked ball that night, I remembered, to celebrate the birth of Athénaïs's latest son, to be named Louis-Alexandre. Nearly all of Athénaïs's seven children to the King were named either Louis or Louise, with their second names chosen to flatter.

Athénaïs would, of course, be present at the ball — even though her baby was less than a day old — for the King would not permit anything to stand in the way of his own pleasure, not even the pain and exhaus-

tion of childbirth. If I went to the ball —
cloaked and masked — I could hear, perhaps,
what the gossips were saying. I could, perhaps, see the Marquis. I could, perhaps, manage to speak to Athénaïs.

I acted on the thought. Within moments, I
had called Nanette, found myself a mask and
a cloak, changed my dress, concealed my
striking blue-black hair behind a froth of
feathers and silk flowers, hidden the marks of
my tears behind thick white powder, red-
dened my lips and placed three patches on
my face for courage. I seized a fan, drew on
my high-heeled dancing slippers and was out
the door and on my way before Nanette had
much more than a chance to say, 'But Bon-
bon!'

The ball was being held in the gardens, with
merry laughing courtiers being ferried about
by sedan chairs, their dwarves running alongside, turning clumsy somersaults and hand-
springs. It was impossible to guess who
anyone was, for all wore extravagant masks.
In just a few bewildering moments, I saw a
troubadour with a lute, a jester in motley, a
maiden who seemed to be made all of flowers, a man in a golden robe with a mask of
gold, a knight in full armour, a fat man
dressed as a baby, and a young girl dressed
as a Siamese princess. One woman was
dressed as a shepherdess, with a small bleat-
ing lamb tied to her with a silken ribbon;

another was dressed in white fur, despite the heat, with a white cat's mask and pink velvet ears. All the servants were painted white and dressed in white robes, pretending to be statues. Candles floated down the Grand Canal, and lanterns were strung through the trees, casting a golden light into the night.

I wandered here and there, listening to snatches of conversation. For a long time, I heard nothing. I felt sick and weary, my feet aching cruelly. Then I heard my name.

'. . . Mademoiselle de la Force . . .'

'Have you not heard the news? No one can talk of anything else.'

I recognised the German-accented voice and, legs trembling, went close to the group, accepting a goblet of champagne from a white-painted impassive-faced servant.

It was the Duchesse d'Orléans speaking, my old friend Liselotte. I had hardly spoken to her since the time I had seen her laughing at Michel's story of my proposal of marriage. Even though she wore a mask of peacock feathers and a gown so heavy with jewels she must have been close to fainting in the heat, she could not disguise her portly figure, her round red face or her guttural accent.

'The Grand Condé tricked him into his carriage and whisked him away to Chantilly, determined to break him of this absurd engagement to Mademoiselle de la Force,' she boomed.

'So it was true, they really were engaged?' someone asked.

'Oh, he was utterly smitten,' someone else said.

'Just wait till you hear the story,' Liselotte cried. 'The Grand Condé assembled all the poor man's relations, all weeping and begging him not to throw himself away on some poor provincial miss.'

I am Charlotte-Rose de Caumont de la Force, granddaughter of the Marshal of France, I thought angrily. *How dare you!*

'But the Marquis was adamant, he must marry Mademoiselle de la Force,' Liselotte went on, with a dramatic flourish of one plump hand. 'The Grand Condé threatened to cut him off. In despair, the Marquis rushed out and would have flung himself in the lake if two of his cousins had not caught him and wrested him away from the edge. In the struggle, a small bag that he wore hanging about his neck broke and fell to the ground.'

Liselotte paused and looked around at the circle of bizarre painted and gilded masks, bent close to hers. 'A bag that Mademoiselle de la Force had given him . . .' Her voice trailed away meaningfully.

'What happened?' someone asked.

Liselotte waited until everyone was listening breathlessly, then said, 'At once, the Marquis' head cleared, his feelings underwent a sudden change and Mademoiselle de la

Force seemed to him as ugly as she really is.'

Tears prickled my eyes. I turned aside, afraid my expression would give me away, and pretended to watch the dancers.

'So she had cast a spell on him?'

'What was in the bag?'

'Was he bewitched, then, to offer her marriage?'

Liselotte leant forward, her red-painted mouth stretched in malicious enjoyment. 'You'll never believe it. The Grand Condé searched the gardens for the bag and, when they found it, opened it up and, inside . . .'

'What?'

'Tell us!'

'What was in it?'

'Two toad's legs, all wrapped up in a bat's wing and a paper of spells and ciphers.' Liselotte looked around in triumph to see her audience's shocked reactions.

'No!'

'She ensorcelled him?'

'Black magic!'

'Really? It was sorcery all the time?'

'Why else would he have wanted to marry her?' Liselotte said contemptuously, and she waddled away to tell the tale again.

I swear I heard the echoes of their words follow her through the crowd: 'Did you hear . . . Mademoiselle de la Force . . . black magic . . . why else?'

The dark phrases rang through my brain. I

stumbled away, my stomach twisted like a wet sheet in a laundrywoman's strong red hands. Then I saw the Marquis. His eyes fell on me. I do not know how he recognised me in my mask. Perhaps it was the long lean length of me, which he had measured against his own body so many times. Perhaps it was my full-lipped mouth, which he had kissed so passionately, or perhaps it was the heady scent of the perfume he had given me. I saw the moment of recognition in his face, though, and then a look of acute distaste. He turned and walked away, and I was left alone in the midst of a tumult of twirling masked strangers, a parade of jeering devils.

The Abbey of Gercy-en-Brie, France — April 1697

I woke in the dullness before dawn, my skull rattling with nightmares. I had not thought of my humiliation by the Marquis de Nesle in many years, locking it away in the darkest cellar of my mind. He had married some dimwit with a sizeable dowry and gone on to gamble it all away. It disturbed me that his memory still had the power to upset me.

I heard a thin whistle, then a slap, followed by a low moan. The sound repeated itself. Whistle. Slap. Moan. I crept out of bed and put my eye to the crack in the curtain between my cell and Sœur Emmanuelle's.

The novice mistress was kneeling on the

floor, her clothes folded down onto her hips, whipping herself with a knotted cord. Her naked back was very thin, the bones of her spine and ribs protuberant, the pale skin marked all over with criss-crossing welts and scars. The knotted cord flailed her once more, and a fresh welt sprang up, beaded with blood. Her moan was as much rapture as pain.

The church bell rang out. Sœur Emmanuelle folded up the knotted cord and stowed it away, crossing herself and mumbling a prayer before she rose with difficulty to her feet. Then she drew up her clothes. I had to catch back a gasp as I realised that she wore a hair shirt under her robe, drawing its roughness up over her lacerated skin. No wonder her shoulders were always so hunched, her face so awry. Sœur Emmanuelle was in pain all the time. Pain she had inflicted on herself.

I stumbled back before she turned and saw me peering at her through the crack. I felt sick and cold. That poor woman. What demons resided inside her that she felt could only be driven out with a whip?

As we went out into the garden after chapter, I asked Sœur Seraphina as tactfully as I could for Sœur Emmanuelle's history.

Sœur Seraphina sighed. 'I don't know much, I'm afraid. All I know is what Mère Notre told me the night she came. Apparently, Sœur Emmanuelle had been betrothed to marry some nobleman. Her trousseau was all sewn and the wedding date set. Then her father told her that her brother had gambled away the family's entire fortune. She was brought here that very night, the abbey being so poor that they would accept her with the few *louis* her father could scrounge together.'

I nodded, filled with pity for her. One day, a young woman with her future bright before her, the next an unwilling acolyte in a run-down old abbey with nothing to look forward to at all. No wonder she was so unhappy.

Sœur Seraphina lifted her worn old face to the sunshine. 'It is a great shame. She was brought here against her will, and so never found her way to acceptance and peace. Her soul is locked away as securely as her body, behind bars of her own making.'

I bit my lip, sure that I too would never find my way to that peace Sœur Seraphina seemed to have found. The hag-ridden dreams of the night before still haunted me — mocking laughter, the faces of devils, the scald of my humiliation. I drew a deep breath of the clean air and squared my shoulders. Here, perhaps, in this enclosed square of garden, with honest labour of my body, I could at least drive the memories away.

I bent to crush lavender leaves between my fingers, breathing in its calming scent. 'The girl . . . in the tower,' I prompted. 'Did she ever escape?'

RHAPSODY

It grows half way between the dark and
    light;
Love, we have been six hours here alone,
I fear that she will come before the night,
And if she finds us thus we are undone.

'Rapunzel'
William Morris

Bella E Bianca

La Strega wanted Margherita to love only her.

She wanted Margherita to kneel at her feet and throw her arms about her waist, burying her face in her lap so La Strega could stroke her hair and chide her. She wanted Margherita to cuddle up to her in bed at night, kissing the nape of her neck and fitting her small narrow feet into the shape of La Strega's longer ones. She wanted all Margherita's tenderness to be for her, and only for her.

As the years passed, Margherita prayed to Minerva, the goddess of the rock, for help. She dreamt of escape, of rescue, of love in many different forms. But still the heavy braid of hair dragged at her temples, still the invisible fetters bound her to the tower, still day followed day with monotonous predictability, till she was sixteen, skinny, bony, ungainly, only her rebellious red curls refusing to submit to the witch's authority.

One summer morning, when La Strega had climbed down the ladder of hair and ridden away, Margherita took advantage of a new sack of flour to make herself fresh bread with honey, and climbed up on the windowsill to eat it, her bare feet tucked under the hem of her dress.

It was mid-morning, and a cool wind was blowing from the north. The lake glittered with white-edged wavelets, and the snowy heights of the mountains were sharp against a blue sky. Margherita sat on the windowsill and ate her warm bread slowly, savouring every mouthful. No matter how careful she was with her supplies, she was always running short by the end of the month. And La Strega liked to keep her thin. She liked to be able to count Margherita's ribs and complain about how sharp her knees were in bed.

Margherita often daydreamt about feasts. Tables groaning with food, servants bringing her platters laden with golden-skinned chicken, carrots roasted in honey, cakes encrusted with sugar. Like so many of her daydreams, imagining food was as much a torture as a delight.

Yet it was the dreaming that kept her sane. While she had dreams, she had hope. Margherita clung to that stubbornly.

Not wanting to feel sad today, with the sun shining and a pantry full of supplies, she reached for her lute and began to strum softly, singing a lullaby she thought — she wished — she might have learnt from her mother.

'*Farfallina, bella e bianca, vola vola, mai si stanca, gira qua, e gira la — poi si resta sopra un fiore, e poi si resta sopra un fiore.*' Butterfly, beautiful and white, fly and fly, never get tired, turn here and turn there — she rests upon a flower . . . and she rests upon a flower.

She could remember so little. The tower blotted out the past. Her childhood was like a secret walled garden that she couldn't enter. Sometimes, she smelt an enticing perfume, like cinnamon, and a flash of memory came, brief and tantalising. Most of the time, the past was a great blur. All she knew was what the sorceress had told her.

Was it true that her parents had sold her for a handful of bitter greens? Surely it was not easy, to give up your daughter to a witch. Had her parents been very poor? Had they been starving? To sell her for a chicken or a pig would have made more sense. Salad greens soon wilted and made only a mouthful or two, nothing of substance there to keep a starving couple alive. Was it the threat of punishment? La Strega had said once that thieves in Venice had both their hands cut off. That would be hard to face. If it was up to her, would she choose to keep her baby but lose both hands, or would she rather keep her hands and give up the child? What if the penalty was death? La Strega said thieves were hanged if caught stealing too often. Surely no one would hang a man for plucking a handful of greens?

Maybe her father had been afraid of the sorceress? Margherita could understand that. She was afraid of La Strega. Even now, after all these years, she watched the moon swell with a sick feeling of dread in her stomach, even though the coming of La Strega meant the coming of food, and company, and conversation.

Or had her parents decided to give her up simply because all children must grow up at some stage and make their own way in the world, and so being taken by La Strega was simply another choice? She could have been sent into service, apprenticed to a craftsman, enclosed in a convent or, in time, married — all of these were different types of imprisonment. She knew, because La Strega told her often how lucky she was to be saved from them all.

There were no answers to any of these questions. Margherita could not ask La Strega, since any mention of her real parents filled the sorceress with rage. She could only ask herself and try to understand.

All the while Margherita was thinking, she was strumming her lute and singing.

Then a voice called to her from far below.

'Petrosinella, let down your hair, so that I may climb the golden stair.'

Margherita jumped to her feet, her lute falling from her hand. Instinctively, she looked for the moon, but it was broad daylight and the sun was high in the sky. *But she left only this morning. She never comes back.*

'Petrosinella, let down your hair, so that I may climb the golden stair.'

The voice was deep. It sounded like it had laughter in it. Surely that was not La Strega speaking? But who else could it be?

Her heart beating rapidly with shock and dread, Margherita unfastened her silver snood and uncoiled her braids. Pressing herself close to the wall, she wound the upper part of the braid around a hook driven into the stone and tossed the remainder out the narrow window. In a few moments, she felt the end of the hair seized, and gritted her teeth as someone began to climb. Every jerk brought tears to her eyes. She clung to the braid with both hands, up near the base of her skull, trying to ease the pressure on the roots of her hair. Jerk, jerk, jerk. The pain grew intense. Just when she thought she must scream, the climber reached the windowsill. Margherita backed away, her hands at her mouth, as a complete stranger stepped through into her tower room.

He was tall, with curly black hair and lively black eyes. He was dressed in skintight hose embroidered with gold thread, a fitted doublet with full sleeves, slashed to show the sheer white fabric of his shirt, and a richly embroidered red velvet cape. His curious glance took in Margherita, the plait wound about the hook and snaking over the windowsill, the tiny room with its narrow bed, the hipbath, the richly coloured carpet and the hooded fireplace with coals glowing orange, and the lack of a door or a stair.

'Merciful Mary, what is all this?' he demanded.

Margherita only stared at him. As he stepped closer, she flinched back, throwing up a hand to keep him away.

'Don't be afraid. I mean you no harm. I was just curious.' He spoke in a soft gentle voice, keeping his distance from her. 'We were sailing past, up the lake, and I heard singing. Such singing! It enchanted me. So when we came to port, I told my men I planned to ride north again. My uncle must have the owner of that voice for his *concerto delle donne,* I thought. They did not approve so I pretended I wanted to go hunting.'

He spread his hands ruefully. He wore a curious ring with a shield on it, emblazoned with five red balls. 'But though we asked in the village, they knew of no singer. A siren in the lake who sings to lure men to a watery death, one said. A witch who lurks in an old abandoned tower and turns into a wolf howling at the full moon, said another. A goddess who walks the woods, singing and collecting flowers for her ancient shrine, said someone else. Just my imagination, said most. I knew it was not my imagination, though. Was not this mysterious songstress singing a lullaby my nurse used to sing to me?' He hummed a few bars, then sang, *'Farfallina, bella e bianca, vola vola . . .'*

Margherita did not speak, though her heart leapt like a hunted hare at the sound of her song on his lips.

After a moment, he went on: 'So I came out last night to see if I could find the girl whose voice haunted me so. And what did I see but a tower without a door, and a woman calling up for a golden stair, and then such a stair come tumbling down, a rope ladder of purest rose-gold. So of course I decided I must climb that stair and see where it led. Wouldn't you have done the same?'

All the time he had been speaking, the stranger had been walking around the tower room, picking up things and putting them back, lifting the curtain to stare in at the latrine, bending to pick up the heavy braid and weigh it in his hand. He kept his distance from Margherita, speaking in an easy conversational way as if he had known her for years. Margherita said nothing, only followed his movements with wide eyes, scarcely able to breathe. He wore a dagger at his belt, and the tightness of his clothes showed the strong muscles of his thighs and calves.

His eyes met hers. 'Don't be afraid. I really won't hurt you. What is your name? Is it really Petrosinella? Doesn't that mean Little Parsley? What are you doing in this old watchtower? How do you get in and out?'

'I don't,' Margherita said in a croaky voice.

'She speaks.' The young man pretended to swoon in surprise. 'I had thought you must be mute. Tell me, please! Was it you singing?'

Margherita nodded.

'You have the most beautiful voice. But you must know that. Oh, the effect coming across the water at dusk, the mountains floating above the blue mist, the full moon just rising . . . it was magical. Spellbinding. I must tell my uncle, see if he can recreate it at home. Of course, we don't have a lake — merely a river, but it's pretty enough. Maybe a barge of young beauties at sunset, all playing the lute and singing. Is this your lute?'

Margherita nodded again. He bent and lifted it, examining it closely. 'You play well. Where were you trained?'

'At . . . at the Pietà,' she answered, her voice coming almost naturally.

'In Venice? Ah, that explains it. You're one of the singing foundlings. I heard that their choirs sound like angels come down to earth. But you haven't told me. What are you doing all the way up here?'

Margherita did not know how to answer. She had grown so used to silence. So used to being alone.

'How did you come to be here?'

Because my parents sold me for a handful of bitter greens. She could not bear to say the words. They had the power to make her heart catch with hurt.

'Are you a prisoner? Why? Who keeps you here? Was it that woman I saw, the one who climbed your hair?'

Margherita spread her hands helplessly.

'I'm sorry, I'm going too fast, aren't I? My *nonna* says I always run when everyone else walks. Let us introduce ourselves. My name is Lucio . . .' He hesitated for a moment, then said, 'I come from Florence. What's your name?'

'Margherita.' It sounded strange, speaking her name out loud. She had not shaped those four syllables in many years. They were so sharp they could cut her tongue.

'So Petrosinella is not your name?'

She shook her head, then, with a burst of bravery, said, 'It's what *she* calls me.' Immediately, she shrank back, aghast.

'She?' Lucio asked. 'The woman who came last night? She's the one who keeps you captive?'

Margherita nodded.

'Who is she?'

'La Strega.'

'A witch?'

Margherita nodded again.

'Does she have a name?'

But Margherita could not tell him.

'But why did she lock you up in this god-forsaken tower? What does she want with you?'

Margherita could not answer that question either.

Lucio set one hip on the table, grabbing an apple from her bowl. He crunched into it thoughtfully. 'A mystery, by God. To think I cursed my uncle for making me come all this way for nothing more than a bushel of lemons. What a bore, I thought. But instead I find a girl locked away in a tower by a witch. It sounds like a mad Persian fairy tale. How long have you been here?'

'More than four years.' Margherita thought of her tally marks. Fifty-two moons, fifty-two cuts on her arms. 'I was twelve when she brought me here.'

'Twelve! You look about twelve now. Are you sure you're sixteen?'

She nodded.

'You are so thin and so pale,' he said. 'Look at your skin — not a freckle on it anywhere.' He took her by surprise by leaning forward and grasping her hand. 'Look, just a few here, on your lower arm. Is this where you reach out into the sun?'

She could not move or speak, barely able to breathe.

He turned her hand over. 'You truly are *bella e bianca,*' he said in a low voice. Suddenly, he stepped away, dropping her hand. Margherita looked down and saw his gaze fixed on her scarred wrists. Abruptly, she hid them in her sleeves. He turned away, eating the apple, pretending not to have seen anything. He seemed so large, as if he took up the whole tower room. Lucio, his name was. It meant light, she thought. If so, he was well named. It was as if he had a lamp suspended over his head, casting its radiance upon him, while the rest of the room sank away into dimness.

'Have you any more food?' He pitched the apple with deadly accuracy at the latrine, then threw up his arms and cheered when it fell straight down the hole.

'I have a little,' she answered.

'Good. I stayed up all night, watching the tower, wondering what you were doing up here. I'm starving. Let's eat.'

To her dismay, he proceeded to cheerfully eat his way through more than half of her monthly supplies. It gave her a strange secret pleasure to see him carving up her ham with his dagger, passing her great hunks of it, saying, 'Eat up! You're so skinny. My *nonna* would throw up her hands at the sight of you and tie you to a chair and force-feed you like a baby. She thinks it a grave insult to leave a single scrap on your plate. Have you any more bread? Oh, do you cook it on the griddle? It's like cooking on a campfire, isn't it? I'd never done that before I came on this trip, but now I'm an old hand. Can I have a try? Sit, eat. Let me make you a feast. Do you have any mushrooms? No? Any eggs?'

Somehow, Margherita found herself sitting on her stool, eating more food than she had in years and laughing at his ham-fisted attempts to make bread. In the end, she jumped up, pushed him down to sit and made the bread herself. While she cooked, he asked her more questions, and she answered them as best she could, his charm and his curiosity more than a match for her.

As she told him everything, slowly and stiltedly, his merriment drained away and he grew grave and determined. 'We'll just have to get you out of here,' he cried, jumping to his feet as if intending to throw her over his shoulder and carry her away right there and then.

'How?' she said with a flash of spirit. 'Will you bring me a skein of silk so I can weave myself a ladder? The only way down is by the braid of hair, and that just happens to be attached to my head.'

He held up the dagger. 'That's easily fixed.'

She shrank back, her hand rising protectively to her heavy braid. 'Have you ever tried to tie a knot in a braid of hair?'

'Well, no,' he admitted. 'But surely it can be done.'

'I've tried.' She sat down limply. 'No matter how tightly I tie it, it always unravels. Would you want to risk your weight on a plait of hair that cannot be tied securely?'

He shook his head, though the amusement was back in his eyes. 'Have you ever heard of rope?'

'Of course, I'm not an idiot. But have you seen how far the drop is from this window?'

'I climbed it, remember,' he said with a grin. 'It's a long way down.'

'Where are we meant to find rope that long?' Just saying the words 'we' and 'rope' gave her such a surge of ridiculous childish excitement that Margherita frowned and turned away, not wishing him to see how desperately she wanted all this to be true, and not a dream, or an imagining, or a trick.

'We sailed up Lake Garda on a boat. You've never seen so much rope in your life. I'll go back to the boat, get the rope, come back and get you out of here. Simple!'

Her flare of joyous excitement drained away. 'She's bound me here. With magic. Even if you got enough rope to climb to the moon, you could not get me out of here, not unless you break her binding spell.'

He gazed at her blankly. 'How do we do that?'

'I have no idea,' she answered.

FEASTING

*The Rock of Manerba, Lake Garda, Italy —
June 1599*

The tower room had seemed so small while
Lucio was there.

Once he had gone, it seemed very empty.

All Margherita's peace was cut up. She
could not settle to reading, or sewing, or playing her lute. Drearily, she tidied up the mess
he had made, feeling sick as she looked at
her depleted pantry.

'What do you do all day?' Lucio had demanded. 'Don't you get bored? I'm bored
after just half an hour!'

This comment had hurt her, though she
did not know why. She had turned away, hiding her face, but he had sensed her feelings
and seized her hands. 'I'm sorry. I didn't
mean I was bored with you! I just meant I
can't stand to be confined like this. Doesn't
it make you feel crazy, not being able to go
anywhere or do anything?'

'Of course it does, but *I* don't have a choice.'

He had stayed a while, which was kind of him, she knew. But as the sky beyond the narrow window had faded, and the thin clouds had warmed with colour, he had grown more and more distracted. At last, he had said, 'I'm sorry, I have to go. My men will be most anxious about me. I'll come back, I promise.'

But La Strega had taught her that all men's promises were valueless.

Margherita did not sleep much that night. She lay awake, reliving every moment of Lucio's visit. The way his hair had fallen over his brow. The strength of his hands. His quick laugh. The determined way he had said, 'We'll just have to get you out of here!' She loved the word 'we'. There had never been any 'we' in her life, only 'I' and 'me'. She repeated the words to herself several times: *We'll just have to get you out of here!*

Please, let it happen, let it be true, she thought one moment, and the very next, *Don't be a fool. He'll go away and never come back. Who wants to challenge a witch?*

At last, she slept, her face stiff with salt from her tears. She was woken in the morning by a merry voice ringing out, 'Margherita, Margherita, let down your hair, so I may climb that gorgeous stair!'

She almost fell from her bed, rubbing sleep crumbs from her eyes, stumbling towards the window. She looked out into a bright breezy day. Lucio stood at the base of the tower, a mule piled with sacks beside him, a coil of rope over his shoulder and a basket in his hand. He waved at her. 'Good morning, *mia bella bianca,*' he cried. 'Let me up! I have food!'

Margherita let down her braid, her heart pitter-pattering in her chest, and he tied the rope to it so she could pull it up and tie it to the hook. Then she dragged up sack after sack of provisions till her arms were aching and her cheeks hurt from the broadness of her smile. When she had finished, she could barely take a step for all the sacks of food piled about her room. Then Lucio hobbled the mule and left it to tear at the weeds and grasses growing from the cracks in the rocks, and he climbed up the rope to join her. By the time he arrived, she had washed her face, tidied her sleep-blowsy hair, pulled on her best gown and pinched her cheeks to bring some colour into them.

'I realised, after I got back to the inn, that I had probably eaten all your supplies. My *nonna* always says I eat her out of house and home,' Lucio said. 'It was rather poor fare too. No wonder you're so thin! I couldn't bear to think of you being hungry because of me, so I got up early and went to the markets. I got you everything you already had, plus a host of things besides. Fresh fruit and vegetables, rice, a whole fresh chicken — do you know how to pluck a chicken? Because I have to confess I have no idea.'

Margherita nodded, smiling and crying at the same time. 'How am I to hide all this? As soon as . . . as soon as *she* comes, she will know someone has been here.'

'Oh, we'll have you out of here before the witch comes back,' Lucio said. 'You did say she only comes when the moon is full, didn't you? So we have almost a month.'

Margherita sat down on her bed, her hands covering her face.

'Don't you want to be free?' he asked curiously.

'Oh, yes, of course. Desperately. It's just . . . you don't know her . . . she . . . she is very powerful.'

'Well, so am I,' he answered. 'Or at least, my uncle is, and I bask in his radiance. Don't look so anxious. There's no problem that you can't find a solution to. Or so my uncle always says. Are you hungry? Because I am. Let's eat and make some plans.'

His basket was filled with the most extraordinary delicacies. Fresh white bread made with finely milled wheat flour. Roast lamb, cooked with lemon juice and rosemary, pink and tender in the centre and oozing with juices. A white-bean salad in a small brown ceramic pot with a lid. A cake made with nuts and honey.

A hunger awoke in Margherita unlike anything she remembered feeling. She devoured all that Lucio handed her, sure she had never tasted such delicious food.

'I cannot stay much longer without getting into trouble,' Lucio said. 'I'm meant to be in Limone sul Garda, buying up lemons and limes and blood oranges and pomegranates, to take back to Florence for my uncle. And tubs of snow from Monte Baldo, so his confectioners can make him his favourite ice puddings through the summer. They mix the snow with rose water and sugar and fruit juices, and make the most delicious treats imaginable.'

Margherita tried to imagine eating snow. The idea thrilled her.

'Tell me about your home,' she asked, lying back on her bed, wishing she could loosen her girdle. She had never eaten till she could eat no more.

Lucio told her about a grand city the colour of ochre, floating on a river, surrounded by gentle rolling hills. 'It has the largest, most magnificent cathedral in the world, with the largest dome ever built. It's one of the architectural wonders of the world. And the art we have there! You've never seen anything like it. My favourite artist is Raphael, who lived in Florence close on a hundred years ago. You look just like the Madonna in one of his paintings. The pale serious face and the beautiful golden-red hair. If we put you in a meadow, with flowers growing about you and two curly-haired little cherubs at your knee, you could be the model for him.'

Raphael, she thought. *He has the same name as the angel of healing.* She smiled.

'I wish I could paint like Raphael,' Lucio said. 'I'd paint you! You should smile more often — it's like dawn breaking over a snowfield.'

Margherita bit her lip and looked away, her cheeks burning. As if realising he was frightening her with his dark intense gaze, Lucio looked away too, talking lightly of his family, about their palazzo with its graceful inner courtyard and the chapel decorated with magnificent frescoes depicting the Journey of the Magi. He told Margherita all about his sisters and his mother, and how kind his uncle tried to be to them. 'He has forgotten what it's like to be young, though. He's sixteen years older than my mother, and I swear he was born old.'

'You live with him?'

'Oh, yes, all our family are close. He loves art and music as much as I do, so we have that in common, at least. He has his own *concerto delle donne,* you know. He's very proud of it. He has tempted the finest singers in the world, from Mantua and Padua and Rome . . . he would be thrilled to have you there, *mia bella bianca.* You'd be a shining

547

gem in his crown. Once we get you out of here, I'll take you to Florence and you can sing for him. He'd have you installed in his palazzo with a rich pension within minutes, I promise you.'

This idea was so wonderful, so tempting, that Margherita could scarcely breathe. Lucio grinned at her. 'All we have to do is get you out of here. Are you sure about this binding spell of the witch's? How do you know she laid it on you?'

'I feel it,' Margherita said. 'Like invisible fetters on my wrists and ankles and on my tongue. You ask me questions that I cannot answer. You want me to leave the tower but I can't.'

'This binding spell sounds like fear to me,' Lucio said matter-of-factly. 'Have you tested it?'

'How can I?'

'We'll try it, shall we? You don't need to climb down my rope. I can just lower you down. I'll tie a loop at the bottom for you to put your foot in, and all you'll need to do is hold on. I'd better cut off some of this hair first, though, else you'll get all in a tangle.' He drew his dagger.

Margherita shrank back as if he had just threatened to cut her throat. 'No, no, please,' she gasped.

He drew back, confounded. 'You don't believe I'll hurt you?'

'No . . . but . . . you mustn't cut my hair . . . she'll know . . . she'll kill me.'

'But how will she know? By the time she gets here, we'll be miles away.'

She shook her head, wiping her tears with frantic hands, begging him not to cut her hair, not to try to force her to leave. 'I'm bound here,' she cried. 'Don't you understand? I cannot leave, she bound me here.'

At last, he gave up trying to persuade her and put away his dagger, reassuring her he'd never force her to do anything she didn't want to. 'We have a month,' he said. 'I will try and find out how one breaks a binding spell. Though where I am to learn such a thing, I have no idea. Maybe there's a wise woman in Manerba? I'll ask at the inn tonight.'

'Don't tell anyone about me,' she cried, in a panic. 'If anyone finds out I'm here, she'll be so angry. Please, don't tell anyone.'

Lucio sat and stared at her, frowning. 'I won't tell anyone yet, I promise. I may have to, in the end, if I need help to get you out. But only if I have to.'

She nodded, wiping her face with the heels of her hands, trying not to let him see how terrified she was at the idea of the witch knowing he had been there.

'I'll stay a few more days,' Lucio said, frowning. 'I don't like to leave you here alone. I'll make some excuse, pretend to be sick or something. At least I can make sure you eat some decent food before I go!' He glanced at the window, checking the position of the sun. 'I left a note for my men, telling them I've gone out hunting for the day. They know how much I love to hunt. I'll have to try and catch a few hares or a bird or two on the way back, else they'll get suspicious. I never come home from a day's hunting without a catch.'

'So . . . you like hunting?' she asked, trying to delay the moment at which he would rise and say he must go.

'Oh, yes,' Lucio cried, his face bright with enthusiasm. 'It is what I do most days. We ride out into the hills with our falcons and our dogs, or we hunt on foot with our bows.'

'Oh, you have dogs? I have always wanted a dog, but she never let me.'

'My dogs are great shaggy beasts, used to running long distances every day. They would have gone mad locked up in here.' He looked about him with distaste and moved his shoulders restlessly, as if wishing he could be gone.

'You have a horse too?'

'Yes, a fine black stallion called Nero. I've had him from a colt and broke him to the bridle myself. I could not bring him with me — a boat is no place for a horse.'

'I have never seen a horse,' Margherita confessed.

Lucio exclaimed in surprise, 'Never seen a

horse! But that's terrible. They are among the most beautiful of God's creations.'

'There are no horses in Venice, at least not real ones. And no horses in a tower.' She tried to smile.

'I'll teach you to ride!' Lucio cried. 'You have not lived until you've galloped through a field at dawn, with the mist rising from the ground and all the birds singing their little hearts out.'

She looked at him. 'I'd like that.'

'We'll have to find you a chestnut mare, to match your hair. And a red dog too. You'll cause a sensation at court with hair that colour.'

She flushed and looked away, barely able to breathe. He spoke so confidently, as if sure of the future, while she could see no further than this moment. 'So . . . you really think we can break the spell? You really think I can escape?'

He was surprised. 'Of course! How hard can it be? I've got up and down myself, and so does this witch of yours. You just need to be brave. Now I've really got to go, else they'll have search parties out for me.' He stood up.

Unable to help herself, she leapt to her feet, her hands flying out, not wanting him to leave.

'Don't look so frightened,' he chided her, catching hold of her hands. 'I'll come back tomorrow. I promise.'

She looked up at him pleadingly. Suddenly, he bent and kissed her on the mouth. For a moment, they were locked together, mouths and bodies and souls, then Lucio broke free, stepping back. 'I'm sorry. I shouldn't have . . . it's just you looked so . . . Don't worry. I'll be back tomorrow.'

He smiled at her, though his dark eyes were sombre and troubled, then he grasped the rope, climbed over the windowsill and was gone.

Some time during the night, Margherita was woken from a nightmare with terrible cramps in her stomach. She doubled over in pain, cold sweat breaking out on her skin. *She's found out, she knows, she's sticking a poppet of me with pins,* she thought. *She's punishing me from afar. I can never be free of her!*

The cramps came and went all night, and when dawn came she was so exhausted she did not get up but stayed curled up in her bed, weeping quietly to herself.

The morning dragged on and Lucio did not come. Margherita stayed in bed.

At last, she heard Lucio's voice calling to her. Then the rope went taut and he began to climb up to her. She scrambled out of bed and went to throw on a robe. But then a hoarse cry broke from her. She stood, trembling, staring at her bed. Blood stained the sheets. She looked down at herself. Blood stained her *camìcia.*

'I'm sorry I could not get here earlier,' Lucio panted, climbing over the sill. 'It was all I could do to convince my men to stay another day. And then they insisted on coming hunting with me. I had to lose them in the forest . . . Why, Margherita, what is wrong?'

'I'm bleeding. She knows. She struck at me during the night.' Shaking, she lifted away her hands, showing him the red smears on her white *camìcia.*

Lucio was by her side in an instant, his arm about her shoulders, his gaze flying from her stricken face to her lap to the stained bed. 'But . . . have you never bled before, *mia bella bianca?*' he asked gently. 'It's natural for a woman to bleed.'

Margherita shook her head.

Lucio sat beside her on the bed, pulling her close. 'You should have started to bleed some time ago. My sisters were thirteen and fourteen when they began, and I have heard of girls being even younger. It is nothing to be afraid of. I know it can hurt and make you feel unwell. My younger sister Alessandra always moans and cries and insists on lying down with a hot stone wrapped in flannel clutched to her belly.'

She stared at him in utter bafflement.

'You have never heard of a woman's monthly bleeding before?' Lucio asked.

Margherita shook her head, then hesitated. 'She asks me, every month, whether I bled while she was gone. I . . . I thought she meant . . .' She glanced down at the fresh red welt on her wrist, from the last cut of the rose thorns.

'Why do you do it?' The words burst out of his mouth. He seized her wrists, holding them upwards so both he and Margherita could stare at her marred skin. 'Your beautiful white skin, so soft . . . How can you injure yourself like that?'

Blood heated her face. 'You think *I* do it? No! How could I? I have no knife or razor, nothing I could use to cut myself. No, *she* does it!'

'She cuts you? The witch? *She* made such a mess of your wrists?' Lucio stared at her incredulously.

'For my blood,' Margherita answered fiercely. 'That's why I'm here. She needs my blood.'

'But why?'

Margherita could not answer. She had said too much already. Fear coiled in her belly like a thick black snake.

Lucio bent his head and pressed a kiss on the inside of one wrist, and then the other. Then he laid his forehead against her palms. For a moment, they sat quietly, neither moving, then Lucio got up abruptly and moved away.

'Come, let me heat some water for you to bathe in and make yourself fresh.' He went to fill the bucket with water. 'Have you eaten anything? You must eat. I would not be at all surprised to find out that's why you are so late to start bleeding, being kept half-starved the way you were.'

He busied himself making her clean and comfortable. When she was sitting in bed, in a fresh *camìcia* and fresh sheets, he made her breakfast and brought it to her to eat in bed. All this time, he barely glanced at her, while she kept her eyes steadily on him. The air between them seemed charged with thunder.

'I brought fresh figs for you today,' he said. 'Would you like me to cut one for you?'

'I have never eaten a fig. What does it taste like?'

'Ah, you've never lived until you've eaten a fig!' he cried. 'Here, let me cut you a slice.'

Deftly, Lucio quartered a fig and brought it to her. She looked at it dubiously. The skin was purplish-green, the seeds inside pink and fleshy. He grinned at her. 'Go on, try it.'

Margherita took the soft purple fruit hesitantly, looking down at it, then glancing up at him. He nodded and smiled, so she brought the fig to her mouth and bit it. The fig seemed to explode in her mouth, tasting unlike anything she had ever eaten before. Delicate, perfumed, piquant. Her eyes met his, filled with delight. Greedily, she ate the rest of the fruit, laughing in embarrassment as juice dribbled down her chin. 'It's delicious!'

He did not answer, and she looked up at him in surprise. His eyes were very intent on her mouth. He reached out a gentle finger and rubbed away the juice from the corner. She jerked under his touch and stilled, staring at him with wide eyes. He ran the finger along her soft bottom lip, then leant forward and kissed her lingeringly. Her whole body melted. One arm crept up about his neck, drawing him closer, and her mouth opened beneath his.

At last, he drew away. 'I think you have cast a spell on me,' he whispered, laying his head next to hers on the pillow. 'I cannot think of anything but you, I cannot sleep for worrying if you are afraid and lonely.'

'I cannot sleep for thinking of you either,' she whispered back.

'Have you cast a spell on me? Are you the witch?'

'No!' she cried and pushed him away. He laughed and caught her, drawing her to him and kissing her again. At once, she was back in his arms, kissing him hungrily, pressing her body against his.

He groaned and drew away. 'You intoxicate me. I feel drunk when I'm with you, heedless of anything else. Oh, Margherita, will you not climb down the rope with me? I'll take you with me to Limone. Have you ever been on a boat?'

She shook her head.

'You'll love it. We skim over the waves like a bird, the wind in our sails, moving faster even than a galloping horse. In only a few hours, we'll be far from here. And then I'll take you home with me to Florence. You'll be safe there. She'll never know where you are.'

'Oh, I want to! I wish I could!'

'Why can't you? It's safe. I promise you I'll not drop you.' He kissed her throat.

'The spell,' she managed to say.

All his attention was focused on her breasts, which rose and fell rapidly below the thin fabric of her *camìcia.* Slowly, he drew the fabric down, following the path of his fingers with soft kisses.

'Your skin is so white, it's like translucent silk. I can see the blue of your veins through it,' he murmured. He drew her *camìcia* lower, revealing the red blotch of her birthmark on her left breast. 'Ah, the parsley mark,' he whispered and bent his head to kiss it. Slowly, he laved it with his tongue, then very gently bit it. She gasped and pulled his head closer, and somehow his mouth found her nipple and she gasped again and arched her back.

He sat up, pushing himself away from her. 'Please don't,' he said harshly.

She was hurt, anxious, reaching for him. 'What's wrong?'

'Nothing! It's just . . . don't you understand how much I'd like to . . . and when you make sounds like that . . . and look at me like that . . . I'd better go.' He stood up.

She sat up, clutching the loosened neck of her *camìcia* to her. 'Please don't go.'

He did not look at her. 'I must. It's not right. You're as innocent as a child. You don't understand.' He strode across the room and grasped the rope.

Margherita flew across the room and flung her arms about him. 'Lucio! Please!'

He made a guttural noise deep in his throat and drew her into his arms. For a long moment, they swayed together, kissing desperately, one of his big hands wrenching away her *camìcia* to find her naked breast, the other sliding down from her waist to cup her bottom. Her golden-red hair fell all about them in wild disarray. He turned and pushed her back against the wall, his hand wrenching up her *camìcia.* Then his fingers found the moist cleft between her legs. He gasped and shoved his body hard against hers. With his other hand, he struggled to undo his hose. He brought his other hand up to assist, then suddenly gasped and broke away from her. His fingers were all bloody.

'Margherita . . . *mia bella bianca* . . . I can't. I mustn't,' he gasped.

'Lucio,' she pleaded, not knowing what it was she wanted, just knowing she could not bear for him to go.

He averted his eyes, grabbing the rope and swinging out the window. 'I'll be back, I promise.' Then he was gone.

UNBINDING

The Rock of Manerba, Lake Garda, Italy —
July 1599 to April 1600

The days dragged past.

Margherita had never been lonelier. She longed for Lucio to return, his words making the world seem so much grander than she had ever imagined. She longed for his touch, his kiss. Her body felt different — sensitive and womanly. She paced her room all day, tossed sleeplessly in her bed all night. At dusk, she sat in her window and poured all her longing and desire into her songs, hoping he would somehow hear her and return.

And he did. About three weeks after he had left, Lucio returned.

As he climbed the rope up the tower, Margherita hung out the window, smiling at him through her tears, her bronze hair all loose and waving about her body. She did not speak, just held out her arms to him as he reached the windowsill. His mouth found hers. For a long instant, they kissed, then Lucio broke free, clambering into the room, drawing her close.

'It's not safe for me to kiss you till I'm on solid ground. You make my head spin so much I'm in danger of falling,' he said. 'Oh, *mia bella bianca,* I've missed you!'

'And I you.'

They kissed again, lingeringly.

'I've brought you something,' he said at length, drawing her to sit on his knee. 'Look.'

He drew a small golden ring out of his pocket. 'It's a type of binding spell. If you wear this ring, it binds you to me, and all other binding spells are broken.'

'It's a wedding ring,' she said wonderingly, trying it on her finger.

He laughed. 'Even locked away all your life, you still know what a wedding ring is. Girls!'

'My mother wore one.' Her voice was constricted with pain and love and fear.

'If I could, I would marry you in the cathedral, with all the usual chanting and incense and weeping, but there is no priest and no cathedral in this tower, so this will have to do until I get you to Florence.'

She nodded her head slowly. He bent his head and kissed her. 'Can we make promises to each other, as if we were truly married? Can we swear to be true and faithful and love only each other and all those things? Because I'm in such pain, Margherita, I need to have you, I need to know that you're mine. I've

561

been in torment since I first saw you. No, since I first heard you singing from your tower height. Please, *mia bella bianca,* please let us swear to each other. Love breaks all spells, I know it does. Wear my ring and let me know —'

She stopped his words with her mouth, cupping both hands about his face. Then she sat back to show him the ring on her finger. 'I swear it all. Is that good enough? Because I really need you to kiss me again.'

He kissed her tenderly. 'I swear —'

'Sshhh,' she said and lifted his hand to her breast. His breath caught; his hand closed tight. Then he lifted her and carried her to the bed.

For a night, all was perfect between them. They loved more deeply and passionately than anyone had ever loved before, or so they said to each other, holding each other's face in their hands, watching each other's eyes as they moved together in the soft candlelight. Then dawn came, and Lucio stood up, drawing on his clothes, saying, 'Come, my darling, let's go home.'

Margherita could not go.

Lucio begged her, enticed her, ordered her. It made no difference. She would not take one step towards the window. 'I can't, I can't,' she said helplessly, while he raged and shouted and even wept. And when he seized her in his arms and dragged her towards the window, she cried out in agony and fell to the floor.

'I can't stay. I have to go,' he told her angrily. 'Don't you understand? I have already stayed far too long. This trip was meant to show my uncle how mature and responsible I am. He will think me a shiftless fool, to take a month to get a few lemons. He will never understand. I meant to take you with me, to have you dazzle him with your beauty and your voice, to show him I was serious about my intentions towards you. The men suspect I've been sneaking off to visit a woman. They'll tell him. He'll think it just a boyish affair. Margherita, please, I beg of you. I need you to come with me!'

But she could not.

After he had left, she wept inconsolably all day. The sun sank and the tower room grew dark. She built up the fire and began to make herself a desultory meal, tears occasionally trickling down her face as another memory assaulted her. Then she sat on her windowsill to eat.

The moon was rising. It was almost full.

Panic twisted her gut. She stood up, looking around the tower room, seeing the many signs that Lucio had been there. The golden ring upon her finger. The cornucopia of food. The sheets, stained with his seed. The rope, still knotted to the hook. The dagger he had insisted she keep, to defend herself if needed.

Every time La Strega came, she was angry if even a candlestick was an inch out of place. Her tawny lion's eyes saw everything.

Margherita began to clean frantically. She washed the sheets, though it hurt her to wash away Lucio's smell. She unknotted the rope, her last and only chance to escape, and coiled it, sobbing with despair. She tried to hide it under the bed, but kept imagining La Strega finding it. Then there was the problem of the food. Strange sacks, different containers, food she had never had before. She could fling it down the latrine, but perhaps La Strega would see it all smashed on the rocks below.

Eventually, Margherita slowly and laboriously chipped away the makeshift concrete around the trapdoor and opened it once more. The smell that rolled up from the depths of the tower made her gag. It smelt of death and abandonment. But she lit a candle and went down the steps again and again, carrying sacks of food to hide on the floor below. When the last sack was hidden, she sat for a while on the edge of the trapdoor, her limbs trembling with exhaustion, her stomach roiling with nausea. She was filled with a black fatalism. Her chance to escape had come, yet she had failed to break free of the binding spell the witch had placed upon her soul. She had been given love, passion, freedom, a future . . . yet even the magic of Lucio's love for her had not been enough.

Margherita would stay in the tower till she died.

La Strega came with the rising of the full moon, as always. She seemed to sense at once that something was wrong, standing on the windowsill and looking all around the tower room with frowning eyes. Margherita kept her eyes down and her face meek.

'Did you miss me, Petrosinella?' La Strega asked.

'Yes, of course . . . Mama,' Margherita replied, her face feeling too hot, her body too large.

'Mama? That is not like you, Petrosinella, to be so sweet.'

'I'm sorry,' she cried, twisting her hands together in anxiety.

'What is wrong?' La Strega's voice was sharp.

'Nothing! It's just . . . I've been lonely. This month seemed so long. The sun does not set till so late in summer and rises so early, the days seem to last forever. I'm sorry, I do not mean to complain. I'm just pleased to see you. Will you not sit?' Margherita gabbled.

'I'm hungry. Let us bring up the food and you can cook something for me. Don't you wish to know what present I've brought you?'

'Oh, yes,' Margherita said blankly, then assumed an expression of eager interest. 'Oh, yes! I've been so good! What have you brought?'

La Strega looked around the tower. It was immaculate. All the sacks and jars were in perfect symmetrical alignment. The bed was without a wrinkle. Yet still she frowned.

Margherita clasped her hands together like a little girl and did her best to look eager, sweet and shy.

'I have brought you sweetmeats and a new songbook,' La Strega said slowly, her eyes on Margherita's face.

'Oh! Thank you!' A month ago, Margherita would indeed have been excited and grateful, but Lucio had exploded the confines of her life like a lit barrel of gunpowder. She fixed her eyes on La Strega's face and smiled till her cheeks began to hurt. Then, she busied herself knotting the rope La Strega had brought around the hook and throwing it down to Magli, chattering as artlessly as a child till at last La Strega stopped scrutinising her face so closely and seemed to relax. They ate a simple meal, then Margherita began to draw water for La Strega's bath. Her heart felt heavy and muffled in her chest, pounding too insistently. She wondered how she could possibly bear the witch's hands upon her tonight, now that she knew what true love was.

When La Strega relaxed in her warm bath, the rose petals floating in the scented water, Margherita silently offered her scarred wrist. 'Have you bled this month?' La Strega asked.

'No,' Margherita lied.

La Strega nodded, satisfied, and gashed the rose thorns across Margherita's thin blue veins.

The summer slowly faded into autumn, the days growing shorter, the moon in its waxing and waning reflecting the points of high tension in Margherita's life and the long lax days when nothing at all happened.

In November, Lucio surprised her by returning.

'I had to see you again, I had to know you were all right,' he said at high speed, stepping over the windowsill. 'You look well, you look beautiful! Not nearly so skinny. I persuaded my uncle I should come back for the olive harvest, that maybe mountain olives would taste better than olives from the plains.' As he spoke, he was undoing his sword belt and flinging it on the ground, wrenching his shirt over his head. '*Mia bella bianca!* Is all well?'

'Yes, now that you are here,' she replied, springing forward into his arms. 'I thought you'd never come again! I was afraid —'

'Stop talking,' Lucio ordered, as if he was not the one who never stopped talking. He kissed her as if he wanted to swallow her whole. 'Oh, sweetheart! I missed you!'

'Yes!' Margherita unknotted her hair from her snood, drew her loose gown over her head and helped him drag down his hose. They fell onto the bed, laughing, burrowing through each other's clothes.

Later, satiated, they lay in each other's arms, talking, telling each other all that had happened in the months they had been apart. Lucio stayed all night and most of the next day. Once again, he begged Margherita to find the courage to leave the tower. Once again, Margherita was unable to.

Winter passed. Each month, La Strega came at sunset on the night of the full moon, despite the gales and the snowstorms. She complained of feeling the cold as she never had before. She complained of aches and pains and said, ruefully, holding her hand to the fire, 'Look how wrinkled they are, just like an old lady's.'

'It must be the cold,' Margherita said desperately. 'Isn't it the coldest winter ever?'

In bed at night, La Strega shoved at Margherita. 'You're growing so big, Petrosinella, you're taking all the room.'

'No, no! There's plenty of room,' Margherita said, trying to make herself as small as possible.

A flash of memory came. Eight small skeletons laid out like the spokes of a wheel. Margherita was now taller than any of those skeletons. And it was true she was putting on weight. Every time Lucio came to see her, he brought her marvellous feasts. He loved to see her eat and he loved the changes in her body. Her breasts were full and heavy now, big enough to fill his hand. Her belly was softly rounded instead of thin and concave. What Lucio gloried in, La Strega found distasteful. So Margherita did her best to keep her body hidden from La Strega and to make her content so her hand did not come creeping in the middle of the night, searching for some tenderness.

Although Margherita kept the tower room spotless, and never raised her eyes, or answered back, or asked any awkward questions, La Strega was cranky and short-tempered. She cut back Margherita's rations. 'Obviously, I'm feeding you too well. You're getting quite fat,' she said cruelly. If it had not been for Lucio's sacks and barrels, hidden under the floor, Margherita could well have starved to death. For she was ravenously hungry all the time, as if eating was the only link she had to Lucio.

In early spring, La Strega found a grey hair at her temple. She slapped Margherita. 'Have you lied to me? Have you begun to bleed?'

'No, no!' Margherita said, and indeed she did not lie. Her blood had come only that once and never again, making her doubt Lucio's easy assumption that all women bled every month. La Strega examined all her *camicias* and sheets but found no stains. She said no more, but her gaze seemed to rest on Margherita suspiciously, so Margherita did her best to play the part of a sweet lovable little girl, who wanted only to make her mama happy. She felt as if her secret was ballooning inside her, threatening to break free from her ears and eyes and nose and mouth, like a gush of blood.

As soon as La Strega had gone, Margherita dug out her wedding ring from the depths of the flour sack and slid it back on her finger. 'Lucio,' she whispered, holding the cool band against her cheek. 'Lucio, where are you?'

In April, soon after Margherita's seventeenth birthday, Lucio came back. Joyously, she took off the silver snood and tossed it on the dresser, and she unbound her hair from its silver ribbon so she could lower the long plait from the window for him to climb. By the time he was framed in the window, she was already eagerly untying her bodice. He held up one hand to stop her, sitting down on the chair and drawing her to sit on his lap.

Mia bella bianca,' he said, his breath soft on her cheek. 'I have spoken to someone about the binding spell. She says . . . she says only you or the witch can break the spell. No one else.'

'It cannot be broken?' Margherita felt dazed.

'No! You can! Only the one who cast the spell or the one on whom the spell was cast.

Don't you see? You can break the spell, you can!'

She shook her head. 'But how?'

'She said you must look in your heart. She said you will know how when the time is right.'

'But I don't! I don't know how!'

'Think, Margherita! You've been here five years. Have you learnt nothing from the witch?'

'I've tried,' she whispered. 'But what can I do? Lucio, you don't understand! She . . . she sees everything, she knows everything. I cannot withstand her.'

'Does she know about us?' Lucio demanded.

Margherita shook her head. 'I don't know. I don't think so. She suspects . . .'

'But she doesn't know! She doesn't know everything. Please, Margherita, you must think. I don't know how much longer I can wait for you.'

Margherita began to weep, and Lucio rocked her in his arms and begged her pardon and kissed away her tears. Soon, they were once again meshed in each other's bodies like the cogs of a clock, which had no purpose apart from each other.

Later, he told her about the old woman. She had been an ugly old crone, gathering tufts of sheep's wool caught in the brambles at the edge of the forest. She had been so old and bent, struggling to carry her basket while leaning on her distaff, that Lucio had hurried to help her. She had thanked him, and blessed his handsome face, and wished she could do something to repay him. That is when he had asked her.

'But I don't know how to break the spell. Oh, couldn't she have told you more?'

'That's all she said. That only the one who cast the spell or the one on whom the spell was cast can break it. And that you must look in your heart, that the answer is within.'

Margherita said angrily, 'Do you think I would not have left long ago if the answer was so easy? That old woman was spinning you moonshine!'

Lucio got up and got dressed, every line of his body taut with anger. 'Margherita, I love you, I truly do, but this is no life for me. I am sick with longing all the time I am away from you, and sick with frustration all the time I am with you. I want a wife, someone to share my life. I am going to Limone now. I'll be back in a few weeks. If you have not managed to find some way to leave this tower by then, I'm never coming back again. Do you understand?'

Margherita nodded, white and tearless. When he had gone, she lay huddled in her bed all day, unable to find the will or the energy to get up.

It was the sight of the moon, swollen as a

body louse on the horizon, which at last gave her the strength to rise from her bed. Margherita could not bear the idea of the witch's cold hands touching her again. She took the dagger Lucio had given her from under her bed and held it to the scars on her wrists, then laid its silver sharpness against the golden softness of her hair, billowing unbound about her. Dead girls' hair. If she cut it off, would that break the spell? But what if it didn't, and La Strega came and found her with her head shorn? What would she do? Kill her, Margherita was sure.

But then she would rather die than lose Lucio, her lover, her love.

She sat on her windowsill, looking at the dark horizon, the snowy peaks of the mountains edged with the last rays of the sun. An eagle was flying high above the lake, soaring and swooping with the motion of the wind. Every fibre of her being wished she too could be free. She tried to remember the spell that the witch had used to bind her. There had been words, a rhyme, nine drops of blood, hair bound into her hair.

Her breath coming fast, like a cornered animal, Margherita lifted the heavy burden of her hair and cut a single strand, at the back, close to the scalp. It came free in her hand, long and sinuous as a golden ribbon. Carefully, she examined it till she found the place where the other girls' hair had been woven into hers, whether by magic or artifice Margherita had never known. She cut it away from her hair, whispering under her breath, 'Goddess of the rock, hear my words. Give me the strength to fly free like a bird.'

Courage lifted her up. She threw the shorn end of the lock of hair out the window and watched the bright strands blow away in the wind and disappear. She was left holding a lock of her own hair in her hand.

She coiled her hair in a ceramic pot and anointed it with oil scented with rose, then lit the squat red candles, setting them into a triangle about the bowl of hair. Then, as the sun set and the full moon rose, she pricked her finger and squeezed nine drops of blood into the bowl:

> With my own blood, three by three,
> No longer shall I be bound by thee.
> No longer bound to this dreadful tower,
> Never again to cringe and cower.
> As I burn this hair, a part of me,
> Let my heart and soul be free.

She hardly knew where the words came from — a dark secret place deep within her. As she chanted them aloud, she lit a taper from one of the candles and held it to the hair until it shrivelled and burnt away into foul-smelling ashes. She then tipped the ashes out into the luminous night. They were gone in seconds.

Her heart was beating fast now, her hands shaking. Hurriedly, she packed a sack with provisions and got out her warmest shawl and her sturdiest shoes. She then rolled back the rug and began to frantically chip away at the paste of flour and water she had made to smooth the edges of the trapdoor. The rope was hidden down there. She could not escape without the rope.

'Petrosinella, let down your hair so I may climb the golden stair.'

Margherita sat back on her heels, as still as a girl turned into a pillar of salt. The chant came again, the witch's voice angry. Margherita scrambled to her feet, almost falling as a wave of dizziness swept over her. She kicked the dagger under the bed and dragged the rug back into place over the trapdoor. Her dress lay discarded on the floor. She stepped into it and dragged it up over her body, but her fingers were so stiff and clumsy that she could not do up the laces. She knotted them as best she could and hurried to the window-sill. The great length of her hair was all in a tangle, but she had no time to comb it. As she wound it about the hook and let it drop, a flash of gold caught her eyes. She wore Lucio's ring. Desperately, she tugged it off and dropped it in the nearest sack.

When La Strega climbed through the window, she was angry at the delay in answering her call, angry at the untidy room, with the bed unmade and the snood and ribbon and comb lying discarded on the dresser. She glared at Margherita, who stood with hands folded and eyes downcast like a little girl caught stealing sweetmeats.

'What took you so long? What were you doing? Why is this place in such a mess? You lazy layabout, what have you been doing all day? Look at you! Do up your gown properly!'

Glancing down, Margherita realised her laces had broken and her dress was gaping open over her breasts. She gasped and pulled her bodice closed. 'I'm sorry, it just burst undone. My dress is too tight, I don't know why.' Anxiety made her words tumble out.

La Strega reached out and grasped her wrist. Her face was white, her eyes glittering as she scanned Margherita from head to toe, noticing the round swell of her belly, her heavy breasts. 'You little whore,' she whispered. Her eyes darted to the unmade bed then back to Margherita, who shrank back in terror. 'You slut!' the witch cried. 'You've betrayed me!' She slapped Margherita so hard that she fell to the floor, sobbing, her hand to her cheek. 'Who is he? Who have you let in?'

'No . . . no one.'

'You liar! How long? How many months? I knew something was wrong! I knew the spell was not working as it should. I thought you were grown too old but all the time you were lying to me.' La Strega drew her dagger. 'You'll pay for this!' She seized Margherita's hair, wrapped it three times about her left wrist, and slashed at it with the knife. The knife sliced through her hair, so that Margherita tumbled back to the floor. The witch was left with a waterfall of fiery tresses cascading from her hand. She brought it to her mouth and kissed it, then let it fall.

'I will never forgive you,' La Strega said icily. 'You're worthless to me now.'

And she raised her knife to strike.

FUGUE

Let down your hair,
That cloudy-gold lure,
The delicate snare
That holds me secure.
Delight and despair
War with me now —
Let down your hair.

Shake out each curl
Swiftly, and be
Like Spring, a wild girl
With her hair flying free.
Bury me there,
And be buried with me . . .
Let down your hair!

'Rapunzel'
Louis Untermeyer

THE AFFAIR OF THE POISONS

The Abbey of Gercy-en-Brie, France —
April 1697

The abbey bell sounded out, wrenching me away from Sœur Seraphina's story and back to the real world of the convent and its high enclosing walls.

'Oh, no, not now,' I cried, looking back towards the church and its bell-tower.

'To think how reluctant you were to first come out into my garden. Now, you never want to leave,' Sœur Seraphina teased.

'It's so beautiful here.' I looked around at the neat squares of earth, misting over with green as seeds sprouted. Birds sang with gusto as they darted about the enclosure, pulling at worms in the earth or carrying straw in their beaks to build nests, and bees hung above the lavender. 'But it's the story, you know that. I want to know what happens next.'

'There is a good reason why St Benedict counsels us to be patient,' Sœur Seraphina replied. I rolled my eyes and she smiled. 'We will come to the garden again tomorrow, never fear. Though I must finish planting out these cuttings of rue before we go to vespers, else they'll wilt. Will you help me?'

I emptied my bucket of weeds onto the compost heap and came to kneel beside her. Sœur Seraphina had taken cuttings from a silvery-grey plant and now she passed me a great bundle of them. I flinched away, dropping the bundle of rue to the ground. A strong unpleasant smell wafted up from the bruised stems. 'What a horrible stink!'

'It's a powerful smell. That's why it's so effective against fleas and devils. I make rue water for the servants to scrub our floors with in summer, and rue water for the priest to sprinkle the altar with before High Mass.'

She smiled at me but saw no answering gleam of amusement in my eyes. The smell of the rue made me nauseous. I stood up and stumbled away, my hands held out in front of me. 'I cannot stand the smell. How do I get it off me?'

Sœur Seraphina stood up creakily, dusting away the dirt on her skirt. Her honey-coloured eyes regarded me in puzzlement. 'Come along in. I'll give you some lemons to rub on your hands. It will help get rid of the smell.'

But the disagreeable odour lingered on my skin and in my clothes all evening, and I could smell it still as I closed my eyes that night to try to sleep. It smelt of prison.

Versailles, France — 1679 to 1680
The witch La Voisin was arrested by the police on 12th March 1679.

I heard the news at the gambling table, and it caused such a disagreeable twisting sensation in my stomach that I felt quite sick. I got up and hurried towards the door. I had to warn Athénaïs.

As I pushed through the crowd, I heard snippets of conversation from all sides. The court was abuzz with the news.

'I heard they found an oven in her summerhouse with the charred remains of babies' bones.'

'And dug up thousands more in her garden.'

'Holy Mother Mary!'

'They say she used to sacrifice babies in satanic rites.'

'She had a laboratory where she made poisons.'

'Did you hear they've arrested a hundred or more witches in Paris alone? They have a list of names . . .'

'I'd like to see that list. I'd wager I know half the names on it. There's barely a lady at court who hasn't gone to have her fortune told at least once.'

'They'll torture her, of course, to find out who her clients were. They'll break her on the wheel or crush her legs in the boots.'

'She'll burn at the stake for sure.'

All I heard from all sides was 'poison', 'murder', 'sorcery', 'torture'; the court could talk of nothing else. I scratched on the gilded panel of Athénaïs's door. She screeched at me to go away, but I insisted she must see me. When her maid let me in, I found Athénaïs lying on her pink velvet couch, beside a small gilded table laden with an empty decanter of wine, a golden goblet, a vial of hartshorn and various medicaments and cure-alls. She held a damp cloth drenched with lavender to her head. 'Whatever it is, I cannot help you. I have troubles enough of my own,' she said.

Athénaïs was not looking her best. Her waist was nearly as thick as it had been before the birth of her son the previous summer, and heavy jowls dragged down either side of her mouth. The battle between Athénaïs and Françoise over the affections of the King had been raging all winter. The King tried to intervene between the two women, which only made things worse. Françoise said that all her best efforts were misunderstood, and that perhaps it was best if she resigned from her position as governess and retired to Maintenon. The King ordered Athénaïs to apologise, but she refused. She retired to her rooms for two days, but for once the King did not hurry to comfort her.

Eventually, Athénaïs rose, had her stays tightened as much as she could bear, put on her most gorgeous gown and sallied forth to win back the King's good will. He was cool to her and made a point of visiting Françoise for an hour after lunch, instead of his habitual sojourn in Athénaïs's apartment. Françoise's maid said coyly that they were reading sermons together; it was a testament to the strength of Françoise's character that we all wondered if that was true.

Desperate to break Françoise's inexplicable charm on the King, Athénaïs pointed out a beautiful young girl who had only recently come to court as lady-in-waiting to the Duchesse d'Orléans.

'Look, sire, at that statue,' she said, pointing to Angélique de Fontanges, who was standing, stiff with shyness and awe, by the wall. 'Does she not look as if she was carved by a master sculptor? Would you be surprised if I told you she was alive?'

'A statue, perhaps,' the King replied, 'but good God! What a beauty!'

By the next day, it was all over court that the King had presented the beautiful eighteen-year-old with a pearl necklace and earrings. A few days later, it was whispered that he had discreetly made a visit to the Palais-Royal, the Duc d'Orléans' residence in Paris, where the young lady-in-waiting resided. There, the King was quietly shown to

Angélique's room. I don't know whether Angélique expected him, or even if she wanted him, but it was not long before she was given an apartment of her own at Versailles, a new coach with eight grey horses (two more horses than poor Athénaïs ever got), and a bevy of servants to wait on her hand and foot, all dressed in grey to match the celebrated colour of her great grey eyes.

Both Athénaïs and Françoise were forgotten. The first raged and wept; the second shook her head in quiet disapproval and said she would pray for the King's soul.

The King barely noticed. He had eyes only for Angélique. When she lost her hat while hunting and tied back her hair with her lace garter, it became at once the fashion to wear one's hair loose and au naturel, bound back with a length of lace. Only Athénaïs refused to take up the new hairstyle, resolutely wearing her hair in the mass of tiny artificial ringlets that had once been copied so widely. Suddenly, she seemed out of touch with the times.

Athénaïs took her revenge in her usual dramatic way, her pet bears 'accidentally' finding their way into Angélique's sumptuous apartment and tearing it to pieces.

All of this I observed because I had taken the position of Athénaïs's lady-in-waiting, left vacant after Mademoiselle des Oeillets was dismissed for making a scene begging the

King to recognise her illegitimate daughter. I had not known what else to do. I was penniless and ostracised after the failure of my engagement to the Marquis de Nesle, the Duchesse de Guise had refused to employ me again and my sister had written to tell me sadly that her husband refused to let me set foot inside his chateau.

Kept busy tending to my demanding mistress's needs, I had gradually seen my own scandal forgotten as other, newer scandals seized the court's attention. Slowly, I had felt my terror at being accused of witchcraft fading. Athénaïs had reassured me by saying impatiently, 'Half the women at court have bought aphrodisiacs before, and half the men too. No one cares about a little love spell, Charlotte-Rose.'

Ashamed of how naive I had been, I determined to be as sophisticated and worldly as Athénaïs. I forgot all that my mother had taught me and spent my days gambling and drinking champagne and whispering scandal behind my fan as the King moved among us, immutable and enigmatic as gravity. He was the Sun King, and we could no sooner change our course than the smallest and most distant planet.

All my hard-won sophistication had deserted me now. I remembered again how the court had turned out to watch the poor tortured body of the Marquise de Brinvilliers being burnt at the stake, and how the stench of her cooking flesh had tainted the air, making us all hide our faces in our pomanders. I was sick with fear that I too would burn, accused of using black magic to win a man's love.

'La Voisin has been arrested. They say she'll be tortured to name her clients.'

'Pardon?'

'They've found the bones of hundreds of aborted babies in her garden, and a laboratory where she made poisons.'

'*Sangdieu!*' Athénaïs started to her feet, knocking over the table and sending the decanter crashing to the floor. 'I must go to Paris. *Mordieu,* it may be too late.'

'You cannot go to Paris. I tell you, the police are there, at her house. They've already taken her to the Bastille.'

'You don't understand,' she said. 'I went . . . I went to a friend of La Voisin's, someone who said she could help me get rid of Mademoiselle de Fontanges.'

I felt cold. 'Get rid of?'

'Not kill her!' Athénaïs said. 'Of course not. No, I just wanted . . . I don't know, for her to get the pox, or lose all her hair, or something. But I'm afraid the police will misunderstand my intentions. Louvois is my enemy. He resents my influence with the King and has done everything he can to bring me down. He will seize any chance to blacken my name.

I must . . . I must stop him finding out.'

I nodded, understanding at once. The Marquis de Louvois was the minister for war and the King's spymaster. He was a big, broad, red-faced bully of a man, servile only to the King, and rude and peremptory to everyone else. He was a bitter enemy of Monsieur Jean-Baptiste Colbert, the chief minister, who was the King's right-hand man and advised him on everything. The Marquis de Louvois wanted to be the King's only advisor, so he worked secretly to bring Colbert down. Since Colbert was an old friend of Athénaïs's family, and she had often supported his appeals to the King, Louvois hated Athénaïs too.

'What will you do?' I asked.

'I don't know. Find out what is happening. Make sure Colbert is keeping an eye on proceedings. He is my friend and will keep a check on Louvois. Maybe I can bribe the interrogators not to torture La Voisin. She'd say anything under torture. Anyone would.'

I started to protest, thinking this a foolish idea, but she did not stay to listen. Without even affixing a patch to her face, she caught up her shawl and her purse and hurried out of the room.

She returned a few days later, pale and haggard. When I asked her anxiously if all was well, she shrugged and said simply, 'I have done all I can. We must just hope for the best.' Then she made a little moue with her mouth and said, 'Such a shame we cannot go and buy ourselves a good luck charm. But there's not a fortune-teller left on the streets of Paris. They've seized them all.'

The arrests and interrogations continued.

The King ordered the chief of police to set up a Chambre Ardente, a name to strike terror into the heart of any Huguenot, as it was last employed as an Inquisition for heretics in the days of the St Bartholomew Massacre. Some said the Chambre Ardente was so named because interrogations took place in a room from which all daylight was excluded, the only illumination coming from flaming torches. Others said it was because so many of the accused ended up burning at the stake.

The Chambre Ardente began its interrogations in April. One by one, the sorcerers and fortune-tellers of Paris were questioned. Most were tortured. Everyone in Versailles was hungry for details, but all was rumour. The King seemed imperturbable, though silver goblets were suddenly banished from court and crystal glass became all the fashion, since all knew that glass could not be impregnated with poison.

Françoise spent her days praying and doing good works. Athénaïs spent her days gambling and alternatively storming at the King and trying to charm him. Neither strategy worked.

The King was icily polite and gave Athénaïs a new position as the *surintendante* of the Queen's household — an honour that allowed her to be treated as a duchess, including the right to sit down in the Queen's presence. Athénaïs was in despair. 'He always gives away such favours when an affair is over. He made Louise de la Vallière a duchess. It's like paying off a servant. I won't have it.'

But she did not turn down the position, or rail against the King any more. Indeed, Athénaïs seemed weary and defeated. Her weight once again ballooned, and people began to make cruel jokes about the size of her thighs. In May, several of the Parisian fortune-tellers were burnt to death. The fourteen-year-old daughter of one was forced to watch so she would not be tempted to follow her mother's career. Another witch, it was said, had died in the torture chamber. My sleep was tormented by nightmares.

'Don't be ridiculous,' Athénaïs said when I confided my fears to her while airing out her petticoats one evening. 'You are nobly born. Your grandfather was the Duc de la Force, your father was the Marquis de Castelmoron. You are distant kin to the King himself. They will not dare accuse you.'

In June, Madame de Poulaillon was tried at the Arsenal. She came from a noble Bordeaux family; my own mother had known her parents. Young and beautiful, she was accused of trying to poison her wealthy husband so she could marry her lover. By all accounts, the prosecutors had wanted her to suffer the punishment of torture and beheading, but the Chambre Ardente took pity on her and sent her to a severe prison for 'fallen women', where she was condemned to hard labour for the rest of her life. 'She was nobly born,' I told Athénaïs. 'Yet they dared to put her on trial.'

'Charlotte-Rose, this is not like you. What has happened to Dunamis?'

I didn't know. All my courage, all my boldness, seemed to have leaked away from me. I slept with a chair jammed under my door handle. I woke often at night, all my senses preternaturally acute, afraid I had heard someone standing over me, breathing. If someone touched me unexpectedly, I'd flinch. Worst of all, I no longer stole time to write my stories. My quill was stuck hard in the dried ink of my inkpot. I did not even write to my sister.

All summer, the tortures and executions continued. The *Paris Gazette* was full of hideous details. One witch had her right hand amputated before she was hanged. Another was strangled before being broken on the wheel. Yet another was tortured cruelly before being hanged. Meanwhile, La Voisin remained in prison, interrogated again and again and again. The royal spymaster Louvois brought reports to the council, but none of us could tell anything by the King's face. He remained as impassive as ever. Only the sight of the beautiful Angélique seemed to soften his adamantine expression.

On New Year's Eve, at the beginning of 1680, Angélique arrived at mass dressed in a billowing gown of gold and blue brocade, trimmed with blue velvet ribbons. When the King arrived a few moments later, a buzz rose through the crowded chapel. He was wearing a coat of exactly the same material, embellished with blue velvet ribbons. The Queen uttered a distressed squeak and pressed her hand to her forehead. Athénaïs stood motionless, clutching her prayer-book so tightly her knuckles turned white. Françoise folded her hands in prayer, turning her eyes heavenwards.

Angélique smiled and sat down.

Normally, such a breach of etiquette would have enraged the King — a mere *mademoiselle* to sit in the presence of the Queen! But he only smiled and gestured for the mass to proceed.

Two weeks later, Princesse Marie-Anne — the thirteen-year-old bastard daughter of the King's first mistress, Louise de la Vallière — was married to her cousin, Louis Armand de Bourbon, the Prince de Conti.

A grand ball was held at the Château de Saint-Germain-en-Laye after the wedding.

591

There were so many hundreds of guests that the royal carpenters built four new staircases from the terrace to the first-floor windows so everyone could mount to the ballroom without causing too great a crush. A long table was set up in the gallery, lined with golden baskets filled with sweet-scented hyacinths, jasmine and tulips, as if it was spring instead of the dead of winter. Outside, snow swirled down; inside was golden light and warmth and laughter and music. The King moved about the crowd, nodding with immense dignity and condescension to his guests. The Queen sat in her chair, a tiny dog on her lap, trying to pretend she did not care about all the thousands of *livres* being spent on the King's illegitimate daughter. Princesse Marie-Anne herself danced as wildly as anyone else there, gulping down glass after glass of champagne and enduring much teasing about the wedding night to come. I wondered if she was afraid, but there was no sign of it on her face or in her bearing. She simply tossed her fair curls, so like her mother's, and looked as stiff and pretty as a doll in a huge white dress glittering with diamonds.

'He had best do as well by my daughters when it comes time for them to marry,' Athénaïs said to me, sotto voce. 'I swear I am about to expire with the heat! Charlotte-Rose, would you be a darling and go and find me another fan? These ostrich feathers look divine but just do not cool me down.'

Indeed, her chubby cheeks were scarlet and her ringlets hung limply on her neck.

'Of course,' I said and made my way through the crowd. I saw Françoise standing with a few other devotees along the wall, looking like a line of owls with their drab clothes and disapproving faces. I smiled at her, but she did not smile back, just regarded me coolly. I did not let my smile fade but swept ahead, taking another glass of champagne as I went. I saw the King standing in a cluster of courtiers, all bowing and smiling and uttering fawning compliments. He was frowning and looking about him, and I wondered where his lovely young mistress was. Angélique was never normally found more than a few paces away from him.

Ten minutes later, I was hurrying along one of the wide corridors, carrying Athénaïs's fan, when I heard a low moan. I stopped and listened. Whimpering came from behind a half-closed door. I pushed open the door and saw the shape of a woman crouched on a low divan. I dropped the fan on a side table, took a candelabra and tiptoed in, my throat constricted. The light fell upon a golden head hanging low and a bowed back covered with oyster-coloured satin.

'*Mademoiselle?*' I asked.

Angélique turned an anguished face towards me and lifted her hands. They were drenched with blood.

'What is it? What's happened?'

'I don't know. I've been feeling so sick . . . I had such bad cramps I thought I was going to die. Then all this blood gushed out.'

I suddenly understood. My hand shook so much that the candelabra tilted and hot wax ran onto my skin. I put it down on a side table.

'And there's . . . there's this thing . . . this monster . . .' Angélique pointed at the ground. A blood-soaked shawl was all bundled up. My pulse banging, I unwrapped the shawl. Within lay a red naked creature, blind and mute like a newborn kitten. A tiny penis, scarlet in colour, was coiled like a snail between the floppy red legs. His bald head was much bigger than his spindly body, and a long, thin, slack cord hung from his stomach, its end ragged and torn and leaking blood. His foot was no bigger than my fingernail.

'It's a little boy,' I managed to say. 'You've had a baby.'

'That's not a baby. It's all red and black. It's an imp from hell. I'm being punished for my sin.' She began to sob again. I saw that her satin dress was saturated with red from her lap to her knees.

'Ssssh, don't weep. You've had a miscarriage. That's all it is.' I wrapped the poor little limp thing back up again, my hands trembling.

She shook her head, the tips of her loose golden curls stained with blood. 'I don't understand.' She began to rock, clenching her hands together, pushing at her lap. 'Aah, it hurts.'

'We need to get you a doctor. Sit still. Please don't cry any more.' I looked around for some wine, but the room was empty of anything but paintings and statues and vases and silly little couches on legs so delicate they looked as if they would break if you sat on them. 'Wait here, I'll —'

'Don't leave me!'

'I must. Just for a moment.'

As I ran to the door, she screamed, 'Don't go, don't leave me with that thing.'

I found a footman and sent him for wine, for hot water, for napkins, for a doctor. 'Find the King,' I babbled, then thought better of it. 'No, no, call Athénaïs, call the Marquise de Montespan.'

Athénaïs did not let me down. Sweeping into the room, she understood the situation at a glance. She took Angélique's hands in her own, chafing them gently. 'There, there, all will be well. Were you all alone, you poor child? What an ordeal. Never mind, it's over now.'

I showed her the dead baby in the shawl.

'How . . . how terrible. The poor little

thing.' I did not know if she meant the dead baby or her hated rival, the nineteen-year-old girl now weeping on her shoulder, ruining the priceless cloth with snot and blood and tears. Athénaïs looked up at me. 'The King will be furious. He must not know, at least not until the wedding is over. We must get her to her bedchamber without a whiff of gossip. Will you help me?'

I helped her lift Angélique to her feet. The couch beneath her was horribly stained. Athénaïs wrapped her in her own silver-embroidered shawl, I took up the dead baby and together we helped the King's mistress stumble to her room.

'I cannot stay here,' Athénaïs said. 'There will be a terrible scandal. It'll be seen as a dreadful omen on the night of the King's daughter's wedding. If Mademoiselle de Fontanges were to die too . . .'

Although Athénaïs spoke in an undertone, Angélique must have been listening, for she cried out now in terror. 'Will I die? I don't want to die.'

'You'll be fine. The doctor will be here soon.' I did my best to soothe her but her fresh nightgown was already stained with a slow creeping red tide.

'I must go. My absence will be remarked upon. Charlotte-Rose, you must not stay either. You can afford no more scandal.'

I looked at Angélique, who clung to my

hand. 'Don't leave me!'

Athénaïs went out, biting her lip. I took a deep breath and sat down beside Angélique, murmuring, 'It's all right, I won't leave you. Rest easy now, the doctor will soon be here.'

When the King's chief physician, Antoine Daquin, at last arrived, his face and fingers shone with grease, and he carried a half-full glass of wine. His heavy wig was slightly askew, framing a pockmarked face with drooping jowls.

He lifted the coverlet, glanced at the red pool in which Angélique lay and frowned at the sight of the tiny naked corpse.

'What did you do to her, *mademoiselle,* to induce the bleeding?' he demanded of me.

'Nothing! I found her like this. All I did was help her to bed.'

'If a child is aborted after its quickening, it is considered murder.'

I steadied myself with one hand on the bedside table. 'Mademoiselle de Fontanges did not seem to even know she was with child. I certainly did not know! Nor did I do anything except help her to bed and call for you. She has lost a lot of blood. Her gown was soaked in it.'

He bent over Angélique. '*Mademoiselle!* What have you done? Did you not want your baby? To murder your own child is a grave sin on your conscience. What did you do? Did you drink a potion? Or insert a metal tool of some kind? Who helped you?'

Angélique was so white even her lips were pale. 'No! I didn't hurt the baby. I didn't know . . . I just felt sick . . . then there was all this blood . . . I thought I was being torn apart by demons.'

'It's all right,' I murmured, gently stroking back her tumbled hair.

Daquin cast me a suspicious look but pressed Angélique back down into her pillows. 'Very well. We'll need to bleed you, to drain out the bad humours in your body. *Mademoiselle,* since you are here you may make yourself useful and hold the bowl.'

'But she has already lost so much blood.'

'Are you a physician, *mademoiselle*? I think not. Kindly hold the bowl and do not attempt to advise your betters.'

I held the bowl and did my best to catch the spurt of blood as Daquin cut a small incision in the delicate blue vein of her wrist. The bowl filled quickly, and Angélique swooned back against her pillows. The doctor held his greasy thumb over the cut and instructed me to wrap it in a bandage. I did as he asked, feeling rather faint. The doctor emptied the bowl into the chamber pot, packed it and the bloodstained lancet away in his bag, and then drained his wine glass. 'Call a servant to dispose of the foetus. If I am quick, I might get back to the feast before all the food is gone.'

Without another word, he went out, and I was left standing by the limp figure of the King's young mistress and her dead baby. Distantly, I heard the swing of dance music and the high hum of chatter and laughter. In the shadowy bedchamber, there was no sound at all. I looked down at myself and saw that my hands were red with blood. I held them away from my body, unable to breathe or move for the horror of it all.

A week later, I was arrested on suspicion of black magic and taken to the Bastille.

The Bastille

Paris, France — January 1680

I was locked in a stone cell. A barred window, high in the wall, let in a shaft of light, enough for me to see a low wooden bench, a reeking bucket, a scatter of sodden straw on the paving, a streak of green slime in the corner.

I sat, clutching my shawl about me. It was silk and did nothing to ward off the cold. My teeth chattered and my limbs trembled. I stared at the iron door, willing someone to come in and bow, saying, 'Pardon, *mademoiselle*. Our mistake.'

No one came. Slowly, the shaft of light faded. All was dark. The cold was so intense my bones hurt. I curled up on the wooden bench, my shawl wrapped around me, my stockinged feet tucked under me. At some point, I must have slept, for I woke from a dream in which my mother had been calling me. Tears were brittle on my cheeks.

Dawn slithered in like a fat grey slug. I put on my frivolous high-heeled slippers and began to pace the cell. My skin was crawling. Lifting away my shawl, I saw my arms and breast were peppered with fleas. Frantically, I began trying to catch them, crushing them beneath my fingernails. Soon, the nails of my thumb and forefinger were black with blood, but there was no cessation to the onslaught of the hopping biting insects. At regular intervals, a bell tolled out.

The wedge of light moved slowly across the wall of the cell, showing the scribbled names of countless former prisoners. Still, nobody came. It must have been past noon when at last the iron door scraped open. A fat man came in, a basket in his hand. He wore a stained jerkin over rusty chain mail and had not shaved in a week.

'Provisions for you.' He put the basket down.

'What am I doing here? I demand to see someone in charge, *tout de suite*!' My voice shook.

'No *tout de suite* around here, sweetheart. You'll be taken to the Chambre Ardente when they're good and ready for you, and not a second before. And my guess is it'll be a while. This place is bursting at the seams and so is every prison for miles.'

'I am Charlotte-Rose de Caumont de la Force, cousin to the Duc de la Force!'

He snorted. 'I've got dukes and countesses and marquises coming out my bung-hole!

Half the bloody court's here!' He went out, clanging the door behind him.

Swallowing hard, I picked up the basket and looked inside. Wrapped up in a napkin were a fresh baguette, some ripe white cheese and two roasted pigeon legs. All rested upon a thick woollen shawl.

Blessing Athénaïs, I pulled the shawl out and wrapped it around me. A small note fell to the floor. I opened it.

24th January 1680

To Mlle de Caumont de la Force,
Mademoiselle, as humbly as I may I recommend me to your good grace, knowing that all my thoughts are with you at this dark time. Do not despair; it is indeed certain that your time in such a dreadful place must be just a short span, for all your friends are exerting themselves to their utmost on your behalf.

You are not alone in your most miserable affliction. There is scarce a man or woman at court who has not seen the dark finger of suspicion fall upon them. You are in grand company indeed, for no lesser personages than the Duc de Luxembourg, the Vicomtesse de Polignac and the Marquis de Cessac have all been arrested as well. Many others have been summoned to appear at the Arsenal, including the Comtesse du Roure and the Princesse de Tingry. Is it not impossible to believe? I wonder that the King allows such severe indignities to be enacted upon those of such ancient and noble lineage.

I should share with you the most scandalous news of all. The Comtesse de Soissons was to have been arrested as well, but her brother-in-law, the Duc de Bouillon, arrived at her house at midnight and warned her to flee. She packed up her cashbox and jewels and a few gowns and drove out of Paris at three o'clock in the morning. They say she tried to poison her husband! Though Lord knows why, he was the most complaisant of husbands. The only question remains, how did the Duc de Bouillon know to warn her? Someone must have informed him of the arrest warrant, but who, I wonder? His Majesty the King has ordered guards to pursue her, but far too late to stop her before she crossed the border.

I have heard it whispered that her sister is to be questioned as well, even though she is such a favourite with the King. Knowing the Duchesse de Bouillon, I fully expect her to turn up with a paramour on either arm and her devoted husband carrying her train.

You can imagine how all is chaos here at Versailles. Everyone is most astonished and frightened, particularly since so many named are linked by blood or friendship to us all. They say another hundred are to be named in the next week, so that even I — who as you know is the most pious and devout of women — feel a shade of anxiety. Luckily, I know that I too have friends, who will defend any such malicious accusations and take care not to drag my noble name through the mud.

Your loving friend,
Athénaïs de Rochechouart
de Mortemart,
Marquise de Montespan

I read this letter many times over the following few hours, having nothing else to read. It was clear to me that Athénaïs was warning me to keep my mouth shut. I was also most intrigued to know I was not the only one arrested, and that those accused included such old friends of the King as the Comtesse de Soissons and her sister, the Duchesse de Bouillon. These two were the last of the Mazarinettes left in France, those bold and beautiful nieces of Cardinal Mazarin, who had been among the King's only playmates and, later, his mistresses. If the King had allowed the chief of police to accuse the Mazarinettes, there was no hope for me.

The long hours passed. Once, I heard an iron door grating open and boots marching past. I ran to my door and pressed my ear against it, but the footsteps faded away and I heard nothing more. Slowly, my intense fear faded and was replaced by something almost as difficult to endure: boredom. As the light was fading, my own door scraped open and a tall, thin, scrawny gaoler came in with a bowl of pottage and a jug of dirty-looking water.

'Some supper for you,' he said, putting it on the bench.

'You're a Gascon,' I cried, hearing his southern accent. 'Oh, how lovely to hear a voice from home.'

He stared at me. 'You a Gascon too? I thought you a fine court lady. Where you from?'

He spoke not only in the Gascon dialect but in Garonnais, the language of my home valley. Only those who grew up in the Garonne Valley would know this particular vernacular. I replied rapidly, and we worked out exactly where we had both grown up, and how many acquaintances we shared, and what had brought each of us to this peculiar (and, I hoped, fortuitous) meeting in a prison cell in the Bastille. His name was Bertrand Ladouceur, he had grown up near Bazas and had come to Paris looking for work after the failure of the harvest in southern France a few years earlier. But Paris had not been kind to Bertrand.

'Parisians . . .' He hawked and spat at the

floor. 'They think we Gascons imbeciles. Give us all the dirtiest jobs, like cleaning out the cesspits or collecting dead bodies from plague-houses. Best job I could find, this.'

'You must find it hard.'

'I do, I do.'

'We Gascons are independent souls. We don't like being ordered about or locked away from the sky.'

'That's right.'

'I fear I'll end up in the Asylum de Bicêtre if I am kept locked up in this foul place much longer. I suppose you couldn't tell me when I am to be brought before the court?'

He looked wary. 'I couldn't say.'

'We Gascons need to stick together. If you carry a message from me to a friend of mine, I'll make sure you're well paid. And I need something to do in here if I'm not to go crazy. Will you not bring me the *Gazette*? I need to know what's going on.'

He thought about this for a moment, then decided that carrying messages and bringing me the newspaper would not do any harm. I did not write my message; a note could be too easily discovered. What I did instead was make a mental list of things I needed — a clean pillow, a blanket, some rue water to try to kill the fleas, some books, a candle to light the long dark hours of the night, some fur-lined boots to keep my icy feet warm, some more food, some clean handkerchiefs — and then asked Bertrand to repeat the list till he had remembered it off by heart. Then I told him how to find Athénaïs. He went out, locking the door behind him. I sat and killed fleas, telling myself stories to keep myself amused.

Some time later, Bertrand returned with a thin fold of newspaper and a jug of small ale, which I drank eagerly, having determined not to drink the water no matter how thirsty I was. The newspaper was full of *L'affaire des poisons,* as the scandal was being called. I discovered that the Vicomtesse de Polignac had made a dramatic escape from her country house only minutes before the royal guards arrived, and that the Comtesse de Soissons, the King's former mistress Olympe Mancini, had arrived safely in Flanders but that the people of Antwerp had closed the city gates against her and pelted her carriage with squalling cats.

Bertrand returned the next day with a heavy basket. I fell upon it with joy, finding everything I had asked for plus a few other small thoughtful gifts, such as a pomander of dried orange studded with cloves. Included was a heavy tome of La Fontaine's *Les Amours de Psyché et de Cupidon.* Once again, I blessed Athénaïs. She had obviously paid Bertrand well, because he asked me eagerly if there were any other messages to be carried.

'Soon, perhaps. If I had any news I could

give her . . . but I don't know what is happening! If only I could listen to the trials.'

'I don't think they'd allow that,' Bertrand said, screwing up his face.

'It could do no harm . . . and I would then have news to send to the 'Marquise de Montespan.'

He shook his head. 'You don't want to be watching the interrogations, *mademoiselle,* not a gently bred young thing like you. But if you like I will bring you what news I can.'

'Bertrand, you're wonderful! I'll get you a job at court!'

'I'd rather you got me a job at the Château de Cazeneuve. I miss the country.'

'I'll write to my sister,' I promised. 'She is the Baronne de Cazeneuve. She'll find you a job you like.'

He nodded in pleased thanks and went out, leaving me alone to douse my room and my mattress with rue water. It smelt foul. I lifted my pomander to my nose but it did little to disguise the stench. I sat and read through the newspapers but found it hard to concentrate on the text. Were those faint screams I heard? Was that distant sobbing? Or was it just the wind wailing about the towers of the Bastille? As soon as it began to grow dim, I lit my candle with shaking fingers and lay curled in my damp and stinking bed, sick with fear.

Every day, my Gascon gaoler brought me a

basket of simple provisions and a few scraps of news. The Duc de Luxembourg was being questioned first, Bertrand told me. No one knew what he was accused of, but it was said he had made a pact with the devil to be invulnerable on the battlefield, to be as wealthy and loved as the King, and to have many women fall in love with him. People were saying he had taken part in black masses and orgies, but I found this hard to believe, given what a stiff-necked old aristocrat he was.

The next day, Bertrand told me the guards were all sniggering about the interrogation of the Duchesse de Foix. A letter from her had been found at La Voisin's house, questioning the power of a breast-enhancing potion the Duchesse had bought. She had written to the witch, 'The more I rub, the less they grow!'

'She was surely not charged for that,' I said.

Bertrand shrugged. 'They let her go. They asked her all sorts of other questions about what she had bought from the witch, but she was adamant that was the only thing.'

A few days later, the Princesse de Tingry was questioned. She came out of the inter-rogation room in tears, Bertrand told me, after they had accused her of aborting the Duc de Luxembourg's children three times, their bodies dried and powdered for use in spells.

'It seems impossible. She's a princess!'

'A great many fine court ladies being brought before the court,' Bertrand said darkly. 'You're up this afternoon, I heard.'

I clutched his arm in sudden anxiety. 'Bertrand, they won't . . . they won't torture me, will they?'

He shrugged, looking uncomfortable. 'I can't say. A sweet-faced thing like you? I wouldn't think so. Not unless they find you guilty.'

I tidied myself with trembling hands, wishing I could wash and put on a fresh dress. The stink of the rue water hung about me, seeming to smell of fear and despair. All I could do was shake out my crumpled skirt, paint my face and try to tidy my rat's nest hair, combing it with my fingers and pinning it up as best as I could without a mirror.

I was taken out of my cell and down into the centre of the Bastille by Bertrand. As I stumbled along the corridors, I heard sobbing and pleading from various cells, and then, from deep in the bowels of the building, a blood-curdling scream.

'The brodequins,' Bertrand told me. 'They crush the legs.'

I put my hand to my mouth and staggered, almost falling. Bertrand put his hand under my elbow and drew me down to sit on a little bench in a corner. 'You just take a few deep breaths,' he advised me. 'Remember, a Gascon is dashing and bold.'

I bent my head down, sucking in air. Just then, a door swung open and a small black-haired woman in full glittering court dress paused in the doorway, spreading wide her arms, making a dramatic entrance.

At once, a crowd of gaily dressed courtiers surged forward. '*Madame!* What news?'

It was the Duchesse de Bouillon. Often called the prettiest of the Mazarinettes, she had a plump round face, flashing black eyes and a saucy expression. So well known was she for her affairs that it was said the King had chosen her to be the first mistress of his son, the Dauphin. Her lover, the Duc de Vendôme, was the King's cousin and her husband's nephew, and, it was rumoured, the father of her youngest son. To my astonishment, I recognised both her husband and her lover in the crowd around her.

'What did they ask you?' asked her lover, rather anxiously.

'Just a whole lot of questions. Really, I never would have thought men who are supposed to be wise would ask such silly things.'

'What kind of questions?' asked her husband.

'They asked me if it was true I had bought poison from La Voisin so I could murder you, darling,' she answered. 'I told them what nonsense! If you were afraid I meant to poison you, would you have escorted me here?'

'Indeed,' her husband answered drily.

'What else did they ask?' her lover asked.

'The rapporteur asked me if I had seen the devil there. I answered that I had, and that he was dark and ugly, just like him,' the Duchesse replied airily. A roar of laughter went up and she was borne away by her supporters, all talking merrily. The last I heard of her was her loud confident voice floating back down the stairwell. 'Well, that was a waste of an afternoon. Shall we go to the theatre since we're here in Paris? I hear Monsieur Corneille's latest play, *The Fortune-Teller,* is all the rage!'

'It's your turn now, *mademoiselle,*' Bertrand said. 'Chin up!'

I rose and went slowly towards the open door, trying to hide the sudden shaking of my knees. Within was a small room, hung with black cloth. The only light came from a few candles, clustered about a stool on a dais, so that I would sit in the blaze of their light while everyone else in the room was sunk in shadows.

I looked about me as I made my way towards the stool, seeing only the shapes of men in enormous wigs and long robes. Occasionally, I saw a flash of an eye, the shape of a hooked nose, the hunched backs of clerks seated at writing desks. Then I had to seat myself and saw nothing but the dazzle of candlelight on my eyeballs. I was cold and had to grip my hands together to try to stop them trembling. I was asked my name. As I answered, I heard the quick scratch of quills against paper and the click of steel nibs in glass inkpots.

The questions came swiftly, and I did my best to answer them.

'Did you ever visit the witch La Voisin?'

'Yes. Once.'

'Why?'

'To purchase a love potion. I'd heard she made such things.'

'Who told you this?'

'The whole court knew of her, didn't they? People were always going to consult her about their horoscopes, or such things.'

'Did she supply you with a love spell?'

'Yes, but it didn't work. The man I wanted didn't fall in love with me.' Heat was creeping up my body. I dropped my eyes and breathed deeply, hoping my cheeks weren't burning red.

'Who was this man?'

I waved one hand. 'A nobody. His name does not matter.'

'Was it the Marquise de Montespan who introduced you to La Voisin?'

I did not know what to say. I did not want to lie and so perjure my soul, but neither did I want to incriminate Athénaïs. Reluctantly, I said that it was, but then added that it could have been anyone, since it was quite the fashion among the court ladies to visit fortune-tellers.

'Maybe so, but you say it was the Marquise de Montespan who first introduced you to this witch?'

'Yes,' I replied in a low voice, silently apologising to Athénaïs.

'Did you take part in a black mass at the house of La Voisin?'

I jerked in surprise. 'No! Of course not.'

Like bullets from a musket, the questions kept firing: 'Are you saying that you never offered your own body as an altar for the black mass? Did you see any infants being sacrificed to the devil? I ask again, did you see the throats of newborn babies being cut? Did you drink any blood? Did you know that La Voisin took part in child sacrifice? Did you know that she used their entrails for her foul sorceries? Did the Marquise de Montespan, to your knowledge, ever take part in such a ceremony? Were you a party to any orgies? Did you go to La Voisin in order for her to abort a bastard child? Did you purchase any poison from her? Did you see the Marquise de Montespan purchase poison? Did you see her purchase aphrodisiacs? Did you hear her ask for any spells to get rid of her rivals? Did the Marquise de Montespan ever talk about drinking blood? Have you ever seen a phial of blood upon her person? Has she spoken to you about using black magic to gain her desires? Did she ask you to buy a potion to make Mademoiselle de Fontanges lose her unborn child?'

Amazed and sickened by their questions, I said, 'No!' to everything. My feelings must have been clear on my face, because at last they stopped the relentless cannonade of questions and allowed me to step down.

'No charges will be laid at this time,' the judge said sternly. 'You are free to go, but only if you understand that you must be prepared to present yourself for further questioning if required.'

I nodded and made my shaky way out of the interrogation room.

Bertrand, my faithful gaoler, was waiting for me outside. He drew me down to sit in a quiet corner. I wiped my eyes with my handkerchief and took a gulp from the flask of Armagnac he offered me. It burst like fireworks inside my belly. I was able to sit up again and thank Bertrand. It was at that moment that I saw the next person being escorted into the courtroom. It was the Marquis de Nesle. At once, my head swam, my stomach clenched.

'Bertrand, will you go and listen for a while? Tell me what that man says.'

Willingly, Bertrand slipped back inside the courtroom. He came back a while later, to shrug and tell me the Marquis had said nothing much.

'Did he mention a bag of spells?' I asked

urgently. 'Did he mention . . . me?'

'No,' Bertrand answered in surprise.

'Then why was he there?'

'He bought a love spell from the witch, that's all.' Bertrand shrugged again.

'A love spell?' I asked blankly.

'Yes. A bottle of perfume that the witch promised would make any woman fall willingly into his arms. It had the flesh of vipers in it, and other such things.'

I stared at him for a long moment, then suddenly bent my head down into my arms, laughing uncontrollably. And then I cried. Between these two states, I managed to rise and make my way out of the Bastille, occasionally having to lean against the wall as another gust of hysterical laughter shook me. Bertrand accompanied me, his face pinched with worry, and put me into a hackney carriage.

'Versailles,' I said. 'Oh, please, take me home to Versailles.'

Burning the Witch

Châlons-sur-Marne, France — February 1680
On 22nd February 1680, La Voisin was burnt to death at the stake.

That same day, the King left the chateau at Saint-Germain-en-Laye to travel to Châlons-sur-Marne to meet the Princesse de Bavière, who had been chosen as the bride for the Dauphin. Angélique managed to get herself up from her sickbed to travel with him. She knew the King could not abide any ailment that interfered with his pleasure.

I went with Athénaïs. To her irritation, her coach was a considerable distance away from the front, where the King and the Queen travelled together. She was used to being in the lead.

Five days later, the long procession of coaches and outriders and baggage carts and soldiers and servants and camp followers arrived in Villers-Cotterêts, and there the Duc d'Orléans threw a grand ball for the King.

Accommodation was restricted in the ancient chateau where the court was essentially camping out. All the ladies shared one vast chilly bedchamber, straw pallets thrown down on the floor. It was there that I had my first sighting of Angélique since her miscarriage.

I was shocked. She was puffy-faced and heavy-eyed, with deep shadows under her eyes and red patches high on her cheekbones. The cut on her wrist where the doctor had bled her was swollen and festering, and she could barely sit upright.

'*Mademoiselle,* you are not well,' I said in concern.

'I am quite well! I have to be well. The King . . .'

'You shouldn't be out of bed.'

'You don't understand. I must . . . I must be well enough to go to the ball. The King . . . don't you understand, he hasn't been to see me, not once.'

'He doesn't like to see sickness. Come, you must lie down. I will ask for some feverfew tea for you.'

'No! I must go to the ball.'

'But you're sick. It makes no sense.'

'She is afraid she will lose her hold on the King if she does not take part,' Athénaïs said from behind me. 'She's right, of course. He will be angry if she continues to keep to her bed.'

'But look at her! She's very ill.'

Athénaïs tilted her head to one side. 'I can

618

do something about that. Come sit here, my dear. If we cover up those shadows under your eyes . . . and blend in a little colour on your cheeks . . . and paint your lips . . . no, not crimson, it'll make you look too pale. Perhaps just a hint of softest pink . . . *voilà*!'

As she spoke, Athénaïs whisked her haresfoot over her rival's young and beautiful face, then coaxed her long golden curls to fall loosely down her back. 'You must tie it back with a lace ribbon, as you did hunting that day. And your dress . . . something white, I think, and pretty. Yes, I think that might just do the job.'

Athénaïs sat back to admire her handiwork. Angélique did indeed look enchantingly pretty. Beside her in the mirror, I looked thin and sallow and every single one of my soon-to-be thirty years. Athénaïs looked like a stout country matron. We both turned away from our reflections.

I picked up Athénaïs's shawl and fan and fussed over her for a moment, then — when the young girl had risen and walked unsteadily out of the room — I said to her quietly, 'Why did you do it? Do you *want* the King to keep her as his mistress?'

'My time is over,' Athénaïs replied. 'The King has not come to my bed in months. Sometimes, he cannot even bring himself to be polite to me . . . and you know how important courtesy and etiquette are to the King! I fear he knows I gave him aphrodisiacs to drink. Or perhaps I am just too old and fat now.'

'But surely it is hard for you to see another take your place?'

'Well, yes. Though, to tell you the truth, I do not particularly want the King back in my bed. It is everything else I want. My chateau and my apartment. The ambassadors paying me compliments in the hope I'll whisper in Louis' ear. The power. That's all I ever wanted.' She sighed. 'Mademoiselle de Fontanges is only a child. Her family sent her to court in the hope she would catch the King's eye. He took her and ruined her. If she loses the King's favour now, what is left for her?'

A life like mine, I thought bitterly. *No chance of love or marriage or children of one's own. A life spent serving others, always hovering on the fringes of other people's lives. You're thirty years old this year, Charlotte-Rose, and what have you achieved? Nothing. Nothing!*

Together, we walked down the corridor towards the great hall. Music was playing, couples were twirling about the room in a farrago of bright silks and ribbons and lace, shrill chatter hurt my ears. We came into the great hall to see Angélique walking straight through the crowd like a stiff-jointed marionette. She ignored the Queen — a solecism that caused gasps and snickers from all around the room. The Queen studiously ignored her, putting one fat hand on her son's pink satin sleeve to keep him from staring at her. It occurred to me suddenly that Angélique and the Dauphin were almost exactly the same age. I wondered distractedly whether the Dauphin cared that his father had taken such a young mistress, and whether he ever wished to be in his father's place. Certainly, Angélique looked beautiful tonight, more pale and ethereal than ever. She reached the King and sank into a curtsey right to the ground.

'Why, my dear,' the King said, caught between embarrassment and secret gratification. 'So pleased to see you are feeling better. Would you care to dance?'

'I would, sire.' Angélique rose rather unsteadily to her feet. He took her hand and led her onto the dance floor, looking massive and dignified in his great, rigidly curled wig, his step rather more ponderous than it used to be. She danced with him, leaning her head against his shoulder. He bent his head to speak with her.

For a while, I stopped worrying about her. Angélique was back in the King's favour, her cheeks glowing with colour, her eyes scintillatingly bright. I unfurled my fan, sipped a glass of champagne and looked about me with interest.

Outside was a bleak winter's landscape, seen only as glimpses through narrow window slits. Inside was a gaudy summer garden, roses and peonies and poppies bowing and twirling and tossing about to the sweet strains of violin music. Jewels glittered on bare necks and wrists; heavy curls hung down silken backs; high-heeled shoes clattered on the stone floor.

'Mademoiselle de la Force!'

I turned at the sound of my name and saw Princesse Marie-Anne, thirteen years old and newly married, hurrying towards me. Her young husband, Prince Louis Armand, was close behind her. Rumour said that their wedding night had been disastrous and she now refused him her bed. She looked so young to me, I rather hoped the rumours were true.

'Is it true you were thrown in the Bastille?' Princesse Marie-Anne asked breathlessly.

I took a deep breath and lifted my chin. 'Yes, *madame,* it is indeed true.'

She clasped both hands together. 'Oh, was it as awful as they say?'

'Worse. Much, much worse.'

'Oh, were you absolutely and utterly terrified?' she asked.

'Did you see anyone being tortured?' Prince Louis Armand asked.

'Yes to you, and no to you,' I replied, smiling. I hesitated, and then said, 'I did hear the sound of screaming.'

Princesse Marie-Anne clapped one white-gloved hand over her mouth. 'No!' She then

622

turned and called to some of her friends. 'Come here, come and listen! Mademoiselle de la Force is telling us about the Bastille. She heard people being tortured!'

Soon, there was a flock of brightly coloured girls and boys about me, asking me eager questions.

'What happened? What did they do? Did you truly hear someone being tortured?'

'It was the most blood-curdling sound I've ever heard,' I told them. 'A scream of the utmost agony. All I could do was clap my hands over my ears and try not to imagine what they were doing to that poor soul.'

'How awful!'

'You must have been so frightened.'

'Did you think they'd torture you too?'

'I hoped they wouldn't. I told myself, "They would not dare torture me. I am Charlotte-Rose de Caumont de la Force, cousin to the Duc de la Force, second cousin, once removed, to the King himself!" But then I would hear the crying and the moaning and the shrieking, and I remembered that the King had demanded an exact justice, with no consideration to be paid to rank or sex, and all I could do then was fall to my knees and pray to God that the judges would realise my innocence.'

There was a little collective sigh.

'So you were vindicated?' Princesse Marie-Anne asked. 'They set you free?'

I nodded and unfurled my fan, waving it gently. 'Such a refreshing change, to be innocent for once.'

They all laughed, every single one of them. I hid my smile behind my fan and realised I was enjoying myself for the first time in a very long time.

'Were you not afraid?' the Prince asked.

'Oh yes, I was terrified,' I replied. 'Apart from the screaming, there was this constant, high, eerie wailing, as if the dungeons were haunted by all those who had suffered there for so long.' *Not a bad line,* I thought. *I must write that down.* 'Then there was the rustling and squeaking of all the rats.'

'Rats!'

'Huge black ones, with eyes that shone in the darkness like little gateways into hell.'

'Oh, horrible!' Princesse Marie-Anne cried.

'I was quite sick with terror, but then I thought to myself, "Well, if I don't want them gnawing on my bones, I'd better find some way to keep them off." '

'What did you do?'

'Oh, I tamed them. I fed them bits of food till I had them dancing on their hind legs for me.'

'Oh, Charlotte-Rose, you did not!'

'Yes, I did. I had thought of training one to carry messages to you, *madame,* but then I thought about what you'd do if you woke up and there was a huge black rat sitting on your pillow.'

'I'd have screamed the place down!'

'And probably tried to crush the poor thing with a poker,' I said. 'I would have been crouched all alone in my freezing stinking cell, thinking, "Any minute now and the Princess will be along to save me," and instead my poor messenger would be lying on your bedroom floor with his brains leaking everywhere.'

'Oh, Charlotte-Rose, don't! That's disgusting!'

'I am inured to disgust now. After what they served up for breakfast, I can no longer be shocked by anything.'

'Was the food really that bad?' Prince Louis Armand asked.

'Worse. Try and imagine gruel that's simply heaving with maggots.'

'Oh, Charlotte-Rose, was it really?'

'Absolutely.'

They all moaned and pretended to gag. 'Luckily, I have friends,' I said solemnly. 'Yes, those rats of mine dragged in a few rotten apples and stinking fish carcasses for me.'

'You're jesting! Aren't you?'

'Of course,' I said with a laugh. 'Do you really think my friends would let me wallow in filth and maggots? No, no! A dozen gold coaches drove up to the Bastille every day, with footmen carrying silken counterpanes and cushions for me, and baskets filled with the very best foie gras and lobster. Why do you think those rats were dancing the ballet for me? They'd never seen anything like it.'

Princesse Marie-Anne giggled and cast me a sparkling look of admiration. 'Well, I think you're very brave.'

'Thank you, *madame.* Indeed, it is not for nothing that my family was named de la Force.' I struck an attitude like a knight holding forth a sword, and everyone laughed again.

It was true, I wasn't afraid any more. It was as if I had travelled through such terror that the world of Versailles now seemed as bright and shallow and safe as a child's wading pond. If the Marquis de Nesle had walked in just then, I could have acknowledged him without the blood rushing to my face. I even felt a sort of regret, that we had made such a mess of our chance at love. If I had not bought the bags of spells, and if he had not bought the aphrodisiacal perfume, would things have been different?

His family would still not have permitted you to marry him, I reminded myself. *Not without a rich dowry.*

Looking up, I saw that the Dauphin had drawn near. His dark eyes met mine. His mouth twisted sideways into an almost-smile. I smiled back, knowing in that moment that I had true friends at court. His new wife, the

Dauphine, smiled too, more tentatively. Many women at court would call her plain. I thought she had a sweet face, full of light.

I heard a gasp and turned to see that Angélique had staggered. She put one hand on the wall to steady herself. With horror, I noticed a red stain on the back of her gown. 'I do not think I can dance any more,' she said.

'No?' the King replied. 'You are still not well. Perhaps you should retire from court until you are recovered. Madame de Maintenon, would you care to dance?'

'Indeed I would,' Françoise answered and stepped forward to take his hand. She looked elegant and poised in a simple gown of solid black, the uniform of a lady-in-waiting to a princess. Françoise had finally resigned her position as royal governess, the King's illegitimate children having all grown rather too big to need her. Promptly, she had been appointed as the mistress of the robes to the new Dauphine, the second most important woman at court. It was an astonishing elevation for a woman born in a prison, married to an impoverished poet and then employed as a governess to bastards. So astonishing that all believed Françoise must be the new royal mistress or else had some kind of hold over the King that no one really understood.

I hurried to Angélique's side. 'You should be in bed.' I draped my shawl about her to hide the ugly stain spreading across the back of her gown. 'That's enough dancing for one night.'

'She preached at me.' Angélique watched Françoise smiling in the King's arms as he danced down the room with her. 'She told me I risked my soul's salvation by being with the King. I said to her, "Do you think throwing off a passion is as easy as taking off a chemise?" Yet it seems to be so for him, doesn't it? He never cared for me at all.'

'Let us get you to bed,' I said unhappily.

As obediently as a small child, she followed me down the hall and let me tuck her up in bed. I brought her a hot brick wrapped in flannel and some old rags to help staunch the bleeding, and I did not call the doctor.

In April, the King made Angélique the Duchesse de Fontanges and gave her a rich pension. At last, she was entitled to sit in the presence of the Queen. It gave her little pleasure. She received the court's congratulations from her sickbed at her sister's convent. She rallied long enough to make another appearance at court in May but it was to be her last. Slowly, she faded away. In the summer of the following year, Angélique died. She was only nineteen.

Many at court believed that Athénaïs had poisoned her. The Marquise kept her head high and continued to try to influence affairs of state, but the King no longer visited her or allowed her any moments alone with him. Françoise ruled the court in all but name.

I don't believe that Athénaïs poisoned poor Angélique. I hope that she did not. All I can say with any surety is that Athénaïs was never able to bear the dark again. All night, she kept the candles burning, and if the wind ever blew out the flame she would scream in terror until someone came with tinder and flint to light her candles again.

REVOCATION

The Abbey of Gercy-en-Brie, France —
April 1697

Words. I had always loved them. I collected them, like I had collected pretty stones as a child. I liked to roll words over my tongue like a lump of molten honeycomb, savouring the sweetness, the crackle, the crunch. Cerulean, azure, blue. Shadowy, sombre, secret. Voluptuous, sensuous, amorous. Kiss, hiss, abyss.

Some words sounded dangerous. Pagan. Tiger.

Some words seemed to shine. Crystal. Glissade.

Some words changed their meaning as I grew older. Ravishing.

Charles had always seemed a rather ordinary name, as common as a duck. I was wrong. Charles was an enchanted name, a shibilant like chalice and chain and hush, charm and charred and flush. As he bent his dark head to kiss my throat, I would sigh his name. *Charles*. As he stroked his hand down my thigh, I would sough, *Charles, Charles*. As he swirled his tongue in my most secret, soft and hidden places, I would sob, *Charles, Charles, Charles*. And now it was the sound of sorrow, loneliness and loss. *Charles, my love, where are you?*

We were married, you know.

Not simply a holding of hands and a vow to be true, though Charles and I did that too. No, we were married by a priest in a church, the light of candles falling on our faces as we swore to have and to hold from this day forward, till death us do part. My sister was there to witness us pledge our troth, weeping with relief into her handkerchief. Nanette wept beside her, and Marie's little daughter — my niece, whom I had never seen before — carried flowers and stared at me with curious dark eyes.

We really believed we had outwitted them all. 'You can do anything,' I had told him, 'as long as you're bold enough.'

Charles was my one true love, the one I had been dreaming of all this time. Ah, if only I had waited! If only I had been patient. If I had been the good, pious, respectable maiden everyone had wanted me to be, maybe they would have left us alone. If I had smelt of roses, instead of the lingering reek of scandal and sorcery and sex, perhaps I would now be an old married woman with a horde of little Charleses and Charlotte-Roses running about, instead of a lonely middle-aged woman locked up in a tumbledown old convent in the middle of nowhere.

Yet would Charles have fallen in love with me if I had been pious and respectable? Would we have had those mad giddy months of dancing at Marly, hunting in the forest at Fontainebleau and sneaking off to make love in the garden at Versailles? Would we have had those few days when the King himself called me 'Madame de Briou' and it seemed I had at last found that little corner of the world to call my own?

I refused to have any regrets. If I had not seen death and been so determined to seize life with both hands, if I had not tried to steer the craft of my own life, if I had not learnt how to give and take pleasure, if I had not been so determined to love with all the force of my being, would Charles have fallen in love with me at all?

I do not think so.

Versailles, France — October 1685
'What shall we do today, Charles?' I asked, joining my lover in the courtyard at the Palais de Versailles. 'It's a beautiful day.'

'I can see you wish to ride,' he said with a brief smile, indicating my forest-green riding habit with one hand.

632

'I thought we could have a picnic,' I said. 'The forest is so lovely in autumn, and soon it will be too cold to sit on the ground . . . or lie, as the case may be.' Charles did not respond to my impish grin, and I frowned. 'Is anything wrong?'

'Let us go for a ride in the forest. We can be private there.'

'Very well,' I said, a little daunted by his demeanour, which seemed cold and pre-occupied. 'I'd love a gallop!'

Soon, we were cantering down the smooth turf under the thick gnarled branches of ancient oak and beech trees. Crimson and orange leaves swirled up under the horses' hooves and spread a spectacular canopy overhead. A red squirrel darted up a tree like a streak of fire.

'This is wonderful!' I cried. 'How I love being out in the woods! I wish we could ride on forever.'

Charles smiled, but it was not his usual carefree grin. He looked pale and strained. I reined my horse in. 'Charles, what's wrong? Something is wrong.'

He dismounted and cast his reins over a broken branch protruding from a fallen log nearby. He then held up his hands to help me down. I unhooked my leg from my pommel and let him lift me down. He held me close for a moment, then stepped away, drawing me down to sit on the log.

I resisted. 'What is it? Has someone died?'

'Ma *chérie,* there is something you should know. The King . . . the King has signed a new law, revoking the Edict of Nantes.'

The earth seemed to rock under my feet. 'What?'

'You heard me. It's now illegal to be a Protestant. All Huguenots must convert to Catholicism or risk death by burning. All Protestant churches will be pulled down. All Protestant schools will be closed. Bibles and psalm books will be burnt.'

'This must be a jest.'

'I'm sorry, *ma chérie.* I came as soon as I heard.'

'He cannot do such a thing!' My legs felt so weak I put my hand out, seeking support.

Charles caught it, drawing closer so I could lean against his shoulder. 'He has. It's done. He signed the new edict this morning.'

'But there are hundreds and thousands of Huguenots in France! They will all migrate. They'll go to the Netherlands, or Germany, or somewhere. Half the artisans and merchants in France will go! Does he know what he is doing?'

'It is now against the law for any Huguenot to migrate, or leave France. Anyone caught trying to leave will be sent to the galleys, or imprisoned, all their possessions confiscated. Anyone who helps them to escape will be sent to the galleys.'

'He can't do that!'

'He can. He has.'

'But Charles . . . what are we all to do?'

He was silent a moment. 'I cannot make any suggestions for the rest of your family, but I have a solution for you, which I hope you will like.'

I hardly heard him, unable to think for the sudden hammering of fear in my ears. I was remembering all the stories: Huguenot babies spitted and cooked over fires; Huguenot women gang-raped and then killed; Huguenot churches burnt down with all their parishes locked inside; Huguenots tortured and enslaved . . .

'You could marry me,' Charles said.

'What?'

'You could marry me. Won't you, Charlotte-Rose? I love you and I want to keep you safe.'

'But we cannot marry,' I said stupidly. 'Marriages between Catholics and Protestants are against the law. Our children would be declared illegitimate.'

'You'll have to convert,' Charles said.

I simply could not understand what he meant for a moment. My head felt as if it was stuffed with lambswool, and my feet and hands were cold and heavy and strangely far away from the rest of my body. Gradually, the meaning of his words soaked through, and I felt a heady rush of anger.

'I can't! Don't you realise? My mother . . .

my family . . .' In those few words, I tried to tell him everything.

Charles was speaking quickly. 'As my wife, they will not dare touch you. I'll be able to keep you safe. The King will be pleased with you. He'll make sure you are not bothered too much. He'll probably pay you some kind of compensation.'

'I can't, I can't.' I broke away from him and ran to where my horse was grazing. Somehow, I managed to get up into the saddle, hitching my long riding skirt up above my knees. I wheeled my mare about and spurred her into a gallop.

'Charlotte-Rose!' Charles called.

I kept on riding. Now, the glorious autumn display seemed like the fires of the heretic's pyre, the very flames of hell.

Sometime later, I at last reined in my sweat-lathered mare. I had lost my hat, my hair hung half over my face, and my skin was scratched with twigs and brambles. I was panting and in tears.

What should I do? What should I do? I did not want to burn. I did not want to try to flee, hiding in some empty beer barrel, or in a cart of straw, to be stabbed by some over-zealous soldier or dragged out by my hair. Where would I go? How would I live?

I stood in a clearing among a stand of beech trees, leaves as red as rubies, branches black as jet. It was sunset, and shafts of richly coloured sunlight struck through the delicate pillars of the tree trunks, as if through the lancet windows of a cathedral.

Fragments of psalms and sermons rang through my mind. *Let God arise, let his enemies be scattered, let them that hate him flee before him. As smoke is driven away, so drive them away; as wax melteth before the fire, so let the wicked perish at the presence of God. But let the righteous be glad; let them rejoice before God: yea, let them exceedingly rejoice.*

Where were the righteous now?

My mother had always said that the afflictions sent against us, the elect, were signs of God's good will towards us, that they were a test of our faith, and that by taking the cross upon our shoulders and following Jesus Christ we would be rewarded with salvation. Yet how could anyone endure such terrible persecution?

I say to God, my rock, why have you forgotten me?

I had lost God long ago. I had lost my mother, my father, my family. I had nothing left but the love that had bloomed between Charles and me like a snowdrop unfurling through snow.

He wanted to marry me.

Heat rushed up my cheeks. I felt my eyes fill with tears. I was too weary to try to mount my horse again. I grasped her reins and began to walk back through the forest, regretting my madcap flight, regretting I had hesitated even for a second.

Charles found me some time later, stumbling along in the twilight, footsore and exhausted. I dropped the reins and ran towards him, seizing him about the waist. 'I'm sorry . . . of course I'll marry you . . . of course.'

He clasped me close, bending his head to kiss my mouth. I kissed him back passionately, my knees weak, my head spinning.

'You taste of salt,' he said a little while later. 'Like a mermaid.'

'You taste divine. Like manna from heaven. Are we truly getting married?'

'We might need to elope,' he answered rather shakily. 'My father's . . . rather difficult.'

I could understand why his father would be horrified at the idea of Charles marrying me. Apart from the fact that I was a Huguenot, apart from my lack of dowry, apart from my scorched reputation, there was the insurmountable chasm of the eleven years between our ages. I was thirty-five; Charles was not yet twenty-four. He would not come of age for another twenty months.

'I'd love to elope. I can think of nothing I'd rather do. When shall we do it?'

He laughed and kissed me again. 'If we

could get the King's permission . . .'

I bit my lip. The days when Athénaïs could crook her little finger and the King would come running were long gone. She had lost her sumptuous apartments at Versailles and was now relegated to the third or even the fourth carriage in any procession of the King's. Françoise, the Marquise de Maintenon, was now the favoured mistress. Some said she was even the King's secret wife, having married him at midnight in a clandestine ceremony some time after the Queen's death. She now had the most magnificent rooms at the palace, across the hall from the King's, at the top of the grand staircase. The King spent all his free hours there. He had taken to wearing plain brown clothes like a bourgeois, without any rings or diamond buckles or jewelled pins, and he frowned on all those *divertissements* he had once loved.

Yet Françoise, like me, had been born into a Huguenot family, even though she was now so devoutly Catholic. She had been trying to save my soul for a decade. If I spoke to her . . .

'He who never undertook anything never achieved anything,' I said, quoting one of my mother's favourite proverbs. 'I will talk to the Marquise de Maintenon. If anyone can convince the King, she can.'

It took some doing.

Gone were the days when one could stand

and gossip with the Marquise de Maintenon over a cup of hot chocolate. It was almost as hard to get an audience with her as it was with the King.

And Françoise was much occupied with the recent marriage of Princesse Louise Françoise, Athénaïs's eldest daughter, to the grandson of the Grand Condé. Princesse Louise Françoise was only eleven, and so, after the ceremonial bedding with her husband, she had gone back to the schoolroom and the loving care of her governess. Except Princesse Louise Françoise despised the Marquise de Maintenon and refused to submit to her authority. Add to that her elder half-sister's outrage that Princesse Louise Françoise now outranked her and the court was in an uproar.

In addition, the King had a boil on his leg the size of a plum and was in such pain that he could not walk. He had to attend council lying on a couch and could only shoot from his little carriage, which enraged him so much he was in a perpetual foul mood. Françoise was kept busy nursing him and trying to keep him happy — a task that left her pale and tired and preoccupied.

At last, though, I managed to catch Françoise's eye and made a begging motion with my hands. She came to greet me, a stately woman dressed in sober clothes that nonetheless rustled richly.

'Mademoiselle de la Force, is there something you want from me?'

'My conscience is troubled,' I said. 'I need spiritual guidance.'

'Do you not have a confessor?'

'*Madame,* you forget. I'm . . . I'm . . .'

She looked surprised. '*Mademoiselle*, have you not yet recanted? The King will be most displeased. Have you not heard of the new laws against heretics?'

'I have. I am most troubled in my heart. I wish to be a good and loyal subject to the King, and to confess and mend my ways, but I feel a duty to my dead parents.'

Her face softened. 'Indeed, I understand. Come this afternoon and we shall talk and see if I cannot help you in your dilemma.'

That evening, I crept out to meet Charles in the palace gardens. The palace glowed with candlelight from nearly every window, and I could hear music and shrill laughter and the clink of glasses. Outside, though, all was quiet, the lawns and paths frosty-white under the moon, the canals and fountains glimmering, the shadows black and deep. It was chilly, and I drew my velvet cloak close about my shoulders.

Charles was waiting for me near the fountain, a tall, broad-shouldered figure wrapped in a dark cloak. In the moonlight, his face looked different — all hard planes and dark hollows — but he smiled at the sight of me and stretched out both hands, and I ran forward with a low cry of delight.

'All is arranged,' I whispered. 'If I abjure my faith, the Marquise will talk to the King and persuade him to sanction our marriage. She says he may even give me a pension.'

Charles caught me in his arms and whirled me around. 'That's wonderful! Oh, my father will not be able to deny us his permission when the King himself supports us!'

I wound my arms around his neck, running my hands under the stiff edge of his wig, nipping at his lower lip teasingly. 'I'll be Madame de Briou.'

'You will,' he asserted. He walked me backward towards a small grove under a circle of trees, his hands busy undoing my bodice. My own hands were unbuttoning his waistcoat. 'We'll be able to sleep all night together like an old married couple. No more sneaking around at the dead of night.'

I pretended to pout. 'Really? I rather like our clandestine assignations.'

'In that case,' he said, and he tipped me backward over his arm, lowering me to the ground.

I gasped and laughed, clutching at his strong arm, my skirts billowing about me.

'Why must you always wear so many clothes?' he said, untying my cloak and tugging my dress away from my shoulders. 'It's so hard to get inside them.'

'I'd have thought you'd have had enough practice by now,' I responded, helping him strip off his coat. He took off his wig and flung it aside, then lay beside me, kissing down my bare shoulder to my breast, one hand deftly unfastening his breeches, the other sliding up my thigh, seeking the soft naked skin above my garter.

'That'll be the best thing about being married. I can have you naked in my bed whenever I want you.'

I opened my lips to say something teasing in response, but he seized possession of my mouth. His hands did their best to unravel me from my layers of skirts and petticoats and stockings and stays, till I was as naked as he could get me. The ground was cold and damp underneath me, and I shivered and snuggled closer to him.

In one swift motion, Charles rolled me over and lifted me so that I sat astride him, my knees on either side of his hips. Eagerly, he guided himself inside me, thrusting up his hips so I cried out in surprise and pleasure. I had never made love in such a way before; I felt him penetrate deeper than I would have thought possible. I arched away and then slammed back down upon him, and arched again, feeling a sudden surge of power and control as I heard him whimper and strain to follow me. Clenching my knees, I bent to my task, our bodies moving together in an ever-escalating rhythm, as if I was riding a galloping horse. My head fell forward and I grasped at a tree trunk, bracing myself, feeling the familiar wild sweet explosion. 'Oh, God, Charles. I love you! I love you!'

He gasped his response into my neck as I collapsed upon him, his hands upon my bare buttocks, rocking me a little as if he could not bear to stop that exquisite motion. *'Ma chérie,'* he whispered tenderly. 'Soon to be my little wife.'

EASTER EGGS

Versailles, France — April 1686
I sat with my quill in my hand, the ink drying on the nib, and looked down at the blank white page before me.

A sort of paralysis had hold of me. I could not write the words, though I knew what I must say: 'My dearest sister, I write to let you know that I have decided to obey His Most Christian Majesty, the King, and my own conscience, and embrace the One True Faith . . .'

I could not bear to think of Marie's face as she read the words. I could not bear to imagine what she would think of me. I had only seen my sister a few times in the past twenty years, but she was still blood of my blood, bone of my bone, flesh of my flesh. Together, we had listened to stories at our mother's knee and learnt to read from the Bible. Together, we had seen my mother seized and dragged away, locked up in a convent against her will. Together, we had endured the hard years of our guardian's rule. We were bound together by something much more potent than time.

'I can't,' I said, laying down my quill. 'She will never forgive me.'

Then I thought of Charles, I thought of the horror of being locked up in prison or burnt at the stake, and I took up my quill again, its feathered plume trembling.

'My dearest sister,' I wrote tremulously, ink blotching the page with black tears. I wished fervently that I could go on and tell Marie all that was in my heart, my feeling that I had lost God and that God had forgotten me, my fear that my mother had been wrong and that we were not the elect of God but cursed by our own arrogance, my conviction that love was the only thing of worth in this graceless world of ours.

Yet I did not dare. All mail sent anywhere in the kingdom of France was opened and read by the King's spies. I would have to write a private letter to my sister as if making a public acclamation before the court, and I could only hope that Marie would understand the necessity.

It was at that moment I heard a faint scratch at the door. Nanette came in, her hands clenched before her, her face pursed with anxiety. '*Mademoiselle,* a messenger has come from Cazeneuve, bearing gifts from your sister, the Baronne, to celebrate Easter.'

I stared at her in utter perplexity. We *ré-formés* did not celebrate Easter. And Nanette never called me *'mademoiselle'* unless in company. I looked over her shoulder and saw Bertrand, the man who had been my gaoler in the Bastille, standing behind her, a basket in his hands. Two hard-faced palace guards stood behind him.

'Thank you, Nanette. A parcel from the country is always welcome.' I rose and went towards Bertrand, who fixed his dark eyes upon my face in some kind of unspoken warning. I smiled at him. 'How lovely to see you again, Bertrand. Country air seems to be agreeing with you. What has my sister sent me?'

'Eggs.'

'Eggs! Lovely. Let me see.' I lifted the napkin and saw a dozen gaily painted eggs nestled in straw.

'Those soldiers wanted to search the basket, but Bertrand was worried the eggs would be broken,' Nanette said in a neutral tone.

'Yes, that would be a shame. A gift from my sister is a precious thing!'

'We need to be sure no treasonous or heretical messages are contained within,' the soldier said. 'That man's a Gascon, and the dragoons have been having a great deal of trouble in Gascony.'

'Indeed? I am sorry to hear that. I don't think you'll find anything heretical in a basket of Easter eggs, though.' I smiled at the soldiers, though my pulse was thudding loudly in my ears.

'Need to check.'

'Well, let me take the eggs out first.' I put the basket on my bed and sat beside it so my body concealed as much of it as possible. The soldiers craned their necks suspiciously, and I smiled at them and began to carefully remove the painted eggs, one by one. Most had been hard-boiled — I could feel the weight of them in my hand as I lifted them out of the basket — but a few were light as air and I heard a faint rustle from within. I laid them down carefully and then rummaged through the straw. An envelope was hidden within. I tried to draw it out discreetly, but the guards saw it and strode forward at once to seize it, filling the tiny room with their bulk. 'It's a letter from my sister,' I protested as one ripped it open, but they ignored me.

'It says "Happy Easter",' the guard said blankly and threw the note back on the bed. They then upended the basket, scattering straw everywhere. There was nothing else to be found.

'Just you look at the mess you've made,' Nanette scolded. 'You like making work for poor old ladies, do you? Out! Out! Go on, be off with you.'

As the guards backed out, mumbling apologies, I read the brief message on the card, in my sister's familiar neat script, then loudly admired the painted eggs. 'I wonder if my niece helped make them,' I said to Nanette. 'She must be quite a big girl by now.'

The moment the door shut behind the guards, I leapt up and seized the four eggs that had been blown empty. Very carefully, I broke them open and found within tiny scrolls of paper, covered on both sides with miniature script. They had been poked through the holes at either end of the egg, where the yolk and whites had been blown out. As Nanette tidied up the straw, I unrolled the scrolls and found they made a letter, cut into quarters. My sister had written in Garonnais, our local dialect. Drawing near the window, I endeavoured to decipher the tiny handwriting:

Ma chérie, I write to you in haste, to try and explain news that you will soon no doubt hear. I wish I did not need to tell you this. Théobon and I have recanted. I weep as I write this, and I beg of you to forgive me and try to understand. There has been much burning and bloodshed here in the south. The dragoons have no mercy. A whole parish of *réformés* was butchered in Bordeaux, women and babies among them. An army descended on Nîmes and there enacted so cruel a dragonnade that the whole city recanted in little more than a day.

You can have no concept of the horror of it all. All kinds of cruelties and obscenities are taking place here, and we have no choice except to recant, or flee, and you know I will not abandon the land or the people who have been placed into my care. The Duc de Noailles himself warned my husband that dragoons would be billeted at Cazeneuve if we did not publicly abjure our faith immediately, so that is what we have done. May God have mercy on my soul. I beg you to forgive me, and to have a thought to your own safety, your loving sister, Marie.

I sat for a long while, holding my sister's letter in my hand, feeling faint and sick. Then I bent and poked the little scrolls into my lantern. They flared into flame and, in seconds, were gone. Smoke stung my eyes. I found I was weeping. *As smoke is driven away, so let God's enemies be driven away . . .*

Nanette came and sat beside me, passing me a handkerchief. I mopped my eyes and blew my nose. 'She has abjured,' I said.

'It is like the old days,' Nanette said in miserable bewilderment. 'I thought such things could never happen again.'

I looked at Bertrand. 'Thank you so much for coming. You took a grave risk, carrying such a message for me.'

He bobbed his head in acknowledgement.

'Are things really so bad in Gascony? What

has been happening there?'

The story he told us had both Nanette and I in tears. Sealed within the artificial world of the royal court, we had known nothing of what was happening in the French countryside. The Huguenots were being maltreated on all sides: fined, flogged, hanged, burnt and stabbed to death. In one village, Bertrand told us, a few hundred *réformés* had gathered in the winter to christen their newborn babies. Some had travelled a long way, since their own churches had been wrecked or burnt. They found the church barred to them by soldiers, who herded them all into a field and would not permit them to go home until they had all knelt and received absolution from the army chaplain. The *réformés* refused, even though it was snowing and bitterly cold. All night, they huddled together in the icy field, singing psalms to keep up their courage. In the morning, all the little newborn babies were stiff and cold, frozen to death on their mothers' breasts, and many others had died too, mostly the young and the elderly. The *réformés* were not permitted to bury their dead in consecrated ground, the soldiers flinging the corpses into a ditch by the side of the road.

'Why didn't they just submit?' I said, wiping away my tears. 'Those poor little babies.'

'Life on earth is short and brutal,' Bertrand said, 'but the faithful shall live forever in the glory of heaven.' His eyes were lit with the fervour of a true believer and I looked away, feeling shame, indignation and fear all at the same time.

'Why did they not flee, then?' I demanded. 'Surely it'd be better than freezing to death in a field?'

'Many tried,' Bertrand said. 'They hunted them down like rabbits and dragged them back. I've heard of ladies staining their faces with walnut juice and dressing as peddlers, or pretending to be servants, walking in the mud while their husbands rode, for it's the women who have suffered the most, you know, soldiers being what they are. Some pretended to be old women, hoping that the soldiers would leave them be, but still had their clothes torn off their backs and the soldiers having their sport with them before they were killed.'

'It's so terrible.' Nanette looked more knotted up in her face and body than I'd ever seen her look. 'What kind of world do we live in?'

'No one dares help any more,' Bertrand said. 'There was a man who was guiding people through the Languedoc to the sea and helping them find passage on ships. He was discovered and tortured cruelly before he was hanged. And the poor people he was helping were loaded with chains and forced to march through every village and town for miles around, with the soldiers beating them with whips till their clothes were in tatters and the blood running freely, so everyone could see, before being sent to the galleys. A bishop saw what was happening and tried to stop the soldiers, and so he was sent to the galleys as well.'

'I heard yesterday that the King had sent one of his own councillors to the galleys when he refused to abjure,' I said. 'One of his oldest friends!'

'We are laden with chains,' Nanette said in a voice of heavy resignation. 'We are driven into the wilderness once more.'

On Easter Sunday, I prepared myself for my public humiliation by candlelight, dressing myself in a plain dark dress with a simple lace collar.

'At least I'm not expected to wear sackcloth and ashes,' I said bitterly to Nanette. 'Or crawl to the cathedral on my knees.'

The ceremony of abjuration was not to take place at the private chapel at the palace, but at the new church built in the township. A majestic pile, it was nonetheless built low so it would not dominate the town. Only the palace was permitted to do that.

I was not the only one abjuring my faith that day. The sentencing of the King's own councillor, Louis de Marolles, to the galleys had caused much shock at court, and many

— both courtiers and servants — had decided it would be best to recant as soon and as publicly as possible.

Nanette was to go with me. We knew the King's soldiers-of-God would care nothing for her age and frailty, and, besides, although she did not understand why the King should make a law forbidding her to sing the psalms she loved so much and forcing her to worship in a way that made no sense to her, Nanette was at heart a practical woman and had no wish to die a martyr's death.

It was dark outside. With Nanette beside me, a woollen shawl draped over her thin shoulders against the sharp nip in the air, I carried my candle through the dark quiet corridors of the palace. Slowly, other *réformés* joined me. Some looked sulky and recalcitrant, others ashamed. Only a few walked with head held high, or with faces shining with true conviction. I myself was one of those who walked with head lowered, unable to bear the thought of meeting anyone's eyes. I felt as if my gown had been ripped from my shoulders, as if some hidden part of myself, usually concealed from prying eyes, was now on display to be mocked. All was quiet. Not even the birds had yet begun to sing, and all the church bells were mute. Yet deep inside my head I could hear the echo of long-ago singing.

Whither shall I go from thy Spirit?
And whither from thy time shall I flee?
If I ascend up into the heavens, there thou
    art;
If I lie down in the sepulchre, behold! thou
    art there.
Should I rise on the wings of the morning,
Should I make my bed in the depths of the
    sea,
Even there thy hand shall lead me,
And thy right hand shall hold me fast.

How often had I heard this psalm being sung? Nanette had sung it to me as I drifted into sleep, the cook had sung it as he kneaded the dough, the goose-girl had sung it as she brought the geese home at the end of the day, my mother had read it as a blessing at the beginning of a meal. How many times had I sung it myself, in the small white chapel at Cazeneuve, the voices of everyone I knew singing together, word and note bound together in plainsong, many voices singing as one?

Tears burnt my eyes. *Forgive me, Maman, forgive me, Papa, forgive me.*

The sombre-faced procession walked down the long driveway to the magnificent gilded gates, candles bobbing along slowly. To the east was a streak of red like a sabre cut. A few blackbirds began to warble. I could not remember the last time I was up early enough to hear blackbirds. We went through the gates and into the town. Smoke rose from a few chimneys, and lantern-light shone through the chinks in a few curtains, but otherwise the town was still and dark. I smelt bread baking. Behind me, someone's stomach grumbled noisily and we all smiled, the sound lightening the grave atmosphere.

A few more minutes and we were at the church. I steeled my nerve and went through the arched doorway into the nave. It was huge and shadowy and smelt of damp stone and incense. Our wavering candlelight caught glints of gold on all sides. Everything was richly decorated, with paintings and statues and embroidered banners and mosaics everywhere. Nothing could be more different to the Protestant church at Charenton, where I usually went to services, seven miles outside Paris. The King had never allowed a Protestant church to be built within the city walls, of course. Us poor *réformés* had always had to travel and be uncomfortable for our faith.

The dawn vigil was being held. Cold and bored, we suffered through it all and then were rocked and shaken by peal after peal of bells, the first time in days that the bells were permitted to ring. There was chanting and many signs of the cross and genuflections, and waving of smoking censers, and choirboys singing and priests intoning, all wearing heavy copes and stoles and surplices and whatnot, much embroidered with gilt thread and strange symbols. Candles glowed everywhere, and the air was thick with smoke and incense. The King came, massive and inscrutable, in clothes more gorgeous and gilded than even the priests'. Françoise was with him, regal in dark purple, plus the Dauphin and his ugly young wife, and a whole crowd of lords and ladies in festive silks. Then came Charles, dressed soberly in brown wool, his face stern and hard. He scanned the pews anxiously. When our eyes met, he smiled. It was like sunshine breaking through a thundercloud. His face was transformed; I was transformed; the whole sombre smoky church was transformed. I smiled back at him, all my heart in my eyes, and felt my head lift and my shoulders straighten. *It's all worth it, to be with him.*

When it came my turn to abjure, I did so with a steady voice and a lifted chin. 'With sincere heart and unfeigned faith, I detest and abjure every error, heresy and sect opposed to the Holy Roman Catholic Church. I reject and condemn all that she rejects and condemns . . .'

I received absolution from the priest, having confessed my sins. I will not say this was easy for me, but I did it. Then I had to take into my mouth the bread of the Eucharist. My body rebelled and I gagged. Somehow, I managed to choke it down. *It is only stale bread,* I told myself. Beside me, Nanette obediently swallowed hers, though her face was so twisted with distaste that her jaw looked dislocated. We sipped the wine a little more willingly — wine is wine, after all — and then it was over. I felt my knees weaken with relief. We were allowed to go back to our pew, and there was a great deal more singing and praying. At last, we were permitted to rise and make our way out.

Charles found us among the great throng of people. He took my hand. 'All right?'

I nodded. 'I'm glad it's over.'

He slipped one arm about my waist, under cover of the crowd, and gave me a little squeeze, then drew away.

As the congregation all filed out, the King went to the altar and stood, flanked on either side by huge candles set upon ornate golden candlesticks. The light cast a long shadow before him. He looked immense, tall as a giant, with his great stiff wig on his head, his long-tailed coat and his high-heeled shoes. A long queue of people waited to see him; they all looked like frightened children, their backs hunched as if expecting a blow, their skinny hands pressed together in a gesture of appeal. I gazed at them curiously as I passed. They were all marked in some way, with nasty sores and hideous swellings upon their faces and necks and groins. Most were poor, dressed in little more than rags, their limbs pitifully thin. One by one, they were pushed towards the King and made to kneel in his shadow. The King dipped his hand in a golden bowl of holy oil and anointed them swiftly on the brow, saying, *'Le roi te touche, Dieu te guérit.'* Then the supplicant was given some money and the next shuffled forward, the King repeating the gesture and the words.

'What is he doing?' I asked Charles.

'He's touching them, to cure them. They have the King's Evil. Scrofula, you know.'

I gazed at the King as long as I could, astonished to see him touching so many poor, sick, deformed people. I had always thought that the King believed the suffering peasants would simply disappear if he ignored them long enough. Out of sight, out of mind. Yet here he was, laying his hands upon them, breathing in their tainted breath, allowing their cringing infected eyes to meet his. It shook me somehow, making me feel tearful and off-balance. I clutched Charles's arm and let him lead me out of the church.

The queue of sufferers stretched all around the square and down the street. There were hundreds and hundreds of them, standing patiently in the rain, some holding sacks over their heads. I wrenched my eyes away and hurried with Charles and Nanette to where his carriage waited, hoping he would think the wetness on my face was rain.

UNDER SIEGE

Versailles, France — December 1686 to January 1687

On a chilly evening not long after Christmas, with mist wrapping the trunks of the trees in cotton wool and a faint star hanging low on the horizon, I went out of the palace to meet Charles in the courtyard. We planned to go to a musical soirée being held at one of the private residences in the town. Charles had a two-seater sedan chair waiting for me.

'Don't you look a picture?' he said, handing me into the chair. 'Though I'm going to have to run along behind the sedan. There's not room in there for me and you and your dress.'

'Our gowns are getting rather ridiculous. They're going to have to widen all the doorways soon, so we don't need to go through them sideways.'

'They'll have to raise the ceilings too. That thing on your head just keeps getting higher and higher.'

'I'll have you know it's the absolute *height* of fashion.'

'Oh, you are most amusing.' Charles managed to squeeze himself in beside me, though I had to loop my train over my elbow and fold my skirt out of the way.

'I'm so glad you think so. I do try.'

'Aren't I a lucky man, marrying a girl both witty and pretty?'

'Oh, compliments will get you everywhere.'

He tried to kiss me, but, what with my billowing sleeves and lace headdress and the jolting of the sedan chair, he only managed a peck somewhere around my ear. 'If I was the King, I'd outlaw those things,' he complained.

I laughed at him. 'The King has tried, but for once we ladies of the court will not obey. Soon, our *fontanges* will be three feet tall!'

'I'll have to send instructions to the chateau carpenters at Survilliers to modify the old place. I can't have my wife banging her head everywhere she goes.'

'I love hearing you say that. Say it again.'

He quirked one black eyebrow. 'Banging?'

I hit him with my fan. 'No! I mean calling me your wife.'

'Oh, that. You like that, do you?' He squeezed closer, sliding one arm about my waist and whispering in my ear. 'My wife. My wife.'

I pretended to swoon and moan, and he gave my earlobe a little nibble and then kissed

661

the pulse below. 'I'm sorry about my father,' he said. 'Can you believe he still refuses to give us permission?'

'It's been a year,' I said. 'How can he continue to deny us when the King himself has given us permission?'

'He's a stubborn old goat.'

'Maybe you should have gone home for Christmas, like he wanted you to.'

'I told him I will come home when I can bring my chosen wife, and I meant it.'

'So who's the stubborn old goat?' I said teasingly.

'He needs to learn that I am a man now and will not be scolded like a child.' Charles's strong jaw was thrust forward in a way I knew well. I caressed it with one gloved hand.

'Perhaps if you'd gone home for Christmas, you could have talked with him, made him understand.'

'There's no talking with my father. He's utterly determined to get his own way in everything.'

I sighed. 'So what are we to do?'

'We just need to wait till I'm twenty-five.'

'When will that be, my cabbage?' I asked teasingly, although I knew very well just how old he was. The twelve years between us was a problem I gnawed at constantly, like a hungry dog with a stolen bone.

'Not till April,' he answered gloomily.

'Oh, well, it's not so long. I was afraid you'd

say in five years' time!'

'I'm not that young!'

'But such a sweet little baby face,' I crooned.

He pushed me back into the corner of the sedan chair, squeezing my breasts with his big hands. 'The earliest chance I get, I'm showing you just how much of a man I am!'

'I can hardly wait,' I said and kissed him on the corner of the mouth. Slowly, I let my lips wander towards his ear. He sighed and stroked the cloth of my bodice with his thumb. I felt my nipple harden, even through all the layers of whalebone and cloth. He turned his mouth to mine, and I smiled and wound my arms about his neck. Our kiss deepened.

'I'm glad you didn't go away for Christmas,' I whispered. 'Thank you.'

The sedan chair jerked to a halt. Charles took a moment to kiss me again, before opening the door and climbing out. He then turned to hand me out. I eased out one high-heeled slipper, holding my skirts down firmly with both hands, before venturing out the other foot and ducking my head down to my knee as I wiggled forward. Sedan chairs were very difficult to get in and out of decorously while wearing a ruffled mantua and a high lace *fontanges.*

'Don't mind me. I'm happy to get a glimpse of your ankle any day,' Charles said.

'I'm sure the sedan-carriers would be pleased too,' I retorted.

The red winter sun had slipped down behind the tall houses of Versailles, and the only light shone from a lantern hung above the front door of the chateau. Our breath puffed white in the cold air. Charles offered me his arm and we went towards the steps, chatting gaily together.

Suddenly, two men ran out from behind the wall. Cloaked and hooded, they seized Charles by the arms, dragging him away from me. I screamed and caught the arm of one of the attackers, but he pushed me away roughly.

Charles struggled to get free, but they had a sack over his head and were wrestling him towards a large travelling coach half-hidden by the wall. I flew at the men, hitting them over their heads with my muff, kicking at their shins with my sharp-pointed slippers.

Again, I was shoved away, so hard I stumbled and almost fell. *'Putain!'* one of the men jeered at me.

I recovered my balance and ran again to try to stop them. This time, the hooded man slapped me. I fell, sprawling. The men heaved Charles into the coach. I heard his muffled cry and the slam of the coach door. Then a whip cracked, and six horses heaved the coach forward, breaking into a gallop. The wheels clattered over the cobblestones. The coach teetered sideways as it veered around the corner, crashed back down on all four wheels and accelerated away. I ran after it but saw only its dark square shape racing along the road out of the town.

I ran back towards the house, calling for help. I found that people were already spilling out, alerted by my screams and the yells of the sedan-carriers, who had seen the entire scene.

'Why did you not help?' I cried.

The sedan-carrier held up his hands. 'They looked like they meant business, *mademoiselle*. Not much use me getting my head kicked in, was there?'

I was helped inside the townhouse, almost incoherent with shock and fear. Madame Moreau, the lady of the house, took me to a small parlour and brought me a cool damp cloth for my cheek, and some hartshorn for my nerves.

'But who could do such a thing? Why? Where have they taken him?'

'I imagine they were men employed by Monsieur de Briou, *mademoiselle,*' Madame Moreau said. 'I hear he is most disapproving of this match between you and his son, and swears it will not go ahead.'

I looked up at her in astonishment. 'Surely he would not kidnap his own son!'

'By all accounts, Claude de Briou is a severe and autocratic man. He's the president of the sovereign courts, you know, and rules them with an iron fist.'

'But to seize Charles like that! To be so . . . so violent . . . so rough.' Tears rose in my eyes again, and I cradled the cool cloth against my burning cheek.

'I believe Monsieur de Briou has commanded his son to break off the engagement and leave Versailles several times, and Charles has always refused.' Madame Moreau poured me a glass of ruby-red wine. 'It is his right,' she said. 'Charles is still legally under his dominion.'

'He turns twenty-five in April!'

'Well, then, you must just hope that Charles remains steadfast in his regard for you until then.' She rose to her feet again. 'I'm sorry, my dear, I must attend to my guests. Shall I order another sedan chair for you? You'll wish to return to your quarters.'

I nodded, my lips pressed together. Anger seethed in me. How dare Charles's father do such a thing! How dare he kidnap and imprison his own son!

I went back to the palace and sought out anyone who I thought might be able to help me, but no one could — or would — offer any assistance. Claude de Briou, Baron de Survilliers, was a rich and powerful man, and the law, so everyone kept telling me, was on his side. The crime was committed not by the father but by the son — in persisting in an engagement of which his father disapproved.

'He'll escape,' I said. 'He'll soon be back, just you see.'

New Year's Eve came and went, and I began to lose heart. I could not help remembering the awful outcome of the affair with the Marquis de Nesle and feared that Charles was being so threatened and coerced that he too would seek to drown himself in his despair. Or, even worse, be persuaded to give me up. I could not sleep or eat, no matter how Nanette coaxed me. She brought me all my favourite childhood fare: duck confit, cassoulet, *poule-au-pot,* apple and Armagnac croustade, Christmas pudding made from crushed chestnuts and cream and a dozen eggs. I tasted no more than a few mouthfuls of any of it.

'You're too skinny, Bon-bon,' she scolded me. 'Men like some meat on their bones.'

'You speak from experience?' I answered, rather cruelly, because Nanette was both as skinny as a church mouse and had, as far as I knew, never had a lover.

'You'll fade away to nothing.'

'I'm just not hungry.'

Nanette folded her lips together and took the feast away, probably giving it to some poor family in the town, if I knew my Nanette. I wrapped my softest shawl around me and went back to staring into the intricate red heart of the fire, longing for Charles to return.

In mid-January, Françoise had some news for me. 'He is being kept at the family's chateau in Survilliers until he swears to throw you over,' she told me, looking grave. 'By all accounts, he is being recalcitrant, and so his father has locked him up in his bedroom. He's not even allowed out into the garden in case he should seek to escape.'

'That's barbaric!' I cried.

'Monsieur de Briou has sworn he will not allow his son out until he has made a sacred oath to marry as he is bid.'

I paced back and forth, my stiff skirts swaying. 'But it's so unfair. We love one another!'

'When has love ever had anything to do with marriage?' Françoise replied wearily. 'There is nothing you can do but submit, Charlotte-Rose. Write to Charles and tell him you release him from the engagement.'

'I won't! His father has no right.'

'He has every right,' Françoise replied. 'You think you two are the first lovers in the world to be forced to give each other up? It's a worn-out tale, I'm afraid. Duty to one's family and to the custom of society must come first.'

I refused to listen. I went to my room and rang imperiously for Nanette. She came in a hurry, looking anxious.

'Pack for me *tout de suite*!' I commanded.

'I am going to Survilliers.'

'Oh, Bon-bon! Should you? It is so far, my cabbage. How will you get there?'

'I'll hire a carriage,' I said. 'You must come with me, Nanette. I cannot travel alone.'

'But how will you pay for it? You've spent nearly all your wages this quarter already.' She twisted her bony hands together.

'I'll pawn my pearls,' I cried. 'Charles will buy them back for me once he's free again.'

'Oh, Bon-bon, is this wise? There could be bandits. The coach could break down and we'd be stranded. And what do you possibly think you can do once you get there?'

'I'll think of that on the way!'

It was an abominable journey to Survilliers.

Between Versailles and Paris, the road was reasonably well cared for, but once past the capital we might as well have been driving over the fields. We had to change horses twice, and both Nanette and I felt that every bone in our bodies had been rattled loose from our joints. When we finally arrived in the small village of Survilliers, it was all we could do to stagger into the inn and beg for some beds.

The next morning, I was woken by the hideous clamour of a farmyard rooster. I groaned, pulled my lumpy feather pillow over my head and tried to dive back down into sleep. The incessant clucking, quacking, mooing and squealing made sleep an impossibility, though, so at last I rose and called Nanette, who soon came back with a simple breakfast of fresh hot croissants and the worst coffee I had ever tasted. When I had eaten, Nanette helped me dress in my most becoming winter gown — a rich dark crimson, the colour of old wine, and trimmed with luxurious black fur — and together we sallied forth to spy out the land.

The chateau at Survilliers was misnamed. A more accurate word would have been 'fortress'. It was a grim, old, grey structure with a moat, a barbican, crenellated battlements, arrow slits, murder holes and every other possible defence that a suspicious-minded medieval architect could conceive. It loomed over the village, being built on the only hill for miles, with a dark and dank-looking forest stretching out on either side.

I girded my loins, so to speak, and walked quickly up the road to the castle, Nanette trotting behind, looking more worried than ever. Though I stared up at the windows, I could see no sign of anyone within. I imagined Charles confined to a stone cell, as cold and malodorous as my cell at the Bastille had been. Fresh anger surged in me.

I crossed the drawbridge over the moat, which was not green and stinking like I had imagined but really rather pretty, with water lilies floating in it. At the far end of the drawbridge was an enormous wooden door, studded with thick iron bolts and reinforced with iron struts in the shapes of wheels and arrows. Cut into this massive door was a smaller door, for mere mortals to pass through. I used the heavy iron knocker to bang on the door, my stomach feeling quite unnerved by all this medieval grandeur.

Some time later, the door was opened — not by a thug in chain mail with an iron mace in one hand, but by an urbane-looking man who stood with both eyebrows raised, asking in some surprise, 'Can I help you?' His small beard was neatly clipped into a point, which was rather out of date, but otherwise he was dressed completely normally in a heavy wig, a silk lavender coat, tight black satin breeches over clocked stockings, and a beribboned cravat.

'May I see Monsieur de Briou, please?' I asked sweetly.

'I'm sorry, the Baron is currently not in residence,' he replied.

'I beg your pardon, I meant the younger Monsieur de Briou. I believe he is here?'

'Yes, *mademoiselle,* he is here but not, I'm afraid, accepting visitors. You will excuse me . . .' He began to shut the door.

I lunged forward, catching hold of his silken sleeve. 'I am sure he will see me.'

He gave a cold austere smile and brushed my hand away. 'Monsieur de Briou is not free to choose who he will hobnob with, *mademoiselle.*' He spoke rather nastily, and I pressed my lips together. Nanette gave a little hiss of disapproval.

'Indeed? How strange. Why don't you ask him if he will receive me? I'm sure he'd be delighted.'

'My apologies, *mademoiselle.* If you will permit?' He continued to close the door.

'Perhaps I could write a note?' I called, but he shut the door in my face.

'What a rude man!' Nanette said. 'How dare he speak to you in that way? Hobnob indeed!' Her bony face was so screwed up with disapproval she looked as if she was chewing walnuts.

'This is not going to be easy,' I said, drawing my mantua around me against the winter chill and walking away from the castle with as much dignity as I could.

'Will we go back to Versailles now?' Nanette asked. A simple Gascon soul, she had always hated the royal palace, but now her voice was filled with yearning.

'Give up so easily? Not I!'

Nanette sighed.

I spent the day wandering about the countryside, viewing the castle from all different angles. It seemed impregnable. I had been angry with Charles for not escaping and galloping post-haste back to me days ago, but now I realised that he truly was imprisoned, and all my will was bent towards rescuing him.

When Nanette and I got back to the inn, my satin shoes and the hem of my gown were besmirched with mud, and we were hungry, weary and chilled to the bone. I walked through the inn door, only to pause with surprise. This morning, the public bar had been empty of all but a somnolent cat. Now, it was crammed with people, who all turned and stared at me with curious eyes.

'News travels fast,' I said in an undertone to Nanette, crossing the bar with my head held high.

'It always does in the country,' she replied.

'I will need a private parlour,' I said to the innkeeper, as haughtily as I knew how. Seeing his two daughters peeping around the edge of the door to goggle at me, I added, 'And a parlour-maid. *Tout de suite!*'

Gratifyingly quickly, the covers were whisked off the furniture in the front parlour and a fire lit in the grate by the eldest daughter, a plump girl with a face like a currant bun, remarkable for its profusion of dark moles. She looked rather like a fine court lady unable to choose where to put her patches, except that she wore a coarse brown gown with a long apron tied over the top and clumsy wooden sabots. A linen kerchief was tied up over her hair, the knot in the front a rather pitiable attempt to copy the fashion *à la fontanges.*

'Thank you,' I said, when she sat back on her heels, dusting off her ash-smeared hands. 'What is your name?'

'Paulette, *mademoiselle,*' she answered shyly.

'Paulette, I am Charlotte-Rose de Caumont de la Force. I'm sure you would have heard of my grandfather, the Duc de la Force, who was the Marshal of France. I need your help.'

'My help?' Paulette was round-eyed and round-mouthed. 'You want my help?'

'Indeed, yes. You see, the cruel Baron has separated me from my one true love and holds him captive in the castle. I must help him escape!'

'Oh, *mademoiselle,* it sounds just like a story!' Paulette cried, clasping her red chapped hands together. 'I'll do anything I can!'

But, willing as Paulette was, she could do nothing.

It was no use bribing the Baron's servants. I did not have enough money to tempt them, and, besides, Paulette said they were all too terrified of the Baron to ever risk his anger. 'He's a right Tartar,' she said.

It was no use trying to blackmail anyone. Paulette told me that the castle's servants never came to the village and certainly never seduced a milkmaid, or cheated at cards, or stole a hen, or did anything at all they would wish to keep concealed from their martinet master.

It was no use smuggling myself into the castle disguised as a laundry-maid. The castle maids did all the laundry themselves and had apparently been employed at the castle since before the Flood. Any stranger at all would be looked at with suspicion, and strangers in Survilliers were as rare as a two-headed calf.

It was no use disguising myself as a peddler. The Baron's servants would just set the dogs on me, Paulette said.

Nor was it any use trying to scale the walls, or dig under the foundations, or creep through a side gate left conveniently unlocked. The Château de Survilliers had withstood many an attack from generals far more versed in warfare than me, and, as Paulette said, 'Why would they leave the side door unlocked? The Baron would have their hide!'

'So, is there a secret passage of some sort?' I asked.

Paulette looked bewildered. 'Secret passages? No. At least, I don't think so.'

'There must be! It looks just the place to have a secret passage.'

'It wouldn't be so secret if the innkeeper's daughter knew about it,' Nanette said sourly, knitting by the fire.

'There must be some way in!'

But there wasn't.

675

COILS

'So, shall we go back to Versailles now?' my long-suffering Nanette asked, three days later, as I at last admitted defeat and called for a carriage.

'No! I could not stand it. All those malicious gossips, whispering behind their fans, and all those detestable devotees with their upturned eyes and clasped hands. Faugh! We'll go to Paris.'

'Paris in February,' Nanette moaned. 'Save me!'

'It can't be worse than Survilliers in February. At least the coffee will be drinkable.'

'And where do you intend to stay?' Nanette said, as if fully expecting me to return to the Bastille and beg them for a room.

I bit my lip. I could not return to the Louvre, having lost my quarters there when I was dismissed as lady-in-waiting to the Queen. I could not stay at the Palais-Royal, having never forgiven Liselotte for her

676

scandal-mongering after my affair with the Marquis de Nesle. I could possibly stay with Madeleine de Scudéry, except that her house was already overflowing with impoverished poets and ambitious young playwrights. Besides, Madeleine de Scudéry was rather fond of working real-life dramas into her novels and I had no desire to fan the flames of scandal. All I wanted was to leave my disreputable past behind me and marry the man I loved.

'I'll go to Henriette-Julie's,' I declared.

Nanette shut her eyes, leant her head back and moaned.

'It's a very good plan,' I said, reviving some of my spirits. 'Henriette-Julie will have some good ideas.'

Henriette-Julie was the daughter of my mother's cousin, the Baron de Castelnau, but had grown up in Brittany, so we had never met as children. Like me, she had been sent to court at the age of sixteen in the hope of making an advantageous marriage. Unlike me, she had succeeded, marrying the Comte de Murat a year later. It was after her marriage that I had made her acquaintance, and we had found we had a great deal in common, in particular a love of books and the theatre. Although only seventeen, Henriette-Julie had already caused a great stir by making her first court appearance dressed in the traditional peasant costume of her homeland, a less-than-subtle rebuke to the King, who seemed to think that any place outside of Versailles existed for the sole purpose of paying him taxes. By all accounts, her elderly husband was impotent and she had already taken a few lovers, but that could merely have been gossip. As I knew full well, gossip had a way of taking a glance and turning it into a caress.

'So you have not given up this mad idea of rescuing Monsieur de Briou?' Nanette asked.

'Of course not! I just need to think of a plan.'

But what could I do?

I needed some kind of disguise.

A disguise that no one, no matter how suspicious, could possibly guess hid me, Charlotte-Rose de Caumont de la Force.

A disguise that would give me access to Charles.

A disguise that would somehow allow me to smuggle Charles away.

All the way to Paris, I thought and thought and thought, until my brain felt like it was about to burst. Hundreds of ideas came to me; all of them were too deeply flawed to occasion me more than a few minutes' pause.

It was sleeting in Paris. The sky was the colour of a dead toenail, the snow on the street churned into muddy grey slush. The carriage jolted forward over the filthy paving stones, the smell coming through the windows so strong that both Nanette and I pressed scented handkerchiefs to our noses.

A man in a long muffler was roasting chestnuts on an open fire and selling them in a twist of paper. My mouth watered at the smell, and I called to the coachman to buy me two twists. He passed them in the window, and Nanette and I devoured the sweet white kernels, the hot shells in their paper warming our frozen hands.

Ahead, there was some kind of commotion. Putting my head out the window, I could see a corpse being dragged along the street by a mule. It was the body of an old man, dressed only in a nightgown, a rope tied around one skinny bare ankle. An old woman, dressed in the plain modest style of the Huguenots, wept in the arms of a young woman, who stared blankly before her, ignoring the hoots and jeers of the mocking crowd that had gathered. A boy, no more than twelve, struggled furiously in the arms of two laughing dragoons, sobbing and shouting, *'Grand-père! Grand-père!'*

'Réformés,' Nanette said, looking out beside me.

'What has happened? Why are they doing such a thing?' My voice shook.

'He'd have refused the last sacrament,' Nanette said, her face twisted in pity. 'Poor old man. His grandson will be sent to the galleys, his wife and daughter to prison.'

'All because he refused Extreme Unction! That's . . . that's barbaric.'

'It is hard, sometimes, to conceal one's true beliefs at the time of death.' Nanette sat wearily back in her seat. 'That is why the King demands that everyone must have a priest called to the deathbed to perform the last rites. Anyone who doesn't is called a heretic and their bodies dragged about the streets. The King pockets any legacy that's left, of course.'

'It's wrong! That poor family!'

'Perhaps he felt salvation worth the cost,' Nanette said. Her conscience was still badly troubled by our abjuration. No matter how many times I reassured her that God would understand, she felt that we had done wrong and wished that we had at least tried to flee. But I would not go, and she would not leave me.

Our carriage jolted forward, leaving the pitiable scene behind us. Our progress was slow, for the spectacle had drawn a crowd. Pie-men pushed their way through, shouting, 'Pies! Hot pies!' A girl carried a tray piled high with ribbons and fans and silver pins; another was calling, 'Hot gingerbread! Hot gingerbread! Try my hot gingerbread!' Beggars held out imploring hands. One was a friar in a coarse brown robe and sandals; another a ragged soldier who had lost one leg in the wars.

The coach edged forward, the driver flicking his whip at the crowd to clear the way. I saw a thin shabby boy cut the ties of a purse belonging to a fat merchant and make off into the crowd. The merchant pursued him, shouting furiously. A footman in a tall white wig minced through the rabble, carrying a letter on a salver. A tavern was doing a roaring trade, a young blowsy woman in a low-cut dress carrying round trays filled with foaming mugs of ale. Nearby, a dancing bear shuffled its paws to the lively tune of a pipe and tabor, played by a shaggy-haired boy in a tattered coat several sizes too small for him. A barefoot little girl in a ragged brown dress did cartwheels and handstands nearby, calling out shrilly, 'It's warm inside! Come in for some hot mulled cider! Hot soup and a nice nip of brandy. Come along inside and get yourselves warm.'

Her feet must be so cold, I thought. I called to her, throwing a coin out the window. With a gap-toothed smile, she caught it and then, with a dexterous twist of her fingers, it disappeared inside her clothing somewhere and she did a one-handed backflip in joy.

'We'll have every beggar in Paris descending on us now,' Nanette said. The little girl had been so quick, though, no one else had noticed, and we swayed our way forward and turned the corner, leaving the crowd behind us.

We passed through the towers of the

Bastille, and I hunched my shoulders in an instinctive attempt to hide myself, a shiver passing over me at the memory of my time within its dreadful walls. On the far side, the Rue Saint-Antoine was wider and cleaner, the carriage trundling along smoothly. As dusk fell, lamplighters pulled down the great lanterns to light the candles within. Our carriage turned down the Rue des Tournelles, medieval houses leaning close overhead, and then we turned again and found ourselves at the Place des Vosges, where my cousin's husband had a house. It had once been the height of fashion to live here, looking across the square with its clipped linden trees and the statue of Louis XIII, but since the King had moved to Versailles the houses were now occupied mainly by elderly noblewomen and rich bourgeoisie. It was still a pretty place, though, with rows of tall houses with steep blue-slate roofs facing onto a wide square.

Our carriage-driver found my cousin's house, looking rather dark and shut-up in contrast to its neighbours, and carried my bags through the vaulted arcade to bang on the front door. Nanette and I stood waiting, shivering in the cold night air, for what seemed a very long time. At last, the door swung soundlessly open and a tall man stood before us. He wore a long dark satin vest, a white wig and spotless white gloves.

'I've come to stay with my cousin,' I said,

too cold for any polite preamble. 'You may take our bags, thank you.'

Henriette-Julie was lying on a chaise longue in her gloomy old-fashioned drawing room, flicking through a magazine of fashion plates. She shrieked at the sight of me and jumped to her feet, both hands held out. 'Charlotte-Rose! What a delicious surprise. I was about ready to die of ennui. Can you believe my boring old husband insists we have Christmas here in Paris? Who stays in Paris in the winter? I think he hates me. He's punishing me because I'm all the rage. But can I help it if people find me amusing?'

She was a slim pretty girl with a riot of chestnut curls, green-flecked hazel eyes shaded by long curling eyelashes, and a pouty-lipped mouth that was almost as large as mine. While she babbled on, she drew me down to sit, rang the bell for some refreshments and then exhorted me to tell her what I was doing in Paris.

'Charles's father has abducted him, to stop him marrying me,' I said, taking off my crimson-feathered hat and tossing it on a table. 'He has Charles locked up in his castle and won't set him free unless he casts me aside.'

'No!'

'Yes! I know it's unbelievable. I must rescue him. I've been to Survilliers, but they wouldn't even let me in to see him.'

'How medieval,' Henriette-Julie said.

'Exactly. I knew you'd understand. I was hoping I could stay with you a few days, until I have some kind of plan. Versailles is simply unbearable.'

'Of course you may. And the Comte can say nothing at all about it. How can I turn away my own cousin? And I simply cannot allow you to languish from boredom. The Comte forbids me to go out at night during the winter. He says it is too hard on the horses. But now you are here, I have an excuse.' She clapped her hands in joy. 'We must go to one of the salons, and then perhaps to the opera. No doubt, you'll have seen it already. It's such a bore, that rule of the King's. Why must we always wait for a new ballet or opera to be shown at court during Carnevale? It means we don't get the new shows in Paris until after Easter. No wonder no one stays in Paris at this time of year!'

'So is it *Armide*?'

'Yes, have you seen it?'

I nodded and made a small moue of distaste with my mouth. Although it had caused a sensation at court a year earlier, I had never liked it. The opera told the story of a sorceress who ensnares a Christian soldier with her magical spells, but when she raises her dagger to kill him, she finds herself falling in love with him and so casts a spell so he will love her in return. He is rescued from her coils by his friends, and she is left alone, in despair. It cut a little too close to the bone for me, so I had little desire to see it again.

'Oh, well, we'll see something else,' Henriette-Julie said. 'Though Paris in winter is dreadfully thin in company. At least Carnevale begins soon. If you stay till then, we can mask ourselves and go out and join the revelries. The Comte never needs to know. He says it's only for the peasantry and all sorts of unsuitable things go on. He is such a bore. That is exactly why Carnevale is so much fun. And if I'm masked and in disguise, no one needs to know I'm a comtesse.'

Her words gave me the smallest inkling of an idea. Carnevale was indeed only a few weeks away. Traditionally taking place in the days before Lent, it was a time of feasting and merry-making, food fights and masks, tomfoolery and mock-battles. At the Château de Cazeneuve, such celebrations were frowned upon as pagan rituals disguised as papist nonsense. However, Carnevale had been celebrated in Paris for hundreds of years. A raucous parade, called the Promenade du Bœuf Gras, wound its way through the streets and alleyways. A young boy rode a well-fattened ox, wearing a flimsy gilt crown and carrying a wooden sword and sceptre painted with jewels. Around him marched the city's butchers, all dressed as women with

paint on their faces, beating drums and playing fifes and pipes and violins. People danced
in the streets, made love in dark doorways
and fought drunkenly throughout the night. I
wondered idly if Survilliers celebrated
Carnevale . . . they were all Catholics
there . . .

'There's the walk of masks,' Henriette-Julie
continued jubilantly. 'Thousands of people
come, all wearing the most extraordinary
disguises and masks. And then there's the
masquerade party at the Opera. We simply
must go to that. Oh, say you will stay,
Charlotte-Rose. You might just make winter
in Paris bearable!'

The door opened and a tall stoop-
shouldered man limped into the drawing
room, leaning heavily on a walking stick. He
was dressed in sombre black, the only colour
the heavily jewelled crucifix that hung on his
breast. His wig was white and heavily curled.
The face beneath the wig was cavernous,
lined and malicious. He seemed the kind of
man who looked forward to Lent because he
gained so much enjoyment from seeing other
people suffer.

'I am sorry to hear you speak so,' he said to
Henriette-Julie, who shrank back in her chair.
'It is unbecoming to the Comtesse de Murat.
Please guard your tongue.'

'Yes, sir,' she answered meekly.

He regarded me with cold eyes. 'And who,

may I ask, are you?'

'I am Charlotte-Rose de Caumont de la Force,' I answered haughtily, rising and giving him a graceful curtsey, exact in its depths for his rank.

'I have heard of you,' he said unpleasantly.

I raised an eyebrow. 'Indeed? I am afraid, *monsieur,* that I have not heard of *you.* Perhaps you do not frequent court very often.'

His thin brows drew together. He stared at me icily, and I met his gaze, tilting my head in polite enquiry. He answered reluctantly, 'My health does not permit.'

'That is a shame. The King does not care for those who shun court.' He stared at me and I smiled. 'And those the King does not care for notice a gradual eclipse in their fortunes. Indeed, the King is like the sun. Those who do not bask in his approval live in eternal winter, while fortune and influence are won by those who exist in his sphere. Though perhaps you have no need of influence?' I looked dismissively around the room, which was richly, if sombrely, furnished.

His frown deepened, though his gaze was abstract, no longer focused on me.

'Perhaps it is a good thing I have come to visit my dear cousin,' I suggested. 'I'll be able to give her some hints on how to get on at court . . . if you should decide to remind the King of your existence.'

He nodded, cast one calculating look at his young and pretty wife, and limped out of the drawing room. Henriette-Julie stared at me, for once completely lost for words. Then she leapt up, clapped her hands and danced about the room. 'Oh, I am so glad you've come! No one ever speaks to the Comte in such a way. Do you think . . . perhaps he will relent and let me go to court after all? I will tilt my head, just so, and remind him that the King does not care for those who absent themselves. Oh, it's priceless. His face! All he cares for is money, and the thought that his fortune may suffer . . . Charlotte-Rose, I love you.'

The next week was a whirl of parties and soirées and visits to the ballet and morning visits to the few nobles unfashionably lingering in the capital.

I borrowed Henriette-Julie's gowns, my clever Nanette easily lengthening them with an extra flounce or fall of lace. Still I found it hard to sleep, haunted by strange dreams in which the Marquis de Nesle had Charles's face, dreams in which I ran through empty medieval castles, dreams in which I smelt the whiff of rotting toads' feet.

All this time, I pondered my idea. What if I went to Survilliers at Carnevale time, dressed in some fantastic disguise?

One evening, Henriette-Julie and I visited

the salon of Anne-Marie-Louise, the Duchesse de Montpensier, where a throng of
elegant world-weary Parisians drank champagne, nibbled on larks' tongues, and listened
to rondeaux and sonnets and stories, each
one spoken loudly to be heard over the roar
of conversation.

I could not help remembering my first
meeting here with Charles, two years ago,
and how scandalously he had seduced me in
a room down the hall. The memory brought
an ache to my heart. I felt fragile, as if on a
knife blade between hilarity and tears, and
wished I had not come. Henriette-Julie —
who had never been before — was exhila-
rated.

'Is it true she has many lovers?' she asked
behind her fan, gazing in rapture at Madeleine de Scudéry. 'And women as well as
men? I've read her books. She says one must
have a heroic soul.'

'Indeed,' I said, as if I had never thrilled to
this same sentiment.

'Charlotte-Rose!' Madeleine came and
grasped my hands, looking searchingly into
my eyes. 'We have not seen you for so long. I
hear you are living a grand adventure?'

I shrugged. 'I think I have found that you
are right, Madeleine. Some days, I despair
that I am a woman.'

Her brows drew together. She slid one hand
about my shoulders, drawing me close so she

could kiss my cheek. 'No, no, my sweet. Never despair! This is not like my Dunamis.'

'I am sick of love,' I said.

She laughed at me, tapping my breast with her fan. 'Love makes mute those who usually speak most fluently! Come, Charlotte-Rose, will you not tell us a story?'

I sighed. 'Not tonight.'

'What of your little friend? Does she tell stories too?' Madeleine turned to smile at Henriette-Julie. I nodded at her encouragingly. I knew that my cousin, having being brought up in Brittany, had a vast storehouse of tales about fairies and ghosts and giants. During the past week, we had amused ourselves by telling each other stories from our childhood, and I had even shown her my precious bundle of stories, which I always carried with me in the court's peregrinations from chateau to chateau in the hope I'd find some time to myself to write. Rather shyly, Henriette-Julie had shown me some of her own stories, and I had encouraged her to memorise a few to tell at the salons.

Henriette-Julie began, with great gusto, to tell a story about a beautiful princess who was wooed by the king of the ogres. Despite her revulsion, her father the king agreed to the marriage, as he feared his kingdom would be overrun. The princess's handmaiden, Corianda, travelled with her to the ogres' land, where the ogre king revealed himself in his true form. The princess, overcome by horror, fainted, and the furious king of the ogres stamped off to hunt bears. Corianda suggested the princess hide herself in the skin of a bear, and sewed her into one, but, to their dismay, the princess was turned into a she-bear. She ran away into the forest, wailing with grief, and there was found by a handsome young prince, who could not bring himself to kill a bear with tear-tracks on its face. In time, the prince learnt her secret, for the she-bear turned back into a princess at night. In the end, love prevailed, despite the murder of their two sons by the ogre king and the condemning of the princess to death by burning.

I was impressed. It was a vivid tale, filled with reversals and unexpected twists, and Henriette-Julie told it with all the drama and simplicity of a true storyteller.

Afterwards, the Duchesse came and kissed me goodnight. 'You may bring your little cousin again,' she said. I knew Henriette-Julie was launched into Parisian salon society.

She chattered ebulliently all the way home, but I was quiet and distracted. 'Is all well?' she asked at one point.

'Of course,' I answered, but as soon as we were home I claimed I was weary and begged leave to seek my bed. Henriette-Julie was disappointed; we had spent many a night drinking wine and talking long past midnight, and she wanted to gloat over her triumph. I insisted, however, and climbed the stairs to my stately guest room, where Nanette sat waiting to disrobe me, a hot brick wrapped in flannel already warming my bed. I let her remove my gown, untie my stays, wash my face and brush out my hair, but I barely spoke, my brain seething with ideas.

In the morning, I rose, put on my crimson gown trimmed with black fur and went to find my former lover, the actor Michel Baron.

SKINNING THE BEAR

Paris, France — February 1687 to July 1689
'Why should I?' he asked.

'You owe me,' I said.

'But we always make a lot of money at Carnevale time.'

'I'm sure the people of Survilliers will be grateful.'

He groaned. 'They'll probably want to pay us in pigs and chickens.'

'At least you'll eat well.'

'What if they won't let us in?'

'Of course they will. A theatrical troupe from Paris, led by the famous Michel Baron, author of the hit play *The Man of Good Fortune*?'

'So you saw it? What did you think?'

'It seemed popular enough.'

'But did you see it?'

'I did not realise my good opinion meant so much to you.'

He groaned again and clutched at his wig. 'For God's sake, Charlotte-Rose, did you see my play? What did you think?'

I took pity on him. 'It was extraordinary. I cried for days.'

'Really?'

'Absolutely.'

He sighed in gratification.

'Will you do what I've asked?'

'But what if we're discovered? My reputation . . .'

'Your reputation as a libertine and an adventurer, you mean?'

'Don't think harshly of me, Charlotte-Rose.'

'I'm meant to think of you kindly? The man who seduced me, ruined my reputation and made mock of me to all of society?'

'Very well, I'll do it. We'll need to be paid, though.'

'Think of this as penance for your sins. I'm sure God will take note.'

'Charlotte-Rose, you've grown hard and cruel in your old age.'

'You've grown soft and flabby.'

'I swear that's not so. If you'd just lay your hand here, I'll show you just how hard I can be.' He took my hand and guided it towards his pelvis.

I snatched it away. 'No, thank you!'

'Not even for old times' sake?'

'Especially not for old times' sake. Let's just focus on business now. This is what I need from you.'

As I told Michel my plans, his long narrow face — prematurely lined with marks of dissipation — broke into laughter. '*Mordieu!* I'll do it! What a jest! Charlotte-Rose, you're a woman in a thousand. I should never have let you go.'

'Far too late to think that now,' I said. 'So you think it'll work?'

'Oh, it'll work. They won't suspect a thing. No one in their right mind would ever think of such a plan.'

'Thank you.'

He laughed again. 'Oh, it's divine madness, *ma chérie,* never you fear!'

I crouched in the back of a jolting canvas-covered wagon, huddled in furs, sure I was about to perish with the cold.

Around me crouched those players of the Comédie-Française whom Michel had persuaded to join our mad escapade. Among them was his ten-year-old son, Etienne, a bright-eyed boy eager for adventure. It made me feel old, knowing Michel had three children . . . and one old enough to appear on stage.

All the actors were in costume, face masks resting on their laps. One was dressed in a doctor's robe with a hideous plague mask in the shape of a bird's beak. Another was dressed as Il Capitano, in a short Spanish cloak and a huge stiff ruff. His mask was flesh-coloured and had a huge bulbous nose and an enormous moustache with upturned ends. Michel was dressed as Harlequin, in a costume made of red and black diamonds. His mask was moulded from leather to suggest exaggerated surprise and amusement. Etienne, his son, wore a miniature version of the same costume. Next to him sat Pantaloon, dressed in red with a black velvet cloak and hat, a fat jingling money-pouch at his belt (though it was filled with scraps of old iron, not coins, Michel had told me, just in case there were any cut-purses in the crowd). His mask was dark-visaged with a cruel hooked nose.

The women were all dressed in various pretty outfits. Columbine was dressed as an idealised milkmaid, with a frilly apron and a lace mask to cover her face. Two other women were dressed as fine court ladies, with gilded and feathered masks on a stick. Their *innamorati* were dressed as court gentlemen, with towering wigs and high-heeled red shoes and silken coats of pale pink and lavender frothing with lace and ribbons.

In the far end of the wagon slept a shaggy brown bear, a ring through its nose and an iron cuff and chain about one hind leg. Curled up against its furry flank were two children, a ten-year-old boy named Yves and his seven-year-old sister, Miette. When I had first seen them, performing outside an inn in

Paris, they were barefoot and in rags. Now, both wore the bicoloured hose and jerkin of jesters, with soft boots on their feet, belled hats on their heads and a heavy cloak to wrap about them.

It had been easy enough to entice Yves and Miette away from their job at the inn. I had only had to show them a little purse of coins that I promised would be theirs and raise the possibility of more work with Michel's troupe. Yves and Miette had been working for no more than some scanty food and a bed of straw in an old shed. They were both as scrawny as newborn chicks. It gave me real pleasure to see them tuck into a good meal of hot pottage and fresh-baked bread, and they had been glad to discard their soiled rags and have some new warm clothes, no matter how bright and peculiar.

Michel had gladly provided the clothes and the promise of work. 'A dancing bear will be useful, and we can always use a tumbler or two.'

The troupe had left Paris before dawn. We marched into Survilliers in a gloomy winter's twilight, shaking tambourines or playing pipes and tabors, dancing and singing, while Michel, in the lead, rang a handbell and shouted, '*Ayez, ayez!* The Comédie-Française has come to town!' Two dancing bears shuffled on their hind legs at the end of the procession. One was Yves and Miette's bear,

Tou-tou. The other bear was me.

I was concealed inside a shaggy brown bearskin, the snarling head drawn over mine. Michel's wife, Gabriele, had cleverly sewn it so that I could put the bearskin on like a coat, my legs and arms within the bear's, my feet hidden under the hind paws. I was able to look out through the jaws, and, when I gestured with my hands, the bear's claws rent the air.

The real dancing bear did not much like me, but Tou-tou was a poor old thing, broken down after a lifetime of hardship and hunger, and did little more than sniff at me suspiciously. Yves and Miette's parents had once been part of a travelling circus, but they had both died a few years earlier from smallpox, leaving their children nothing but a few rags and their bear. Both children loved Tou-tou, and they had begged Michel for some honeycomb for it and a good meal of fish.

We gave a performance in the village square to an audience of delighted rustics, with much hoarse singing and banging of wooden tankards as our accompaniment. Then, Michel shouted, 'To the castle!' In the cold winter evening, we wound our way along the muddy laneways, singing and banging tambourines, the men carrying smoky flambeaux to light the way. Most of the village came with us, happy to see the performance all over again. Tou-tou went down on all fours after a while, and reluctantly I copied her, bedraggling my fur with mud.

We did not need to hammer on the castle doors. They were gaping wide open, the steward himself standing in the doorway, curious faces peering at us from behind. With a great deal of noise and laughter, we all trooped up, Michel shouting out his patter.

'I guess you can come in,' the steward said. 'Though not one of you is to leave the great courtyard, do you hear? And I'll count you coming in and count you going out, and if there's any silver missing tomorrow, I'll have the police on your trail.'

'What, do you think we're thieves and vagabonds?' Michel roared. 'We're the Comédie-Française! I've played to kings and popes and admirals, and had them all on their feet, cheering the house down.'

'No offence meant,' the steward said. 'Though one could wonder what the Comédie-Française is doing all the way out here in Survilliers.'

'Have you not heard the news? Lully, the King's composer, has wounded himself in the King's service. Conducting a *Te Deum* to celebrate His Majesty's recovery last month, he struck his big toe while beating time with his staff. Now, it's gone gangrenous, and Lully looks set to die. All ballets and operas in the capital have been cancelled. So we decided to take the show on the road. Just

699

like the good old days!'

'Indeed?' The steward looked taken aback. For a moment, he frowned, as if thinking such a story too bizarre to be true. But then, apparently deciding it was too bizarre *not* to be true, he stood aside and let us in. It was a good story, I had to admit, and, unfortunately for the King's composer, all too true.

'Call all your people out,' Michel cried. 'It's Carnevale!'

A dour-looking guard spoke in an undertone to the steward, who frowned and shrugged. 'Very well,' he said in a low voice. 'Else we'll have mutiny in the ranks. No one will want to miss the show by staying and guarding him. Just keep a close eye on him.'

'Yes, sir.' The guard stumped away. Inside my shaggy bearskin, I exulted, sure they were speaking of my love. Soon, I saw him. They brought Charles down to the courtyard, a guard on either side. He looked thin and pale but was as richly dressed as usual, and my anxious eyes — peering out the bear's snout — saw no sign of any bruises or cuts.

The show began, the players all doing their best to put on such a lively and funny show that the steward and the guards would all be absorbed and pay no attention to an old dancing bear. I shuffled about on my hind paws like Tou-tou, waving my claws about and turning in circles, making my way closer and closer to Charles. Miette went with me, for she had hold of the chain that was attached to an iron cuff about my hind foot. She spun and twirled on one toe, and capered about, and many of the guards laughed and threw her coins, not paying any attention to me.

At last, we were standing right next to Charles. He was laughing and watching the show, but he looked down kindly at Miette as she tugged on his velvet sleeve. 'Would you like to see my bear dance?' she asked, lisping sweetly and smiling her gorgeous, funny, gap-toothed smile.

'Of course,' he answered with a smile.

She tugged on his sleeve again and he stepped back, his guards all laughing uproariously and slapping their thighs as Pantaloon chased Harlequin around the courtyard, trying to beat him over the head with his stick. Harlequin ran up a wall and somersaulted over his head, then bashed him in the behind, before racing away again. Miette tugged again and Charles stepped further into the shadows, till he was so close I could put out a paw and touch him.

I did. He flinched back in surprise, but I whispered, 'Charles, it's me. Charlotte-Rose.'

The expression on his face was almost as ludicrously surprised as Harlequin's mask.

'I'm in disguise. They would not let me in to see you, and that steward of your father's has seen my face. I had to see you.'

'Charlotte-Rose?' he whispered, peering into my snarling bear's face. 'Is that really you? In a bearskin?' His voice shook with laughter.

I nodded. 'There's very little time. I need to know, do you still love me?'

His face softened. 'Of course.'

'You still want to marry me?'

'With all my heart.'

'Then we need to get you out of here! I don't want to wait for you any longer.'

'My father will never permit it.'

'Then we'll elope. Can't we? Please?'

'He says he'll keep me locked up in here till I swear on my family's Bible that I will not marry you.'

'Couldn't you just do that? And then, when you're free, we could run away and get married.'

He frowned. 'That's not very honourable, Charlotte-Rose.'

'Neither is keeping you locked up against your will!'

His frown lingered. 'I cannot perjure my soul.'

'Not even for me?' I pleaded.

His face relaxed a little. 'You know I'd do anything for you, *ma chérie* . . . anything that is not dishonourable.'

'Couldn't you tell him something that will put his suspicions to rest? Tell him you cannot bear to be locked up any more, and that you will swear not to return to Versailles, or get in contact with me. And then, when he lets you out, you can come and meet me in Paris. You won't have lied to him, or perjured your soul, or anything dastardly like that. Wouldn't that do?' As I spoke rapidly, in a low voice, I turned my snout from side to side, making sure no one was paying us any attention. Everyone's gaze was fixed on the play-actors in their circle of flambeaux, though, and we were half-hidden in the shadows.

Charles frowned and bit his lip.

'I abjured my faith for you! I dishonoured the memory of my family. Does that mean nothing to you?'

One of the guards glanced over his shoulder at us, and Miette at once did a nimble handstand, calling, 'Look at me, *m'sieur,* look at me.' Obediently, Charles looked and smiled and clapped, and he gave her a coin. The guard looked away.

I was crying inside my bearskin. Charles heard me take a sobbing breath, the bearskin heaving unhappily, and he relented. 'Of course it does. I'm sorry. That's what I'll do. I won't lie to him, though, or swear not to do anything I mean to do.'

'Meet me in Paris, at the house of my cousin, the Comtesse de Murat,' I said. 'She lives at Place des Vosges, near the Bastille. She will hide us until you come of age. Then we can be married. Oh, Charles, do not fail me! These last few weeks have been so awful.'

'For me too,' he said and put out his arms as if to embrace me. He could not hug a dancing bear, though, and his arms fell down. 'I wish I could kiss you,' he said unhappily. 'I'd like to tear that bearskin away from you!'

'Jean de la Fontaine said "Never sell the bearskin before you've killed the bear",' I said rather shakily. 'Oh, Charles, please, make it soon!'

Charles and I signed our marriage contract on 22nd May 1687, my thirty-seventh birthday. Two weeks later, on 6th June, we were married by a priest, before witnesses, at the Eglise Saint-Sulpice, one of the largest and grandest churches in Paris, second only to the Notre-Dame. It was a dark, vast, gloomy place, but my happiness made it bright and warm. The priest blessed us, and Nanette and my sister, Marie, wept with joy.

My husband and I spent a few glorious days in Paris. We walked hand-in-hand along the Seine, went to the theatre and the ballet, and made love every night in our own consecrated marriage bed. 'At last!' Charles exulted. 'No more making love with all our clothes on.'

'We had better go and confess,' I said, after a few days. 'The King did give us his permission, after all.'

So we packed our bags and went to Versailles, to present ourselves to the King and beg his pardon for marrying without notifying him first.

The King was looking weary and sick, his pendulous cheeks purple as eggplants. He simply nodded and said, 'Ah, young love. You are of age now, Monsieur de Briou?'

'Yes, sire,' Charles replied.

'Very well. Ask the maître d'hôtel to find you an apartment. And Madame de Briou?'

'Yes?' I answered, thrilling to the words.

'Let us have no more scandal.'

It was too much to hope for. Ten days of happiness was all I had, ten days of being called 'Madame de Briou', ten days of going to sleep in my husband's arms, ten days of waking to his kiss, ten days of midsummer madness.

Then the Baron de Survilliers contrived to have our marriage dissolved by an Act of Parliament. I had, he said, seduced a minor and married him without his family's consent. Charles raged and declared he was of age and could do as he wished. I wept heartbrokenly. It did no good. Charles was imprisoned once again, this time in the old leper hospital at St Lazare, which had been turned into a gaol for people who had proved an embarrassment to their families. The Baron offered me a bribe to revoke my marriage vows. Icily, I refused. So the *putain* took me to court. The whole court came along to watch the proceedings. I was called a strumpet, a sorceress, a succubus. Jean de la Fontaine, shocked at my treatment, wrote a few verses in my support. At once, he was mocked and vilified, and people said I had worked my wicked wiles on him and made him fall in love with me too. The court proceedings were nothing but a brouhaha, designed to humiliate me in every way possible.

On 15th July 1689 — more than two years after our ill-fated wedding — Parliament declared that there had been an abuse of position, and I was fined one thousand gold *louis.* This was as much as a year's pension from the King. Charles was fined three thousand gold *louis.* Even the priest who had married us was fined. Charles was set free from the prison but joined the army at once and was sent away to fight in one of the King's never-ending wars. I never saw him again.

The Abbey of Gercy-en-Brie, France — April 1697

I did not sleep well again that night, the sour smell of rue on my skin bringing back such dark memories. From the creaking of Sœur Emmanuelle's bed, I guessed she too was sleepless. Before dawn, I heard her rise and whip herself again, mumbling heartbroken prayers. Part of me wanted to rush in and take that knotted cord and fling it out the window, but I lay still, my ears buried beneath my hands.

I could not take refuge in the garden for the next few days, for it was Easter and the nuns had their vigils to keep and their Exultet to chant. I wondered what all my friends at court were doing. Feasting, probably, glad that the long days of Lent were at last over. I ate my pottage dourly and wished that I was at the Château de Meudon, playing cards with the Dauphin and the Princesses de Conti, drinking champagne and eating foie gras, a fire roaring on the hearth.

It was the Great Silence of the abbey that I found hardest to bear. It was hard for someone who loved words so much to be forbidden to speak for the greater part of the day. Only in the early evening, as we gathered by the fire in the parlour, were we permitted to talk among ourselves. Sœur Emmanuelle always sat behind the novices, her cane resting against her knee, ready to strike out at any sign of frivolity.

On the evening of Easter Monday, I noticed, as I came into the parlour, how the girls drew their chairs away from their novice mistress, closing her out of their circle, exiling her to the cold edge of the room. I saw a flash of pain in her eyes before she folded her lips grimly and bent her head over her sewing. For a moment, I hesitated, then I drew a chair beside her. 'I believe you were once at

707

court in Paris, Sœur Emmanuelle?'

She glanced at me in surprise. 'A very long time ago.'

'I went to court in '66. Were you still there then?'

Her face twisted. 'No.'

I soldiered on. 'Were you in Versailles for the great fete of '64?'

'I was.'

'I have always wished I was there! I've heard it was an astonishing spectacle. Is it true they shot fireworks into the sky that made the shape of two intertwining *L*s, to signify Louis and Louise de la Vallière?'

'Yes, it's true,' Sœur Emmanuelle answered. 'We did not know whether to be shocked or jealous. The King was very handsome back then.'

I think she surprised herself as much as she surprised me by this rejoinder. She bit her lip and jabbed at her sewing with her darning needle.

'Is it also true that the King had his menagerie paraded through the fete on golden chains?'

She nodded again. 'Lions and tigers and an elephant, the biggest creature I had ever seen.' Her hands stilled on her sewing. 'It had a silk tent on its back where its keeper rode. And all the servants were dressed as fairy gardeners, carrying around trays of ices in all the colours of the rainbow. I ate so many I was almost ill and my mother wanted me to go back to the palace, but I would not. I wanted to see the ballet and then, of course, Molière was putting on his new play, *Tartuffe*.'

'*Tartuffe!* I never got to see it. The King banned it straight afterwards and it was never staged in public again.'

'Justifiably so. It was most irreligious.'

'But very funny, I believe,' I said.

For just a moment, her thin lips quirked. 'I must admit that Athénaïs and I thought it very funny at the time. We laughed till we wept. Girls can be very silly.' She cast a look, half amused, half exasperated, at the novices who were peeping over their shoulders at us.

'Athénaïs! She was the first friend I made at court. You knew her?'

'We were great friends when we were girls. But then our paths parted. It has been many years since I have paid her much thought.' Sœur Emmanuelle's voice had cooled again.

'I was her maid of honour for a while, till she fell out of favour.'

'She was a vain and silly girl when I knew her.'

'I always thought her very kind.'

Sœur Emmanuelle twisted her lips. 'She was kind, I suppose. Although the Montemarts had the cruellest wit of any family at court, when they wanted.'

I nodded, knowing this was true.

'She was most unkind to her poor husband,'

Sœur Emmanuelle went on. 'The Marquis de Montespan was devastated when she became the King's mistress. Did you know he had the gates of his chateau taken down because he said his cuckold's horns were too high for him to pass beneath them?'

'No! Really?'

'Oh, yes. He even had his carriage decorated with antlers. I think he went a little mad.'

'Poor man.'

'He had an effigy of Athénaïs buried in the graveyard and made their two children wear mourning for her. I believe he orders a requiem mass to be sung in her memory every year.'

'Wouldn't that be awful? For her, I mean? Being mourned as dead when you're still alive.'

'She did sin against him.'

'Yet what other choice did she have? The King will brook no resistance to his will.'

'Well, I believe she was exiled to a convent in the end, just like us,' Sœur Emmanuelle added with more than a touch of malice in her voice.

'Except the King gave her a dowry of half a million *francs*,' I answered.

'I warrant she does not have to sleep on a pallet of straw with a blanket as thin as a wafer.'

I smiled and, to my surprise, saw Sœur Emmanuelle's lips twist in what was surely a smile too.

The next morning, I went with quick steps to the garden to meet Sœur Seraphina, who was cutting chervil to make soup. She said, teasingly, 'I'm guessing you wish to hear the rest of the story.'

'Yes, please,' I replied, pulling on my gardening hat and gloves.

'Well,' she said, 'this is what happened . . .'

Fantasia

There are more wings than the wind knows
Or eyes that see the sun
In the light of the lost window
And the wind of the doors undone.

For out of the first lattice
Are the red lands that break
And out of the second lattice
Sea like a green snake,

But out of the third lattice
Under low eaves like wings
Is a new corner of the sky
And the other side of things.

'The Ballad of St Barbara'
G. K. Chesterton

ALONE IN THE WILDERNESS

The Rock of Manerba, Lake Garda, Italy —
April 1600

The dagger plunged towards Margherita's throat.

She caught the witch's wrist. To her surprise, she was strong enough to force the dagger away. La Strega had always seemed so much bigger than her. Yet Margherita now realised she was as tall as the witch. She wasn't a little girl any more.

The dagger clattered to the ground. Margherita scrambled to her feet, looking around for some kind of weapon. La Strega seized her dagger again, lips drawn back over her teeth, her breath hissing as the silver blade flashed down. Margherita stumbled back. Her hip banged into the dresser. She groped with her hand for something with which to strike the witch. Her hand found the heavy silver snood. She flung it at the witch with all her strength.

In her heart was a wordless shout.

Somehow, mid-air, the snood twisted, spread, transformed. It fell over the witch, vast as a fishing net. It pinned her to the ground.

For just an instant, Margherita was trans-fixed, staring in astonishment. Then a great joy flooded her. Enunciating each word very clearly, she said:

By the power of three times three, I bind
    you to me.
Thou may not speak of me, nor raise a
    hand to me
Nor stir from this place where I have cast
    thee.

The witch gasped and put one hand to her heart. Her tawny eyes were dark with rage and fear. She struggled to speak, but her tongue refused to obey her. Margherita laughed shakily. She caught up her winter cloak and the sack with her provisions. Her hair felt strange, so light and soft, brushing the back of her neck. Hastily, she fished in the flour sack and drew out her wedding ring, blowing the flour dust towards the helpless witch.

'He loves me, and I love him. You poor thing, have you ever been able to say the same?' She slipped the ring onto her finger. The witch's dagger lay gleaming on the floor. She picked it up with a fold of her cloak and tossed it out the window — she would touch nothing that had been La Strega's — and fished under the bed for Lucio's knife. She strapped it about her waist, a dangerous giddy exhilaration taking hold of her.

Now, how to get out? La Strega was pinned to the carpet by the silver fishing net, heaving with all her strength against its weight. There was no way that Margherita could roll back the carpet and prise up the trapdoor to find the coil of rope Lucio had left her. Her wild raking glance took in the comb and the coils of silver ribbon discarded on the dresser. The snood the witch had given her had turned into a net to bind her. What could Margherita do with a comb and a ribbon?

Margherita laughed. She caught them both up, shoving the comb into the pocket of her cloak and hurriedly tying one end of the ribbon to the hook in the wall. As she tossed its silken end out of the window, it twisted and thickened and transformed into a sturdy silver rope that snaked down the dizzying fall of the tower, disappearing into darkness.

Margherita clambered out of the window and began to climb down the rope, the sack slung over her back. Her hands were slick with the sweat of terror. Her body was heavy and weak, her arms trembled. She concentrated on stepping down one foot after another, not allowing herself to think of the dreadful fall below. Her sack grew heavier and heavier.

The climb down seemed endless. At last, though, the wind heaving at her body grew less and the sounds of the night changed, growing more intimate. She risked a look down and saw that the blackness of the ground was nearby. When at last her questing foot felt something solid below her, all her muscles gave way and she collapsed onto the ground.

'*Signorina,* what is wrong?' a high squeaky voice said from behind her. A giant loomed out of the shadows. Margherita screamed and reached into her pocket, flinging the comb at the giant's feet. A thicket of thorns at once sprang up around him, and Margherita ran away into the darkness.

The slope was steep, rough and stony, lit only by the light of the moon. She fell often, grazing the heels of her hands, tearing her dress. Her stomach cramped with pain. She tried to moderate her pace, to have a care, but fear was a hellhound baying at her heels. She ran on blindly.

I must find Lucio, she thought. *He was headed north, to the place where the lemons grow.* She was not sure which way was north but she followed the curve of the lake away from the tower, remembering a casual gesture of Lucio's hand.

Every rustle in the shadows made her gasp, her heart jerking. The world seemed immense and dangerous. She soon could run no more. She sat for a while, a sharp stitch in her side, then got up, staggering on through the night.

The panorama of dawn was the most beautiful thing she had ever seen. Vast and strange, the sky stretched above her, streaked with long clouds like a girl's hair flying, coloured crimson and rose and blue and gold. The lake shimmered with the same vivid shades. Everywhere she looked was a new sight to delight her eyes. Mountains stretching as far as the eye could see, tipped with indigo and bronze. A boat sailing on the water, its sail ochre-coloured, its twin flitting along beneath. Birds sang and warbled, every note delighting her ear.

A small village lay nestled in the curve of the bay, smoke drifting from tall chimneys. Margherita limped closer, wondering if she could go there and beg for help. Surely someone would help her? But then she saw men on the shore, their brawny arms bare, shaking out fishing nets. The sight stabbed her with fear, and she remembered the witch struggling under the silver net. Surely La Strega would have got free by now? Surely she'd be close behind?

Margherita turned away from the village, pressing on through the forest.

The day passed slowly. Margherita walked and rested, walked and rested. Her feet hurt dreadfully, and her stomach was swollen and distended, as if something she had eaten disagreed with her. By midday, she had reached another town, but she gave it a wide berth, frightened by the idea of having to speak to anyone or trying to explain her predicament. Her only thought was to find Lucio.

Mountains began to press down upon the shoreline, immense and grey. By dusk, there was no way forward. The sides of the mountain rose directly from the lake and soared high into the air, as steep as — and infinitely higher than — the walls of her tower.

Margherita was so exhausted she could not take another step. She wrapped herself in her shawl and lay down under a tree, so cold and uncomfortable she thought it impossible she could sleep. Somehow, though, she did.

In the morning, she lay for a while under her cloak, too stiff and weary to move. Frost glittered on the cloak's hem. She heard a rustle in the bushes behind her and sat up, gripping the hilt of her knife. A deer stepped delicately out of the undergrowth, its liquid black eyes fixed on her. Margherita sat still, enchanted. It paced past her and disappeared into the bushes. She rose and followed it along a faint rough path through the trees.

The path led her to a clearing in the forest. An old woman sat on a rock, spinning handfuls of lambswool into a smooth thread with a distaff and spindle. She was dressed in the rough clothes of a countrywoman, with silver hair twisted up and secured with a clasp made of leather and wood. Her dark eyes were heavily hooded. She looked up and smiled as Margherita stepped out of the shadows.

'Good morning,' she said creakily. 'Lovely day for a walk.'

Margherita nodded shyly, instinctively drawing away.

'Are you hungry? I was just about to break my fast and would love some company.' The old woman put down her distaff and lifted a basket into her lap, unfolding a napkin to reveal fresh dark bread, filled with nuts and fruit. It steamed gently in the chilly air. Margherita's stomach grumbled loudly. The old woman grinned, showing a mouth full of gaps. She broke off one end of the loaf and passed it to Margherita. It smelt so good it was all she could do not to cram her mouth full.

'Are you thirsty?' the old woman said, gnawing at the heel of the loaf. 'I have fresh goat's milk.' She drew a ceramic jug out of her basket, uncorking it and passing it to Margherita, who drank thirstily.

'So where are you off to this fine morning?' the old woman asked.

Margherita summoned up enough courage to tell her. 'Limone. Can you tell me which way to go?'

'Limone?' the old woman answered. 'The best way to Limone is by boat. If you go down to the port at Desenzano, you'll be able to buy passage on a cargo boat.'

'I have no money,' Margherita said.

The old woman looked troubled. 'It's a long hard way if you don't have a boat. Are you sure you wish to go there?'

'Yes,' Margherita answered. 'I must.'

'There's an old mule track over the mountains,' the old woman said doubtfully. 'It's steep and rough and wild, though.'

'I have to try it,' Margherita said. 'I don't know what else to do.'

'Can you not wait here? I live in the forest nearby and will gladly give you shelter if you need it.'

'I cannot wait.' Margherita imagined the witch and the giant stalking her through the shadowy forest, coming ever closer to her. She dared not wait a moment longer. So the old woman told Margherita the way through the mountains, though her wrinkled face was worried.

'Thank you so much!' Margherita cried.

'Take it easy along the way,' the old woman advised. 'You don't want to bring on the birth of your babies too soon.'

'Babies?' Margherita was amazed and frightened. 'What do you mean?'

The old lady pointed her spindle at Margherita's rounded belly. 'Did you not know?

There's a baby in there — two if I'm not mistaken.'

'A baby? Two babies?' The thought filled Margherita with sudden fierce joy. Babies of her own. Hers and Lucio's. No wonder her dress had been tight. Her desire to find Lucio grew even more urgent. She looked up at the mountains with grim determination.

'I hope you find him.' The old woman picked up her distaff and spindle and began to spin again.

Margherita followed the faint path up, up, up, leaving the forest behind. Her legs and lungs burnt. Many small waterfalls surged out of the cliff face, running over the path and making the rock slippery. She kept her hand on the cliff face, picking her way through slowly and carefully despite her longing to find Lucio.

Each twist of the path revealed another panorama of mountains and valleys and swift foamy rivers. Wherever the path widened out, she would rest. There were few trees, but whenever she saw one she gathered together fallen twigs and branches and stuffed them in her sack. If she wanted a hot meal, she would need a fire.

A little after noon, Margherita came out onto a high spur of land and saw for the first time the lake spread out below her. The sight of it, dark jade green etched with silver, made her catch her breath with painful joy. She had begun to be afraid the old woman had sent her in the wrong direction, as she had been travelling away from the lake the whole way.

It was an exhausting and difficult scramble after that, the mule track leading upwards at a sharp angle. Margherita supported her belly as best she could, filled with wonder at the thought she carried new life within her and determined to protect her babies.

It grew colder. Snow lay in the shadow of the cliff and draped the round boulders above her. There were no longer any trees, only stubborn grasses clinging to crevices in the rocks. Margherita gathered the dry leaves for kindling, though they cut the skin of her cold numb hands.

The path soon led her to a pulpit of stone at the very crest of the mountain, offering a sweeping view of the lake below, and snowy peaks of mountains stretching in all directions as far as she could see. The cold wind buffeted her, but she spread her arms wide, tears freezing on her cheeks. *This is what an eagle would see,* she thought, *as it soars above the lake. I am free like the eagle!*

On she went, leaning on a broken branch. She passed a rocky crag shaped like a giant's thumb, just as the old woman had described to her. She was on the right track.

The afternoon was spent climbing again, though the incline was much easier now. The track wound through green valleys and up stony spurs, taking her to the top of another crest and another panoramic view of the lake. It was so cold it hurt to breathe, and her feet were numb. Margherita huddled her hands in her shawl and kept on walking.

Every step hurt. Every breath stabbed. Again and again, she stumbled, only to catch herself and keep on going. The sharp pain in her side was like a spur, goading her on. The sun slowly set behind her, the snow on the crests of the mountains turning violet and rose. They seemed to go on forever, those mountains, soft undulating ranks of them stretching into blue infinity. Margherita began to fear she would never find her way free of them. Surely, she was lost. The old woman had said it was a day's walk. Perhaps she had gone too slowly. Margherita began to hurry.

By the time the moon rose, golden and mis-shapen as a clipped coin, Margherita had begun to realise that the sharp stabbing pains in her side were more than just a stitch. They came more rapidly, with greater intensity. Each time the pain came, she had to stop, crouching, panting, the world receding from her. Her legs trembled so much she could scarcely keep her balance.

She stopped to rest. The pain came in a red roaring wave. Margherita could only wait for it to recede before she stumbled on, looking for somewhere she could take shelter. At last, the path rounded a bulge of stone and opened into a small protected valley between high cliffs. At the back of the valley was a shallow cave. Nearby, a spring of fresh water burbled from a cleft in the rock. Margherita knelt to drink from it. The water was icy-cold and delicious. When she tried to get up again, the world whirled about her and a sharp pang lanced through her stomach. She gasped, feeling like a kitten swept away on a flood-tide.

Eventually, the pain ebbed away. Margherita realised she had only a few moments before it came again. She staggered into the cave and quickly emptied out her sack, tossing all the kindling she had gathered into a pile. Her hands shook so much it took a few tries before she managed to strike a spark and light the messy pile of twigs and branches. Firelight began to dance all over the walls of the cave, bringing her as much comfort as warmth.

She collected water in her pot, setting it to heat in the fire. When the water was warm, she took off all her outer garments and washed herself as best she could. She knew very little about giving birth, but she felt sure it was best to be clean.

Pain rippled over her belly. She bent, gasping, her hands on her knees. When at last the tide of pain receded, she set herself to tear her petticoat into rough squares of linen. She would need clouts for the baby and for herself. She had only managed to rip the material in half when the pain came again, more intense than ever. She began to sob.

'Mama, I need you,' she said. The sound of her own voice steadied her, making her feel less alone. 'I wish you were here. I wish you knew I was alive. I know you loved me. I never believed her. I mean, I tried not to believe her. Oh, Mama, I wish you were here!'

She was afraid she might die there, alone in the wilderness.

Pain came like a rabid dog, tossing her as helplessly as a rag doll. She crouched on the floor of the cave, feeling as if her belly was being ripped apart. A deep primal scream forced its way out of her throat. Then she felt a sudden intense relief, and a rush and slither between her legs. She reached down and eased a baby into the world. It was a boy, red-faced and red-haired, screaming and punching his tiny fists at the air. Harsh sobs racked her chest. Margherita sat back on her heels, cradling the baby to her chest. She could do nothing but weep for a while, but his insistent crying roused her and she wrapped him in one of the squares of linen, rocking him helplessly in her arms. His curls were the colour of the firelight, the colour of a new minted copper coin. His eyes were scrunched tight. He kept on screaming, high and piercing as a seagull. Memories of paintings of the Madonna feeding her child came to her. She lifted the baby to her breast and awkwardly inserted her swollen nipple into his mouth. In an instant, he began to suck hungrily.

Margherita felt a corresponding tugging deep inside her. Then her distended belly rippled with acute pain. She gasped, tears coming to her eyes. Her son made a little dissatisfied noise as she jerked. Margherita clutched him to her, sobbing, then quickly laid him down, screaming, on the pile of rags. She was only just in time. Her pain demanded her surrender. For a moment, she seemed to black out; all knowledge and sensation of the world swept away. Her body exerted itself with all its strength. She felt another child slide from her. This child was blue and silent. A little girl with damp dark curls. Margherita lifted her to her breast, but she was limp and unresponsive. Frantically, Margherita clutched her close, whispering, 'Oh please, oh please, someone help me.' The little girl was covered with a white scum of mucus. Margherita tried to wash her clean, rubbing the rag over her tiny body. As she grew more frantic, her movements became more urgent. 'Please, don't let my baby die,' she cried and clutched the little girl to her. The baby gasped for air and began to cry. Weak with relief, Margherita wrapped her in a clean rag and brought her to her breast, then scooped up her screaming son with her other hand and tucked him next to his sister. Silence fell. Margherita sat, dazed and exhausted, gazing down at the two tiny heads nestled against her. One fiery red, the other dark as night.

Dead Man's Bells

Lake Garda, Italy — April to May 1600

At last, the little ones slept.

Margherita had just enough strength to throw some more branches on the fire, then she lay down on her cloak, drawing the heavy shawl over herself and her children. She slept.

Just for a moment, it seemed. Then her son awoke and began to scream once more. His noise woke his sister. Margherita did her best to feed and soothe them, but her breasts were hard as rock and hot as lava, and she ached all over. Blood was still seeping from between her legs. As they suckled hungrily, she felt a familiar surge of pain in her womb. 'No,' she moaned. But all that came out this time were two horrible messes of bloody flesh, tied to her babies by thick, grey, twisted ropes. She waited till her babies had once again slipped into sleep, then cut the ropes and buried the messes at the back of the cave under some rocks. She bandaged the bloody stumps as best she could, sobs shaking her, and lay down again.

The night passed in a blur. The babies woke and screamed and fed, woke and screamed and fed. It was always her son who woke first and who fed the longest. Her little girl was weak and fretful, crying more than she drank, her wails becoming weaker as the endless hours of the night crept past.

In the dawn, Margherita dressed herself again and made a sling from her shawl to carry her babies in. She felt sick and dizzy but knew she needed help. It had been a long time since she had eaten, and although she felt no hunger she knew she must find food and warmth and shelter soon if she and the twins were to survive.

She trudged slowly along the old mule track, the babies lulled into sleep by the motion. It was nastily cold at first, but as the sun rose higher the air warmed and she began to move more easily. Many times, she had to stop and lean against a rock; the stain of blood on her skirt was growing larger. Midmorning, she fed her son, but she could not rouse her daughter to drink.

Margherita saw Limone as she came over the crest of a hill in the golden hour before sunset. It lay below her, a tiny stone village, crammed between the precipitous cliffs and the deep shadowy waters of the lake. The air was sweet with the smell of lemon blossom, for all available land had been terraced and planted with lemon trees, the delicate flowers protected from the cold by high walls of stone covered with panes of glass that glowed in the sun. The stone walls were joined by wooden trellises where grapevines grew.

The mule track had turned into a narrow cobblestone road, steep as a waterfall, set with steps at irregular intervals. Panting, with sharp pains in her legs and side, Margherita stumbled down to the port, cradling the weight of her babies in her arms. It was warm down there, the sun reflecting off the grey stone and catching sudden glints of crystal. The fishing boats were coming in, men deftly furling their red sails, casting ropes to the shore to be tied down safely, nets filled with wriggling silver fish. Women in rough brown gowns and aprons, kerchiefs tied over their hair, were filling the baskets on their hips. The setting sun dazzled on the water, hurting Margherita's eyes, making her head ache.

Margherita pressed her hand to her heart, sucking in deep breaths, trying to calm her anxiety. She could see no sign of Lucio, even though it seemed the entire village was crowded into the tiny square, talking and laughing. As she made her hesitant way towards the port, people turned to stare at her in surprise. Margherita shrank back. It had been so long since she was last in the midst of a crowd. The noise and the smell of them made her feel sick.

Her heart beating uncomfortably fast, Margherita went up to the nearest woman, busy gutting and scaling fish with a wicked-looking knife. 'I'm sorry, I'm wondering if you have seen a young man . . . his name is Lucio. He comes from Florence.'

The fishwife looked surprised. 'Do you mean Signor Lucio de' Medici? The nephew of the Grand Duke?'

Margherita stared at her in stunned disbelief. Lucio was a de' Medici? The wealthiest and most powerful family in all of northern Italy? The blood drained from her face, leaving her cold and trembling.

'He was here last night,' the fishwife said. She called to the crowd. 'Has anyone seen Signor de' Medici today?'

A burly fisherman looked around. 'Ah, yes. Young de' Medici. I saw him this morning. He set out at dawn.'

'He's gone?' Margherita felt a sickening drop in her stomach.

The fisherman nodded. 'He was up bright and early, very anxious to be on his way.'

Anguish racked her heart. She was too late; she had missed him. Where would Lucio go? Would he go back to the tower? What if La Strega was still there? She remembered La Strega's snarling face as she had sought to throw off the silver net. The witch would seek revenge on Lucio. She would hurt him or kill him.

She looked about her. The mountains towered all around. Her heart quailed inside her at the idea of having to climb back up that precipitous track and retrace all those cold stony miles. But the only other way was by boat, and Margherita did not know how to sail, nor did she have any money to pay for her passage.

She gazed imploringly at the fisherman. 'Please, will you take me in your boat? I need to . . . I need to find Lucio!'

'The wind's blowing the wrong way,' the fisherman said. 'You must sail in the morning if you wish to head south. At this time of day, the *ora* is blowing. It'll take you all the way to Riva if you're not careful.'

'I don't care! I must go after him. I must stop him! It's a matter of life or death.'

He looked at her as if she was mad. 'I tell you, it's no use. We'd have to row the whole way with the wind and the current against us.'

She looked around at the circle of faces. Everyone was staring at her. 'I have to find him.'

'In the morning,' the fisherman said. He put out one huge rough hand as if to seize her. Margherita jerked her arm away, a sharp jolt of dread going through her.

'No need to be afraid,' the fishwife said, stepping closer. Her knife was still in her hand, dripping blood.

'No!' Margherita cried. She spun, ready to flee, but the ground rocked beneath her, then tilted. Darkness engulfed her.

Stars dazzled her vision. Time was fractured. Glimpses came to her: faces bending over her, people shouting at her, babies screaming. She was hot, and then cold, small and light, then huge and heavy, awake and then caught in a nightmare.

She dreamt she was back in the tower room again. The four walls closed in on her, pressing upon her lungs. She saw herself pacing the floor, her hair catching the light of the fire. Then the pacing figure turned and looked up, and Margherita saw she had the face of the witch. Terror froze her. She could not move or speak, or scarcely breathe.

The witch continued to pace, her eyes filled with madness, her fists clenched. Dawn brightened the window. Faraway birds began to twitter and sing.

'Margherita, let down your hair so I may climb the golden stair!' a merry voice called from below.

Please, no, Margherita whispered to herself.

The witch paused mid-step. For a moment, she was still, her white face like a mask, then she picked up the long coils of golden-red hair and flung one end out the window.

Lucio! Margherita screamed. But she made

no sound. The braid jerked as someone began to climb. The witch braced herself, struggling to bear the strain.

Margherita tried to shriek a warning to her lover climbing the braid. She tried to seize the witch and knock her down. She had no more force or substance than a ghost.

Lucio swung his leg over the windowsill. *'Mia bella bianca!'* he called. Seeing the still figure in white, he reached for her, only to recoil as he realised it was not Margherita who stood waiting for him but the witch La Strega.

'You wish to see your dearest girl, but the pretty bird sings no longer in the nest.'

'Where is she?' Lucio cried furiously.

'She's gone. You'll never see her again. I'll make sure of that!' As she spoke, La Strega dropped the braid and whipped out her dagger, lunging at him. Lucio lost his balance and fell with a scream. Down, down, he fell, tumbling head first into the thorny bushes that had sprung up from Margherita's comb at the base of the tower. The branches caught him, saving him from being dashed against the rocks, but when he lifted his head, groaning, blood was trickling from his eyes.

Margherita woke with a start. 'Lucio!' she sobbed. 'Oh, Lucio!'

'Ssssh, now,' a woman's voice said kindly. 'We'll be there soon.'

'Where? Where are we going?' Margherita's

voice was creaky. She opened her eyes and saw a pale blue sky above, flecked with tiny clouds like brightly coloured fish. The light hurt her eyes. She winced and covered her face with her hand. It seemed as if she was lying in a bed, but the bed rocked weirdly beneath her and she could hear water lapping. She tried to sit up, but her limbs felt weighted down. Panic flooded through her. Struggling up on one elbow, she realised she was in a small boat, wrapped up in blankets. Her tiny babies were tucked in beside her. Her son was awake, sucking furiously at his hand, his indigo-blue eyes staring up at the sky. Her daughter lay limply, her face deathly pale.

'Just you lie still and rest now,' the woman said. It was the fishwife from Limone, a shawl wrapped about her head. 'You've got milk fever. But don't you worry now. We're taking you to the wise woman. She'll know what to do.'

Even though Margherita heard her words, it was hard to understand their meaning. Everything felt so strange. She looked down at the little heads tucked up against her. Their birth seemed like a dream. But it had been real. Did that mean that Lucio's fall from the tower was real? Tears choked her. She wanted to leap up, to shout, to run, to hurry to Lucio's side. But she could scarcely lift her head.

'Try and rest,' the fishwife said. 'The wind

is with us. We'll be there soon.'

The little boy began to wail. The sound made Margherita's stomach clench with anxiety. She tried to feed him, but her breasts were hard as rock and throbbing with heat. It was agony to even brush her fingers against them.

The fishwife took him. She dipped the twisted end of a square of linen into a bucket of milk, then let him suck on it. It kept him quiet a moment or two, but then he began to scream even more loudly, his face turning crimson.

'The wise woman will know what to do,' the fishwife said hopefully, dipping the kerchief in the milk again.

Whenever the twirl of milk-sodden linen was held to his mouth, he sucked eagerly, then cried till it was dipped in the milk again and he could suck again. The little girl did not stir, and Margherita held her close, pressing her face to the dark curls, still matted with blood and mucus. Tears dampened her eyes. She shut them and felt again that sick giddiness, that sense of time and place being out of joint. *Where are you, Lucio?* Margherita thought. *Oh, please, be safe!*

When next she opened her eyes, it was to find the boat sailing into a small bay. The mountains towered above her, rising straight out of the water on either side but pulling back in one spot, like a woman lifting her

skirts. In that one spot was a grove of blos-
soming fruit trees, a tendril of smoke curling
up from a low stone cottage in their midst.

'She's here,' the fishwife said in relief.

The boat was being skippered by a burly
man with skin coarsened by long years in the
sun. He carried Margherita to shore, despite
her instinctive recoil, and through a garden
riotous with herbs and flowers. She knew
some by sight: parsley and sage, and rosemary and thyme, and the pretty blue flower
of rapunzel. Against one wall was a pomegranate tree, its grey branches bursting with
scarlet flowers. Margherita knew what the
tree was called because at the Pietà they had
worn pomegranate flowers in their hair when
they performed.

The fisherman carried her in through a narrow doorway, ducking his head to avoid banging it on the stone lintel. The room was bless-
edly cool and dim inside. An old woman sat
knitting by the fire. She rose to her feet. 'Lay
the poor girl here,' she said.

He laid Margherita down on a narrow bed
against the wall, and the old woman brought
her a cup of fresh water flavoured with some
kind of herb. Margherita gulped gratefully.
She did not think she had ever been so thirsty.

Margherita was staring anxiously over the
fisherman's shoulder. 'My babies?'

'Giuseppe will go and get them now. You
need to just lie back. Let me see what I can

do to help you.'

'Lucio,' Margherita said, turning her head restlessly against the bolster.

'You did not find him?'

At these words, Margherita drew her gaze back to the woman's face. Hollow-cheeked and wrinkled, with hooded dark eyes and silver hair coiled out of the way, it was the face of the old woman who had given her directions in the forest. 'It's you.'

'Yes. I'm sorry to see you in such straits. Let me take a look at you.' The old woman lifted Margherita's skirt and examined her quickly, then laid one hand on her swollen aching breast. 'I wish you had stayed with me. I could have helped you.'

'I had to find Lucio.' At the words, Margherita's eyes filled with tears again. She had gone through so much in her search to find him, yet had failed.

'You'll find him again, don't you fear. Let us just make you and these little ones of yours well again.' The old woman laid cold compresses on Margherita's breasts and forehead. 'I will pluck you some cabbage leaves as soon as I can. There is nothing better for sore and swollen breasts.'

The sound of a baby roaring came up the path. The old woman turned swiftly to help as the fisherman and his wife carried the twins into the cottage. The little boy was red-faced and squalling. The little girl lay as limply as if she was dead.

The old woman brought the little boy straight to Margherita. 'You need to feed him. I know it hurts, but it's the best thing for you both. Feed him for as long as you can stand the pain.'

Hot agony lanced through Margherita as her son fastened greedily onto her nipple, but she gritted her teeth and endured. To her surprise, the pain soon eased a little. She watched anxiously as the old woman bent over the little girl. She felt her forehead, tested her thin arms and legs, then pressed her ear to the tiny concave chest. Her face was grave.

'What's wrong?' Margherita cried.

'Her heart is very weak,' the old woman replied. 'Don't be afraid. You are all safe here. Keep feeding your son, and I'll be back in a moment.'

'Don't leave me!'

'I won't be long.' The old woman picked up a basket and a knife from the table and went out the front door. Margherita lay still, supporting her son's head and gazing at the still body of her daughter with anxious longing. She looked so small and pale and helpless. Margherita longed to hold her.

In a moment, the old woman came back, her basket full of herbs and flowers. She put the basket down and took out a bunch of purple-blue foxgloves. Margherita felt her heart constrict. Her grandmother had always called foxgloves 'Dead Man's Bells' or 'Witch's Gloves'. The old woman stripped away the leaves of the flower and tossed them into a bowl with some wine, which she then warmed on the fire.

'What are you doing?' Margherita gasped, as the old woman lifted the limp body of her daughter.

'Giving her foxglove tea,' she replied. 'It will help her heart. Don't worry, I know not to give her too much. Just a spoonful to begin with.'

Carefully, she spooned a mouthful of the potion into the baby's mouth, massaging her throat and heart to help her swallow. The baby choked, spluttered and began to cry. Smiling, the old woman wrapped and tied a square cloth about her bottom, then swaddled her in a soft white knitted blanket and tucked her in beside Margherita. 'There you are, my little lamb. You have some milk now.'

As Margherita wearily guided her daughter's mouth to her nipple, the old woman took away the little boy, expertly changed the sodden rags about his bottom, wrapped him up in another white knitted blanket and tucked him back beside Margherita. He was fast asleep, his soft mouth puckered in a contented smile.

Tears slid down Margherita's cheeks, but she could do nothing except blink them away, both hands filled with her babies. Her own little children. Margherita could scarcely believe it was true. She wept with joy as much as with pain and exhaustion. The old woman smiled at her and came to dab away her tears and lift a cup of warm herbal tea to her lips so Margherita could drink.

'How can I thank you?' Margherita said.

'Grow well and strong again,' the old woman said. 'You look as if you may have lost a lot of blood, and you're far too thin. You must look after yourself so you can look after your babies.'

'I don't even know your name.'

The old woman smiled. 'You can call me Sophia.'

She brought Margherita a bowl of fish soup and let her drink. 'You must build up your strength. Heaven knows, you'll need it with two little ones to look after. What shall you call them?'

Margherita looked down at the two little heads, one dark, the other bright bronze-red. They were so small and so new, their skin as soft as rose petals. 'I think I'll call my little girl Rosa,' she said, thinking of the skeletons lying entombed in the tower. It seemed so unfair that they should be forgotten. 'And maybe . . . if you don't mind . . . Sophia, after you?'

'I would be honoured,' the old woman said.

'Rosa Sophia,' Margherita said and bent to

kiss the downy dark head. She then gazed down at her son. Lucio, after his father? Alessandro, after hers? She wanted him to have a name all of his own, though. Then an idea came to her. 'Raphael,' she whispered. The angel of healing, and the name of Lucio's favourite artist. She remembered how he had described the painting of the Madonna in the Meadow, surrounded by flowers and with two little ones at her knee. 'Raphael Lucio,' she said and hugged him close.

That night, she dreamt of Lucio again. He stumbled through a forest, his eyes all swollen and crusted with blood, his hands groping outwards.

Margherita woke with a cry of anguish. 'Lucio!'

'Ssssh, now,' Sophia soothed her. 'You don't want to wake the babies.'

'Lucio . . . he's hurt. Oh, I need to go to him!'

'You cannot be going anywhere just now,' Sophia said. 'It'll be days before you can even walk. Look, you've woken the little ones. Let me help you get them settled.'

'They cannot be hungry again,' Margherita said in disbelief as the thin wails of the babies filled the room.

'Indeed they can,' Sophia said. 'You'll find they do little else but eat for the first few weeks, the little darlings.'

Margherita found it intensely frustrating.

All her sinews and nerves urged her to go and find Lucio, but she could barely rise and make her way to the chamber pot. The twins seemed to cry all the time. Raphael ate greedily and soon fell asleep, but Rosa was much more unsettled. Sophia made her some chamomile tea and fed it to her with a teaspoon, then held her up against her shoulder, rocking her gently and singing to her till at last she fell asleep.

'I don't know how I'd manage without you,' Margherita said.

'If you had not been so strong and sensible, the three of you could have died out there in the mountains,' Sophia said. 'Many a young girl would not have done so well. Rest up, and tomorrow if it's warm enough you can go and sit out in the sunshine.'

'I need to go and find Lucio!'

'So you shall, just as soon as the three of you are strong enough.'

Margherita trusted her enough to close her eyes and try to sleep. This time, she dreamt of singing.

THE GODDESS OF SPRING

*The Rock of Manerba, Lake Garda, Italy —
May 1600*

The tower on its high rock cast a long shadow over the shining waters of the lake. As the small boat sailed into its coldness, Margherita shivered and pressed her twins closer to her.

'Not long now,' Sophia said.

She brought the boat in as close to the shore as she could, and Margherita kilted up her skirts and waded to shore, the twins snug in a sling made from her shawl. 'Thank you!' she called, and Sophia blessed her and bid her farewell with a troubled glance.

Margherita put her wet feet into her boots and made her way along the rocky beach. Birds sang, and the sun filtered through the soft green leaves of downy oaks. The twins slept peacefully in their sling.

'Lucio?' Margherita called. Now that she was here at the Rock of Manerba again, she did not know how to find him. She was terribly afraid of La Strega. Was the witch still here, lurking nearby, waiting for Margherita to return?

She circled around the hill, looking for any sign that Lucio might be near. But all was still and quiet. Slowly, she began the steep climb towards the crest of the hill. The top of the tower was visible through the leaves. Margherita thought she saw a flicker of movement at the window and ducked behind a tree. Her heart was beating so hard it made her feel faint. She waited till its pace slowed, then crept forward.

To reach the base of the tower, Margherita had to climb over ruined stone walls all overgrown with brambles. She thought she heard La Strega's voice, calling her. *Petrosinella! Petrosinella! How could you leave me here? Petrosinella!*

It's nothing but the wind, Margherita told herself. *La Strega is long gone.*

At last, she reached its square foot and the thicket of thorn trees that had sprung up from her comb. Tatters of cloth were caught in the thorns. Margherita untangled one and held it to her face. It was the red velvet of Lucio's doublet. On the stone was a dark bloodstain. With tears in her eyes, Margherita touched the stain gently. Then she began to follow its trail through the rocks and the brambles. A glimmer of gold caught her eyes. She saw, twisted through brambles, the long rope of braided hair. It took her a long time to disentangle it, but at last Margherita managed it and coiled it at the bottom of her sack. Then she went on, following the spots of blood.

Many times, she thought she had lost the trail, only to find a broken branch or a shred of cloth on a thorn.

Petrosinella, the wind called.

She found a place where the blood had pooled, as if Lucio had fallen there. It was hard to follow the trail after that. Margherita could not be sure whether it was Lucio who had bent back the grasses or a hare, or a deer. Once, she found the imprint of a shoe in the dust, but it seemed far too large for her lover.

The hours passed. The babies woke and demanded to be fed. Afterwards, Margherita ate some of the bread, cheese and olives that Sophia had given her. On she went, searching, calling, her voice thickening with despair.

As dusk fell, she found a place to camp down near the shore. It was cold, and she gathered driftwood and made herself a small fire. She fed her hungry babies, then made a little nest for them in the grasses while she heated up a small pot of rice and vegetables that Sophia had made for her. The babies were cold and unsettled, so when she had eaten she gathered them in her arms and sang them a lullaby.

'*Farfallina, bella e bianca, vola vola . . .*'
Butterfly, beautiful and white, fly and fly . . .

Sparks from her fire spun up like tiny fireflies. Above, the sky was midnight-blue velvet sewn with countless silver sequins. An owl hooted nearby. Margherita felt her misery seep away. *I'll keep on searching,* she vowed. *Lucio, wherever you are, I will find you.*

She sang the lullaby again, her voice strengthened with new hope. Then, out of the darkness, came a hoarse cry. 'Margherita!'

She scrambled to her feet, looking about her with dilated eyes. 'Lucio?'

'Margherita!'

A dark figure stumbled out of the darkness, his hands stretched before him. Margherita lay down the twins in their nest of soft grasses and leapt to meet him. In an instant, they were in each other's arms, kissing, talking, laughing, weeping.

'Where have you been? I've been searching.'

'I thought I'd lost you forever.'

'What happened? Are you hurt? Let me see.' Gently, she drew Lucio towards the fire. His gait was slow and unsure, and he gripped her hand tightly. As he came into the light of the fire, Margherita saw his face was bruised and badly scratched, his eyes sealed shut with dried blood. She drew him down so he lay with his head on her lap. 'Oh, my darling, what have you done?'

'I'm blind,' he said.

Margherita began to weep. He reached up to draw her closer, his breath sharp and uneven with grief. The tears flooded down her face and, as she bent to kiss him, fell onto his eyes. 'Oh, my darling, I'm so sorry,' she managed to say. 'It doesn't matter. I love you with all my heart. I will love you and look after you all of my life. I will be your eyes and you will be my strong arm.'

'I love you too,' he croaked.

Still she wept, her tears falling on his face like spring rain on a battlefield. He put up his hand and gently wiped them from her cheeks, then rubbed at his own wet eyes.

'I can see,' he said wonderingly. 'Just a glimpse, a slash of something bright.' He reached up one hand and touched a tendril of her red-gold hair, hanging down over him. 'It's your hair . . .'

'You can see?' Margherita scrambled to her feet, laying his head gently on the ground. 'Wait just a moment!' She caught up her sack and drew out some of the soft cloths Sophia had given her for the twins. She ran down to the lake and dipped them in the dark water. In a moment, she was back by his side, gently cleaning his face. Lucio cried out and flinched away, then submitted to her ministrations, his hands clenched by his side.

As the crust of dried blood was washed away, Lucio was able to prise open his eyelids. 'I can see firelight. It's blurry, but I can see it!'

'Your eyes are intact,' Margherita said in

relief, peering down into his face. 'The thorns did not put them out, thank heavens! I'll wash them properly in the morning, with herbs steeped in clean water. Perhaps then you'll be able to see more clearly. Oh, Lucio, I'm so glad! You're not blind at all.'

'Thanks to you. Your tears healed me. It's like a miracle.'

'The miracle is that you were not killed, or crippled, by your fall!' Margherita stroked back his dark curls.

'I thought I would die. But someone came to help me. He lifted me and carried me away from the tower, and bound up my wounds.' Lucio lifted his shirt to show that rags, now bloodstained, had been wrapped about his chest. 'He brought me water mixed with honey, and a kind of soup made with herbs and fish, and built a fire for me to sleep by. I'd have died of cold and despair if he'd not been there.'

'I was helped too,' Margherita said. 'By an old woman named Sophia.'

A thin high wail cut through the night. Margherita was on her feet in an instant.

'What's that?' Lucio asked, startled.

'That, my love, is your son. His name is Raphael Lucio. He's hungry, but if you sit up I'll put him in your arms for a moment so you two can meet.'

'My son?' Lucio looked down at the tiny bundle in his arms in amazement. 'He has your gorgeous hair,' he said after a moment, winding a bright curl around his finger.

'While your little girl has *your* gorgeous black hair,' Margherita said. Carefully, she propped his daughter into the crook of his other arm. 'Her name is Rosa Sophia.'

'Two babies. I can hardly believe it.'

'It was rather a surprise to me too,' Margherita said with a laugh. She took the babies back and expertly settled them in the crook of her arms to feed. 'I had no idea I was expecting! La Strega knew, though. My dress was too tight.'

A spasm of hatred passed over Lucio's face. 'I thought she had killed you.'

'She tried to, but I escaped.' Margherita remembered her deliverance with wonder. 'It was amazing, Lucio. This tower is built on a place of power, a shrine to an ancient goddess. I prayed to her for help . . . and somehow that help came.'

Lucio looked uneasy. 'It must have been merciful Mother Mary helping you.'

'Maybe,' Margherita said. 'Whoever it was, I'm grateful.'

'Well, at least now La Strega is having a taste of her own medicine. I wonder how much she likes her tower now.'

Margherita stared at him. 'She's still there?'

Lucio nodded. 'I've heard her screaming for help these last few days. But no one can hear her here.'

'She's screaming for help? She's locked in the tower?'

'I guess she has no way of climbing down. The braid fell out the window with me.'

'I bound her there.' Margherita was frozen in horror. 'Oh, my heavens, I bound her there with my spell.'

'Serves her right,' Lucio said.

'No, don't you realise? I cannot leave her there. I know what it is like to be locked up, to fear you'll be left to starve. I cannot do that to her. I cannot have it on my conscience. We have to rescue her.'

Lucio was silent for a long moment, then he nodded. 'Very well. We'll never be free of her otherwise. What do you want me to do?'

'You can shoot a bow and arrow, can't you?'

'Of course,' he replied. 'Standard training for all young men of noble birth.'

'Could you shoot an arrow through the window of the tower?'

'Almost impossible,' he answered. 'But I can try.'

'I know you can do it,' she said, kissing him.

'In the morning.' Carefully, he laid down his sleeping daughter, then picked up his son and laid him beside his twin. 'Tonight, I want to sleep in my wife's arms.'

In the morning, Margherita washed Lucio's eyes clean again, and he was able to see the glory of the rising sun above the mountains and the shimmering reflection in the lake below. He kissed her in gratitude and stroked his babies' soft cheeks, filling his eyes with their innocent beauty.

Hand-in-hand, they walked through the forest, each carrying one of their twins. The babies slept peacefully. The tower loomed above them, dark and lonely.

Lucio had stashed his bow and quiver of arrows under some rocks at the base of the tower. Once he had retrieved them, Margherita tied the end of her silver ribbon to one of the arrows. He looked at her sceptically. 'She cannot climb down a ribbon.'

'I did.'

He quirked his eyebrows, shrugged and searched for the best vantage point.

La Strega must have heard their voices, for she appeared at the window. 'Please, you must help me! I'm a prisoner.'

Then La Strega saw who stood at the base of the tower and fell silent. Her head drooped in defeat.

'You stole me from my parents, you bound my will and locked me away in this tower for five long years,' Margherita called up to the sorceress. 'I should leave you here to die like those other girls whose skeletons lie in the cellar. But I won't. I don't want your death on my conscience.'

Margherita drew the long heavy rope of hair out of her sack and coiled it on the stone.

Then, with her dagger, she cut branches from the white-flowering thorn and built a pyre about the hair. From far above, the witch watched, her own hair touched to bright colour by the sun. Margherita gathered handfuls of dry leaves and twigs, and thrust them into the heart of the kindling. Then, with steady hands, she lit the fire with her flint and steel. Bright flowers of flame burst open on the twigs. She sliced open her palm with her dagger, letting nine drops of blood fall down on the fire:

> With my own blood, three by three,
> I burn this hair and set you free,
> All of you bound by another's curse,
> Let the evil spells reverse.
> I wish only that you may gain,
> Kindness, mercy and love's sweet pain.

Then Lucio let loose his arrow with its streaming tail of silver. It flew true, straight through the window, the witch dropping to her knees so it did not impale her through the heart. Somehow, the ribbon transformed into a rope of tightly twisted silver cord, and La Strega was able to climb down. By the time she reached the ground, she was weeping with relief. The few days she had spent in the tower had changed her enormously. She was haggard, her hair streaked with grey, her face graven with deep lines. She dropped to her knees before Margherita and begged for forgiveness.

'It is not easy for me to forgive you,' Margherita said. 'You stole my freedom, you stole my youth, you almost stole my life. Yet if I do not forgive you, my life will be warped by what you did. And without you, I'd never have known what true love is.'

La Strega raised a ravaged face. 'I'm truly sorry.'

'You need to show true repentance,' Lucio said sternly. With his dagger, he cut two branches from the thorn tree and bound them into a makeshift cross with the silver cord. He gave it to La Strega. 'You could do so much good in this world. Till now, you have chosen darkness and evil. Can't you choose another way now? To show you truly repent?'

'I'll try.' La Strega took the crude cross in one hand. With the other, she scooped up handfuls of the hot ashes and streaked them on her face and arms. 'I don't know where I'll go. I know one thing, I'm free of Venice at last! The witch Sibillia bound me there, you know, bound me against my will.'

'As you bound me,' a man's voice rang out. Magli stepped forward from the shadow of the tower. His voice was as clear and sweet and powerful as a bell. He smiled at the sound of it. 'Listen to me! I can speak. I can even sing.' He opened his mouth and began to sing the lullaby Margherita had sung so many times in her lonely prison: *'Farfallina, bella e bianca, vola vola.'* Fly, fly . . .

'You sing beautifully,' Margherita said. All her old fear of this huge man melted away. She thought of the story that Lucio had told her, of the stranger who had helped him when he was wounded. She remembered the huge footprint in the dust and held out one hand to him. He took it and bowed low over it.

'I used to listen to you sing and long with all my heart to be able to sing like that. You've set the music in me free again. I can never repay you!'

'She bound you too?' Margherita cast an angry look at La Strega, who rose to her feet.

'I needed him!' she cried then flushed and dropped her eyes. 'I'm sorry,' she said.

'Come back to Florence with us,' Lucio said to Magli. 'I will tell my uncle you saved my life. With a voice like yours, he'll be glad to give you a place at court.'

'I must go back to Venice first,' Margherita said. Lucio looked at her in surprise. 'My parents . . . I must find my parents.'

'Of course! We'll go back to Venice, find your parents and show them their grand-children. Maybe we'll get married there? I'd like to have it settled before I go home. My uncle is kind, but he does rather think he's in charge of our lives. If we're married and have your parents' blessing, and two fine children already, well, what can he say?' Lucio grinned at her with his old merry expression, and Margherita was flooded with love for him.

La Strega went west, barefoot and streaked with ashes, carrying nothing but the cross of thorny branches. Magli headed south, taking messages to Florence. Lucio and Margherita headed east to Venice, each carrying a sleeping baby in their arms.

It was a long way, and they were both sick and weary, and, very soon, footsore. A young man gave them a lift in his cart. His name, he told them, was Giambattista Basile, and he was a Neapolitan looking for work in the Venetian Republic.

'What I'd like to do,' Giambattista said with a sigh, 'is write stories, but I guess I'll have to be a soldier instead.'

'That seems a shame,' Lucio said politely. 'Do you not like fighting?'

Giambattista shuddered. 'I hate it, but I hate being poor even more. I'm hoping to make my fortune in Venice, and then I can retire and write scurrilous stories. You two look like you have a tale to tell. Will you not share it with me?'

'You'd never believe it,' Margherita said with a shaky laugh.

'Try me,' Giambattista challenged her.

So she and Lucio told him most of their story, if not all. Some things were too hard to tell. He gasped and scowled and shook his fist in all the right places, and in the end — as they came over the hill and saw Venice floating in a sunset haze on the lagoon — he said, 'I'd have had it end differently! You should have strangled her with that silver cord, or turned the comb into a wolf to eat her.'

Margherita sighed and shook her head, but Lucio said, 'Perhaps you'll be a better soldier than you think, Giambattista.'

He grinned. 'Ah, well, it'd make a better story, don't you think?'

Dusk was falling as their gondola drifted through the shadowy canals towards San Polo and the small shop of a mask-maker. Margherita was so exhausted she could barely support the weight of her two hungry babies. Lucio drew her back to lean on him, putting his strong arms under hers, gently cradling his children. Margherita let her head rest on his chest, feeling the beat of his heart beneath her cheek. 'I wonder if they're still there. Maybe they're dead, or moved away . . .'

'We'll find out soon,' Lucio said.

Margherita had dreamt of her return so many times. A narrow dark alleyway, a window opening into a treasure trove of strange exotic masks, bright with sequins, nodding with coloured feathers. She would fling open the door and cry, 'I'm home!' and her parents would rush to embrace her.

So this is what she did. And though her parents were slow to reach her, their bodies bent and old now, their grief-numbed minds slow to realise their daughter was truly home, when at last their arms encircled her their embrace was as fierce and glad and loving as she had ever imagined it would be.

Palazzo Pitti, Florence, Italy — October 1600
On 6th October 1600, a grand entertainment was staged in Florence to celebrate the marriage of Henry IV of France and Maria de' Medici, the younger sister of the Grand Duke, Ferdinando I.

Called simply the *'opera'* (the 'work') by its exhausted creator, Jacopo Peri, it was the very newest of entertainments — a combination of music, song, dance and acting. Held at the Palazzo Pitti in Florence, the idea was to prove to the world how brilliant was the Florence court, and how exceptional its singers, dancers, actors and musicians. Peri had chosen as his theme the story of Orpheus and Euridice but had changed the ending to a happy one so as not to cast a blight on the nuptials. Henry IV of France had already been married by force once, to mad Margot, his wedding precipitating the St Bartholomew's Day Massacre. No one wanted a shadow to fall upon his second wedding day.

Margherita was to sing the role of Proserpina, the goddess of spring. It was a mark of huge favour. The only other woman in the cast was Peri's own daughter, Francesca, who played the title role. All other women in the opera were played either by castrati or by a single pimply-faced soprano-voiced boy. The castrati were all squeezed into flouncing gowns and tightly curled wigs, the boy tottering on high heels to try to raise him to the same height as everyone else. Magli had flourished so well under Margherita's tutelage that he had been given the role of La Tragedia. He towered over everyone else on the stage, his lugubrious face painted with a single tear.

Margherita wore her own red-gold hair hanging loose, at the insistence of her husband, Lucio, and was dressed in a gorgeous gown of silvery-green silk embroidered all over with flowers. She stood, her palms damp with perspiration, her stomach fluttering with nerves, in the wings, waiting for her cue. At one point, she peeked around the curtain, smiling to see Lucio sitting in the front row, his twins perched on his knee. Margherita's parents sat on either side, dressed in their finest, while nearby sat the Grand Duke and his wife, the haughty Christina of Lorraine, the King of France and his new bride, plus countless richly clad noblemen and noblewomen.

Margherita heard the beautiful notes of her introduction. She took a deep breath, squared her shoulders and stepped out onto the stage, letting her voice soar with the music. Lucio gazed up at her, his dark eyes filled with pride and tender love. She smiled back at him.

Here I am, she thought, *singing before kings and queens, just like I always dreamt I would do. I can travel the world, see camels and elephants if I want to, visit mountains that touch the sky and oceans that pour over the edge of the world.*

I am Margherita.

I am loved.

I am free.

POSTLUDE

I'm redeemed, head light
as seed mote, as a fasting
girl's among these thorns, lips
and fingers bloody with fruit.
Years I dreamed of this:
the green, laughing arms
of old trees extended over me,
my shadow lost among theirs.

'Rapunzel Shorn'
Lisa Russ Spaar

A Tongue of Honey

*Château de Cazeneuve, Gascony, France —
June 1662*

I was always a great talker and teller of tales.

'You've honey on your tongue, *ma fifille,*' Maman once said. 'If you'd lived in earlier times, you could have been a troubadour.'

'Girls can't be troubadours,' Marie said, nose in air.

'Oh, but they can,' Maman said. 'There were some famous troubadours who were women. They were called *trobairitz* and wrote some of the most beautiful poems and songs we know. My mother used to sing me one by the Comtessa de Dia, and I used to sing it to you when you were just a tiny flea. Don't you remember?'

My sister and I shook our heads.

She sang in her low voice: 'You give me such joy, enough to make a thousand who weep, merry once more.'

'I do remember it,' I said in wonder, hearing a faint sweet echo from my babyhood.

'Troubadours used to travel from court to court, telling stories and singing songs. They often carried news, which, in dangerous times, they would disguise as fables or fairy tales. Sometimes, they would stay at the court of a king and queen, but other troubadours travelled all over the known world.'

'That is what I would like to do,' I said with utter certainty. 'I'll be a . . . what was the word for a girl troubadour again?'

'*Trobairitz,*' Maman said. 'It's Occitan.'

'*Trobairitz,*' I repeated carefully, the word sounding strange on my tongue.

'There aren't any troubadours any more, are there, Maman?' Marie said. 'And if there were, girls wouldn't be allowed to be one.'

'Probably not,' Maman agreed sadly.

'I'll be one anyway,' I said with determination.

Maman smiled and pulled gently on my hair. 'I'm sure you will, *ma fifille,* a clever girl like you. You can do whatever you like in this world, if you just have courage enough.'

The Abbey of Gercy-en-Brie, France — April 1697

I lay on my thin hard pallet, looking up at the shadowy arches of stone above me, just rising from the invisibility of night. My eyes smarted with tears, and there was a lump like a bite of unchewed apple in my throat. My life had seemed so open when I was a child, a land of infinite possibilities filled with castles and snow-capped mountains, flower-filled meadows and green valleys, cascading waterfalls and deep hidden gorges where the bones of giants might lie. Now, my life was so grey and narrow. It was bounded by bells and the chanting of prayers and iron-bound doors that were locked three times. I was caged.

I thought of the strange tale that Sœur Seraphina had told me, of the girl locked in a tower without stairs or a door. She had sung, and her song had been heard. It had haunted the distant listener in the forest until he had come and helped her to escape. But I could not sing. Who was there to listen to me in this prison but the other prisoners? And God.

I took a deep breath and pressed my fingers to my wet eyes. When I took my fingertips away, my eyes were dazzled. I blinked and looked up. Above me, a shaft of early sunlight had pierced the narrow mullioned window in the wall behind me. Before I had gone to sleep the night before, I had shoved the window as wide as I could in the hope of some fresh air and a glimpse of some stars. All I could manage was a few inches, not even enough to slide my hand through. Yet it was wide enough for the rising sun to find a way in, and there, rotating slowly in the shaft of golden light, were three honeybees.

I lay still, feeling an inexplicable shiver pass

over my skin, raising the hair on my arms and on the nape of my neck. The bees glowed like jewels, amber banded with jet, wings flashing with diamond fire. Their eyes were huge and dark and shiny. For a moment longer, they hung above my head, humming with life, then one by one they rose and flew away through the window.

To the garden, I thought. Without a second's thought, I swung my feet to the floor, caught up my heavy cloak and my sabots and went quietly, barefoot, down the narrow hallway between the canvas curtains. I could hear soft snoring and the rustle of straw as someone rolled over. The stone was so cold underfoot it felt like I was walking on knives.

Through the sleeping convent I crept and found the door into the garden. I paused for a moment, afraid it might be locked, but lifted the latch. It swung open under my touch. I stepped through into the dim hush of dawn. Above the dark walls, the sky was luminous, the palest of blues. The mullioned windows of the dormitory wing glinted with sunshine, and the air smelt delicately of apple blossom and early violets. I breathed deeply, thinking of my mother. *You have honey on your tongue . . .*

My pulse quickened. I was aware of a deep thrumming in my blood, a subtle trembling in my body from the soles of my feet to the tips of my hair, as if a giant was drumming deep underground. I was both afraid and exalted. Something was happening — I didn't understand what. The thrumming deepened. Then I saw it, a strange dark cloud, like a storm of blossoms, at the far end of the garden. Bees, hundreds and thousands of them, reeled drunkenly through the air.

I felt at that moment both acutely alive and acutely vulnerable. The bare skin of my arms and face prickled with apprehension; my stomach lurched; my heart sang. For a moment, I hesitated, gazing at that small living whirlwind, then I turned and ran back into the convent. I knew where Sœur Seraphina's cell was; I had seen her go in after vespers. I scratched at the door with my smallest fingernail, then, remembering I was not at court, knocked a rapid staccato with my knuckles. It felt oddly liberating. I knocked again.

The door opened and Sœur Seraphina looked out. She was dressed only in her chemise, her cloak wrapped hastily over the top. Her short hair straggled about her face, a pale reddish-blonde colour. She looked at me questioningly.

'The bees are swarming,' I whispered.

Her face changed at once. She opened wide her door, stepping back to bend and search for her shoes under her cot. I caught a quick glimpse of her room. A warm rug woven in jewel- like colours lay on the floor, and a thick eiderdown of yellow silk was flung back on the bed. Hanging on the wall was the most extraordinary drawing of a penitent St Mary Magdalene, tear-filled eyes turned to heaven, ripples of thick lustrous hair falling down about her, barely hiding the full ripeness of a bare breast. On the other wall hung a simple wooden cross made of two thorny branches tied together with a tarnished silver ribbon.

Sœur Seraphina caught up her shoes, and then we hurried down the corridor to the garden. 'I hope I am not too late,' she whispered as she opened the garden door.

The sky was brighter now, and sunlight gilded the top of the church spire and outlined the brazen buds of the pomegranate tree. The humming was louder; it sounded like a watchman's rattle, warning of danger.

Sœur Seraphina sprang forward, heading straight towards the dark whirl of bees. I ran after her, feeling again that prickle of apprehension. I'd been stung by a bee as a child, and I well remembered the pain. Sœur Seraphina did not seek to grapple with the swarm, though, but went to the hut and got out some thick gloves, a veiled hat, a long-handled pan with a lid, a tinderbox and a set of small bellows, passing them out to me one by one. I put the hat on hastily, drawing down the veil, and shoved my chilled hands into the gloves. Swiftly, Sœur Seraphina filled the pan with dried tansy flowers, like fragrant brown buttons, and then used the crumpled brown leaves as tinder, striking a spark from her flint with her steel. Soon, the tansy was alight, and thick grey smoke billowed up from the pan.

'Put the pan on the wall over there,' Sœur Seraphina instructed. 'We must try and stop the bees from crossing it. They do not like the smoke. If they come close to you, use the bellows to puff smoke at them.'

As I obeyed, she hacked at a wormwood shrub with her gardening knife and tore away a long branch, rubbing her hands up and down the stem, bruising the silvery leaves. 'Bees do not like the smell of wormwood,' she explained, and rubbed her hands over her bare face and neck. Holding the long wormwood branch in one hand, she then went and found an empty straw skep. Holding the bellows tightly, coughing a little as the fragrant smoke drifted across me, I watched the swarm of bees in utter fascination. They flickered and swirled like a school of glinting minnows, gauzy wings whirring, their mesmerising hum resonating inside my head.

Sœur Seraphina smiled encouragingly at me and gathered up a handful of earth, throwing it under her right foot, chanting:

I've got it, I've found it:
Earth masters all creatures,

768

it masters evil, it masters deceit,
it masters humanity's greedy tongue.

She then scraped up the earth again and
flung it over the swarm of bees, saying in a
gentle sing-song:

Sit, wise women, settle on earth:
never in fear fly to the woods.
Please be mindful of my welfare
as all men are of food and land.

I stared in wonder and a kind of fear, thinking, *Who is this nun? What heathen magic is
this?* Her hair caught the sun, glowing like
the embers of a fire within ash. Her eyes
glowed as golden as the bees' striped bodies.
She had flung off the heavy dark cloak, and
so was dressed all in white like some ancient
pagan goddess, her arms and feet bare.

Carefully, she raised her wormwood branch
and gently stroked the edges of the swarm.
The bees recoiled from the branch. She
swooped the branch back and forth through
the air, like a conductor directing a *Te Deum.*
The cloud of bees responded like music.
Slowly, she directed them down into the
straw skep; they obeyed her every gesture and
soon were contained within the beehive, all
but a few that buzzed about at the entrance,
checking all was well before shooting away to
begin the job of gathering nectar once more.

'I am amazed,' I said and meant it.

She smiled and cast away her wormwood stick. 'I am glad you woke me. I might have lost them otherwise. How did you know?'

'I could not sleep,' I said. 'Three bees came through my window, buzzing about above me. I thought I'd come out to the garden . . .' My voice trailed away. I could not explain the impulse that had led me to follow the bees.

She nodded as if it all made sense. 'Homer says that the sun-god Apollo was first given the gift of prophecy by three bee-maidens.'

'How do you know all these things? You don't talk like a nun at all.'

She smiled faintly. 'I have lived a very long time, and most of it was not as a nun.'

'But where did you live? How do you know so many strange and wonderful things?'

She regarded me thoughtfully for a long moment, with eyes as intent and golden as those of a lioness. 'Have you not yet guessed?' she asked in her soft foreign accent. 'I am Selena Leonelli. I was a courtesan in Venice for many, many years. I was muse to the painter Tiziano — he painted that canvas of me that hangs upon my wall — and I was the sorceress who owned the secret walled garden in Venice and grew the bitter green herbs that Margherita's father stole. It was I who found the tower in the forest, I who bathed in the blood of virgins, I who worked magic by the power of the full moon so that I would keep my beauty forever.'

'But . . . but that's impossible,' I stammered.

'Is it? Two hundred odd years I've lived, by my reckoning, and slowly, slowly, the spells I wrought are fading away. My hair is grey now, my skin is sagging, my back is bowing under the weight of all those years. And all this time, I have tried to make reparation for the evil I did.'

I could only stare at her. 'That painting . . . in your cell . . . that is you? I mean, you were the model?'

She nodded. 'Tiziano painted me many, many times.'

'You were very beautiful.'

'I was. It's a long time ago now, so long ago it feels like a dream or a story someone else told me.'

'How is it that you are permitted to keep the painting? And those other things of yours, the rug and the eiderdown and those fine candlesticks?'

Sœur Seraphina gave that faint enigmatic smile of hers. 'I was once a very wealthy woman. When I sold all I owned in Venice, I had a trust fund set up that pays me an income each quarter. I pay that to the convent. It is almost the only income they have now. Mère Notre allows me a few indulgences in thanks, though none that can be seen by the other nuns. The painting is one of them. It is all I have left of my own life, and it reminds me of why I am here.'

Bells began to ring out. Sœur Seraphina smiled. 'Come, my dear. It's time for matins. There's plenty of time for me to tell you my story. I'll tell you while we work in the garden.'

I nodded and felt a sudden sunburst of joy at the idea.

All through the long morning service, I thought and wondered and made plans. 'By good grace or ill grace,' Sœur Seraphina had said to me, but I had struggled against my fate, choosing ill grace at every step. I remembered now a favourite saying of Athénaïs's. 'We must play with the cards God has dealt us,' she used to say. Her cards had been beauty and wit and breeding; all I had were words.

At chapter, I begged permission from Mère Notre to speak. Looking surprised, she granted it to me.

'I am ready now to take my vows,' I said. 'As a gesture of my good faith, I beg you to take the golden gown and sell it, using the funds to mend the church roof.'

Small cries of pleasure and astonishment rang out. The bursar, Sœur Theresa, clasped her hands together and raised her eyes to heaven.

'I have jewels that may be sold too. I have no need of them any more. And soon I will be receiving my pension from the King. I would like to turn it over to your hands, Mère Notre, to do as you see fit.'

'Thank you, *ma fille,*' she answered rather breathlessly.

'In return, I'd like to request one or two small things for myself. I would like a cell of my own, if you permit, Mère Notre,' I went on, hands folded demurely. 'With my little writing desk in it, and some quills and an inkpot. I have learnt so much working with Sœur Seraphina these past few days, I wish to make a record of it so the knowledge may be passed down to future generations.'

'A worthy ambition,' Mère Notre answered. 'We have cells to spare, now that our number has dwindled so much. I see no reason why you should not have one if you wish.'

I thanked her and made arrangements to meet with Sœur Theresa and go through my chest. All this time, Sœur Seraphina sat quietly, the corners of her mouth compressed with amusement.

In a few days, it was done. My court clothes and jewels were all packed up and sold to the ecstatic daughters of the local nobility, raising more than enough money to fix the church roof. I kept only one small bee brooch from my favourite dress, which I set on my writing desk next to my inkpot and my jar of quills.

My cell was bare and austere, but it had its own window, which looked onto the garden, and I convinced Mère Notre to spend most of my first pension from the King on sheep fleeces for all the nuns, to spread on the cold damp stone floors, and on thick eiderdowns for our beds. 'I'm sure God does not want us all to die from pneumonia,' I'd said. My eiderdown was not rose-pink silk, as I secretly desired, but it was at least soft and deliciously warm.

I sat at my desk, sweet-scented air from the garden wafting across my face, and carefully chose a quill and sharpened it. I drew a piece of my best smooth white paper towards me and wrote across the top, with a most beautiful flourish:

Persinette
Once there were two young lovers who at last managed to overcome all difficulties to be married. Nothing could equal their ardour, and all they longed for now was a child of their own. Soon they discovered their wish was to be fulfilled . . .

Each word was shaped with certainty, and I felt, more strongly than ever before in my life, that I had at last found my true path. I knew the story would change as I told it. No one can tell a story without transforming it in some way; it is part of the magic of story-telling. Like the troubadours of the past, who hid their message in poems and songs and fairy tales, I too would hide my true purpose: to beg pardon from the King and persuade him, as subtly as I knew how, to release me from my imprisonment.

It was by telling stories that I would save myself.

AFTERWORD

Charlotte-Rose de Caumont de la Force wrote the fairy tale 'Persinette' while banished from court to the Abbey of Gercy-en-Brie. It was published in her collection of fairy tales, *Les Contes des Contes,* in 1698, under the pseudonym Mademoiselle X. It was one of the first collections of French literary fairy tales.

While imprisoned in the convent, Mademoiselle de la Force also wrote several more historical novels and her memoirs. With the money earned from her writing, she was permitted to move to a wealthier convent in Paris in 1703 and, a few years later, allowed to live in retirement at the Château de la Force.

In 1713, she was at last granted her full freedom. She moved to Paris, where she became a celebrated member of the salons and was named a member of the Accademico dé Ricrovati di Padova. She also joined a secret society set up by the Duchesse de

Maine, wife of one of Athénaïs's royal bastards. Called La Mouche à Miel, or the Order
of the Honey Bee, the thirty-nine members
all wore a dark-red satin dress embroidered
with silver bees and a wig shaped like a
beehive.

The Abbot Lambert wrote of her, 'We
admire the purity and the elegance of her
style, her imagination is vivacious and brilliant, she is a genius, a flame, an elevation, a
force.'

Charlotte-Rose died in 1724, at the age of
seventy-four.

ACKNOWLEDGEMENTS

Bitter Greens is, of course, a work of imagination. As Charlotte-Rose de la Force herself wrote, *'Bien souvent les plaisirs de l'imagination, valent mieux que les plaisirs réels',* which translates as 'Often the pleasures of the imagination are better than real pleasures'.

Help in writing *Bitter Greens* came from many quarters. I first read about Charlotte-Rose de la Force in an essay by the writer and editor Terri Windling called 'Rapunzel, Rapunzel, Let Down Your Hair', published in the Endicott Studio's Spring 2006 *Journal of Mythic Arts,* in the early stages of my research for *Bitter Greens.* I was immediately smitten with Charlotte-Rose's character. Someone who disguised herself as a dancing bear to free her lover was exactly my kind of woman! I wanted to know more about her and so began my long journey to discover the life of this virtually unknown writer.

After long months of detective work, I

found a biography of her life, *Mademoiselle de la Force: Un Auteur Mèconnu du XVII Siècle,* by the French academic Michel Souloumiac. However, it was only published in French. So I enlisted the help of a translator, Sylvie Poupard-Gould, who not only translated Michel Souloumiac's work but also translated an autobiographical sketch by Charlotte-Rose and a number of her fairy tales. Since the first was written in dense academic terminology and the second in Old French, complete with the letter 'f' looking like the letter 's', this was no easy task, and I am incredibly grateful to Sylvie for all her hard work and the strain upon her back and eyesight.

I read many other books in the making of this novel, far too many to list here, though you can find them on my website. A few helped me so much, however, that I'd like to mention them here. Martin Calder's memoir, *A Summer in Gascony,* helped me enormously in understanding the Gascon personality and allowed me to first hear Charlotte-Rose's voice. *Love and Louis XIV* by Antonia Fraser and *Athénaïs: The Real Queen of France* by Lisa Hilton illuminated the Sun King and his mistresses. *The Splendid Century: Life in the France of Louis XIV* by W. H. Lewis brought the world of the French court to life, while I cannot recommend *The Affair of the Poisons: Murder, Infanticide, and Satanism at the Court of Louis XIV* by Anne Somerset enough for anyone interested in discovering more about this extraordinary chapter in French history. *A Social History of the Cloisters* by Elizabeth Rapley helped me to recreate the daily life of cloistered nuns in the seventeenth century, plus I'd like to thank Robert Nash, secretary of the Huguenot Society of Australia, for helping me to understand the beliefs and practices of seventeenth-century French Protestants.

Thank you also to Gabrielle Doucinet and Catlin Jeangrand from the Agence de Guides-Interprètes in Pau for all their help in setting up my research trip to Gascony; to Dr Jean-Pierre Constant for all his help in illuminating the literary world of seventeenth-century Paris; and to the Comte de Sabran-Pontevès for showing me around the Château de Cazeneuve, where Charlotte-Rose was born and lived till she was sixteen.

I am also greatly indebted to my wonderful guides in Venice: Dottore Alvise Zanchi, who took me on a tour and answered endless questions about life in Renaissance Venice; Loredano Giaomini, who showed me through the many hidden gardens that once belonged to convents and palaces and perhaps even witches; and Cristina Pigozzo, who led me and my children through the spooky alleyways of Venice at night and told us riveting ghost stories, some of which worked their way into this book.

Thanks also to my doctoral advisors at the University of Technology, Debra Adelaide and Sarah Gibson, to my lovely agents — Tara Wynne at Curtis Brown Australia, and Robert Kirby at United Agents in the UK — and a very big, heartfelt thank you to my wonderful publisher Susie Dunlop at Allison & Busby, who has shown such faith in my novel and has worked so hard to bring it to a whole new audience. Thank you to Christina Griffiths, for designing the gorgeous cover, and also my heartfelt gratitude to Lesley Crooks, Sara Magness, Chiara Priorelli and Sophie Robinson at Allison & Busby — I'm very proud to be published by you!

I am also very grateful to the gifted poets whose Rapunzel poems have been quoted throughout the book: Arlene Ang, G. K. Chesterton, Nicole Cooley, Adelaide Crapsey, William Morris, Anne Sexton, Lisa Russ Spaar, Gwen Strauss and Louis Untermeyer. I do hope you'll go on to read more of their amazing work.

I could not have written this book without my research trip to Paris, Venice, Gascony and the Italian lakes. Thank you to my three amazing children, who came adventuring with me, and to my husband, Greg, who stayed behind to pay the bills.

I love you all!

ABOUT THE AUTHOR

Kate Forsyth is the bestselling and award–winning author of more than twenty books. Her books have been published in fourteen countries. *Bitter Greens* is her first hardcover adult novel published in the United States. Kate is currently undertaking a doctorate in fairytale retellings. She lives in Sydney, Australia.